We Hear the Dead

We Hear the Dead

Dianne K. Salerni

SCHOLASTIC INC.
New York Toronto London Auckland
Sydney Mexico City New Delhi Hong Kong

ISBN 978-0-545-30237-1

12 11 10 9 8 7 6 5 4 3 2 1   10 11 12 13 14 15/0

Printed in the U.S.A.   40

First Scholastic printing, September 2010

Cover design by Marci Senders

For Bob,
who believed in me

Contents

Author's Note

This is a work of historical fiction, although the story of Maggie Fox is a true one. I have fictionalized the narrative, using my own interpretation of documented events. Some of the dialogue is taken from correspondence and published writing of the time. On occasion, I have changed the sequence of events to fit the story line and have altered details of place or circumstance.

CONFESSIONS

Maggie

I began the deception when I was too young to know right from wrong. No one suspected us of any trick, because we were such young children. We were led on by my sister purposely and by my mother unintentionally.

Only with the passing of time did I come to understand the consequences of my actions. As Doctor wrote to me: "Weary! weary is the life by cold deceit oppressed."

Kate

My sister has used the word "deception." I object to her use of that word, for I do not believe that I have ever intentionally deceived anyone.

Maggie has a different understanding of all the events that have happened since that night in Hydesville long ago. To her the spirits were always a game. For my sister Leah they were a means to an end. For my mother, a miracle.

And for me they were my life's calling. I have no regrets.

Kate

PART ONE:
THE HAUNTING OF
HYDESVILLE

Chapter One
Maggie

My earliest memories always include Kate. With three years between us, there must have been a time when she was a toddling child in infant's clothes and I an independent youngster, but I do not remember this. As long as I can remember, we were together, friends and sisters, inseparable companions. Later we would come to be known as the Fox sisters, named by the newspapers as a single entity. We grew up together and yet alone, separated from our older siblings by more than fourteen years and allowed to run wild and free by parents astonished to have produced a second batch of offspring.

We were a mischievous pair, playing tricks on each other, on the neighbor children, and on our parents. Household objects such as my father's spectacles and my mother's hairbrush were always going astray. Kate usually discovered the missing objects and was praised for her cleverness. Feeling a bit jealous, I once asked Kate peevishly if the next time she stole some object, she couldn't let me be the one to find it. She stared at me silently for a moment, her violet eyes steady upon me, and then replied, "Just because I find them doesn't mean I stole them."

A fine thing to say to her companion in devilment! I tied the string to the apple with my own hands when her six-year-old fingers were too clumsy to secure the knots. We used to drop the apple out of bed and let it thump on the floor, then draw it quickly back into bed when my mother tried to find the source of the noise. This was a great game, and after several repetitions my mother would mutter superstitiously about spirits and devils. Kate always wanted to push the boundaries of common sense, dropping the apple when our mother was close enough to see.

"We shall be caught," I whispered nervously.

"No, we shan't," she murmured back.

And we never were. My mother never could see anything but good in us. I believe she must have used up the sharpest of her mothering instincts on my siblings, and by the time we came to her, she was weary.

My mother's life had not been an easy one. In my father's younger years, he had battled a drinking problem, and my mother left him for a time. She moved with her two children, Leah and David, into her sister Catherine's home. Although these events took place long before I was born, I have had ample opportunity to hear Leah talk about her life without a father and the hardships she endured. I know it was partly to escape poverty that Leah ran away and married Bowman Fish when she was only fourteen years old—not that it did her any good.

Eventually my father's reformation and conversion to Methodism resulted in reconciliation with Mother and an attempt to make a living on a farm in Ontario. By the time I was born, David was approaching adulthood and Leah had already presented my parents with a grandchild. Kate's arrival, three years after me, surprised them even more. Sometimes my father would squint at us through his spectacles as if he were a little confused about who we were and how we came to be living in his house.

Kate and I spent our earliest childhood years living on the farm, and when that venture failed, my father moved us to Rochester, New York. We spent some years there, with my father now trying to make a living as a blacksmith. David eventually married and moved to Wayne County, near the town of Hydesville. He spoke to my father about a tract of land near his farm, and in the early part of 1848 my father decided to build a house there.

I was not happy about leaving the cheerful and bustling city of Rochester for the dreary, vacant countryside of Wayne County. I had just turned fourteen, and I thought that being banished to "frontiersland" would be the end of my life.

To make matters worse, the rooms that my family rented in Rochester had become unavailable because the owner, Mr. Isaac Post, had sold the house. It was necessary to move out of our lodgings before the new home was built, so my father rented a small house within the town limits of Hydesville.

Hydesville wasn't much of a town, as far as I was concerned, and ours wasn't much of a house. Its best feature was a south-facing parlor with several windows to brighten the room. The kitchen, however, was dark and dreary. The house's single bedroom received sunlight only in the morning. There was a buttery off the kitchen, and a cobwebbed attic over the back half of the house. The absolutely most horrible part of the house was the cellar.

Kate and I explored it while Father and David moved furniture above us. Foul water squelched around our shoes, bubbling up from the damp earth floor. The wood beams supporting earthen walls leaned inward at an alarming angle, giving the unsettling impression of imminent collapse.

"It smells like an open grave," I stated in disgust.

"To be sure," answered Kate, "and there lies the corpse." She pointed at the darkest corner of the cellar, where I could dimly make out a mound of loose earth piled carelessly against a crooked wall.

"What are you girls doing down there?"

The voice made us jump. We turned and saw my father leaning in through the doorway, peering at us in the dim light.

I opened my mouth, ready to burst out with fresh complaints about moving into a house built over a pauper's cemetery. But Kate took my hand firmly and spoke before me. "We were just curious, Father." She led me toward the stairs, and I followed silently, without voicing my opinion.

Hydesville was less a town than a cluster of houses and farms that had grown up around a tavern, which later closed down and left the townsfolk wondering why they had come. My mother, I know, was relieved to see the boarded doors on the old Hyde's Tavern. She had forgiven her husband for his years of drunkenness but had never quite forgotten.

We had lived in the Hydesville house less than two weeks when a letter from my sister Leah arrived, telling us to expect her daughter to arrive by canal boat within a few days. Lizzie was coming "to lend us a hand." Only Leah could imagine that feeding and housing another person under our present circumstances would be a help. Especially Lizzie, a great big horse of a girl with the brains of a cow and the liveliness of a fence post.

Leah obviously needed to be rid of Lizzie for her own purposes. Perhaps she wanted to put a boarder in the girl's room to make extra money. Leah held piano lessons and rented rooms but always seemed to be in an endless state of acquiring funds. Whenever she could persuade my parents to feed, clothe, and shelter her daughter, she did so.

Anticipating Lizzie's arrival did not improve my outlook on the house, Hydesville, or the dismal end of my former life. Kate and I moaned and threw fits, but Lizzie was already on her way, and our mother actually looked forward to her arrival. Honestly, I cannot tell why, unless it was simply because she was the eldest grandchild and the daughter of her precious Leah. Lizzie did not resemble my sister, who was pretty and bold and the center of any gathering of people. I never met Mr. Bowman Fish, who ran off to marry a rich widow when Lizzie was only a baby, but I imagine that he must have resembled his own name and passed those features on to his daughter.

"Lizzie Fish is a stinky old cod," Kate chanted out of the hearing of our parents.

"Face like a path where the oxen trod," I rejoined, turning the jump rope, which we had tied to a tree.

"Screwed up little eyes and pale, thin hair—"

"For a penny and a half I would push her down the stair."

"How many steps did Lizzie fall down?"

"One…two…three…four…five…six…"

My seventeen-year-old niece, Lizzie, was the least important person in this entire story—and also the most important. She was the reason for everything that was to come: the rapping, the lecture halls, the spirit circles, and the messages from the dead.

Kate and I did not like Lizzie. We did not look forward to her arrival, and we resented sharing our bed with her.

Everything that happened—everything—was originally just a plan to scare Lizzie and make her go home.

Chapter Two
Maggie

We arrived home from school one afternoon that week to find Lizzie Fish sitting on our bed and mending a skirt from the pile of sewing I was supposed to have done but hadn't.

"Good afternoon, Aunt Margaretta! And to you, Aunt Catherine!" Lizzie pursed her lips in amusement at her own joke. Kate and I used to laugh at being addressed as old aunties by our niece when we were perhaps five years old, but the joke had long since worn as thin as the hem Lizzie was mending.

"Hello, Lizzie," I replied.

"Come here and give me a hug, Kate," she said, laying aside the skirt. "Look at your hair, all coming loose. Have you been running in the schoolyard like a boy again? And, Maggie, how about a greeting for your niece? I see you've torn this skirt as well. I'll be working my fingers to the bone, I can tell!"

Lizzie at seventeen was taller than my father and large boned, like a man. She didn't have her mother's pretty, plump face or dark hair and eyes. She was a washed-out beige all over, like clothing left out too long on the clothesline.

We dutifully greeted her, content for the moment to mind our manners. I did not comment on her making my uncompleted chores obvious by overtaking them herself, and although we noticed she had rearranged our meager belongings, we said nothing. Our family was of modest means. Kate and I owned little for ourselves, and most of what we had was in storage in the attic anyway.

Lizzie was full of news from Rochester, but our initial excitement ebbed away when we realized that it wasn't any news that interested us. She could tell us nothing of the handsome boy who had lived across the street, for instance, but knew all about his grandmother's infected finger. She knew who had died but not who had married. She had not seen any plays or stage shows, because she couldn't bear the thought of attending the theater without a gentleman to accompany her. As if any gentleman would be interested in a damp mop like Lizzie!

"What word of Mr. and Mrs. Post's efforts against slavery?" asked Kate. Our family had boarded for two years with the Posts, a Quaker couple active in the abolitionist cause. It was their sudden move to another house that had caused our own premature departure and led indirectly to our renting of this abysmal house. Kate and I had speculated that the Posts' new house was meant to be an active station on the "railroad" that conducted slaves to the safety of Canada, and we had spent long hours imagining their adventures and dangers.

"I am sure I would not know," Lizzie stated stiffly. "As much as I sympathize with the plight of the poor, downtrodden Negro, I cannot presume to know anything about the traffic in fugitive slaves."

It was a most disagreeable afternoon in which Kate and I grew more determined about our course of action. We consulted again that evening when we volunteered to wash the dishes from the evening meal, freeing Mother and Lizzie to join Father upon their knees in the parlor, engaged in prayer.

Never once did we imagine that we were commencing an enterprise that would change the course of our lives.

⚜

Lizzie took the middle of the bed, all knees and elbows, while we balanced on either edge beside her. Darkness still came early, for it was late in March. Mother and Father had not yet retired and were still sitting in the parlor.

Suddenly Lizzie sat upright in bed. "Did you hear that sound?" she asked.

"What?" I yawned sleepily.

"Yes," Kate whispered urgently. "I heard it. I've heard it every night since we moved here."

"What is it?" Lizzie sat still, listening. Only a moment later, there was a sharp cracking sound.

I sat up. "Where is it coming from?"

"It's in the room with us," Kate stated.

Again we heard the sound, but this time twice in quick succession. Lizzie leaned across me and fumbled for the tinderbox on the table beside the bed. It took a few moments to get a light, for another loud rap caused her to flinch and lose the flame. Once she had the lamp lit, however, she quickly slid past me to the edge of the bed. She cast the light at the floor first, searching for mice, I suppose. Then she eased from the bed and began to look around the bedroom. Our parents' bed was still empty. There was a trunk and a chest of drawers. That was all.

Cautiously, Lizzie walked over to the one small window in the bedroom and, holding high the lantern, leaned close to peer outside.

Crack! Lizzie jumped back.

"Did you see something?" I hissed.

She did not reply but strode swiftly across the floor, opened the door, and left the room. Kate and I turned to each other in the dark and linked hands.

Soon Lizzie returned with our mother, and together they cast the light of the lantern around the room. A few moments later, a light bobbed up and down outside our window, and we could clearly see Father looking around. While he was visible, another volley of raps sounded inside the room. Mother jumped nervously, and Kate and I huddled close in the bed, but it was obvious that Father had heard nothing outside.

Eventually he came back into the house and joined Mother and Lizzie. A whispered conversation followed, and Father seemed doubtful about their story. We all listened for a while, but no more noises were heard.

Sleep came slowly and uneasily that night for everyone.

We all heard it again the next night, even Father. Of us all, he turned out to be the most disturbed, because he could not find the cause. On the third night, he searched every room in the house, ascending to the storage attic and descending to the cellar. My mother wrung her hands in nervousness, and Lizzie huddled on the bed with her arms around us.

"You should leave this place," Kate whispered into Lizzie's ear. "You don't have to suffer this haunting like the rest of us. You can go back to your mother's house in Rochester and forget all about these nighttime rappings!"

"As if I would leave you!" Lizzie replied indignantly. "Grandfather will soon discover how these noises are made, and then we'll laugh at our own foolishness! I don't believe in ghosts at all."

"You would if they spoke to you," I said tartly, because I was weary from lack of sleep and wished Lizzie would leave and end it all. Kate gazed at me thoughtfully, and suddenly I regretted my words. I knew my sister well and was fearful of what new mischief she was going to contrive.

As with the first two nights, the knockings eventually subsided, and all of us laid down to a sleep that did not seem to refresh us. On the next morning, which was the thirty-first of March, our rest had been broken for so many days that we were nearly sick. Kate lay in bed most of the day on the verge of one of her headaches. Mother and Lizzie were bedraggled and pale, but together they made broth for Kate and a thin chicken stew for the rest of us. Mother told me I could stay home from school, and Father, instead of going out to work on our new house, spent most of the day in prayer.

In the afternoon, my brother, David, came by in his wagon to find out why Father had not been to the new house that day. Mother and Lizzie explained all about our problem while Father sat silently by.

For just a moment, David's eyes flicked over at me. I believe I met them steadily, because then he turned to Mother and said,

"If you search, I am sure you will find a cause for it, as it must be something about the house."

"I *have* searched," Father said gruffly, almost his first words to us all day.

David paused, then said smoothly, "All the more reason to be out of this place as soon as possible. Can I expect to see you tomorrow at the building site?"

"Yes, of course," Father murmured, looking cross.

"If the rapping comes tonight," said Mother with a false brightness, "we will not mind it but try and get a good night's rest. You are right, David. We have wasted too much effort on what is surely the normal creaking and groaning of a poorly constructed house. We will look forward to a more *silent* home in the future!"

David departed, and we took our evening meal. The sky had hardly turned dark before Mother was urging us all to sleep. Kate had just ventured out of bed when she was suddenly ushered back into it. After sleeping away the day, Kate was the only one of us who had truly rested, and she complained bitterly about being turned back to bed. I should have known that lively events were bound to occur that night!

The raps commenced as usual, when we had all lain down. Lizzie moaned and threw her arms over her head. "'Tis the devil!" she whispered loudly in consternation.

Kate suddenly sat up. "If it is the devil, then let us see his tricks." Speaking loudly, so that our parents in the next bed would not miss it, she said, "Here, Mr. Splitfoot, do as I do!" And then she snapped her fingers four times.

Four raps immediately followed.

"John!" Mother gasped. "John, wake up!"

"Oh, you can hear me, can you?" said Kate, speaking to the air. "Can you see me as well? How many fingers am I showing?"

Three sharp raps startled us all from any chance of sleep. Lizzie squeaked in fear, and we all felt a shiver of cold upon our skin. It was too dark to see Kate, but we did not have any doubt that she was holding up three fingers.

"Count to ten!" I was startled to hear my mother give this command. She was lighting the lantern by then, and she had a shaky but determined timbre to her voice.

By now, nobody was surprised to hear a slow, labored sequence of ten raps. We were too exhausted to be fearful, but there was a strange feeling of being separate from reality. It was as if we were all sharing the same dream, and because it was a dream, there was no reason to be afraid.

"Are you a human being?" my mother asked. When there was no immediate response, she cried, "Are you a spirit?"

"Margaret!" my father protested, taking her shoulder. But she shrugged his hand off and turned her back on him.

"If you are a spirit, give me two sounds," she said, and there came a reply of two sounds almost before she had finished speaking.

"Are you an injured spirit?" Two raps.

"Were you injured in this house?" Two raps.

By this time, Father had moved to the edge of the bed and buried his face in his hands. He sat with his back to us, as if trying to separate himself.

Lizzie, meanwhile, was gripping my arm so tightly that it was starting to go numb, and Mother was pacing the bedroom excitedly with her lantern. "Spirit," she asked, "give me one sound for no and two sounds for yes. Did you die of natural cause?"

One rap.

"Were you murdered?" Two raps.

"In this house?" Two raps.

"Is the person who murdered you still living?" Two raps.

"Are your remains still present in this house?" Two raps.

Lizzie wailed, "Grandmother, stop!" My mother turned around, suddenly becoming aware that there were terrified children in the room.

"Oh, girls!" she cried, repentant. She rushed to the bed and sheltered us with her arms. "Spirit, do you mean us any harm?"

One rap.

"Will you make these sounds before other people if we bring them here as witness?"

A long pause followed, and I had almost started to relax when two sharp raps answered the question. I could hardly believe my ears. Was Mr. Splitfoot, our devil or spirit or whatever he was, going to perform now for people outside the family?

"John!" Mother rushed back to the other bed. "Get dressed quickly and fetch the Redfields. They must witness this testimony."

"Are you mad?" my father whispered harshly, without removing his hands from his face.

"No, I don't believe I am," Mother said indignantly. "And if the Redfields hear this spirit also, then I will know that I am not."

"It is too late." This was a feeble protest, and my father knew it, because he was already on his feet and pulling on his overalls.

"It is barely eight o'clock. While you are out, you can see if the Dueslers are home and bring them, too!"

My mother outweighed my father in bulk and character, and so he was swiftly bundled off to bid our neighbors come visit with our ghost. While he was gone, I contemplated my course of action. Truthfully, I nearly spoke out then and there. I do not know what held my tongue, unless it was Kate's force of will or simply my own destiny. When I heard the front door open and voices in the parlor, the time to confess had passed and I was trapped in the deception.

"Now, what kind of tomfoolery is going on in here?" boomed the voice of Mrs. Redfield, a neighbor from across the street. She bustled into the bedroom, stout and brisk, dressed in what passed for a good cloak and hat in this tiny hamlet of Hydesville. Her commonplace appearance reminded us suddenly that we were all in our bedclothes and that we had invited this woman into our sleeping chamber, where she could see the intimate details of our threadbare lives. I retreated like a turtle into the bedcoverings, and Mother put one hand self-consciously to her hair, which was plaited and hanging down across her bosom.

Then Mother drew her dignity to herself as if it were a cloak much fancier than Mrs. Redfield's and said, "Thank you for coming, Mary. We greatly appreciate your good judgment and wise counsel. Has John told you what happened here tonight?"

Mrs. Redfield drew off her gloves, looking curiously around the room. "He has told me some tale of injured spirits and ghostly knockings. My husband refused to come for what is surely an early Fools' Day prank by some persons who should know better." Her eyes alighted on Lizzie and me. I imagine that I looked very guilty, but Lizzie's surprise was genuine and indignant. Kate was ignored by all. She was eleven years old but gave the appearance of being much younger.

"Spirit," my mother called out, addressing the air like a madwoman, "is our good neighbor right? Are you a manifestation of an April Fools' Day prank? Rap once for no and twice for yes."

One loud knock sounded.

My father's shoulders hunched in apparent embarrassment. My mother looked vindicated. Mrs. Redfield's eyebrows rose sharply, and she took a few steps toward my bed, looking us over carefully. Our hands were all within sight, and we had not moved even the slightest bit.

"Can you count to five for Mrs. Redfield?" my mother continued.

We all heard five raps while Mrs. Redfield scrutinized Lizzie and me for some kind of movement. Finding nothing, she walked quickly around the room, looking in the corners and under the beds.

"If you are the spirit of a murdered person, demonstrate this by two raps," my mother then commanded. By the time we had heard these two raps, Mrs. Redfield had finished her search of the room and her demeanor suddenly changed.

"Girls, you look so terrified!" she exclaimed. I, for one, certainly was, but not for the reasons she imagined! "I am going to bring my husband here to see this for himself, but I admit I am loath to leave you here so frightened!"

Kate reached over and gripped Mrs. Redfield's hands earnestly, looking frail but determined. "We can be brave until your return."

Chapter Three
Maggie

Made bold by our high success with Mrs. Redfield, I regained a little of my own spirit and bounded out of the bed to take my mother's arm. "Mother," I urged, "if Mrs. Redfield is returning with her husband, then we should cover ourselves more decently, don't you think?"

"Yes, child. This haunting has quite addled my wits!" exclaimed Mother. "We are in no state to receive visitors."

Mother and Lizzie put on their housedresses over their nightclothes while Kate and I merely donned our cloaks and climbed back into bed, pulling the blankets up over our legs. I felt excited and giddy. So the house was haunted by the spirit of a murder victim, was it? Surely I had something to add to this story, for I would be ashamed to be outdone by my little sister!

We did not have long to wait. Soon there was a great deal of commotion at our front door. Mother quickly went to meet the visitors, and we heard a confusion of voices talking all at once. Mrs. Redfield had indeed brought her husband but had also stopped at the Dueslers' house and pressed both of them to come, along with Mr. and Mrs. Artemus Hyde, who had just been departing from a visit with the Dueslers. In addition, they were joined by three men all in fishing gear, who had been night-fishing at the creek when they spotted the activity outside our house and decided to investigate. All in all, there were more than a dozen people crowded into the little bedroom of our house, and I had to pinch myself to keep from laughing at the hilarity of it.

Mr. Redfield was a little wisp of a man, not nearly as imposing as his wife. With the Dueslers it was the opposite, for Mrs. Duesler resembled a wilted flower while her husband was large, loud, and athletic, with dark, curling hair and a fashionably large mustache. Mr. and Mrs. Hyde were both tall and dignified, exquisitely dressed as befitted their station as the richest family in town. Mr. Hyde's father had founded Hydesville, and Mr. Hyde owned the house in which we now lived.

Mr. Hyde was proclaiming in a loud voice that he had never heard any complaint about this house before, and it was certainly nonsense that a murdered man was buried here. Mr. Duesler was quick to agree, pointing out that he would know if anyone had been murdered on the street behind his own home!

In this, Kate and I quickly discovered that we had a friend in Mrs. Redfield. Having been convinced herself, she did not wish to be made ridiculous. Her voice rose above the others as she repeated what she had heard.

"'Tis a prank," scoffed Mr. Hyde. "Tomorrow is April Fools' Day, and I am afraid you have been made the April fool, Mary!"

"Artemus, it is no prank. I will vouch for these girls myself! If you used your ears instead of your tongue, even an old dog like you might learn something!" scolded Mrs. Redfield.

As if it had been waiting for its introduction, our ghost suddenly rapped loudly. All present heard it and began to look around uneasily for the source of the sound.

"Is this the injured spirit who communicated to me and the Foxes earlier this evening?" Mrs. Redfield inquired in a loud, dramatic voice.

Two raps.

"Two means yes, and one means no," Mrs. Redfield explained to the crowd.

"Why, someone's having a game with us!" exclaimed Mr. Hyde. "They're in the attic and knocking on the ceiling above us!"

This caused the fishermen to hurry out of the bedroom and into the hallway, where we heard their feet pounding up the attic stairs.

Mr. Hyde followed them out into the hall and called up to them, "There's a cellar as well. The steps lead down from the buttery." The fishermen came down with their light and tramped off to the buttery, where they found the cellar steps and descended. I tried to picture that horrible damp place with its soggy wet floor, and I knew that it was a place well suited to harboring a ghost.

After a brief time, the fishermen returned, reporting to Mr. Hyde that they had found no living soul. A sharp rap followed closely upon this pronouncement, as if our spirit had been waiting to make itself heard.

"Are you the spirit of a man, then?" asked Mr. Duesler, speaking into the air. He received two raps in reply. "Murdered in this house?" Mr. Duesler went on, ignoring Mr. Hyde's huff of indignation. Two raps. "How were you murdered?"

There was a long silence. I wondered if I was going to have to say something, when Mrs. Hyde unexpectedly spoke up and pointed out that the spirit could only give yes or no answers.

"Was it a rope?" Mr. Duesler then asked. One rap.

"A knife?" Two raps.

"Were you stabbed?" Two raps.

"In the chest?"—one rap. "In the throat?"—two raps. "Aha, so your throat was cut?" Two raps.

Mrs. Duesler moaned softly and held hands with Mrs. Hyde. Lizzie covered her face with her hands, but Kate looked as if she was enjoying a deliciously horrifying story.

"Now, Bill," protested Mr. Hyde, "don't you think we'd have noticed if one of our people had disappeared from town?"

"Spirit," continued Mr. Duesler, "were you a resident of Hydesville?"

One rap. Of course not. As Mr. Hyde said, people would have noticed.

"Were you a visitor to town, a guest?"

After a moment, there were three raps.

"Now what the devil does that mean?" asked Mr. Duesler.

"Bill, your *language!*" whispered his wife.

"You asked two things at once," interjected Mrs. Redfield. "A visitor and a guest."

"Were you a visitor?" Two raps.

"A guest of someone in town?" One rap.

"A visitor but not a guest?" pondered Mr. Duesler.

"A peddler!" guessed Mrs. Redfield. That was not what I had in mind, but it presented interesting possibilities. Two raps.

"You were a peddler," repeated Mr. Duesler. "You visited the people in this house, and they murdered you by cutting your throat with a knife."

"Preposterous!" exclaimed Mr. Hyde.

"Who had this house before John Fox?" asked one of the fishermen.

"It was the Weekmans," declared one of the other fishermen. "And they left all suddenlike, without telling anyone they were going!"

Mrs. Redfield spoke up immediately. "They told *me* they were going! Mr. Weekman had an offer of employment back east, and they had to leave at once or lose the position. They could not possibly have done this terrible thing! Why, Hannah Weekman was the mildest of women, and her husband, Michael, was a soft-spoken gentleman!"

Mr. Duesler asked the spirit, "Was it the Weekmans who murdered you?"

One rap. Mrs. Redfield liked the Weekmans, and I liked Mrs. Redfield.

Our neighbors worked their way backward through the former tenants of the home, and finally the spirit agreed that Mr. Bell, a man of whom I knew nothing, had been the dreaded murderer. Mrs. Redfield narrowed her eyes and declared, "I never liked John Bell."

The questions went on well into the night. Mr. Hyde slowly became convinced that he was hearing something extraordinary.

He exclaimed again and again that the newspapers would hear of this crime and that no villain could get away with such an act in a house he owned!

Eventually the raps diminished and vanished. Questions went unanswered and no more sounds could be summoned. Kate was asleep across the bed, and my own eyes were drooping uncontrollably. Mrs. Redfield invited my mother to bring us to her house across the street for the remainder of the night. Her husband, Charles, she announced, would stay with my father and watch the house for further disturbance until morning.

Mr. Duesler gathered Kate up in his arms and carried her from the room. Mr. Hyde himself offered me his arm and helped me out of bed. As the crowd dispersed, my eyes caught those of Mr. Redfield, who was shaking his head solemnly. Speaking his only words of the evening, he stated, "I still say this is a prank."

❧❧

Morning came late for me. I awakened to Kate's low voice, rich with excitement, urging me out of slumber. There were a few moments of disorientation when I opened my eyes, until I was able to identify my place on a trundle bed in Mrs. Redfield's bedroom.

"Maggie, wait until you see!" Kate was saying. "The whole town has come!"

For a moment, I thought she was telling me that the entire town of Hydesville had come to punish the two of us for last night's wickedness. Kate's persistent grin seemed out of place. Finally I pushed myself upright, taking in the full daylight streaming in the windows and hearing the murmur of voices outside the glass. A dress was strewn across the foot of my bed, one of my own, taken from the trunk in my bedroom.

Within a few minutes, I emerged fully dressed onto the front porch of Mrs. Redfield's house. Blinking in the daylight, raising one hand to shield my eyes, I saw an amazing sight.

A large crowd of people stood outside the house in which we lived, just across from the Redfields'. The front door of our house stood open, and people milled in and out as if it were a place of commerce. Several people took note when Kate and I appeared, and there came an excited murmur among the crowd. Men removed their hats and bowed to us. Ladies whispered to one another behind their hands, and a few of them inclined their heads in respectful greeting.

All these people had come to see the house haunted by the ghost of a murdered man!

Throughout the afternoon, our house was the site of a great commotion. Over and over, we heard our mother and Mrs. Redfield repeat the story of last night's events to curious neighbors from all over Arcadia Township. To my vast amusement, the story grew in the telling of it! The more Mrs. Redfield and my mother talked, the more they believed their own words. Kate chimed in whenever they would allow her to speak, agreeing with everything they said, while I smiled behind my hand and Lizzie looked bewildered.

There were many people who searched our house during the day, but of course there was nothing to find. No one seemed surprised by the lack of ghostly sounds in daylight, although everyone was anxious to see what would happen when night fell. There was talk of digging up the cellar to look for the peddler's body, but without my father's permission, nobody wanted to begin such an endeavor.

My father, meanwhile, had left. He had gone to the building site of our new home, just as he had promised David the day before. We learned later that he said nothing to David about the night's excitement, and my brother was ignorant of the events in town until he went home for the evening meal and found a house full of gossiping neighbors.

When evening finally came, it was nearly impossible to find standing room in our miserable little house. People completely unknown to us had arrived by carriage and were pushing and jostling their way into our bedroom. This room, where Kate and I sat unnoticed on our little bed, was the best place to hear the knockings of the peddler's ghost.

Mr. Duesler at once took charge and asked most of the questions for the crowd. He repeated all of last night's questions over again and received all the same answers—that a visitor to town was murdered by having his throat cut. Various committees were formed to go into the attic or the cellar to listen and look while the raps took place. No sounds could be heard in any room except this one bedroom, and eventually Mr. Duesler found out that the murder had taken place in this room!

It was about this time that my brother, David, appeared, gently inserting his way through the curious onlookers. I wasn't sure what David thought when he first heard the raps for himself. I admit that I was nervous. But eventually he suggested what others had been saying all along: they should get some picks and shovels and overturn the cellar floor. Nobody had wanted to do this without the approval of my father, or at least Mr. Hyde, but when David seemed willing to take charge, several men produced the desired digging tools.

The crowd surged out of the bedroom and into the buttery, where the cellar stairs seemed likely to give way under the weight of spectators watching David, shirtsleeves rolled up, breaking up the dirt floor with a pickax. The fever of excitement was catching, and I found myself as anxious as anybody to hear what he found. Kate said calmly that she was sure David's findings would satisfy everyone, and because I had no problem believing that there probably was a body in that horrid cellar, I had little fear of being found out.

Mr. Duesler was distressed to lose his place as the center of attention. He was not quick enough to get a spot among the diggers, and so he returned to the bedroom to recommence his role as spirit questioner. In a moment's inspiration, he offered to recite the alphabet, and if the spirit rapped at certain letters, he could spell out answers other than yes and no. By this process the name of Bell was spelled out again and again as the peddler named his killer.

Mrs. Redfield, not to be outdone by Mr. Duesler, came forward at this point and cried, "Oh, you poor restless spirit! Is there not a heaven for you to attain?"

The spirit rapped yes.

At this, Mrs. Redfield's eyes filled with tears, and she asked if her little child Mary Louisa were in heaven. Very quickly, the sympathetic spirit rapped yes.

Instantly, a chorus of voices called out, asking after a legion of dead relatives and acquaintances. The spirit assured all present that every single one of their loved ones was in heaven with the Almighty.

A great emotional outburst commenced, with women bursting out in tears as they wept for lost children and men blowing their noses into handkerchiefs as they remembered their dear old mothers. Thankfully, there came a great upheaval of men from the cellar at that point, and David appeared with his digging crew, their trousers damp and their shoes coated with mud.

"We cannot excavate any further tonight," my brother declared. "The holes fill up with water as fast as we can dig them. There's a spring under this house, and it's going to require a pump to do any kind of thorough search."

My mother inserted herself into the crowd and urged everyone to leave. "We can resume our contact with the spirit tomorrow evening, or rather Monday, as it would be unseemly to conduct this on the Sabbath," she said.

"Agreed," Mr. Duesler concurred. "We can allow a *reasonable* number of people access to this room in order to communicate with the spirit. This constant crowd is a distraction to those of us trying to pose a serious inquiry into the affair."

"Here, Bill!" shouted out the voice of a man I did not know. "What gives you the authority to decide what questions to ask or who gets to listen to the ghost jaw on about how he was killed?"

Mr. Duesler turned bright red and seemed quite speechless for a moment. Mrs. Redfield jumped in immediately. "If you have some doubt about what's been happening here, Demosthenes Smith, then I will invite you to attend Monday night's investigation your-self. I am sure Bill Duesler would be happy to stand down in his role, if you so desire. Wouldn't you, Bill?"

Mr. Duesler had no choice but to agree to allow someone else to ask the questions, although he looked unhappy about it.

Slowly, the crowd began to disperse. David stayed for a while to speak to my parents. Father especially seemed unhappy with the idea of digging up the cellar and adamantly refused to allow any activity to take place the next day, on the Sabbath.

For my part, I refused to be removed from my bed. Kate snuggled down beside me, and we did not allow any room for Lizzie Fish, who had to go home with Mrs. Redfield.

The spirit was very quiet for the remainder of the night.

Chapter Four
Maggie

One of the most amazing things about those strange days was that Kate and I were caught in the act more than once. Still, most people never believed we could be responsible for what they were hearing.

The first person to accuse us was that loud-voiced man, Demosthenes Smith, who embarrassed Mr. Duesler on the night of April Fools'. He did not return on Monday, as suggested, but came later that week. By then we had grown accustomed to receiving a limited number of people in the bedroom at dark. My mother would shut the door to close out distractions, lighting only a small candle in the corner of the room "because the spirit preferred it that way."

Kate and I had become rather bold and, I daresay, overconfident about our own cleverness. Therefore, it was with a sense of shock and disbelief that I felt a great hand grasp my foot during the rapping. My leg was abruptly pulled out from beneath the covers and over my head.

"I have the ghost!" shouted Mr. Smith. "I have the ghost!"

Mother quickly reached for the candle and brought it around to light the area near my bed. There I was, exposed, certainly with a look of shock and fear on my face, while Mr. Smith held my foot triumphantly in his hand, his unpleasant face twisted with smugness.

There was a long, long moment of silence in which I imagined being soundly thrashed with a rod by my father and shunned forevermore by all the good people in the town.

Then my father's low voice growled, in a tone of anger I had never heard before, "Mr. Smith, I will ask you to release my daughter at once."

It was only then that I realized how my dress had fallen away, baring my legs. The women in the room had all turned furious faces upon Mr. Smith, who suddenly seemed to realize the liberty he had just taken with a young girl. He dropped my foot and took a step backward. I scooted away from him to the head of the bed and pulled my dress down over my ankles.

Talk of the town for the next two days was how Demosthenes Smith had presumed to lay hands on one of the Fox girls and how John Fox had run him out of the house. No one wanted to know why Mr. Smith thought my foot was the ghost.

In fact, the ghost originated from four feet and a couple of knees. Kate had always been able to loudly crack her toes. With practice, I had learned to do so also, although not as reliably as Kate. For really loud raps, Kate popped her knee joints. When possible, I concealed two thin blocks of wood under my dress. Loosely holding them between my knees, I could bring them together for a sharp rap if nobody was closely observing me. This was the reason Kate and I so often drew the bed coverings over us during the rapping.

The next person to guess our secret was the town doctor. It happened under particularly frightening circumstances, and I came close to confessing everything in that moment.

Visitors continued to arrive at the house nightly. My mother never turned them away, even people unknown to us. Night after night, the murdered peddler answered questions about his own death and the heavenly disposition of every departed soul known to the questioners. In addition, David had brought a pump to try to reduce the water level in the holes he had dug in the cellar. The pump made a ghastly noise by day, and the spirit knocked long into the night. We were exhausted.

Kate's health had always been fragile. She was prone to severe headaches, which made her violently sick to her stomach and left her weak for days. One afternoon, after a bad spell of vomiting, she fell to the floor like a stone and became stiff and insensible. I screamed for help, and Mother and Lizzie came running. Mother cast me out the door, bidding me run for the doctor.

Run I did. I banged loudly upon the door of Dr. Knowles. His daughter-in-law opened the door and, finding me frantic with worry, called for the doctor. I begged him to come attend my sister.

We arrived back at the house within minutes, the doctor having taken pity on me and broken into a run beside me. We found Mother and Lizzie anxiously standing over the bed in which they had placed Kate, wringing their hands and alternately moaning and praying. Kate was still stretched out to her full length, with her feet extended and her head stretched back on her neck. As we watched, her limbs began to shake and twitch. A commotion of snapping and cracking sounds rang out from the bed, and to me it seemed obvious that they were coming from Kate.

It was obvious to the doctor, too. He quickly surveyed the situation and said, "She is having a seizure. We must make certain she does not bite her tongue, or worse, swallow it." Swiftly, he removed his belt and began to force it between her teeth.

As quickly as it had come upon her, the fit ended. All her limbs relaxed and went limp. Her head rolled back to its normal position, and the sounds all stopped. She suddenly broke out in a sweat, and her eyes fluttered.

"Kate!" I sobbed, climbing up on the bed beside her and putting my arms around her. She moaned and clutched at her head.

The doctor sent Lizzie out of the room and drew Mother aside. He was a very hesitant and soft-spoken man. He had never come to our house to hear the spirit rapping, but he must have known what had been taking place six houses down from his own. He questioned Mother gently regarding Kate's headaches and looked at the tonic that we usually gave her when she was ill.

"This would be good for her to take now. It will relax her muscles and help her to sleep. I think…today's seizure was perhaps a result… that is to say, the activities in which she has been engaged may have brought on too much excitement." The doctor spoke in half sentences, looking over Mother's shoulder at Kate on the bed. He seemed loath to say what was on his mind. As I listened, burying my face in Kate's hair, I knew that he was about to give us away.

Mother, meanwhile, asked if communicating with the spirit had made Kate fall ill.

The doctor shook his head. "Too much excitement for a young girl…I can't account for the noises, exactly…I mean, I haven't heard them…unless you count today. I think…that is to say, I suggest that a manipulation of the joints or muscles of her fingers and toes…that could be a cause. I would suggest rest for her…away from all of these activities. This medicine has morphine in it. That should prevent…that is to say, make unlikely another seizure."

It was clear to me that the doctor had betrayed us. My guilty mind heard his accusation, and I waited all afternoon for my mother to confront me. My dread turned to bewilderment when she said nothing at all but sat down beside me to hold my hand and watch over Kate's sleep. It was later that I realized that she had listened to the doctor and heard only what she wanted to hear.

When my father returned home that afternoon, Mother informed him of the doctor's opinion that the excitement of the spirit rapping had made Kate ill. She needed to be removed from the house and kept under the sedation of medication to prevent another fit.

Far from being persuaded that her daughters were causing the rapping, Mother had now been convinced that the haunting was a danger to her children's health. She moved us to David's house immediately.

The doctor never said another word about the noises he heard the day Kate had her fit. But Demosthenes Smith chuckled knowingly every time he passed me in town.

Chapter Five
Kate

There is a history of second sight in my mother's family. Great-Grandmother Rutan, for example, was a legend. She was known to rise from her sleep in the middle of the night and walk out of the house and down the road to the graveyard, following a funeral procession that only she could see.

In the morning at the breakfast table, Great-Grandmother Rutan would tell her family all the details of the funeral: how many carriages had attended, who had led the procession, and how many mourners had been present. The family would listen sadly, because the visions that she saw always came true within a few weeks.

My mother's sister Elizabeth was also gifted with the sight. Sadly, she was burdened with a dream vision at the age of nineteen in which she saw her own gravestone. She knew that she would marry a man who had a name beginning with the letter *H* and die at the age of twenty-seven. True to her vision, my aunt married a man named Higgins and died at the foretold age.

Maggie says that if she had been Aunt Elizabeth, she would have avoided all men whose names began with the dreaded letter and would not have moved from her bed for her entire twenty-seventh year of life. But Maggie doesn't truly understand the gift, or she would know that such antics cannot stop a preordained future from happening.

I grew up knowing that I would be the next family member to have the sight. Sometimes I had vivid dreams and knew that they were visions of the future, but upon waking, I would be unable to remember them. I believed that my headaches were a manifestation of my frustration to truly use my gift, and that if I could develop my power fully, the headaches would cease.

It is true that the rapping started as a prank. But quickly I came to realize that the answers I rapped were coming from a source I could not identify. When Mary Redfield asked about her dead child, I felt the strangest sense that some small spirit was reaching out from beyond the veil of life, wishing to comfort this poor woman in her grief. And all of the other neighbors who flocked to me, asking after the loved ones who had passed on—they sensed this gift in me, that I could deliver messages from heaven and thus ease their pain.

After my fit, when my mother dosed me thoroughly with the headache tonic, I heard the voices more clearly than ever. Perhaps that bout of illness was the breaking of a kind of barrier, allowing me to use my gift in a way that had thwarted me before. Although my mother removed us from that sad little house in Hydesville, I knew that my role in the rapping of messages from the spirit world had not come to an end.

As for my sister Maggie—she says that she invented the murdered peddler on an impulse, to entertain me and frighten the neighbors with a good ghost tale. No one was more surprised than she was by what David found in the cellar.

Sometimes people do not recognize their own gifts.

Chapter Six
Maggie

The day after Mother moved us to David's house, we received an unexpected visitor.

"Yoo-hoo!" called the unmistakable voice of Mrs. Redfield. "Margaret Fox! Do tell me you are at home, because I have brought you an important visitor!"

I dropped my sewing in a hurry, because any visitor at all was a welcome break from the dreariness of my brother's farm. David's wife, Betsy, was moving toward the front door at a snail's pace. Wide and slow moving, she was expecting her third child. She was expecting her third child, wide and slow moving. I skirted around her and managed to open the door before Mrs. Redfield could burst through with her knocking.

"Why, Margaretta, fetch your mother," gasped Mrs. Redfield, looking red faced and breathless. "There's someone here to meet her!"

"Who is it?" I asked, peering around Mrs. Redfield. There was a young man coming up the steps to the front porch.

"He's a *writer*," Mrs. Redfield whispered loudly. "He writes for newspapers, and he publishes pamphlets, and he wants to speak to your *mother*."

By this time, Betsy had arrived to greet the visitors, and my mother was coming down the stairs from the second floor. Betsy ushered us into the parlor, where the young man removed his hat and bowed deeply to each one of us as Mrs. Redfield made the introductions.

"This is Mr. E. E. Lewis, come all the way from Canandaigua to write about the supernatural events that have overtaken our town!"

"I received a telegram from Mr. Artemus Hyde," explained Mr. Lewis. This produced the expected reaction of awe, as none of us had ever been the recipient of a telegraph message—they had been invented only four years earlier and still were an amazing modern marvel. Mr. Lewis seemed rather a marvel himself for this backwoods township in the wilds of New York. He wore a tightly tailored cutaway coat and a vest with a shawl collar, showing off his starched white shirt and loosely tied cravat. He had the longest, thickest sideburns I had ever seen, and dark, curled hair coming down to his collar in the back. His eyes were blue and twinkling, and when they grazed over Betsy, she patted her hair and smoothed down her farm dress. When they rested on my mother, she turned quite pink and sank quickly to a sofa, one hand reaching out to grasp mine.

I turned a saucy smile in his direction and asked, "What does the E. E. stand for, Mr. Lewis?"

"It stands for my Christian names," he quickly replied.

"And those Christian names are…" I encouraged him.

"Two names given me by my parents, both beginning with the letter *E*," he said with a returning smile. He pulled a small blank daybook from the inside pocket of his frock coat and turned to my mother. "Mrs. Fox, if you don't mind, I am greatly interested in the events that have so perplexed this town. I would like to take a statement from you regarding this strange affair and your role in uncovering the crime revealed by the ghostly manifestation. With your permission, I shall take down your words and print them for the edification of interested readers across this great nation."

"Land sakes!" exclaimed my mother, fanning herself. "Do you think anyone would be interested in what happened in our house? I don't know where to begin!"

"It is best, Mrs. Fox, to begin at the beginning," the young man reassured her. "You could start by telling me how long you have lived here in Hydesville, and in this house particularly."

My mother began hesitantly, but she quickly warmed to her tale and recounted all the details of the evening when Kate had first commanded, "Here, Mr. Splitfoot, do as I do." Mr. Lewis made notes in his daybook, his blue eyes moving steadily from the book to my mother, as if no one else were in the room. He interrupted her once to ask if I was the daughter who first spoke to the spirit. "No, that was Catherine, my youngest, who is upstairs sleeping. This is Margaretta," replied my mother.

When Mother had finished, Mr. Lewis turned to Mrs. Redfield and asked her to make a statement about her experiences that first night. Mrs. Redfield was more than happy to comply, and she embarked on a lengthy tale that repeated much of what my mother had already said. Mr. Lewis did not seem to mind but wrote every single thing down in his book. Mrs. Redfield's memory of the events wandered occasionally from the truth and sometimes seemed self-serving. She claimed, for example, that she had asked the spirit to rap out her age as a test of its supernatural knowledge. "There were thirty-three raps," Mrs. Redfield emphasized, "and that is my age." My eyebrows rose in disbelief, because I felt sure Mrs. Redfield had bid farewell to age thirty-three a long time ago, but Mr. Lewis showed no such doubt and wrote it down.

I was ready to tell my story next. In my mind, of course, I was the most important person in the story next to Kate, and so it was with a bit of shock that I saw Mr. Lewis rise and close his book.

"I would like to speak to your husbands, ladies, so that I might record their versions of this story as well," he said. "It seems as if I should also speak to Mr. Duesler, and a few other people who were present."

"And you will want to come to the house tonight and hear the rappings for yourself, will you not?" Mother asked anxiously, forgetting that she had sworn that very morning not to set foot in the house again after dark.

Mr. Lewis seemed a bit hesitant. "My task here is to record, not necessarily to witness."

"Oh, Mr. Lewis," exclaimed Mrs. Redfield, "you can't come all this way and not hear the rapping for yourself!"

"I suppose I might want to see the house…and certainly the cellar…"

"Then we shall meet at dusk at the Fox house!" proclaimed Mrs. Redfield, and it was clear that Mr. Lewis would bend to her will, just as so many good people before him had done.

I jumped up as he started to leave the parlor, springing into his path. He smiled and nodded in a polite good-bye. "But, Mr. Lewis!" I began.

"Miss Margaretta?" he raised an eyebrow quizzically.

For a moment I was speechless. I could not ask him why he did not write down my story, because my story was largely a secret. Finally, I said, "Those Christian names, sir. Might they be Edward Enoch?"

He smiled. "They might be. But they are not."

That evening, Father drove the wagon into town, conveying Mother, Betsy, and me to meet Mr. E. E. Lewis at the house. Kate had been left behind, over her protestations and wailing. I know she was angry about being left out, and I had some reservations about creating the rapping by myself. I feared the peddler would be more subdued tonight, and I was not sure that Mr. Lewis would be impressed. I think I was more worried that Mr. Lewis would not even notice me than I was about being caught.

We could see the lights of the house and the lanterns carried by neighbors as we approached. A small group waited upon the doorstep, and my keen eyes quickly picked out Mr. Lewis. Father reined in the horses, and as the wagon came to a halt, someone lifted me down. I gathered my skirts and hurried forward, eager to be at the forefront of the crowd.

Mr. Lewis had his daybook out and was leaning down to catch the words of one of the neighbors when a sudden commotion from inside the house caught the attention of all present. Heavy footsteps and excited voices approached, and then my brother flung open the door. Poor David had been single-minded in his endeavor to dig up the cellar. He felt that there had to be an explanation for the mysterious events in the house, and that if he could find some physical proof of an evil deed committed there, it would shed a good deal of light on the problem. He had even pulled up some of the floorboards in the bedroom to make room for a block and pulley to hoist buckets of mud from the cellar.

Now, with his hair askew, his sleeves rolled up, and his trousers coated with mud to his knees, David looked like a ghostly manifestation himself. He was grinning madly, and he thrust out his hand to us triumphantly with the announcement, "I've found him."

At first it seemed to me that he was holding some fragments of pottery in his hand. And then I realized that I was looking at bone, smashed pieces of bone. Yellow-white, smooth in one part and jagged in another, they were tangled in what might have been hemp but was actually hair. As David jiggled his hand a bit, some of the pieces rolled about and I could see that two teeth were included among the bones.

A hush fell over the crowd as one of the men held up a lantern and David presented his find for the perusal of Mr. Lewis. "What do you think, sir? Is this him?"

Mr. Lewis pushed his hat backward on his head and closely inspected the gruesome collection. He made a move as if to poke at them with his finger, but he drew back before doing so. "I can't say, Mr. Fox. Those look like a man's teeth, but the bone could be anything. Is there more to him?"

David's face fell a bit. "No," he admitted, "not yet, anyway. We're still ankle deep in water down there. I haven't given up, though. If he's down there, we'll find him. The rest of him, that is. Why, if this isn't human, what is it? What else has hair like that?"

"A horse?" came a voice from the crowd.

"Buried in the cellar?" scoffed David. "With a man's teeth?"

"A man could lose his teeth without losing his life," observed Mr. Lewis. "But this bone is very suggestive of some wicked event. I do not doubt that if there is more conclusive evidence to be found, you shall discover it, Mr. Fox."

"He needs a decent Christian burial!" exclaimed Mrs. Redfield.

"Just that bit of him?" asked her husband wryly. "Or shall we wait for more?"

There was some nervous snickering then, and David looked out uncertainly at the crowd, his big hand closing over the bits of bone and teeth protectively. "This is hardly a laughing matter," he said with dignity.

"Indeed, it is not," agreed Mr. Lewis. And although I would have sworn that he had not noticed my arrival or been aware of my presence, he suddenly turned and looked directly at me. "This child is shivering in fear," he stated. With a swift movement, he removed his suit coat and slung it around my shoulders. I had hardly been aware of my own teeth chattering, but when the warmth of his coat settled around me, I looked up at him gratefully. "I suggest we disperse," Mr. Lewis continued. "Allow Mr. Fox to close up this house—or tomb, if that's what it be—and we can continue our investigation into this affair at another time."

The crowd parted as he took my arm and led me down the front steps. He meant to hand me off to my mother, but she was engaged in animated conversation with Mrs. Redfield, and so I had a moment to turn and speak to Mr. Lewis. "I thank you kindly for your coat, sir."

"Miss Margaretta, you owe me no thanks. Where I come from, a man would be horsewhipped for showing any less courtesy to a young lady in need. I am certain that if your parents had known such a grotesque discovery would be made here tonight, they would not have brought you here and exposed you to such a fright."

"A ghost has been rapping in my house for nearly a fortnight," I replied in what I hoped was an offhand manner. "I believe it would take more than a few bones to frighten me now, Mr. Elijah Ezekiel."

"Ah, a very biblical appellation," Mr. Lewis murmured with a smile. "I will be sure to remember it if I am ever graced with a son. But, alas, it does not belong to me."

He bowed, and I curtsied. My father gave me a hand up into the wagon, and then I handed down Mr. Lewis's coat regretfully.

Everybody seemed to think that seeing the bones had shocked and distressed me. They gave me a warm tisane of chamomile and peppermint to calm my nerves and put me to bed. The truth, however, was that I hardly gave those poor, sad bones a second thought. I always said there was probably someone buried in that wretched cellar! I bounded out of bed the next day and spent the morning hanging about the front door, eager to greet any visitors—especially Mr. E. E. Lewis, who might call to inquire about my emotional state and finally put my story into his daybook.

Nobody heard the approach of a carriage and horses that morning except for me. I hurried out onto the porch, patting my hair into place and checking my skirt for its cleanliness.

Unfortunately, the man to emerge from the carriage was a stranger to me. He was of medium height but broad across the chest. His hair was fair, but his eyebrows and beard were dark, giving him a fierce look. He took a moment to brush at his trousers and sleeves, then he looked up, faced the house, and began to stride purposely forward. He showed no reaction when he saw me waiting for him and did not speak until he had mounted the steps.

His voice was a deep baritone. "Is this the house of Mr. John Fox?"

"This is David Fox's house," I replied. "But John Fox is currently residing here."

"Then please inform him that I would very much like to speak with him," the man said. "My name is Bell."

Chapter Seven
Maggie

The little assembly held in David's farmhouse that day was a meeting that no one in my family would ever forget. Everyone was frozen in their places, as though it were a painting.

Mr. Bell stood stiff backed and dignified in the center of the drab little parlor, having declined the offer of Betsy's best chair. My father remained standing, because his guest did, but looked frail next to the visitor, with hunched shoulders and a feeble gaze behind his spectacles. It occurred to me for the first time how much my father had aged since the night before April Fools' Day.

My brother stood a few feet behind Father, lending silent support. David had a slight build, like my father, but his face resembled Mother's in its openness and affability. David was used to being well liked, and it pained him to be seen in an adversarial role. My mother sat on the settee, plump and matronly and demurely dressed like a good Methodist. Betsy had taken a seat in the far corner, pale, weary, with a swollen belly leaving almost no room for two-year-old Ella on her lap.

Lizzie dithered uncertainly in the doorway, with Betsy's younger baby on her hip. Behind her, Kate and I peeped into the room, probably looking like the frightened schoolgirls that we were.

Mr. Bell's gaze swept briefly over us, with a look of consternation to find us in such a state of terror. Little did he know that we were not frightened because we thought he was a murderer, but because we thought he might murder *us* if he found out how we had destroyed his reputation for the sake of a prank!

Everyone had said that Mr. Bell had moved away. Nobody mentioned that he had moved only as far as Lyons, which was still in Wayne County and only an hour away by carriage. Never in a thousand years would I have expected him to hear about how we had maligned his name and come to set the record straight! Of course, neither could I have imagined a hundred people visiting the bedroom of that dismal Hydesville house to talk to the dead or a writer from Canandaigua arriving to record our stories. It was almost as if I had pushed a wagon down a hill without noticing who was in the way and then found myself helplessly watching the aftermath.

Mr. Bell addressed my father formally. "I understand that you have accused me of murder, sir."

"Not I," replied my father.

There was a long moment of silence, as everyone expected that my father would go on, and when he did not, Mr. Bell's eyebrows furrowed in puzzlement. "Have I been misled, then? I understood that there had been an accusation and that it originated with this family." Again his eyes passed over the room, finding only an ordinary, respectable-looking farming family.

David stepped forward and placed one hand on Father's shoulder. "It is difficult to explain, Mr. Bell. But there have been manifestations at your former home that defy explanation."

48

"Ghosts?" scoffed Mr. Bell.

David nodded in agreement. "If you choose to use that term, sir, then yes, ghosts. Or rather, one ghost in particular. And it is true that an accusation has been made against you."

"By this ghost?" Mr. Bell repeated incredulously. "It speaks?"

"Ah…no," admitted David. "Rather he…raps."

It was clear Mr. Bell was having difficulty maintaining his equanimity, his expressive face fighting down a display of temper. But he did not want to give the appearance of a murderous man, and so he was weighing each statement for its measure of innocence before speaking it. Nonetheless, the idea of a rapping ghost was too ridiculous to bear, and impatience won out on his face as he took a breath in preparation for an attack on my brother's wits or sanity.

Before Mr. Bell opened his mouth, however, my father unexpectedly spoke again, shaking off David's hand. "I knew no good would come of it when good Christian people debased themselves by consorting with demons and spooks. I said so myself when all of this devilment began." Father peered up at Mr. Bell and said, "I have had nothing to do with that house in a week. I won't set foot there again. I tried and tried to find the source of those noises, sir, I truly did. Never was a man as vexed as I, trying to find a rational explanation that a God-fearing Methodist could accept. And I have prayed, sir, yes, prayed daily…for deliverance from this burden."

Slowly, Father's voice ran down, and he lifted a hand to his spectacles, removed them, and wiped them carefully on a shirtsleeve, his eyes cast down to the floor. David reached out hesitantly to him, and Betsy rose from her seat, reaching him at the same moment. Father turned and smiled weakly at his daughter-in-law, then allowed her to take him by the arm and lead him out of the room. Mother watched him go with a surprising coldness in her features, then turned her face back to the visitor.

Mr. Bell seemed taken aback by Father's outburst and demeanor. He reined in his temper, and his eyes were more sympathetic when he faced David once more. "I can see that you are sincere," he said in a quieter voice, "and troubled by these events."

"They have indeed been troubling," said David, "and my father, who is a profoundly religious man, has been shaken to the core."

"I have been counseled to seek a lawyer and enter charges of slander," Mr. Bell went on, causing a grieved look to appear on David's face. "But I consider myself a gentleman above all, and I felt it was proper that I should come here before taking any legal action, and meet my accuser face-to-face."

"That," replied David sadly, "will prove to be difficult."

Mr. Bell did not stay much longer. He accepted a chair, and then he and David discussed his next course of action. He wanted to see the house, of course, and hear the rapping for himself. Kate gripped my arm fiercely upon hearing this.

David broke the news to him that remains had been discovered in the cellar, and Mr. Bell was very careful in his response, appearing as concerned as any good citizen but not overly distressed. When David, acting on his natural enthusiasm, offered to show him the box of bones, Mr. Bell recoiled in distaste and almost refused. But he seemed to consider how that might appear to us, and perhaps remembering the old wives' tale about a murder victim's body bleeding afresh when the murderer was near, he changed his mind suddenly and expressed a frank eagerness in viewing the remains. My brother cheerfully fetched the box and proudly showed off his find, apparently not finding it awkward that he was showing it to the purported killer. Mr. Bell solemnly viewed the contents of the box for a respectable number of seconds while Lizzie and I leaned forward, craning our necks. The bones did not bleed.

Finally, David closed up the box, Mr. Bell stood up and shook his hand, and in a procession we led the visitor to the door. Only my mother remained behind in the parlor, her stony expression unchanged. Among us all, only she truly and utterly believed that our visitor had invited a peddler into his home, slit his throat with a knife, stolen his belongings, and buried his body in the cellar.

⁘

Kate's fingernails dug into my arm. "I will not rap for that man!" was the first thing she said when she could get me alone. "If we rap for him, he will catch us!"

"Demosthenes Smith caught us, and it did us no harm," I pointed out.

"This man is different. He has much to lose, and people will believe what he says."

"Don't you feel the least bit guilty that he stands accused of murder because we thought it would be fun to scare everyone?"

Kate shook her head at me sadly and gave me that intense violet gaze that seemed to mesmerize my entire body. "Maggie, that man is not a gentleman. Didn't you see him? He tried to act innocent, but he had to think carefully about every word he said."

"I can see why Mrs. Redfield does not like him," I admitted. "She never thinks a second about what she says before it reaches her tongue. But he was talking about getting a lawyer and entering charges of slander!"

"Who has spoken slander? No one in our family! Who has said that he is a murderer? Who has said it aloud?"

"Why, the people listening to the raps," I said in surprise. "Mrs. Redfield, Mr. Duesler. At least they asked the questions, and the spirit answered with its knocking."

"Then let him charge the spirit with slander and see what a judge makes of it!"

I paused to think this over. Kate took my arm and shook it. "Maggie, do not forget. David found those bones. They are real."

"What do you want to do?" I asked weakly.

"Nothing. The spirit will not rap tonight when Mr. Bell is at the house. We cannot, Maggie. I feel this very strongly."

Kate sometimes had very strong feelings that one thing or another would happen. Sometimes she was right, but just as often she was wrong, and then she would say that the event did not happen because she had foreseen it and diverted it. I was never able to argue a way out of this, because how could I disprove something that never occurred?

"But what will happen when Mr. Bell goes to the house tonight and the spirit does not rap the accusation?" I asked in my final weak plea.

Kate held my gaze. "We won't get caught."

⋙⟡⋘

That night, Kate and I selflessly volunteered to look after Ella and the baby so that everyone else could go to Hydesville. Lizzie stayed behind with us, and Father would not go, but everyone else rode off, eager to hear the spirit rap out his accusation to Mr. Bell. Sadly, the evening was a disappointment to everyone except Mr. Bell, for the spirit remained silent. Mother said the spirit was offended by the presence of his killer. Mr. Bell renewed his doubts about our family, but dozens of people were ready to swear that the Fox family had not made up the story. Mr. Bell was led unwillingly through the house as witnesses explained how thoroughly the premises had been searched for an earthly explanation for the rapping noise.

In the morning, Father collected his tools, as he did every morning, and started on foot for the site of our new house. He had been working long hours, often alone, doggedly trying to finish it so that we could move in.

It was my turn to bring his lunch that noon, and a happy chance that was for me, because as soon as I came within sight of the partially completed house, I could see that Father was not alone. A carriage that belonged to the Hydes was pulled up alongside, but it was not Mr. Hyde who had driven it. When I realized that Mr. E. E. Lewis was speaking with my father, I nearly broke out into a run, with Father's lunch rocking in its basket on my arm.

The daybook was out, and my father was gesturing with his hands, indicating his frustration and helplessness in a way I knew quite well. Mr. Lewis was nodding, slipping his pencil inside his coat, closing his book. I slowed my footsteps as they became audible to the men, and when they turned, I was walking at a demure pace, breathing deeply to conceal my breathlessness and smiling in what I hoped was a fetching manner.

"Margaretta," my father acknowledged me with a nod and quickly relieved me of the basket.

"Miss Fox," Mr. Lewis smiled at me, bowing deeply. "You bring the sunshine with you, I think, for there have been nothing but clouds all morning, and now that you are here, everything is brighter."

"I see you have finally captured my father," I said, still a little breathless and doing my best to conceal it.

"I was finding him a bit difficult to reach, but then someone told me, 'Why, he's out every day laboring at his new house. I can't think why you are unable to find him.' And didn't I feel like a fool when I found him exactly where everyone in town knew he would be?" Mr. Lewis was looking as fashionable as ever, in his spotless cutaway coat and vest. I found my eyes fixed upon the askew loops of his rakishly tied cravat, and my fingers itched to reach out and straighten them.

Father was digging in his lunch basket and paying no attention to us. I turned my shoulders slightly away from him, and Mr. Lewis turned in tandem with me, so that Father was left behind in spirit, if not in distance. "I am rather glad that I have encountered you today," I said, "for I wanted to tell you that I had fathomed your Christian names at last and assure you that your secret was safe with me."

"My very soul quakes at the thought of exposure. Do tell me how you discovered them."

I tipped my head and looked up at him through my lashes. "With your dark hair and complexion, it is obvious that your mother was a red-skinned Indian, probably with the power to tell the future. And envisioning your career as a reporter of mysterious events, she named you Eagle Eye."

He threw back his head and laughed so good-naturedly that my father actually raised his head from his meal and looked at us curiously. "Miss Margaretta," Mr. Lewis exclaimed, "you have made this visit every bit as interesting as that old murdered peddler has. Sometimes even more so, since I understand the peddler was quite silent last night."

"That is what I heard. Was Mr. Bell very angry?"

"I wasn't there, but I was told he was more self-righteous than angry. Look here. This was delivered to me this morning."

He removed a paper that was folded inside his daybook and smoothed it out so that I could read it. It was a petition, stating that the signers knew Mr. John Bell and believed him to be of sound character and completely incapable of criminal activity. It was signed by about thirty people, including almost the entire Hyde family and a few other Hydesville residents.

"Land sakes!" I exclaimed. "There's Mrs. Jewell's name!"

"Does that surprise you?"

"Not especially. Just the other day, she was telling Mrs. Redfield that it was a wonder Mr. Bell hadn't murdered them all in their beds. But Mrs. Jewell's head is stuffed with feathers, so she has trouble keeping track of her opinions from one day to the next."

Mr. Lewis tried to stifle his snickers as he folded the paper and put it back in his book. "Miss Margaretta, you are a caution! If you were a few years older, I would be utterly under your spell."

"I will be a few years older, in a few years," I quipped.

"A fair warning," he remarked, turning to check the horses on the carriage team.

"You weren't at the house last night, then?"

"No, I was not."

"You haven't heard the rapping at all, have you?"

"No, sadly, I have not."

I took a breath. "Mr. Duesler said you will not go to hear the rapping, because then you would have to admit it was real. He said that you are going to write about the people of Hydesville as if we were superstitious bumpkins and make fun of us all."

Mr. Lewis fiddled with the harness for another moment, then turned to face me. "That is not true. I plan on writing about Mr. Duesler and every person I have met here with the utmost respect. But you are correct. I have avoided going to the house to hear the rapping for myself. I came here as a recorder, not as a witness. If I hear the haunting for myself, then I will form my own opinion, and that will cause me to write with bias. I have listened; I have taken down the stories of those who experienced these events. I believe that these people have been unable to solve the mystery of these noises, and that is what I plan to write about."

"You haven't taken my story." The words passed my lips before I could even think of holding them back.

"Miss Margaretta," he smiled. "I can't take *your* story."

I suddenly felt all the breath leave my body. Did he know?

"What do you mean?" I asked in a voice that was nothing but air.

Mr. Lewis looked down on me, and I suddenly felt all the flirtation leave the conversation. "You have to understand, this is how I make my living. I plan on making money from the publication of this story. But I hope that I have enough virtue in me that I refuse to make money by publishing the name of an underage girl."

"But my name is already in your book. I heard my mother and Mrs. Redfield tell their stories. I was there on the night this started. My name is already part of the story."

Mr. Lewis made a slight grimace. "That is the only thing I have changed in their stories. Otherwise, I will quote them word for word."

"What did you change?"

"Your name. I have taken it out. Yours and your sister's and your niece Lizzie's."

I shook my head. "I don't understand."

"I've removed your names," he explained, "wherever they appeared. You'll be grateful later, when you are grown. It is not appropriate to print the names of underage girls in a publication about spirits and hauntings. It would not be a gentlemanly thing for me to do." Mr. Lewis vaulted up into the driver's seat of the carriage. I stepped back and took a fresh look at him.

"You removed my name," I repeated, just to make sure.

"It was the right thing to do," he said. And he bowed to me from his seat, shook the reins, and clicked at the horses. The carriage jerked forward while I stood alongside, staring up at him, with my father somewhere behind me devouring his meal in total oblivion.

⌒⌒

That afternoon, I cornered Kate in a private spot. She had been pestering me for days with ideas to enliven and expand our prank, and I had, for the most part, discouraged her. Now, however, I was irritated enough with Mr. Lewis to take a bold risk. "Do you remember when you wanted to call yourself a 'medium' for the spirits?" I hissed. "Let's talk about that again."

Chapter Eight
Maggie

I learned an important lesson that spring. People can view the same events and interpret them in completely different ways. For example, I thought that I was an important part of the manifestations that occurred in the Hydesville house that year, but Mr. E. E. Lewis thought that I was an irrelevant girl who was best left out of his account of those events. In addition, I thought that through my own cleverness I had convinced an entire town that a certain house was haunted, but my sister believed that she had proved her ability to communicate with the dead. In the end, it was a matter of perspective that was perhaps too complex for me to grasp.

When Kate first suggested that we continue the rapping outside of the Hydesville house, I refused to cooperate. It seemed clear to me that if we rapped outside of the house, we would soon be caught in the act. However, Kate insisted that people already suspected it was our gift of second sight that made communication with the spirit possible. I admit I was easier to convince when I was angry with Mr. Lewis. He had already left town, having gathered the sworn certificates of dozens of witnesses. I promised myself that he would soon return when he learned it was the girl rather than the house that was haunted, but I was wrong. I never met Mr. Lewis again, although he did indeed publish his pamphlet. As promised, it did not include my name or Kate's, but by the time it was printed, our notoriety was already ensured.

When the rapping first descended upon the Fox family farm, a day of chaos and confusion ensued. I distinctly recall Lizzie clasping her hands to her ears and crying, "I won't hear it! I won't hear it!" My poor sister-in-law, Betsy, fell into a state of collapse, sobbing that no one had been murdered in *her* house. The peddler's bones fell under blame, and David ran the box out of the house and into the barn for temporary storage. For my part, I regretted my actions almost at once, out of pity and fear for Betsy. I was afraid she would lose the baby, and this was something I did not intend and for which I would not forgive myself.

Through it all, Kate was a center of calmness and serenity, with her hands folded placidly and her voice firmly stating, "I don't think it is the same rapping. I am sure it is not the same spirit at all."

Of course, it absolutely was the same rapping, caused by the same source, and yet Kate's continued insistence that it sounded different eventually had an effect on the listeners, and they agreed that the sound was not identical to the one heard in the Hydesville house. This surprised me, for I had not yet come to understand the magnificent power of suggestion that would play a role in our future deceptions.

David asked if the spirit would rap for the alphabet, and two knocks were heard for yes. Painstakingly and patiently, David spelled out the alphabet, waiting for a rap to confirm each letter, until the following message was revealed: *We are all your dear friends and relatives.*

This caused another commotion, resulting in David taking his wife to her brother's house, where she could rest in peace, away from the rapping. Before he left, he argued with Mother about the new noises.

"Your sister has the gift," I heard Mother tell him.

"Now, Mother, don't talk superstitious nonsense," David hushed her.

"Superstitious nonsense!" my mother sputtered indignantly. "Did you not just recite the alphabet for a ghost? My grandmother had the second sight—"

"Yes, so you've told us," David interjected. "I've heard the stories."

"Stories! Is that what you think? But surely you remember your aunt Elizabeth!"

"Certainly I remember her—vaguely—but whether or not she actually prophesied her own death..."

Mother gasped. "Do you think I don't know whether or not my own sister had the sight?"

"Perhaps, but I am just as sure that *my* sister does not!" David stared her down stubbornly.

"Then how do you explain all that has happened here this month—and today, here at this house?"

"I don't know, Mother. But there must be an explanation, an explanation that is based on science we don't yet understand. Perhaps in twenty years we will laugh at how ignorant we were today. Perhaps spirit communication will be as commonplace as the post. Think how we marveled at the telegraph only a couple of years ago!" Mother continued to glare at David, with her hands on her hips. He dropped his voice, and I had to strain to hear him continue. "This is not what I want for Kate, or Maggie. Do not give them this reputation. I want to see them married into good families and happy. You must not jeopardize that!"

I was touched by his protectiveness. David, fourteen years older than I and nearly seventeen years older than Kate, was almost a father to us. As for my real father, he packed his own lunch and walked out to the new house that day, turning his back on the rapping for the last time. The new house was partially under roof, and Father moved in immediately, preferring the frigid April wind to living in a house with spirits. Mother never commented on his desertion, and although the house would be finished within a month's time, neither she nor Kate or I ever lived in it as anything more than a guest.

It would be wrong to say that we did not think about him or miss him. But Father's absence did not trouble us greatly.

In spite of David's protests, it did not take long for people to find out that the rapping had followed us to the farm and was heard only in the presence of the two youngest Fox daughters. Mrs. Redfield was soon included in my mother's confidence—and then Mrs. Jewell and Mrs. Duesler. Every evening Mother lit a candle in David's parlor, drew the curtains and closed the door, and then the ladies waited eagerly for rappings from the spirit world. Kate and I sat together on the settee, holding hands, smiling indulgently as the spirits rapped yes and no to questions about their heavenly reward.

It is difficult to justify our deception of these people. We had taken over David and Betsy's house and their life. We had driven a wedge between our parents. We had lied to good people, who had never shown us anything but kindness, and pretended that we had messages for them from beyond the veil of life. Some people might say these were wicked acts. And yet there was never any wickedness intended.

⚜

The excitement of the spirit circle truly infatuated me, and I know this was true also for Kate. In these early spirit circles, we did not dare masquerade as our companions' dead relatives. When pressed by our visitors with the question "Who are you?" we spelled out the answer "many," indicating that several combined spirits contributed to the rappings. We kept to the religious doctrines we knew, and confirmed the rewards of heaven to those souls who kept the faith.

There was no attempt made by the ladies to discover any explanation for the rapping, nor did they ever show any sign of disbelief. I think we were made bold by this simple faith, and thus were unprepared for the scrutiny that would fall upon us later. In fact, Kate and I passed that time in a kind of euphoria, having fallen under the spell of our own artifice.

So well treated were we at the hands of these ladies that we were totally unprepared for what happened the evening that Mr. Duesler came to see David, toting a shotgun in each hand.

He came quickly to the point, not being a man to mince words. "I have received some alarming news. There are a group of men from southern Arcadia who have risen in arms and are coming here tonight."

"My God," David gasped. "What for?"

"It has to do with the Hydesville house. There has been a great deal of talk about what happened there, especially since that man from Canandaigua was here taking certificates from everyone. David, it's because your sister called the spirit Mr. Splitfoot. That smacks of witchcraft in their eyes. And then you dug up bones from the house, and they are saying that your family has raised the devil from the earth of the cellar."

"That's ridiculous!" David burst out.

"Don't I know it?" Mr. Duesler replied in some distress. "But these are superstitious folk, and they take such things seriously. It is very unfortunate that your sister called the spirit Splitfoot, and I take responsibility for repeating the story. I thought it was amusing, and I never imagined that there might be violence."

"I know some of these men, I'm sure," David said mildly. "I have had business dealings in Arcadia. There is nothing to fear."

Mr. Duesler shook his head, and there was a nervous murmur from the women listening. Betsy began to wring her hands, all the color draining from her face, and Lizzie sat down at Mother's feet and put her head in her lap like a child.

"David," said Mr. Duesler. "I feel partly responsible, because I told this story around town like everyone else. I never meant to bring trouble to your house. But if these people get themselves worked up into a frenzy and accuse you of devilish acts, then I fear for what they might do. I suggest you send the women and the children to a neighbor or relative. They can take my wagon. I will stay and defend the house with you."

"Bill, I cannot believe there is any danger. I know these men, I tell you. Nothing will happen." David turned around and looked at each of the women. "Nothing will happen. I pledge my word."

"Nonetheless," said Mr. Duesler. "I will stay the night with you."

Darkness fell, and we all waited on pins and needles inside the house, listening for the sound of voices, horses, or worst of all, the crackling of flames.

Eventually the expected visitors arrived. We all ran to the front of the house, and from the windows we could see the lit torches and the movement of bodies on the road. Betsy and Lizzie ran to get the babies from their beds, and I pulled Kate close and whispered fiercely in her ear, "We have to tell the truth! We have to tell them we faked it all!"

Kate was pale and shaking. "They'll not believe us now."

Mr. Duesler had brought his shotguns, and now he tried to hand one to David. But my brother shook his head. "I don't want that."

"Don't be a fool!" hissed Mr. Duesler. "You need to defend your family!"

"It will be a sorry day when I cannot do that with reason and good judgment alone," replied David. Then he took hold of the handle to the front door, threw it open, and stepped out onto the porch to face the men.

They were armed. I could see the glint of shotguns in their hands. Some held torches, which could easily set the farmhouse ablaze. Through the window, we saw David stride confidently across the porch and down the steps to meet them. My mother pressed her hand to her mouth, and Betsy sobbed, caught between watching her husband through the window and running out the back door with her children.

We heard David's voice ring out: "Gentlemen! Welcome. I understand you have some questions for us regarding events that happened in Hydesville. I would be happy to address these matters with you."

There was a murmur among the crowd, and a voice shouted out, "We heard there are witches and the devil in your house!"

"No, sir!" David called out. "Just my family—my mother, my wife, and my sisters, who are a bit frightened by your presence. Surely you have some daughters or sisters, and you can appreciate how they might feel if approached in the night by armed men with torches! I would ask you to lay those aside, and then you may search my house if you will. I can assure you that you will find nothing unnatural or sacrilegious here. I did find some bones in the Hydesville house, and I suspect there may have been a murder there some years back. I haven't been able to prove it or pinpoint how long they have lain there."

"Dave Fox?" someone spoke out loudly from the crowd. "Is that you?"

"Yes, sir! Ned Burns, is it?"

"Why, I didn't know it was *you* they have said so much about!"

David laughed lightly. "Yes, I am afraid it is me. We've been very busy here, and I haven't been out to see you about that cow like I said I would."

One man stepped forward, holding his torch up to illuminate his own face, and using his shotgun like a walking stick. "I wondered what had kept you!"

"Will you search the house, Ned?" asked David, as though he were inviting the man in for tea.

"No, we won't come in. We'll come back in daylight, properly, as God-fearin' men ought to. No need to disturb your family now. Come on, men! That's Dave Fox, I tell you. He's all right, by God."

And with no other prompting, the crowd vanished back into the darkness, their lit torches dwindling to the size of fireflies in the night. David turned and strode back into the house, walking past Mr. Duesler and his shotguns without a word, having defended his house and family with nothing more than his amiable personality.

In the morning, only one man returned. David brought the box of bones out of the barn. The man poked and prodded the sad little display, commiserated with David on the unlikelihood of proving a crime with such inadequate evidence, and then departed without burning the house down. Thus, the first occasion in which the rapping was denounced as witchcraft ended as quickly as it began, and without violence.

Chastened by our near collision with superstitious zealotry, Mother suggested that we suspend the spirit meetings for a time. Which is why we were surprised to hear a wagon approach the house the next evening around dinnertime. Although the immediate fear had subsided, none of us had quite relaxed yet. We were half prepared to hear that the crowd of agitators had returned or that another group of townspeople had assembled with some demand or accusation. I do not think that any of us were prepared for the new fright actually descending upon us.

"What in the Sam Hill has been going on in this house?"

The voice rang out as clear and precise as a church bell. Lizzie, peeling potatoes in the kitchen beside me, instinctively flinched and hunched her shoulders like a baby bird sinking down into its nest. "Mother!" she whispered hoarsely.

We were done for.

My sister Leah had arrived.

PART TWO:
THE RISE OF A RELIGION

Chapter Nine
Maggie

Leah did not believe a word of it.

"I cannot believe you have been so easily taken in, Mother," she chastised. "Lizzie, give over those potatoes. One would think you hadn't been taught how to handle a peeling knife. I wish you had sent for me sooner! To think I had to hear this from the parent of one of my pupils. I cannot tell you how embarrassing it was to know nothing of what was happening here while my family name was being ridiculed in letters to strangers!"

"You haven't heard the spirits rapping," Mother said indignantly. "You don't know a thing about it."

"I know a humbug when I hear it, even thirdhand. For Pete's sake, you would think my own daughter at least would have written to tell me! But apparently you were all too busy talking to dead people to have time to write the living!"

"I didn't want to worry you, Mother," Lizzie mumbled.

"Oh, it was much better to have Jane Little's mother come and read me her cousin's letter and inquire whether insanity ran in my family! Betsy, don't reach over your head like that; it's not good for the baby. Maggie, fetch that pot down for Betsy instead of sitting there like a bump on a log—that's a girl. Kate, you look like the cat that swallowed the canary. Make yourself useful and set the table."

Leah was tall and large boned, but her years of living lean had not allowed her to attain the girth of Mother. At thirty-four, she still held a flush of prettiness in a face that was a little too round but lit up by lively gray eyes. She wiped her hands on her skirt apron and surveyed the kitchen as though it were her domain while we hustled about doing her bidding. "Where is Father?" she asked, suddenly realizing his absence.

We all continued at our assigned tasks in silence for a moment while glancing sidelong at Mother. After an awkward pause, she lifted her chin and met Leah's eyes significantly. "He moved out to the new house to finish it."

My sister arched an eyebrow. "He's living there alone?" At Mother's brief nod, Leah shook her head and shrugged one shoulder before turning to resume slicing the potatoes.

David put his head in through the back door and handed me a bucket of water from the pump. "Does she want to see the bones?" he whispered to me.

"Not before supper, David, thank you!" Leah called out. "I'll come out to the barn and pay my respects later, if you don't mind." I fetched up beside her with a freshly filled pot and let her slide the sliced potatoes into the water. Then she looked up and met my eyes, murmuring in a lower voice, "I will want a few words with you later, as well."

I nodded mutely.

At supper that evening, Leah told us how she had left Rochester the very day she learned about the hauntings involving her family. She went first to the Hydesville house, only to find that we had all moved out.

"Throughout the trip, I kept thinking that there had been some mistake and I would find that Mrs. Little's relative was ill-informed or a malicious gossip. But the neighbor in Hydesville, your Mrs. Redfield, was quick to regale me with stories about your resident ghost and about the spirit sittings you have held here at the farm."

Mother was eager to tell her own story and launched into a long-winded version of the same tale she had told Mr. Lewis. David and Betsy interrupted to share their own little pieces, and Lizzie nodded along wholeheartedly. When they explained that the spirit rapping occurred only in the presence of her sisters, Leah turned her head to give us a most skeptical look.

Kate stared back with her innocent gaze. "We were awfully frightened at first, but now that we have come to know them, the spirits do not trouble us at all. They so terribly want to be heard."

"Indeed," Leah replied dryly. "I can hardly wait to satisfy their need."

Although we had agreed, for Betsy's sake, to suspend the spirit circles, it was decided to make an exception in honor of Leah's arrival. After the supper dishes had been cleared and after David had taken Leah to visit the bones in the barn, we drew the curtains in the parlor and extinguished all but a single candle.

The spirits would be subdued that night. I had grown accustomed to concealing a block of wood within my petticoats on which I would knock with my hand in the darkness of the parlor.

Tonight, with Leah watching, I could not dare. Mother began as she always did, by summoning the spirits. When they had signaled their presence with a loud rap, she began to ask the usual questions.

"Are we in the presence of spirits from beyond the veil of life?" Two raps.

"Have you any messages for us this evening?" Two raps.

Mother smiled triumphantly and looked significantly at her eldest daughter as she asked, "Do you have a message from my grandfather Jacob Smith this evening?" Two raps.

This great-grandparent, whom I had never known, was a special favorite of Leah's, but she sat impassively as we waited out the rapping through the alphabet, which eventually spelled out: *Welcome my little Annie Leah.*

Leah's only response to this pet name was a raised eyebrow. "Is this the spirit of my great-grandfather, Jacob Smith?"

There came one rap, for no.

Mother leaned forward to touch Leah's arm. "Oh no, he never raps himself."

"Why not? I never knew him to be short on words in life."

"You're not taking this seriously," Betsy observed quietly.

"I *am* serious!" Leah protested, but she was laughing.

"Do you have any questions for the spirits, Leah?" Kate asked sweetly.

"Yes, I do." Leah leaned forward in her chair and addressed the air just below the ceiling, as she had seen our mother do. "Was Adelaide Granger's daughter Harriet really poisoned by her husband?"

It was a pickle of a question. We all knew the story, from our days living in Rochester. The daughter of Leah's friend Mrs. Granger had died of a sudden illness, and poison had been suspected. The husband, who was a doctor, had gone to trial and had been acquitted, but Mr. and Mrs. Granger had never stopped believing that their son-in-law had murdered their daughter.

Rather to my surprise, the spirit rapped twice, for yes. I wondered if Kate knew what she was doing.

Leah also registered surprise. "What should Mrs. Granger do about it?"

David called out the alphabet for us, as he usually did.

Nothing. Be at peace.

"What about justice for the husband?" demanded Leah.

The answer came: *He will receve justice in the next life.*

"That's an interesting spelling of the word 'receive,'" noted Leah. "Perhaps our spirit should have spent more time at its studies and less time rapping on the gates of heaven."

"Oh, Leah!" Mother exclaimed at the same moment that David snorted and said, "Doggone it, Leah!"

Suddenly, Kate spilled out of her chair and onto the floor in a faint, which we had agreed she would do if our sister became difficult. I was the first on the floor beside her, taking her hand as everyone else started out of their seats. "Kate! Kate!" I cried. "Can you hear me?"

Kate turned her head toward my voice and her eyelids fluttered. "Don't fear for me, Maggie. I am simply spent. The spirits have gone away now."

Lizzie was immediately at my side, helping me lift Kate to her feet, and then Mother was there, clucking and fussing over her. Together, we escorted Kate upstairs and put her into the trundle bed in the children's room, and then I lay down beside her, pleading exhaustion myself.

I know the adults spent a long time downstairs talking after that. Kate and I whispered to each other, trying to decide what we should do. We heard footsteps approach and we quieted ourselves instantly. The door opened and someone slipped into the room. I knew without looking that it was Leah. She stood over us silently while we tried to breathe steadily and feign sleep. After a time, she moved away and her footsteps retreated down the stairs.

There was one sure way to avoid Leah the next day—we went to school. Our attendance had been sporadic since we moved to Hydesville, and once the rapping began we had been more often truant than not. The teacher looked none too pleased to have us suddenly appear, as our presence provided a distraction to the other pupils, who were more interested in us than their lessons.

As we were passing through Hydesville on our long walk back to David's farm at the end of the school day, Mrs. Redfield came bustling out of her house to catch us.

"I have so missed our sittings, girls! Mrs. Jewell and I were just saying that we hoped that we could sit with you this evening. With all due consideration to Betsy Fox's nervous condition, I wanted to offer my own parlor. I can send my husband with the carriage for you and your mother—and the sister you have visiting from Rochester. Do ask your mother, won't you, girls? I will send Mr. Redfield around dusk."

"Betsy's nervous condition indeed," muttered Kate as we continued on our way. "She looked pretty sprightly last night when she was watching Leah sharpen her tongue on us."

"She'd boot us all out of the house if David would let her," I agreed. "Shall we go to Mrs. Redfield's house tonight, then?"

"If Mother will allow it," replied Kate. "I'm a little fearful about what Leah will say in front of the ladies, though."

At Mrs. Redfield's house, Leah could not have been more pleasant or polite. The ladies were quite taken with her personable manner and forthright friendliness. Mrs. Hyde asked her, "Where is your husband, dear?"

Leah cast her eyes down sadly and said, "He's dead," which was news to me. But then I saw Lizzie cringe in embarrassment, and I realized that her father was just as alive as ever and probably still living out west with his rich widow.

During our sitting, Leah sat demurely with her hands folded in her lap and listened attentively to the spirits. If she smiled now and again, it seemed only to indicate her pleasure in hearing the uplifting messages from those who had gone before us to heaven. Once she caught me watching her and winked.

It wasn't until the third day of Leah's visit that the blow finally fell. Lulled by a false sense of security, Kate and I had been unwise enough to let her find us alone. Leah caught us in the parlor and shut the door.

"I know you are doing it," she said, without preamble. "I don't quite know how, but I know it is you."

Kate began hesitantly: "It is true that we are the medium through which the spirits…"

"Forget that hogwash, Catherine!" Leah snapped. "I know you are making the noises with your person somehow. There are no spirits at work here."

"I have the gift!" Kate said indignantly.

"The gift of mischief making! But you haven't any sense! Do you have any idea what would happen if you were found out? Stop fidgeting and look at me, Margaretta! Mrs. Redfield thinks you are both the most darling girls. Can you imagine how that would change if she discovered you were making a fool of her? And what about your rich Mrs. Hyde? She's the biggest toad in the puddle here, and if her husband found out how you've tricked them both, he would ride you out of town on a rail!"

I sniffed doubtfully, and Leah turned on me. "Do you think they don't do that anymore, Margaretta? I am here to tell you they most certainly do."

She turned back to Kate. "What about Betsy and David? Have you thought about them? If you are discovered a fraud, their reputation is ruined. They'll have to leave town. Everyone would think they were in on it, especially with David giving people peeks at that box like it was a carnival sideshow! What about Lizzie? She'll be riding that rail right beside you, because no one's going to believe that one out of the three girls was innocent."

It was true. I had not thought about any of those things. I couldn't help flashing a look of alarm and despair at Kate, whose eyes were welling with tears.

"You've gotten yourselves in a fix, girls," Leah said. "It's a lucky thing for you that I came when I did."

⚜

Leah sat Mother down for a long talk. Kate and I stood together quietly in the corner of the room and did just what Leah had told us to do.

"The strain of this gift is too much for such young girls," Leah explained to our mother. "Kate has already had one fit and fainted dead away on another occasion."

"But the spirits just come, every evening," said Mother. "What can we do but listen to them?"

"I propose that we try splitting up the girls." Leah glanced back at us, and we nodded as we were supposed to. If we did not agree, Leah had made it plain that she would reveal our deception to Mother. "I will take Kate with me back to Rochester, and Maggie will remain here with you—for now. If all goes well, you can join us in a few weeks."

Mother's brow furrowed. Kate was her youngest, and I could see how much it pained her to be parted from her baby. "Perhaps you should take Maggie," Mother suggested. I wasn't sure whether to feel jealous at that or hopeful about returning to Rochester or apprehensive about leaving with Leah.

However, Leah's plans were already made. "I will take Kate," she insisted. "Then, if there is another fit, she can see a doctor in Rochester who doesn't take horses as patients on alternate Saturdays!"

"There's nothing wrong with Dr. Knowles," muttered Mother. "But I guess it couldn't hurt to let a city doctor take a look." She brightened. "I could come with you."

"You will stay here," Leah instructed. "Betsy will need your help when the baby comes. I will write you in a few weeks, and if this spirit manifestation is under control, you can bring Maggie for a visit."

In the end, there was nothing Mother could do but bow to her daughter's will. We passed Kate into Leah's greedy hands, not knowing that we were conducting the business of spirit communication into an entirely new realm.

Chapter Ten
Kate

Some people might say I made a bargain with the devil. I suppose it seems so, and yet that is a rather harsh judgment of my sister. I prefer to think of it as an agreement for our mutual benefit. There was nothing, after all, that I wanted more than an opportunity to explore and share my newfound talent.

In many ways, I was fortunate that my gift took this form. I always felt that it must have saddened my great-grandmother that her second sight was attuned only to funerals. The family learned to keep their knowledge a secret, for in those more primitive days Great-Grandmother Rutan might have been branded a witch and blamed for the very deaths she prophesied.

I would have liked to have met Aunt Elizabeth and learned more about her dream visions. Sadly, like those of her grandmother, they always foreshadowed death. However, my mother has told me that her sister was always a lively and cheerful person. Knowing that she was to die in her twenty-seventh year, she never wasted any of the days until that time. My mother recalls that she held her head high and proud on the day she married Mr. Higgins, even though her groom had tears on his face and her sisters wept. She would not allow the foreknowledge of her death to deter her from love.

How lucky I was—my gift allowed me to look backward, at those already gone before us, instead of forward to a knowledge no one really wanted in advance. If my role was to be a medium through which the dead communicated with the loved ones who grieved for them, then I was proud and willing to accept that role. It was not all that different from the service of a clergyman who ministers to a grieving widow in her darkest hour.

In fact, Mrs. Redfield told me that my succor was a greater balm to a suffering heart than the doctrine recited by a well-meaning sermonizer. After one of our spirit meetings, she took my hands and said to me, "Bless you, child. You have lightened my heart in a way that no one else could—not the reverend at the church or any other person who has counseled me on God's will. I believe that my daughter's soul still exists and that she is waiting for me in a better, brighter place, thanks to you."

I had never known that Mrs. Redfield suffered so, for she seemed such a merry and high-spirited person, but apparently she kept her secret grief locked within her heart. I was touched and moved by her plight, and I always made sure to include a special message for her from her daughter.

I was distressed at leaving Hydesville, as Leah had commanded. Being separated from Maggie was like leaving a limb behind. I cried for the first two nights, inconsolable no matter how Leah tried to comfort me, and was stricken by a sick headache that left me prostrate and weak. On the third night, my aunt Elizabeth spoke to me in a dream and bade me take cheer, for my fate was preordained and this temporary loneliness was a small price to pay for the full realization of my gift. After that, I faced my new life in Rochester with more mettle and settled into the role set forth for me by my sister as a medium for the spirits.

Leah made it clear to me that if I wished to continue along this path, I would abide by her decisions in every case, and I agreed. When her plan became clear to me, I faltered somewhat. However, I soon realized that while certain persons were convinced by Leah's tricks and others were entertained, the true believers understood that the value of the experience resided in what I had to say. Before long I had followers whose need was as great as that of the ladies I had known in Hydesville, and it was for the benefit of those persons that I tolerated Leah's tomfoolery.

My sister may have been a trickster, but my own purpose was pure.

Chapter Eleven
Maggie

What a dismal place Hydesville was without my sister. If I had thought it a wasteland before, it was a hundred times more so now. The little farmhouse, full to bursting a few days prior, now seemed lifeless and empty. Mother and I were the only visitors remaining. This may have pleased Betsy, full to bursting herself and preparing for her confinement, but for me it seemed a sentence to a life devoid of any meaning. Consequently, I was ill tempered and quick to anger. When Betsy chastised me for scorching David's Sunday shirt with the flatiron, I burst into tears and exclaimed that no one in this backwoods town would notice a few burn marks.

"If it were up to me," she snapped in return, "I would close you up inside a crate and send you back to Rochester City by post!"

Even the spirit meetings, held now in Mrs. Redfield's parlor, came less frequently. The fact is that I was not as strong without Kate. My heart was not in it, and it became difficult to resort to any subterfuge when all the ladies' attention was focused on me. Cracking the joints in my toes failed me on more than one occasion, and without Kate's assistance in reserve, the spirits often gave conflicting answers, rapping once instead of twice or failing to rap on the correct letter.

"Margaretta is simply not as gifted with the spirits as her sister," I overheard Mrs. Hyde whisper to Mrs. Duesler.

As embarrassing as this was, it was nothing less than the truth.

I did not protest when our meetings ended early and soon ceased altogether. At that time, I assumed that this was Leah's plan for extricating us from our deception. Before she left, I had asked her, "What shall I do in your absence?"

"Continue as you have done," she said, "but be careful and take no risks. Await my first letter, and take guidance for your actions from my words."

I was expecting her letter to report that Kate's power to converse with spirits was diminishing, and I would subsequently "discover" that my abilities had also faded away. The unsuccessful spirit meetings held in Mrs. Redfield's house foreshadowed the end of the entire ghostly enterprise, and in many respects it would be a welcome relief, for I had tired of the game.

As it turned out, I was wrong about Leah.

Two long weeks passed while I languished in boredom and restlessness. Finally, one afternoon, David returned from town with a letter that had arrived by the latest mail carriage. Mother tore it open immediately, just as anxious for news as I was, and after scanning it with a furrowed brow, she read it aloud to the gathered company.

Dearest Family,

We safely arrived in Rochester a fortnight ago. As you know, it was my hope that these ghostly incidents would end if we separated

Kate and Maggie. Alas, this has not been the case, and, if anything, the spirits have grown overexcited in their new stomping ground and have been making their presence known to all.

The rapping began on the boat during our trip and only grew worse once we had arrived at my house. Our first night in the house was a sleepless one, what with the mattress shaking under us and Lizzie shrieking in the night that some cold hand had touched her neck. When the girls cried out for the spirits to leave them alone, first Lizzie, and then Kate, and finally I, too, felt a stinging slap on the face! In the end, I was forced to wake Calvin Brown from sleep and ask him to move down from the third floor and make his bed upon the sofa in the second-floor parlor.

After much reflection, I decided to invite a few very close friends to the house for a spirit circle like the one I attended at Mrs. Redfield's house. I hoped that if the spirits were given this opportunity to communicate with the living, they might cease their nightly pranks. And so it happened that, after an evening of rapping and answering questions for our guests, our ornery spirits were appeased, and we have had no more trouble with them.

Let me assure you, however, that I have not yet hung up my fiddle when it comes to abolishing these pesky spirits. I have a mind to move Kate from this house, which is half a century old and may be just as haunted as your little Hydesville house, and into a more modern residence. I am currently engaged in seeking such a place, although mindful that it must be one in which I can accommodate Calvin, for alone among my boarders I feel a certain responsibility to him. It is good to have him with us in any case, as his presence comforts the girls and provides an anchor against the turbulent waters in which we find ourselves.

I will write again when I have found a new residence that meets my requirements, and I hope at that time Mother and Maggie will join us here.

Your devoted daughter and sister,

Leah

We were all puzzled and disturbed by Leah's letter and the report of these pranks attributed to the ghosts. I had been so certain that Leah would use our separation to abolish the spirits and end the deception without giving our duplicity away. Instead, she seemed to have escalated the falsehoods.

I could not make heads or tails of it. Had Leah been convinced after all that we employed supernatural powers to create the rappings? What was I to make of the cold hand and shaking mattress reported in her account?

Leah stated that she had moved Calvin Brown into her apartment as protection from the spirits. Calvin had rented rooms in the third floor of Leah's house for nearly ten years. He was a mild-mannered and pleasant young man, about David's age. My mother had practically adopted him when she discovered that his parents were dead and that he had no other living relatives. For years we girls had viewed him as a foster brother, just as dear to us as David. Leah was blind to the fact, obvious to the rest of us, that Calvin's regard for her was something more than brotherly. I had no doubt that Calvin would do whatever Leah asked of him, and I wondered if he, too, was now included in the deception.

Three more weeks passed in a slow, countrified agony. Betsy took to her bed in labor and, after two days, delivered a healthy daughter, later christened Althea. I admit staring into the child's red, squalling face with some consternation, viewing her mainly as a source of more laundry that would no doubt find its way into my lye-burned hands.

Mercifully, the expected letter from Leah finally arrived, stating that she had found a suitable house on a more modern street in the city and that we could join her there immediately. I packed my meager belongings in a hurry and was ready to go in an hour—although it took Mother another two days to prepare for the journey. We started out before dawn, with David driving us in the wagon to Newark, where we boarded one of the Erie Canal boats. It was my first trip by boat, and the bedlam of activity was a great excitement for a time, but once the voyage was under way it soon became tedious. Sad-looking horses walking on trails beside the canal pulled the boats, and people on foot easily outpaced us, waving merrily as they passed.

The trip lasted the entire day and into the evening. It was quite dark by the time we set foot on land at Rochester and hired a carriage to take us to Leah's new residence on Prospect Street. Unlike the sleepy little hamlet of Hydesville, the city of Rochester was still awake and going about its business even at nine or ten in the evening. Carriages and wagons bumped along the streets, and pedestrians, many of them walking in couples and dressed for evening social excursions, strolled leisurely along under the gaslights. I smiled at the bustling hubbub of it all. I had missed this background noise of life in the nighttime when forced to fall asleep to silence punctuated only by a cricket or an owl.

Leah's new home was indeed in a more modern and affluent part of town, although it was interesting to note that it adjoined a cemetery, which was a strange choice if she were fleeing from ghosts. I am afraid that we roused the entire household when we knocked on the door, but our arrival precipitated joyful exclamations and exuberant embraces.

Snuggled in bed with Kate that night, I finally heard the story of her month living with Leah. "Oh, she knows how we make the sounds," Kate assured me, "and so does Lizzie, now. You wouldn't believe how furious Lizzie was when she found out. She called me all kinds of horrible names and said that I was bound for hell for deceiving our family and friends. Why, I was so angry I slapped her!"

I began to see the layer of truth beneath the falsehoods in Leah's letter. Our older sister had defended her daughter by slapping Kate back, who had bounced right back and slapped Leah in return!

"I was very peeved with Lizzie," Kate went on, "so I waited until she was asleep and dribbled cold water down her back. She leapt up screeching and overturned the mattress I was lying on. Then we pulled each other's hair out in handfuls until Calvin woke up and grabbed each of us by our night shifts and shook us till we squealed! Leah stomped around angrily with her hair all bound up in rag curls, and Calvin blushed like a girl to see her in her nightclothes, but Leah didn't pay any mind. She gave us a tongue lashing and stamped her feet all the while, until the old lady who boarded downstairs banged on the floor with a broom and asked if we were dancing the Highland fling upstairs!"

She and I giggled and whispered long into the night, two dearest friends reunited, until the comforting rumble of city noises outside lulled us into sleep.

Chapter Twelve
Maggie

Kate and Leah had a few surprises for me when I sat for my first spirit circle in Rochester.

The guests included Amy and Isaac Post, Mr. and Mrs. Granger, and their friend Reverend Clark. Our family had rented rooms in the Posts' old house for years, and Kate and I had grown up playing with their sons. When I first saw them that evening, I greeted them with some awkwardness, knowing that I was about to deceive them.

I was also worried about the Reverend Clark, for Kate had confided that he was a longtime friend of the Grangers and that he had come with the purpose of exposing our fraud and rescuing his good friends from harm. Kate, however, expressed no reservations and assured me that Leah had everything well in hand.

Reverend Clark was short and stout, with shaggy eyebrows and a gruff manner. When first introduced to him, Kate and I were entertained by the sight of his unkempt eyebrows waggling in surprise, for he was clearly taken aback by our appearance. We looked like two innocent children excited to partake in a late evening with the adults, not sinister confederates in a humbuggery!

Leah invited our guests to each take a seat around the table in the center of the parlor. Calvin Brown already had a hand on the back of a chair, which he pulled out for Leah with a shy little smile. She seated herself and arranged her voluminous skirts in a decorative manner with a murmur of thanks. When she dropped her handkerchief, Calvin, always attentive to her needs, quickly knelt and retrieved it for her.

Kate took a chair to the left of Leah, and I sat myself on her right. The remaining chairs were taken by the Grangers and the Posts, with Reverend Clark directly across from Leah. Calvin, Mother, and a sullen-faced Lizzie withdrew to a sofa in the corner of the room. When Leah gave a nod, Calvin put out the gaslights, leaving three candles burning on side tables in the room. Afterward, we sat in silence, with our hands upon the table.

Everyone seemed quite comfortable with the silence, except for the Reverend Clark, who was looking around the faces in the circle with some puzzlement. Just when it seemed that he was about to start asking questions, we all heard a shower of quick, light raps, knocking upon the floor and the table itself. I tried not to show my surprise, because these noises were not the joint-cracking sounds to which I was accustomed.

No one at the table had moved his or her hands, although Reverend Clark leaned back from his seat and tried to peer around the table on both sides.

Leah called out in her bright voice, "Welcome! We have gathered here tonight to commune with the brotherhood of spirits, and if it is the wish of our voiceless guests to telegraph their messages to those present in body, please give us a sign."

Again we heard a shower of gentle raps. Mrs. Granger looked eagerly at Leah, who nodded to her with an indulgent smile. "Harriet!" Mrs. Granger gasped breathlessly. "Is that you?"

We heard two raps, for yes.

This was another shock to me. Never before had Kate and I impersonated the deceased loved one of a person present. We were careful to send messages from a nameless group of spirits, refusing to allow the members of the circle to directly address their relatives. It would be too easy to make mistakes, we had reasoned, and incorrectly answer their questions. Also, we had qualms about the morality of such an imposture. For us, there was a great deal of difference between sending a message from Harriet and pretending to be Harriet.

"Are you at peace, my darling?" Mrs. Granger went on.

Two raps.

"Are you lonely?"

One rap, for no.

The Reverend Clark was looking anxiously back and forth between the wife of his friend and the three of us sisters. Leah looked comfortable and confident and happy for her friend Adelaide Granger. Kate was excited but not perturbed in any way, and I am sure that I looked extraordinarily innocent that night.

After a few more questions and comments by Mrs. Granger and another pitter-patter of knocks, which apparently signified Harriet's presence, Mr. Granger sighed and addressed his daughter's spirit. "Harriet, dearest, we have brought Lemuel Clark with us tonight, and he would like to ask you some questions. Would you be agreeable to taking his test and thus proving to his doubting nature that you are really with us?"

Agreeably, Harriet rapped twice.

"I have a suggestion," Leah intervened. "Why don't you write four answers to a question of your choice, only one of which will be correct, and then after asking your question, you can point to the answers in turn. Our spirit will rap when you point to the correct one."

Reverend Clark nodded thoughtfully and accepted the paper and nib pen that Calvin rose to offer him. He wrote four words upon the paper: *Rover, Pinkie, Bear, Dusty,* and then set the pen aside. "Harriet," he said hesitantly, as though feeling foolish addressing the empty air, "can you tell me the name of the little dog my wife and I once owned, that you so enjoyed playing with when you were a child?"

He pointed to the name *Rover* and, after a moment's silence, moved his finger down to the name *Pinkie.* Immediately, we heard two raps. Mr. and Mrs. Granger sat back in their seats with smiles on their faces, the Posts exchanged a nod, and the Reverend Clark looked up with an utterly astonished expression.

We heard five distinct knocks at that time, and Leah said, "She is calling for the alphabet board." Leah reached down and lifted up a slate that had rested by her chair. When she placed it on the table, I saw that the alphabet and the numerals zero to nine were written upon the slate in chalk. With a start, I realized that this was to replace David's method of reciting the alphabet. Leah pointed to the letters on the board in order, and Amy Post, taking up the paper and pen abandoned by the Reverend in his surprise, recorded each letter that received a knock.

Soon Harriet had spelled out the following message: *Do not persist in your unbelief. I have come not to disturb you but to ease the grief of those who mourn me and promise that all will be as it should be in the land of eternal summer.*

Kate turned to Leah now and, using her girlishly innocent voice, said, "I wish the spirits would *do* something, just to let the Reverend see how strange they act sometimes!"

"Let's invite them," replied Leah. "Would you like to see the table move, Reverend? Let everyone move their chairs back from the table." Under Leah's direction, we did this and then placed our feet upon the chair rungs and our hands in the air over our heads, so that all could clearly see them. No sooner had we done so than the table, with no hands upon it, lurched several inches across the bare floor toward us girls.

I could not contain my gasp, and Mother cried out, "Land sakes!" Reverend Clark, although his shaggy eyebrows waggled in astonishment, stood immediately up, grasped the edge of the table, and pulled it back to its original position. He was just sitting down when the table slid roughly away from him again. Kate clapped her hands in childish delight, and the spirit circle broke up at that point.

The Reverend Clark took each of our hands in turn as he left that evening, stating that we had certainly given him much to ponder and that his entire understanding of the universe had been altered. He cupped one hand under Kate's chin and said, "I see that I was mistaken in my belief that chicanery was taking place in this house.

This child has no more understanding of duplicity than a canary bird, but for all her artless innocence has created a miracle."

Much later, when we were safely alone, Kate poked fun at the Reverend by placing her fingers along her eyebrows and waving them humorously. "If I heard correctly," she said, "that man called me a birdbrain."

"That is only what you deserve for acting like one," I retorted. "Now, if you don't tell me how all those events were accomplished tonight, I shall tear the dress from your body to look for myself!"

I had figured out that Kate was making the new rapping noise by detecting the slight rustling of her skirts each time they occurred. With a rueful grin, she lifted up the hem of her dress and showed me the places where lead balls had been sewn into it. "It was Calvin's idea," she admitted. "He is more devilishly minded than we could have guessed."

"However did you know the dog's name?" I asked.

Kate smiled. "Look, I will teach you to do it yourself easily. When the Reverend began to write down the answers, I watched him closely. He paused a moment before writing the first name, but he moved the pen directly to the second name without thought. He paused another moment before writing the third name and even longer before writing the fourth, because he had to invent them, you see. I find that most people place the correct answer in the second position, because they don't want to write it down first, but they can't think of two more false answers without stalling for time."

"And to think the Reverend compared you to a canary, you wicked thing!" I exclaimed. "How did you make the table move?"

"Leah did that. Calvin tied a length of thread to the table leg and extended it out to the chair in which Leah would sit. He looped it over her foot when he knelt down to fetch her hankie."

I fell upon the bed that we shared, utterly taken in amazement. "I had no idea that you were running a carnival show here in Rochester while I scrubbed my hands raw on Betsy's laundry!"

It took no time at all to sew lead balls into the hem of my "spirit dress," and I practiced tapping them on the floor without making an obvious disturbance with my skirt. As for the trick with the thread, I tried that out as soon as possible, which turned out to be the next day at noon, while Mother was out of the house. Having set up my prank earlier, I waited until I saw Calvin rise out of his chair to reach across the table for the water pitcher. When I saw that he had the handle and was easing back to his seat, I gave a jerk with my foot and was greatly satisfied to see his chair twitch out from underneath him. He sat down heavily upon nothing and clattered to the floor with the pitcher upside down in his lap.

Kate shrieked in laughter, and Calvin good-naturedly joined her, raising the pitcher mockingly, as if to throw it at me. Leah hurled her napkin to the table, exclaiming, "This is totally unacceptable, girls!" But then she broke into uncontrollable peals of laughter and had to hide her face in her hands.

The only person who did not laugh was Lizzie.

⚬≈⚬

Our niece was becoming a problem. She heartily disapproved of all our spirit tricks, and only the force of Leah's will prevented her from revealing our secrets to Mother. Somehow we knew that this would be a disaster and an ignominious end to all our ghostly activities.

Lizzie felt that our pretense was immoral and bound to condemn us to fiery perdition. She was aghast at how we had fooled all the people of Hydesville and ashamed that we were well on our way to doing the same in Rochester. Alone among us, she did not see the miraculous change in the health of Leah's friends, the Grangers, and would not admit that our spirit communications were often a balm to the injured souls of the grieving.

She made her feelings plain in her demeanor and actions. Leah spoke to her daughter privately, and they had a terrible row. While Lizzie sulked in tears downstairs, Leah climbed the stairs to our room and explained to us what she planned to do. Kate and I were having a great deal of fun in our trickery, and because we had not yet realized Leah's comprehensive plan for us, we were amazed that she had chosen to join in our pranks.

On the next evening, as it happened, we were having the Grangers and Reverend Clark back for another spirit circle. The Grangers could not bear to go more than a few days without contact from their beloved Harriet, and the Reverend professed he would like to return to ask the spirits a few questions of theology. Unfortunately, it appeared that the evening was going to be a disappointment. Our meeting began to resemble a Quaker church service in the length and breadth of its silence.

"What can be the matter?" cried Mrs. Granger after a time, growing distressed by the absence of her daughter's spirit.

"I think I know," Leah said fiercely, and she turned in her chair to face her daughter, seated as usual at the back of the room. "You are the cause of this silence. You have been a very wicked girl, grieving the spirits so with your actions!"

"No, Mother!" Lizzie gasped, while at the same time two loud raps were heard, the accustomed sign for yes.

"Spirits!" called Leah, raising her head. "Has my daughter, Lizzie Fish, wronged you?"

Two raps.

Lizzie burst into tears. "I can't help it! I just said what I thought!"

"You must repent if you wish to remain a member of this household," Leah replied sternly.

"See here!" exclaimed Reverend Clark in some dismay, while the Grangers clasped hands for comfort. "What can this poor girl have done to deserve such rough treatment at the hands of her own mother?"

"You do not understand, Reverend," Leah said. "My daughter has been hostile to our gentle spirits, and they are greatly offended by her ill will. She stood in this parlor yesterday and told me that she wished they would go away forever and cease tormenting my sisters."

"Oh, Lizzie," my mother murmured, and Mrs. Granger wrung her hands and vehemently exclaimed how much she relied on Harriet's messages to simply continue in her daily living.

Lizzie was sniveling by now and wiping tears from her cheeks but still as stubborn as her mother in her own way. "I can't repent. I don't see the wrong in what I said to you, Mother. I was sincere, and I cannot repent for it."

Five loud raps called for the alphabet board, and Leah placed it in the center of the table and began to point to each letter in turn. Our guests were much too distraught to write down the message, so we spelled each letter out loud as it was rapped, and the meaning was plain: *Lizzie must go.*

Our niece fell to her knees and, sobbing, begged her mother to have mercy. Kate sent me a plaintive look, and I cringed, feeling just as guilty. Leah turned her back on her daughter and faced her three guests: "The spirits have spoken their will. It shall be done as they say."

Two days later, a pale and tearful Lizzie mounted a hired carriage while the driver hoisted up a trunk full of her belongings. Leah had already wired a curt telegram to her former husband, Bowman Fish, announcing the imminent arrival of his daughter. Lizzie would be visiting with her father, whom she had not seen in years, for an indefinite period.

Leah stood in the street outside our house with arms folded and watched her leave.

"This is harsh, even for Leah," commented Kate, watching from an upstairs window.

"Don't you be fooled," I replied. "Leah loves her daughter. If we get caught in this foolishness, Lizzie will be safe out west. After the performance the other night, no one will ever accuse Lizzie of being a party to our lies."

Chapter Thirteen
Maggie

That summer, it seemed the fashionable thing to do in Rochester, New York, was to make an evening visit to the parlor of Mrs. Leah Fish on Prospect Street to hear the spirit rappers.

Visitors began arriving around teatime, often bringing gifts of jams and bread, sugary confections, or sometimes hair ribbons for me and Kate. Callers who came often, seeing the meager household run by Leah, gifted us with more practical items such as candles or lamp oil. New acquaintances were quickly charmed by the friendly and forthright manner for which Leah and Mother were known, and no one left without remarking on "those pretty girls!"

As darkness fell, we would commence our spirit circles, sometimes holding two in an evening. Spirits rapped, tables moved, the curtains rustled, and bells rang. Participants gasped in astonishment, awed by the physical manifestations and the uncanny ability of the unseen rappers to identify correct answers written on paper. After each long evening, Kate and I would fall to our beds in exhaustion, having played out as much mischief as any two girls could desire.

Still, this swell of visitors flush with gifts did not provide enough to sustain our household. Because Leah had nearly given up her piano lessons, Mother began to fret over how her daughter would maintain her residence in this expensive part of town.

About a month after our arrival, while hosting a spirit circle comprising our closest and most frequent visitors, the Grangers and the Posts, we suffered a long, awkward period of silence from the spirits. It was always uncomfortable when the spirits were not forthcoming, but Leah occasionally required this, and Kate and I were accustomed to obeying her commands. On this evening, after many plaintive but fruitless entreaties to the spirits, Leah finally gave a great sigh and clasped the hands of the people on either side of her.

"Good friends," she began with great reluctance, "I fear the fault is mine. Worries of a secular nature have confounded my concentration, breaking our connection with those spiritual entities who no longer suffer from such troubles."

When pressed by our concerned friends to elaborate, Leah tearfully explained that her income from piano lessons had vanished, as few pupils were still willing to come to her house. "I don't know how I will support the girls and my mother," she confessed. "I don't know what will become of them if I have to give up my place in this house."

Of course, we could have returned to my father's house in Hydesville and received ample support from his blacksmith work and the income from David's farm. This somehow escaped mention.

With downcast eyes and a hesitant voice, Leah then said, "A dear friend of mine has suggested that I require an entrance fee to our spirit circles, and while I scorned this idea from the start, I cannot endure the weight of our debt much longer. I hoped that you, my dear friends, would advise me on this matter."

Mr. Post was quick to respond. "I think it is a capital idea, Mrs. Fish. No one would begrudge you recompense for your time and devotion to this spiritual endeavor. Even the spirits themselves, although they no longer have such physical needs, could not deny you the wherewithal to provide for your family."

"I am in agreement," Mr. Granger added. "It has long been in my mind that you should receive recompense—as Isaac here has put it—for inviting us into your home night after night and exhausting yourself mentally on our behalf."

Leah shook her head as if fighting this unpleasant notion. "But what will people think if I, a woman without a husband, begin to accept money as an entrance fee to my home?"

Amy Post slapped her hand lightly upon the table. "A man can establish a respectable practice of business and charge a professional fee for his service. A woman should not be denied the same right."

Thus my sister, "reluctantly," of course, began the practice of charging a dollar a head for participation in our spirit circles. It happened with scarcely a ripple in the pattern of our lives. To be sure, Kate and I were largely unaware of the exchange of money, for it happened with careful discretion, and because a portion of it went to the purchase of fashionable dresses for the two of us, we were hardly likely to complain. After all, as Leah pointed out to our mother, people wishing to send a telegraph to living relatives must pay a fee. Why not expect that a spiritual telegraph would likewise require a surcharge?

For their dollar, our clients received words of gentle wisdom and, hopefully, solace for their grief. Our spirits were always kind and forgiving, promising an eternity of joy to the well deserving, and in their mercy, almost every person was deserving of heaven. As for those visitors more interested in the mysterious side of spirit communication, we could provide that as well. We kept Calvin's ingenuity busy all summer with our requests for ghostly manifestations.

The window curtain rolled up and down by itself. An unoccupied rocking chair began to rock on its own. A vase untouched by any hand tipped over the edge of a table and smashed on the floor, although Leah was quite vexed by that, and the spirits left her breakables alone thereafter.

It occurred to Kate that we could accomplish even more tricks if the room were darker, and so she asked Calvin if he could contrive a way to make the candles go out by themselves. After some consideration, Calvin hit upon a simple but effective solution. He snapped a candle and cut out the wick in the broken place. Then, by lighting the candle and using the dripping wax to conceal and repair the break, he made his tampering undetectable. Candles so treated burned normally until the breach in the wick was reached. After some experimentation, Calvin became expert at timing the failure of each candle, and so it was arranged that two separate candles, on opposite sides of the room, would sputter and go out within moments of each other, plunging the spirit circle into darkness.

Thus our summer progressed, and a core group of devoted spiritualists soon became the bulwark of our new enterprise. A newcomer to our circle of favorites was Mr. Eliab Capron, who, like my old friend E. E. Lewis, was a journalist, though a novice. Mr. Capron had read the Hydesville pamphlet written by the esteemed Mr. Lewis and was eager to learn more about our communication with the spirits.

The one person who continued to puzzle me was Amy Post. Originally, I had quailed at the thought of deceiving this formidable woman, whom I admired and respected for her advocacy of those who could not defend themselves. I admit to being somewhat disappointed that she was taken in so easily while conversely relieved that she did not expose our deception. As the months passed, I continued to observe her closely, for I was unable to classify her interest in spirit matters.

Once, when feeling brave, I broached the subject with Leah, who had spent the afternoon in private discussion with Mrs. Post. "Does Mrs. Post believe in our spirit rapping?" I asked tentatively, almost afraid of bursting a bubble that no one else had noticed floating among us.

Leah looked up from the letter she had been writing and gave me a sharp glance before asking, "Why do you ask such a thing? She is here nearly daily, and she has brought many important people to our circles."

"Yes, she has," I agreed. "Mrs. Stanton and Mrs. Mott seemed very pleased that the spirits shared their convictions on women's suffrage. Some of the other people at the table were surprised that the spirits were so socially minded that night, but Amy Post and her friends took it very much in stride."

"The spirits are very wise, of course," murmured Leah, who had turned back to her letter.

"Mrs. Mott went so far as to ask me," I continued, "if I couldn't manage to contact a spirit of some historical fame and acquire a testimonial from him regarding women's rights."

Leah's pen faltered and dropped a blob of ink at this news, and she had to reach for a blotter. "What is your point, Margaretta?" she asked in annoyance.

"Do they actually believe, or are they using—"

"They have chosen to publicly state that they believe," Leah said, fixing me with her no-nonsense eye. "That is good enough for me, and it should be good enough for you."

Upon those words I had to be content. Amy Post believed in the spirits, or claimed that she believed, and because I shared most of Mrs. Post's views regarding the abolition of slavery and the rights of women, I was not averse to including support for these progressive issues in our spirits' messages. Part of me wondered whether the feminist portion of Mrs. Post's nature did not admire Leah's gumption at making a living at tricks worthy of Mr. P. T. Barnum himself.

⁕

One event marred our triumphant conquest of the Rochester social scene.

In the early fall, it happened that Kate challenged Calvin to make Leah's piano play by itself. We did not make much of this proposed trick at the time, because it was typical that Kate and I conceived the impossible, and quiet, unassuming Calvin proceeded to make it possible. After a few days of deliberation and examination of the piano mechanism, Calvin began to create his miracle.

He waited until Leah was out of the house, so that she could not prevent him from working on her beloved instrument. Then, selecting a low bass note because of its position farthest from an observer, he attached a dark thread to the hammer, ran it down through the bottom of the piano, along the side of one of the legs facing the wall, and into the floorboards. Under this floorboard, Calvin constructed a clever device that would pull the thread whenever the far end of the board was trod upon. One step on this rigged section of floor, and the thread would pull down the hammer, which also caused the key on the outside of the piano to depress as though by an invisible finger. No matter how I stuck my head inside the piano, I could not discern the guilty thread, even knowing that it was there.

When Leah returned, she screamed something awful, but no damage was done to the piano, and after she calmed down, she had to admit that the effect was very mysterious.

The piano began to toll its lone bass note soon after our first visitors arrived that afternoon. The first person to innocently walk past the piano leapt backward with a cry of alarm when the note rang out by itself. Quickly, others hurried over to investigate, and at seemingly random intervals, the same low note tolled again and again.

The beauty of the device was that none of the Fox family needed to approach the piano; in fact, my sisters and I made a point of keeping our distance. If too long a period went by without a sound from our invisible pianist, Calvin would stroll past, tread upon the board, and leap back convincingly at the consequential *bong!*

Visitors came and went that long evening, some deliciously mystified by the one-note tune, and others frightened. A woman named Abigail Bush wrung her hands together and cried, "'Tis a death knell! It heralds a death! Somebody dear to this family is going to die!"

Kate and I struggled to contain our amusement in the face of Mrs. Bush's dire prediction. My mother, however, was greatly upset, and because of her agitation our guests excused themselves and dispersed. I noticed that Amy Post was one of the last to leave and that she tried to comfort Mother with a different interpretation of the evening's events: "Perhaps it duplicates the Bell of Liberty, commemorating the document of feminine independence that was drafted this summer at Seneca Falls." At a dubious and somewhat resentful glance from Mother, Amy smiled ruefully and said, "Or perhaps it is just a very mischievous spirit, who regrets his lost opportunity in life to learn the piano from Leah."

Calvin was very regretful that he had so distressed his foster mother, and I heard him whisper to Leah that he would dismantle his creation as soon as Mother had gone to bed. Thus, as soon as all the guests were gone, Leah led Mother from the parlor and started her up the stairs.

It was just then that the doorbell rang—once, twice, and a third time in quick succession. Thinking that one of our visitors had left an item behind, I scampered to the door. I heard Leah behind me on the stairs, trying to discourage Mother from going down to answer it. Opening the door, I found a young delivery boy on the stoop with a telegram in hand.

"Maggie!" My mother pulled free from Leah's grasp and came running down the stairs, nearly stumbling in her panic. "Is that a telegram? Who's dead? Oh, dear Lord, who is dead?"

"Mother!" I exclaimed with some irritation, slitting open the envelope with my index finger. "Just because we receive a telegram doesn't mean someone is dead!"

But in this case, it did.

I gasped out loud and put my hand against the wall for support. Mother snatched the message from me, and in a moment she and Leah both were reading it. My mother screamed, and my sister covered her face with her hands and burst into tears.

David's little daughter Ella had been stricken with a high fever and had died that very evening while we were holding our spirit circle with the piano tolling its death knell.

Chapter Fourteen
Maggie

The death of David's bright-eyed little girl devastated our family, and grief brought us together briefly, all our petty disputes forgotten. My poor brother was nearly destroyed. I was shocked by his appearance, for he seemed to have aged ten years in the span of two months.

The funeral service was held shortly after our arrival in Hydesville, and my poor little niece was buried in a small coffin handmade by her father and her grandfather, working side by side. Leah was our source of strength, as always. She almost single-handedly directed affairs, guiding our grief-stricken brother and his wife through the ceremony.

By contrast, Kate was nearly prostrate with hysteria. Immediately after the funeral, she took to a bed and refused to get up. Slipping away from the company of neighbors paying condolence calls, I went upstairs and perched myself on the bed beside her, taking her hand.

"I know what you're thinking," I whispered, "and you need to stop it."

"I caused Ella's death," Kate's lips formed the words, but there was scarcely any breath behind them.

"You know that is nonsense," I said fiercely.

"I predicted it, then," she replied in a firmer voice. "I'm the one who asked Calvin to make the piano toll that note."

"I think you asked him to make it play," I corrected. "I am sure you did not ask him to make it sound like a death knell, and you certainly didn't ask that idiot woman to predict that someone in our family would die! It was a coincidence. Ella had been ill for two days before!"

"I asked Calvin to rig the piano two days ago," Kate said gloomily.

"You did not. It was only one day ago!"

"I don't want this power!" Kate's tear-stained face turned toward me. "I don't want the power to see death approaching! I want to comfort people, not foresee their grief!"

"You are forgetting," I hissed. "You don't actually have any power at all. You crack the joints in your toes to make the rapping, and you are very good at reading people's faces. You are a fraud, just as I am."

Despite my best efforts, Kate remained inconsolable and probably would not have left the bed at all had Leah not barged in that evening and taken her by the ear. Kate was forced to scramble up and onto her feet, lest she lose that particular piece of her anatomy.

"That's enough wallowing from you, you self-centered chit!" Leah scolded. "David and Betsy aren't lying in bed. They're behaving with dignity, and I won't have you overshadowing their grief. She wasn't *your* child!"

I gasped. Kate's health was delicate, and one did not just order her out of bed when she was taken by a spell. However, two red circles of shame appeared on Kate's cheeks, and she scrambled to pull on her dress before Leah could lay hands on her again.

The emotional ordeal was not yet over for us, however. We had scarcely returned to Rochester before Mother began to make us uncomfortable with requests to contact Ella's spirit in a circle. Kate dug her fingernails into my arm each time she asked, and when Mother was not within hearing, she would hiss, "I cannot do it! I will not do it!" However, Mother would not give up the idea, and truly, there was no reason for not doing for her what we did for strangers at a dollar a head. When she asked us in front of our regular group of sitters, Leah gave a resigned sigh and nodded to us girls. Kate cast her eyes down in shame, and I returned a wide-eyed gaze to Leah. What could we do to impersonate Ella, a child less than three years old? She could not spell out any message. What did Mother expect?

Leah had the matter well in hand, however. "Dear spirits!" she cried. "We are seeking the spirit of a small child—a girl very dear to us, who passed into your realm a week ago. Please, help us to locate Ella Fox, for her aunts and her grandmama wish dearly to speak to her!"

We waited in silence. Leah closed her eyes and swayed in her seat. "Ella, are you there? Knock for us, child. Your grandmama is waiting for you."

And there came a small gentle knocking, as if the tiny hand of a child had rapped upon the center of the table.

"Ella!" my mother gasped tearfully. "Ella, darling, is it you?"

"Ella!" Leah said hastily. "Knock two times for yes. You can count to two, can't you, dearest?"

Two tiny knocks were clearly heard in the room, and Mother raised her hands from their customary position on the table and clasped them to her face. "Ella, my darling! Are you in heaven?"

Two raps, tentative and childlike.

"Are you alone, Ella?" asked Leah. "You can knock one time for no, or two for yes."

The spirit of Ella rapped one time, for no.

Leah nodded knowingly. "You are not alone. That is good, my darling. Who is with you—is it perhaps your great-aunt Catherine?"

Acting upon impulse, or perchance because I had grown accustomed to working from Leah's hints, I caused there to be two very strong knocks upon the table.

Mother's eyes lit up, glistening with tears. I rapped out the command for the alphabet board, feeling on sure ground. I did not remember this sister of my mother's, who had died many years ago, but I knew of her from Leah's stories, and it was easy to spell out a message that my mother would believe: *I told you, Peggy, when you left John, that I would care for your children as my own. That is as true now as it was twenty-seven years ago.*

My mother sobbed loudly, but they were cleansing tears, and Leah raised a hand to brush at her own wet cheeks, giving me a quick, grateful glance. We were all hurting from this unhappy loss, but somehow it was very reassuring to think of little Ella in the hands of the indomitable Aunt Catherine, who had taken my mother and her children into her home when they had nowhere else to go.

Adelaide Granger, who was present that evening, put her arms around my mother and pressed a handkerchief into her hands. "How very good it is," she said, smiling through tears of her own, "that you, who have given so much comfort to others, can also reap the benefits of your daughters' precious gift!"

As successful as we were in promoting our new family business, we were unable to convince everyone. Many people left our circles unsatisfied, especially those wanting to make a fortune with their stock speculations or seeking a way to outwit a rival in business or romance. Leah explained that the dead no longer understood the complexities of finance or love, having transcended to a realm of divine contemplation, but these seekers grumbled nonetheless when they received messages that spoke more to patience and virtue than to ambition and avarice.

Some sitters did more than grumble. Jealous women loosed their shrewish tongues to give us a piece of their minds, and a few of the men became angry and abusive, hurling epithets at our faces and calling us heathen witches and frauds. Persons of this temperament generally found themselves grasped firmly by an elbow and propelled swiftly to the front door at the hands of Calvin Brown, who, though mildly mannered, possessed substantial strength in his six-foot frame.

We also received a fair share of attention from the newspapers. The *New York Tribune* frankly called us humbugs, and the *Rochester Courier and Enquirer* doubted that real spirits would spend their time "thumping on walls and rapping on tables." Some favorable press could be found in the *Rochester Daily Democrat*, which stated: "These young women will have to be pretty smart if they have deceived everybody." The likelihood of such a phenomenon was apparently rated somewhat lower than the possibility of real communication with ghosts.

Still, Mr. Capron and the Posts were rather disappointed with the jeers of the press and the public at large. Leah, Kate, and I met with them late in October to discuss the suspicion and skepticism of the Rochester community.

"I am at a loss to know what we can do to further our cause," Leah began with a note of fatalism in her voice. "The spirits have commanded us to make their communications more public."

"Perhaps," suggested Mr. Capron, tapping his fingers nervously upon his pipe, "when I publish my book, we will attract the attention of intellects more scientifically minded than the journalists of the local papers."

"You know that we have the support of Lucretia Mott and Elizabeth Stanton," Amy added. "I also understand that Frederick Douglass has expressed some interest in coming up to hear these raps for himself, and will most certainly publish his experience in his *North Star* paper."

A few moments of silence followed as our friends considered other potential contacts or venues for advancing the idea of spiritualism. Kate and I contributed nothing to the conversation, for we were not expected to have any opinions, but we did cast sidelong glances at each other, waiting for the skillful maneuver that we knew must be coming.

"It does occur to me," Leah finally said hesitantly, "a dear friend of mine suggested a few weeks ago that we appear in a public forum to proclaim the truth of spiritualism and prove it to the doubtful by demonstration. I was aghast at the suggestion, of course."

"Wait a moment," requested the soft-spoken Mr. Post, stroking his beard. "That is not an unreasonable suggestion. Perhaps we should hold a public lecture on the spiritual realm and the immortality of the soul. You could present your work, Eliab," he added, nodding at the journalist. "It would be good advance publicity for your book."

"And a source of income for the ladies," Mr. Capron added virtuously. He drew on his pipe with a thoughtful expression.

Leah shook her head gently. "My dearest companions," she said, "you are forgetting that we are modest and respectable women. I fear it would not be seemly for us to appear on a public lecture stage."

"Mrs. Fish," said Mr. Capron, "I will do the public speaking, and you need only be physically present in order to translate for the spirits. Your reputation will not be injured in any way."

Under Mr. Capron's kind prodding, Leah cast her eyes down in acquiescence. "If you feel it is a wise course, Mr. Capron, then I will, as ever, abide by your judgment. I only think that we should ask the spirits for guidance before making a final decision."

The alphabet board appeared in my hands as if I had somehow known in advance it would be needed. Mr. Capron took it upon himself to ask the question, and the spirits rapped out their answer immediately: *Hire Corinthian Hall.*

Chapter Fifteen
Maggie

Corinthian Hall was the pride and joy of Rochester, a tall and majestic building with vaulted ceilings and tall windows. It served as the venue for countless cultural events and educational lectures; even the famous Frederick Douglass had spoken at the hall that summer. Never in a million years had I imagined that I might stand upon the platform as a fourteen-year-old girl and perform my parlor tricks before a public audience!

Mr. Capron managed to reserve the hall for the evening of the fourteenth of November. I fluctuated day by day between ecstatic excitement and pure terror, one moment reflecting upon a choice of dress, the next pledging that I would lock myself in my room and refuse to come out. Kate, by contrast, was serene and assured, looking forward with almost adultlike intensity to the opportunity, not suspecting that fate would intervene to prevent her from appearing there at all.

It was the only time Mr. Capron ever got the better of Leah. They were discussing their preparations for the event when Mr. Capron said in passing, "Of course, Miss Kate will not be present with us."

For a moment Leah blinked at him in confusion, and then, composing her face, she covered her surprise by agreeing, "Of course not. She is too young to appear on a public platform." Knowing her as I did, I could sense the vexation beneath her calm exterior, but it would have been foolhardy to take any other stance. Leah already strained the boundaries of propriety by allowing scarcely known acquaintances into her home each night, taking money from them, and sitting in near darkness with men who were not related to her by blood. She was daring to appear on display at a public lecture, and without the support and patronage of Mr. Capron, she would certainly have been courting disaster.

"I have had my qualms even about Maggie," Leah went on. "But we certainly must have one of them with us, for the spirits do not rap except in their presence."

"Indeed," Mr. Capron agreed, "but I have been reflecting at length on what arrangements could be made for Kate, and I have exchanged a number of letters with my wife. I may not have mentioned to you, Mrs. Fish, that my wife was a schoolteacher before our marriage, and as you can imagine, education has always been highly valued in our house. For some time now, the lack of schooling for Kate has weighed heavily on my mind. It is one thing for Miss Maggie here, as she has likely taken enough education for a young girl of her social standing, but our Miss Kate is…what, twelve?"

"Eleven," corrected Leah, although Kate had in fact passed her twelfth birthday. My sister was intent on making us out to be younger than we were.

"Far too young to give up her schooling," Mr. Capron said, reaching into his vest pocket to remove a folded paper. "I have here a letter from my wife, Rebecca, inviting young Kate to come and reside at our home in Auburn for a period of time. My wife can tutor her at home, and once she is satisfied with her progress, we will locate a placement for her in a suitable school."

Leah accepted the letter from Mr. Capron and quickly read it. Then, with a fixed smile, she returned it to his hands. "This is a very kind and generous offer. Your wife is obviously a lady of excellent character and a charitable nature. However, I am afraid that my sister is of delicate health, subject to debilitating headaches and even occasional fits. Furthermore, she has never been away from her family and is extremely attached to Maggie and to her mother. To my regret, we shall have to decline your kind offer."

Mr. Capron folded the letter back into his vest pocket, inclining his head politely, and turned the conversation deftly back to the upcoming performance at Corinthian Hall. No doubt Leah thought the subject was closed, as did I, but we had not considered one important fact. Leah was not Kate's mother.

To our great consternation, Mr. Capron took his offer to Mother and convinced her of the need to continue Kate's education. Mr. Capron was passionate enough about his desire to sponsor her education that my mother was completely won over. Soon after, and much to Leah's dismay, Mother had agreed and the travel plans had already been made.

Predictably, Kate became recalcitrant, railing shrilly at Leah and crying piteously to Mother. "I won't go!" she promised our sister with a tear-streaked face. "I'll be ill! I'll have a fit!"

Leah faced her impassively. "Then let us go now to Mr. Capron's lodgings, and you will confess to him that you have been deceiving him from the beginning. We will admit that we have made a right fool of him but that you are tired of the game now and wish to end it."

I sank down upon the bed weakly, even though I knew Leah was only herding Kate into compliance and had no real intention of doing such a thing. For a moment I envisioned what it would be like to confess and heard a great rush of blood in my ears. I truly felt dizzy, contemplating the awful possibility of being found out, seeing the faces of Mr. Capron, the Grangers...

Kate was pale and trembling with emotion. "You don't mean it."

"I do," Leah insisted. "That was our agreement from the beginning. You would do exactly what I told you to do, or I would tell the truth."

Temper subsiding, Kate's eyes filled with tears of sadness and misery instead of anger. "But I don't want to leave you. I don't want to go live in Auburn."

"We need Mr. Capron. If this is what it takes to make him happy, then you will have to show some grit and do it." After a moment, Leah relented and put her arm around Kate. "I'll bring you back as soon as I can. Mother will miss you, and I imagine she will regret her decision as soon as you are gone. Besides, you are sorely in need of tutoring in spelling, as many of our spirit messages have proved!"

Kate sniffed. "What shall I do about the spirits while I am in Auburn?"

Our sister considered. "Continue as you did in Hydesville," she said. "You may hold spirit circles and rap for Mrs. Capron. But take no risks, and it would be better if you kept to your original method of rapping and didn't try any of the new tricks you've learned from Calvin."

Kate turned suddenly and looked at me with worry. "How will you manage without me at Corinthian Hall? Maggie cannot rap as loudly as I can."

I had been worried about this myself for many days. "I dare not bring any bells in my pockets," I said.

Leah shook her head. "Nor any of those lead balls in your hem. We'll be relying on nothing but your toes, Maggie."

"They'll never hear it," I said.

"Calvin and I have some ideas," Leah assured me. "Although I will be on the platform with you, you know I cannot help you make the actual rapping. We will have to depend on Calvin, whom no one will see or pay any mind to. Trust that he will be nearby and serving our cause."

The evening of the fourteenth of November arrived with a frigid blast of northeasterly wind. Kate had departed, sad and unwilling, just two days before. Without her presence and unflagging confidence, I felt panicky about the lecture. How could I possibly crack the joints in my toes loudly enough to be heard in that immense hall?

It was not until Leah had tried and failed to make any noise with the joints in her feet and ankles that I realized it was not a skill possible for everyone. Kate had patiently demonstrated for her, time and time again, exactly the movements we made, but our sister was unable to make a sound. She could crack her finger joints with a sharp noise, but such a movement was obvious and easy for an observer to detect. Feet, ankles, and legs were always hidden beneath long skirts.

Leah assured me that I would not have to rap for any test questions at Corinthian Hall or spell out any messages. "You just need to be heard," she said. "A few loud raps while Mr. Capron is speaking. Calvin has found an entrance to the crawl space beneath the audience hall. If he can gain access undetected, he will create a few raps of his own, and it will appear as if they are coming from different locations." Perhaps I still looked frightened, for she placed a hand under my chin and fondly lifted my face for a sisterly kiss. "Twenty-five cents a ticket, Maggie, and half of it coming to us."

Wrapped tightly in our cloaks against the biting wind, we arrived around seven o'clock in the evening at the side door to the Corinthian, and the manager, Mr. Reynolds, ushered us inside. If I thought the hall immense when I visited it and sat among the audience, it was nothing compared to the size of it as viewed from the raised platform. The tall windows stretched upward on either side of us, drawing the eyes toward the bronze gaslights hanging from the lofty paneled ceiling. Four Corinthian columns, for which the hall was named, stood at the back of the platform before a heavy red curtain. A lectern had been placed near the front of the platform for Mr. Capron, and nearby were four chairs, neatly arranged with two prominently in front and the remaining two set apart and slightly behind the others. There Leah and I would sit on display, with Amy Post and her husband discreetly positioned nearby.

The Grangers escorted my mother to a seat in the front row of the audience, skirting the crowds of people who were noisily progressing to their places in a seemingly endless procession. The echoes of voices rumbled off the walls, and I gripped Leah's hand in cold fear, squeezing her fingers mercilessly. We would learn later that more than four hundred tickets had been sold, and we stood to earn at least fifty dollars from the event.

Mr. Reynolds, the manager, kindly took my cloak and Leah's, and we smoothed our skirts and hair in preparation for walking shakily out to our seats. Calvin had already melted away like snow, unnoticed. Mother thought he would be waiting behind the platform; Mr. Capron assumed he would be seated in the audience with my mother.

The evening proved to be a long, torturous ordeal of sitting patiently and self-consciously in a hard wooden seat, my eyes cast modestly down at my folded hands. I saw more of my own skirt than I did of the audience, although I did peek beneath my lowered lashes, searching for faces I might know, for friendliness, for credibility.

Mr. Capron began by comparing himself to some of the world's greatest men of discovery, such as Galileo and Columbus, who were ridiculed for their findings before humankind was ready to believe in them. Then he went on to recount the story of the Hydesville peddler whose spirit had implored for justice by rapping out a message to a pair of innocent country girls.

My first attempt at creating a rap failed, for I was nervous and afraid of making some kind of visible motion with my foot. On my second attempt, I heard the crack quite clearly, and several people in the front row lifted their heads simultaneously. Clearly, the sound did not carry far, but some heard it, and those who did not hear it would see the reaction of those who did.

"Ah," Mr. Capron said, "I hear that the spirits have joined us." He continued his narrative by explaining how the rapping sounds had followed us to Rochester, and he began to expound on his own theories about communication with the spiritual world.

On the left side of the hall, about two-thirds of the way back, people seated in the audience began to murmur. One man rose from his seat and placed his hand upon the wall, then turned and made some comment to his companions. A few minutes later, some ladies seated in the center of the hall gasped and drew back in their seats, their faces turned toward the floor near their feet. Although I could not hear anything from my position on the platform, it appeared that various spots in the audience were experiencing some unusual phenomena, and I could only assume that our wonderful accomplice had indeed gained access to the crawl space beneath the hall.

Mr. Capron continued with his lecture, unperturbed by the sudden and apparently random disruptions in the audience. Feeling emboldened, I continued to produce the raps at varying intervals, and it was evident that Calvin was freely moving beneath the hall. When Mr. Capron reached the end of his prepared speech, tentative applause broke out in the parts of the audience that had heard the mysterious noises issuing from the walls, the floor, and the air.

But one man rose from somewhere near the back of the hall and began to stride up the center aisle toward the platform. A murmur of anticipation rose from the audience as he approached, and I could see that Mr. Capron stiffened as he recognized the oncoming man. He was short and heavily whiskered, nicely dressed in elegant evening wear, and giving off an air of self-importance. He was clapping his hands as he came, in that slow, deliberate way that showed disdain rather than appreciation. When he was sure that he had the attention of everyone in the hall, he called out in a loud, clear voice, "Very good, Mr. Capron. Very good. A marvelous tale of ghostly drama, but rather short on actual facts. Entertaining, but deceptive."

"Mr. Bissel," replied Mr. Capron, "I fail to see where we have been deceptive."

"Oh, it is very easy to deceive the innocent and the gullible and thus lead them away from a righteous path," answered the man before the platform. "The Bible tells us we must not suffer a witch to live, and what you have presented to us tonight must be none other than witchcraft or fraud."

A murmur rose from the crowd, and my heart froze at the word "witchcraft." But Mr. Capron leaned across that lectern and pierced Mr. Bissel with the intelligent gaze of reason. "We live in the nineteenth century, Mr. Bissel. Rational men do not believe in witchcraft, and I believe that those who have joined us here tonight are neither gullible nor uneducated."

"I am glad to hear that, Mr. Capron," stated the man from the audience. "Then I can assume your 'spirit mediums' would be prepared to undergo scientific tests to determine whether they make these sounds by trickery?"

"What do you have in mind?"

"A committee," stated Mr. Bissel. "Let us say, five men, who will examine your mediums at a time of your choosing, but at a place that we have designated, to see if they can produce ghost noises by any means that we can prove to be false."

I could hear the indrawn breath of many in the audience as they waited for Mr. Capron's reaction to the challenge. Our journalist friend turned to look at Leah, who raised her eyes and nodded briefly, placing her welfare in his hands. Mr. Capron looked out at the audience, then dropped his gaze to Mr. Bissel. "We agree to your terms, sir—but only if a committee can be gathered from the persons already present here tonight, who could be assumed to have an open-minded stance on the issue."

Applause broke out spontaneously from the audience, and immediately a barrage of nominations erupted, with accompanying catcalls and cheers. Glancing at each other, the Posts rose and moved to the front of the platform to supervise the selection process. Leah signaled Mr. Capron, who escorted us from our seats and to the doorway at the back of the platform.

I clutched at Leah, whispering fiercely, "What is happening?"

"They are choosing a group of men to determine whether we are making the raps by deceit." Leah gave me a glance meant as warning, conscious of Mr. Capron's presence at our side.

Still, I pressed on with my anxious inquiry. "How do they propose to determine this?"

Mr. Capron leaned forward to give me a placid and comforting smile. "There is nothing to fear, Miss Maggie, because there is nothing they can find. The spirits will surely prove themselves to be real, so that even a committee appointed by Josiah Bissel and his friends cannot lack satisfaction."

And to this, there was nothing more Leah or I could say.

Chapter Sixteen
Maggie

Before the end of that evening, we learned that Leah and I would be expected to meet the chosen committee at ten the following morning and again at two in the afternoon. A carriage would arrive to take us to the appointed place, which would not be revealed until the last minute for fear that we would plant some mechanism for trickery there.

Leah wanted to know who had been chosen for the committee. Mr. Post told her, "I did the best that I could to make certain it was a fair group, impartial in the balance of votes, if not in the individuals. Josiah Bissel won places for a couple of his cronies, but I managed to acquire two judges of the court who are known to be fair and honest."

I turned to Amy Post and asked her urgently, "Who was that man, that Mr. Bissel?"

Anyone else of the company might have dismissed my question without serious answer, but I knew that Amy would grant me the dignity of a reply. "Josiah Bissel is a dangerous man to run afoul of, with many friends and associates who will do whatever it takes to keep his favor. I would be very wary of his men on the committee, Maggie." Amy took my hand and patted it, seeing the worry in my eyes. "I will be with you tomorrow, and you may call upon me if you need my help. I have faced down enough slave hunters in my time that I am not easily intimidated by the likes of Mr. Bissel!"

The next morning, as promised, a carriage arrived at Leah's house, which transported four of us—Mr. Capron, Amy Post, Leah, and myself—to the location of our first examination, which proved to be the Sons of Temperance Hall. Before our departure, Leah had instructed me privately on my behavior during the tests.

"The spirits will not be answering questions today," she told me. "A few discreet raps will be sufficient, but take no chances. If there is the possibility of detection, make no sound at all. Silence proves nothing—remember that!"

Leah and I were conducted into a meeting room off the main auditorium and given a place to sit. Mr. Capron and Amy were obliged to wait outside the room. One of the men, a lawyer named Mr. Whittlesey, proved to be friendly and not very intimidating. He greeted us, introduced himself and his fellow committee members, and assured us, "There is no reason to be alarmed. You shall have a fair investigation."

One of the other men, a justice of the circuit court, began immediately to ask us questions, challenging us to identify his mother's maiden name and other personal information about himself.

Leah was polite but firm. "You have been misinformed, sir, if you believe us to be clairvoyants. I cannot read your mind."

"But I thought your spirits answered questions," he insisted. "Surely your Mr. Capron told us so in his lecture."

"'The spirit of the murdered man in Hydesville answered questions about himself," Leah acknowledged. "And when we sit in a proper setting, after dark, many of our guests receive answers from their departed kin, but the spirits have never engaged in guessing games."

"Then what are we here for?" grumbled another man.

A gray-haired gentleman with cold eyes and a thin-lipped mouth stepped forward. "We are here to determine the true cause of the rapping sounds produced in the presence of these women. We will be hearing those sounds, will we not?"

"I hope so," Leah replied sweetly. "We certainly entreat our invisible companions to make themselves known." And as if in answer, we heard three sharp raps. The man's eyes shifted to me at once, and I, having resolved to make myself as Kate-like as possible, gazed back at him in wide-eyed innocence, smiling blandly.

"There they are now," I told him.

The gentlemen circled around us, discussing the situation. "They were seated in chairs last night, too," said one of the judges. "Let us have them stand."

"You may address us directly," Leah said brightly, helpfully standing up. I rose from my seat and stood beside her, but the man with the cold eyes, whose name was Dr. Langworthy, put out an arm and moved us apart.

We stood motionless for a minute or two, and the committee members exchanged puzzled glances as we still heard two strong raps. Dr. Langworthy observed us shrewdly for a time, and then he motioned to a table in the center of the room. "Mrs. Fish, I will ask you to sit upon this table with your limbs stretched out before you."

Raising an eyebrow at the questionable dignity of such a position, Leah eased herself onto the table and then gathered up her skirts and swung her legs until they were stretched out on the table in front of her. While she was arranging her skirts to fully cover her ankles, Dr. Langworthy reached out and grasped both of her knees with his hands. Leah let out a startled shriek and drew back from him in outrage.

"Mrs. Fish," the doctor chastised her with a sneer, "I don't know what you may be accustomed to in the country, but accredited physicians generally touch their patients to examine them."

"You are under a number of misapprehensions, Dr. Langworthy, which I will gladly correct for you," Leah snapped. "The first is: I am not your patient. Secondly, I have lived in Rochester nearly all my life, and I am quite familiar with the practices of accredited physicians. And finally, I have seen many Rochester doctors in the course of my life, but never one who would lay hands upon a female patient without asking her permission first!"

"See here, Langworthy!" the lawyer, Mr. Whittlesey, exclaimed. "There is no reason to treat Mrs. Fish or her young sister with anything other than the respect due a lady. If you will not amend your behavior, I will ask you to dismiss yourself from this committee."

The doctor murmured an ill-tempered and scarcely sincere apology and asked for Leah's permission to hold her limbs while he listened for the raps. She agreed, but the atmosphere between them was tense and filled with mutual dislike. I dared not make a sound, and the silence was long and unpleasant.

For the next three-quarters of an hour, Leah and I were asked to submit to a number of indignities. I spent my time upon the table with the doctor's hands upon my knees. They also asked us to stand upon pillows, and they tied a thin rope on the outside of our skirts around the level of our ankles. Dr. Langworthy pressed a stethoscope against our backs to listen to our lungs and held our wrists with his cold, clammy fingers to measure the pulse of our blood.

When Mr. Capron knocked on the door and announced that the agreed-upon time had passed, Leah and I were quite relieved to escape the clutches of the vile doctor. To Mr. Capron's inquiry about the consensus of the committee, Dr. Langworthy quickly replied, "There was scarcely a knock to be heard during the entire hour and never when the ladies' limbs were held."

Amy Post's brow furrowed at the discovery that we had been physically handled, and Mr. Capron looked shocked at the very mention of the word *limb*. But Leah gathered her dignity and turned in the doorway to face the doctor. "Did you determine a method by which my sister and I create the knocks through some mechanism or deceitful behavior?"

Langworthy inclined his head. "No, we did not."

"Then I trust you will report as much when asked," Leah retorted.

Mr. Capron seemed quite taken aback by the obvious hostility between the doctor and my sister. "Will you send the carriage again this afternoon?" he asked tentatively.

"No need," said Mr. Whittlesey. "If Mrs. Post is willing, we would like to make the next examination at her home, because she is well known to you and to us, and the ladies may find themselves more at ease there."

"My home is open to you," Amy replied. "We look forward to meeting you there this afternoon."

<hr>

Our suspicions were raised by their choice of the Post house as a second location for their examination. We were, of course, very familiar with the house and had, on occasion, met there to discuss spiritualism or hold a private sitting.

"I don't know why they have chosen the Post house," Leah muttered. "They think we will be at ease there. Perhaps they believe we will make some mistake that will reveal trickery on our part."

"That is absurd!" exclaimed Mother. She had never stopped believing in the spirits. "What trickery can they possibly hope to reveal?"

I avoided Mother's eyes and made a pretense at eating. We could not freely speak our thoughts in front of my mother, but I understood what Leah was trying to communicate. I must continue to be on my guard and act with the utmost discretion and caution. It would be better to have the examiners fail to hear or see any evidence of a spiritual presence than to have them positively identify us as frauds!

Our prudent planning served us well, as we discovered immediately upon the arrival of the committee at two that afternoon. When the five gentlemen entered the Posts' parlor followed by three stern-faced women, I guessed immediately what they had in mind and was relieved that our foresight had led me to wear clothing without any hidden balls or bells.

Two of the ladies were introduced as wives of committee members, Mrs. Langworthy among them. The third was a relative of Josiah

Bissel. They had been deputized as a subsidiary committee to perform a thorough examination of our bodies and our clothing.

Amy and Leah were irate at this unannounced and degrading affront to our modesty. Mr. Capron could not decide what he thought about it, proving himself an inadequate champion of our cause by declaring that "the girls" had nothing to hide and so there was no reason to object to an examination by other members of the "fair gender."

Fair gender, indeed! There was nothing fair about these women! The doctor's wife had the face of a hatchet, and the Bissel woman's squinty eyes were cold and black, giving her the look of a vicious snake. The third woman was so pale and spiritless that she withdrew to the back of the room immediately and let the other two do as they pleased. As soon as the parlor door closed, with the men and Amy Post on the outside, Mrs. Langworthy snapped, "Doctor thinks the girl is doing it with her feet. Off with your shoes, child!"

Shaking like a leaf, I unlaced my shoes and stepped obediently out of them. Mrs. Langworthy picked them up, shook them, and stuck her skinny, veined hands inside them. Miss Bissel insisted Leah hand over her own shoes, and my sister complied slowly and insolently. Mrs. Langworthy then grabbed hold of my skirts and began to run her hands over the fabric, squeezing and shaking the folds and turning up the ends to examine the hem.

I folded my arms over my bosom in quiet misery, allowing the wretched woman to turn me about as she clutched at my dress in a most personal and humiliating manner. All the while, she was muttering in my ear: "We know you are a liar and a fraud, you little guttersnipe. You might be able to fool the common masses, but you should not have tried to swindle your betters. You deserve what's coming to you!"

Leah was submitting to her own humiliation, allowing the Bissel woman to manhandle her in a similar fashion while staring at the ceiling as if too haughty to notice her own abasement. But I could see twin circles of reddish color in her cheeks, and her lips were pressed together as if locked against the words that were boiling within.

"Take off the dress," snarled my tormentor.

"What?" I gasped, turning a shocked face to the doctor's wife. "No! I won't!"

"I want to look at the inner seams. I believe I feel something inside them, just here!" she said, jabbing me in the ribs.

"That's my corset!" I cried indignantly, and it was the truth, for there was nothing hidden in this dress. She only wanted to embarrass me further.

"We demand you take the dresses off," Miss Bissel chimed in, smiling smugly at Leah. "Or else we will return to the committee and tell them we could feel hidden objects sewn into your clothing that are undoubtedly used to make your mysterious noises."

Tears were stinging my eyes and Leah appeared to me through a blurred haze, but I could hear the misery and defeat in her voice as she told me, "We'll take off the dresses, Maggie. These harpies will not be satisfied with less, and our reputations will only suffer more if they are not able to acquit us of concealing objects on our persons."

Snuffling back my tears, I unfastened my dress and struggled out of it. Never in my life had I undressed before anyone other than Kate and my mother. I wadded up the dress and flung it furiously at the nasty old wife of that horrid doctor. "Here! Take it! There is nothing inside it, as you will see!" I snarled.

Mrs. Langworthy only smiled triumphantly at my display of temper, saying, "Poor breeding always shows when a whelp is cornered."

She examined my dress with great thoroughness, clearly disappointed to find nothing that should not have been there. Leah had also removed her own dress and was standing with her fists clenched at her sides, as if she wanted to box the ears of the woman who was now peering at the seams nearsightedly and making side comments about the quality of the fabric. Mrs. Langworthy next made me take down my hair, and when I did not do so quickly enough, she reached out and pulled it down herself.

When I thought it would be impossible to reach any lower point, my examiner sighed and tossed my dress aside, onto the floor like a rag, and said, "Well, then, let us have off with the rest."

I was already standing in a corset and petticoats; there was nothing that could have induced me to disrobe any further. Leah, likewise left in only her undergarments, put an arm around me and said in a rather shaky voice, "We've had enough of your examination. You won't get another stitch from us."

"I think you'll do as you are told!" the doctor's wife replied as though to a recalcitrant child. She grabbed hold of my arm and tried to yank me out of Leah's grasp.

Breaking out in sobs, I pushed at her blindly and tried to break free. "Amy! Amy!" I cried. "Please help us!"

The parlor door burst open so promptly that I think she must have been on the verge of intervening when I cried out to her. Amy Post was not a beautiful woman, but she looked like an avenging angel to me when she charged to our aid, her face flushed and her eyes alight with fury. "That will be enough from you, Evangeline Langworthy! Unhand that child and leave my home at once! You've accomplished what you came to do and enjoyed it all too well, I suspect."

Mrs. Langworthy sniffed and dusted at her fingers as she released me. "I don't know why you have involved yourself with these two, Mrs. Post. One would think that stuffing Negroes beneath your floorboards would keep you busy enough for two women, let alone adopting a couple of charlatans fit only for a carnival show!"

The doctor's wife gathered her skirts and sailed out of the parlor like a great ship, with Miss Bissel scurrying in her wake. The third woman, who had cowered in a corner throughout our ordeal, retrieved my dress from the floor and thrust it at me in some embarrassment as she passed me. Then she, too, departed, closing the door behind her.

Leah covered her face with her hands, giving way to tears at last. Amy Post put her arms around me, and I pressed my face into the crumpled mess of my dress and sobbed with humiliation.

At that moment, in my heart, I despaired of ever being free from the spirits that I had created, in boredom and devilment, on April Fools' Eve in Hydesville.

Chapter Seventeen
Maggie

We were greatly shaken by our treatment at the hands of "the Ladies' Committee," although Leah recovered her wits sooner than I did. "I cannot say that I ever received much respect from the ladies of society," she observed ruefully while repairing the damage done to her hair, "although this is the first time I have ever been treated like a slave girl! Still, I suffer no pangs of remorse for the lack of friendship from the Bissels and the Langworthys."

"Indeed not," agreed Amy Post, who was combing my hair in a motherly manner. "In fact, they rather remind me of inbred pedigree dogs, which yip and yap all the more fiercely to mask their own inherited deficiencies."

Recalling how the doctor's wife had compared me to a poorly bred mongrel, I shivered and did not join in their merriment, forced as it was. Never in my life had anyone spoken with such hostility to me, and I marveled that Leah could pass it off so lightly. She was tougher than I was, without a doubt!

My nerve broke entirely that afternoon when a letter came from Mr. Whittlesey, the lawyer on the examination committee. Apparently he had received an anonymous note warning him not to attend the public presentation at Corinthian Hall that evening if he found in favor of the Fox sisters, for he would be mobbed. In his letter to us, Mr. Whittlesey tried to discount the possibility of real danger and personally guaranteed our safety.

"Although honor bound to inform you of this unpleasant piece of news," he wrote, "I assure you that no harm will come to any good woman in the city of Rochester while I am resident here, and to this end I intend to escort you to and from the hall in my own carriage."

I began to cry, and even Leah paled somewhat. "I think it would be best if Mother did not come to the hall tonight," Leah said grimly. "I will think of some excuse and ask Calvin to stay with her."

"You can't possibly be thinking of going!" I cried out. "Leah, we can't! Please! Not if there's a mob waiting for us!"

"I don't think there is any real danger," Leah spoke hesitantly, turning to Amy. "What do you think?"

"You must appear tonight when the committee makes its report," Amy replied, "or your guilt will be assumed and your reputation will be shattered. I will go with you; I shall sit beside you and take whatever risk there may be along with you."

"Then I will go, even if it means going to the stake!" Leah resolved, turning to me with a slight smile to show that she was exaggerating. But her words frightened me all the more.

"You'll go without me!" I cried. "I've already had a narrow escape from a mob back in Hydesville, and if it hadn't been for David, we might all have been killed!"

Leah would have argued with me, but Amy put a hand upon her arm to quiet her. "Maggie must do as her heart tells her," said Amy. "To force or coerce her against her will would be wrong."

As it happened, Calvin sided with me when he found out about the threats, and he was furious to discover that Leah wanted to leave him at home. "I cannot remain behind and let you face a lynch mob!" he said in a voice tight with emotion. He bristled all over with tension, and his burning eyes would not leave Leah's face.

She tried reason first. "Mr. Whittlesey has sent a letter stating that he is aware of the threats and that he is acquiring police protection for us in the hall."

"Half the police are in the pocket of Josiah Bissel," Calvin countered. "You know that, Leah."

Leah turned then to another, more personal form of persuasion and, taking his hands, led Calvin to a seat beside her on Amy's settee. Leaning forward and looking directly into his worried eyes, she began to speak softly and urgently to him. Amy motioned for me to join her, and we withdrew from the parlor to give them privacy. After a minute or two, Calvin departed with his shoulders slumped in a way that gave us little doubt who had persevered.

Arrangements had been made with the manager of the Corinthian for our reappearance that evening. A previously scheduled event had been postponed because of the popular demand to see the rappers revealed or confirmed, and the carriage arrived for us at the Post house promptly at seven. Mr. Whittlesey himself called upon us, and when he discovered only Leah, Amy, and Isaac dressed in their cloaks, with me cowering upon the stairs, he exclaimed,

"Why, Miss Margaretta! Aren't you coming this evening?" I shook my head vehemently, wide-eyed and petrified. The lawyer looked startled. "You cut me to the quick, child! I will not let any harm befall you!"

I looked from his face to Leah's, then to Amy and Isaac, feeling more and more foolish. No one else seemed frightened, and for a moment I felt like a small child who had been terrified by a bogey tale. "Oh, for land sakes!" I burst out in a sudden decision. "I cannot let you go without me. Let me get my cloak and I shall come, although I expect I will probably be killed!"

A line of people had already formed outside the Corinthian, jostling their way out of the wind and into the rather narrow entranceway to the hall. As before, our carriage brought us around to a side entrance, and we hurried into the shelter of the building.

My companions seemed calm and at ease on the journey to the hall, and I thought that only I retained a sense of nervous apprehension about the evening's event until we met Mr. Capron inside the hall. He hastened to speak to Mr. Whittlesey as soon as we arrived, his face drawn and pale. The lawyer responded with surprise and alarm. Unable to hear them, I pulled away from Leah and tried to get closer, but all I overheard was Mr. Capron saying that he had "removed it from the hall and dumped it into the street."

Before I could make sense of this, the manager of the hall took our cloaks and once again directed us through the corridors that led to the platform. Even more so than the previous evening, the hall echoed with the voices of an excited audience. It seemed to me that the first row of seats was filled with a different sort of group than the night before, composed of rough-looking young men with no female companions in sight. Resolving to keep my gaze cast downward, I seated myself as demurely as possible and waited patiently for the presentation to begin.

Mr. Whittlesey joined Mr. Capron at the lectern and raised his hand for silence. The audience quieted but did not completely stop talking. Thus, it was evident even from the first minute that the two men did not have the control over the event that we had been promised.

Mr. Whittlesey began by summarizing the previous evening and then describing the examinations conducted that day. When he stated that neither he nor his colleagues had discovered any evidence of deception, several members of the audience rose from their seats and started to make catcalls. The lawyer stammered a bit, taken aback by this reaction. I had given up holding my gaze in my lap and was staring at him and Mr. Capron with growing horror. They had been warned! They both had been warned! How could they have been so foolishly unprepared after promising to ensure our safety?

A sudden battery of loud cracks, like gunfire on a battlefield, erupted at the back of the hall, echoing riotously off the vaulted ceiling. Women screamed in fright, but from my position on the platform I could clearly see the cause of the disruption: firecrackers, set alight at regular intervals along the back row of the auditorium. Instantly, the promised police protection appeared from behind the red curtain. They rushed across the platform, leaped down into the audience, and sprinted toward the back of the hall.

No sooner had the policemen run to the back of the hall than Mr. Bissel appeared out of the crowd and clambered up onto the front of the platform. "This is a fraud!" he shouted. "Perpetrated by frauds, with the collaboration of more frauds! Mr. Whittlesey is a friend of these women! He arrived here tonight in their company, in the same carriage! His committee is a farce! I say we form a new committee right here and now and examine these females to our satisfaction!" Before anyone could react or stop him, Mr. Bissel grabbed me by the arm, dragging me from my chair and thrusting me toward the raised edge of the platform. "Who wants to examine this one?" he challenged, spittle flying from his lips.

I screamed, teetering on the edge of the platform, staring straight down at a sea of faces, ugly with violence.

Then firm hands took my shoulders, pulled me out of Bissel's grasp and backward to safety. Mr. Bissel snarled and aimed a blow at my rescuer, but Mr. Post dodged the poorly aimed fist and responded by punching the smaller man directly in the eye. For a moment, I don't know who was more shocked—Bissel or my gentle Quaker friend! Then Mr. Post took my hand and ran with me toward the back of the platform. "Come, Maggie! This way!"

I could see Leah and Amy ahead, running along the backstage corridors, which had already filled with smoke from the firecrackers. Mr. Capron and the manager of the hall waved us along after them, herding us toward that same side door by which we had entered. As we stumbled outside, the acrid smell of smoke was joined by a sharp, stinging odor that burned my eyes. While Mr. Post pulled me toward the waiting carriage, I turned back and saw quite clearly the source of the other pungent smell.

In the street outside the hall lay an overturned barrel and, in a thick puddle spilling out onto the street, a large quantity of warmed tar.

❧

That night, I shivered in my bed for long, long hours, unable to achieve warmth in spite of the number of blankets my mother and sister had piled upon me. Mother sat beside me for most of the night, horrified by the story that had spilled from my lips as soon as I saw her. She was furious with Leah, and rightly so. Over and over again, I saw the faces of those horrible men in the first row, reaching up for me as Mr. Bissel threatened to cast me down. I smelled the tar, which Mr. Capron had discovered before we arrived, and in my nebulous dream state, I imagined having it poured upon my skin…

"Maggie, wake up. It's noon."

I startled awake, strangling a shriek as I realized that sunlight filled the room and that Leah was seated upon the bed beside me. Mother was gone, and the blankets had been cast aside in my turbulent sleep. I pursed my lips in preparation for some sharp remark, but my sister calmly unfolded a newspaper and held it out in front of my face. "You've made the papers, Maggie. Look."

The headlines were bold and numerous: "Riot at Corinthian over Validity of Spirit Rapping," "Firecrackers Cause Panic," "Pillar of Community Invites Assault of Young Girl on Stage."

"Mr. Reynolds, the manager of the Corinthian, is pressing charges against Josiah Bissel, because witnesses all state that he handed out the firecrackers to the boys who set them off," Leah went on as

I scanned the article in the paper. "The police chief has all but charged Bissel with inciting a riot and soliciting an assault on you. I doubt anything will come of it, but public opinion has already convicted him. The people of Rochester now believe that Bissel and his friends were conspiring to keep them unaware of the truth behind spirit rapping!"

"I suppose you consider that good news!" I snapped, tossing down the paper and trying to hide the fascination of seeing my name in print. "Never mind that we were nearly tarred and feathered, or assaulted—or killed outright!"

"I am sorry you were frightened." Leah picked up the paper and folded it neatly. "Nobody expected him to jump onto the platform like that. No one was prepared for that."

"Nobody was prepared at all!" I retorted. "Except possibly Mr. Post!"

Leah laughed with sudden mirth. "For a pacifist, he packs a mean right cross!"

"It is not funny!" I cried. "We might have been killed!"

My sister shook her head gently and rose from the bed. "I have not led as sheltered a life as you have. I have no illusions about life and death, respectability or poverty. Last night was frightening—no two ways about it—but in the end we came out victorious and virtuous. If you want to lie abed and think about what might have happened, then do so. But if you ever want to grow up, Maggie, then you can get dressed and come downstairs, where the friends who protected you are waiting to be assured of your well-being."

She strode to the door and then called back over her shoulder, "I believe there are five different floral bouquets downstairs, all with calling cards from young gentlemen wishing you a quick recovery from your harrowing experience. It is a shame that you are not well enough to receive any visitors. I shall have to send them away when they call."

Swearing softly with words that would greatly distress Mother, and words that I had, after all, learned from Leah, I swung my legs out of bed and reached for some clothing.

Chapter Eighteen
Kate

Life in Auburn with Rebecca Capron and her daughters was pleasant and lively, and an opportunity for me to explore my powers without Leah telling me what to say. Although I missed Maggie no less, it was difficult to be lonely with the four Capron girls always about, laughing and teasing and including me as one of their own. They were impressed with my gift but not terribly impressed by me—within hours of my arrival they had teased me, petted me, borrowed my dresses, and lent me their own. I was just another girl.

This is not to say that I didn't sit with Mrs. Capron and other interested parties in spirit circles most evenings. If anything, they believed me all the more for my ability to channel the spirit messages with reverence and then, a little while later, join the girls in a mock battle with pillows and flying shoes. "She's such an innocent thing," I overheard Mrs. Capron tell her friends. "She doesn't understand the significance of what she does."

In spite of this, Mrs. Capron did not think I was a featherhead and praised my schoolwork. She said that I was a very apt pupil. There was a particular girls' school near New York City that she wanted me to attend the next fall, and she knew of a newspaper editor and his wife who might be willing to have me stay in their home.

Such a move held little appeal to me. Although it would be exciting to live near a big city, New York was much too far from my family, and I was not quite the city girl that Maggie was. My home would always be with my family, although I was resigned to life in Auburn for now, with the Capron girls making a temporary substitute for my sisters.

It was easy enough to bribe the girls with sweets and other promises to tell me all the stories they knew of their mother and her friends, who gathered each night to speak to the spirits. The Capron sisters hardly had to be enticed at all to listen at keyholes and repeat gossip they had heard, and no one ever linked this girlish pastime with the intimate knowledge of the rapping spirits. Without Leah to direct me, I was free to deliver messages from the spirit world that fostered my chosen purpose: to comfort the grieving, proving by the words of their beloved departed that there was life beyond death.

One might fault me for continuing the carnival tricks that Leah had encouraged, but Mrs. Capron had come to expect them, having learned of the spirit antics from her husband. There was little enough I could do on my own. Leah had made me rip out the hidden seams in my dresses and remove all balls before I left for Auburn, and it was a good thing that she had, because the Capron girls viewed anything belonging to one as available for use by all. Often, the best I could do was to cause the candles to go out while we sat holding hands, and then duck my head under the table in the darkness and bump it around a bit.

I altered the candles myself at night, after everyone else was asleep. Being as cautious as possible, I took them to the kitchen and laid out slabs of bread and jam before going to work on my task. Thus, if anyone came downstairs unexpectedly, I could scoop the candles into my pockets and be scolded for nothing more than an unladylike appetite. It was lonely work. I longed to tell Maggie of things I dared not write in my letters—how I had known the answers to some questions not through reading the face of the asker or listening to gossip but simply through *knowing*. Maggie would have argued as she always did. "Everyone gets a bit of luck sometimes!" she would have cried, or "You must have been told the story and just forgotten." I missed her stubbornness and the challenge of a good debate with my closest and dearest friend.

Letters could not replace her, although I savored each correspondence as a breath of air from home. Things had apparently taken a bad turn at Corinthian Hall, and Maggie was badly frightened by the experience. However, Leah's letter said that the event had only converted more people to a belief in the spirits, and I would venture to guess that she was correct, for even in Auburn people were outraged over the riot. And because Maggie's letters spoke mainly of the flowers and candy she had received from sympathetic visitors, I assumed she had recovered from her shock and was determined to make as much profit from her misadventure as possible.

After several weeks, Mrs. Capron began pressing the issue of the private girls' school in New York City again. The newspaper editor of her acquaintance had offered me a home while I attended that school next year, provisional upon his meeting me.

Eventually I was coerced into meeting this Mr. Horace Greeley, despite my reservations, and it turned out that he was no different from any of the people who came to see me. He had lost his son to cholera and, more recently, a dear friend to a shipwreck at sea. As a newspaperman he wanted to be skeptical, but even more badly, he wanted to believe.

After our successful spirit sitting, Mrs. Capron and Mr. Greeley spoke enthusiastically about my scholarly potential, worthy of a position as governess or schoolteacher. And yet what each of them wanted most from me was something I was already capable of giving them—spiritual peace. How odd it was that those who most needed my spiritual gifts tried so hard to educate me into a role where I could not use them!

Chapter Nineteen
Maggie

I missed my younger sister dearly. My confidant, coconspirator, and greatest ally was far away and living a merry life with a gaggle of girls her own age. There were many occasions when I speculated that Leah was well pleased by our separation, for all that she had originally opposed it. Our entire family was under a sort of bondage to Leah, and she ruled over us as expertly as any benevolent despot in history. When she showered us with gifts, it was easy to forget her moments of anger and coercion. However, any person with absolute power over others is a tyrant, even if that person is amiable and pleasant much of the time.

The months passed quickly, and news of our spirit communications spread across the state of New York. Abolitionists, feminists, Quakers, and forward thinkers everywhere had readily accepted the idea of spiritualism. We had made some enemies, it is true: the Bissels and Langworthys of our city still claimed that we were frauds, and the Catholic Church had denounced us as possessed or depraved. But still, we had many admirers and eventually imitators. We learned that other women, girls, and sometimes boys claimed to attract spirits that would rap messages from beyond the grave.

"It is inevitable that anything successful will be copied," Leah said philosophically. "I am not overly vexed, except that ineptitude by other mediums will give us a bad name. Otherwise, it should not have much impact on us, for we are the original rappers and still greatly in demand."

Yet the possibility of competition caused Leah to consider action that she had previously shunned: traveling to other cities to demonstrate the spirit rapping. For many months, Leah had refused to consider the numerous invitations we received from persons in other cities and towns. "We are not a traveling carnival," she would say. But by the time Mr. Greeley arrived from New York, the possibility of being overshadowed by newer and more interesting spirit mediums had begun to gnaw upon her resolution. The prestigious newspaper editor from New York City merely hastened her decision.

I had received a letter from Kate describing her sitting with Mr. Greeley, and so it was a simple matter for me to impress him with an astounding knowledge of his personal life. Mr. Greeley claimed to think very highly of Kate and desperately wanted to remove her to a private school, but he still never guessed she was capable of writing a letter that included all the information I needed to be successful at his sitting in Rochester. What fools were those men of self-importance who did not credit two half-grown girls with any cleverness!

In addition to his desire for Kate's education, Mr. Greeley dearly wanted us to visit New York and demonstrate our supernatural talent. After much debate, Leah finally agreed to his request.

That summer we embarked on a memorable journey across the state of New York. Departing as soon as we could after Kate's return from Auburn, and leaving behind Calvin, who was suffering from a persistent chest ailment, we traveled first to Albany, then to Troy, and finally to New York City itself. At the height of the summer, after traveling by steamboat down the Hudson River, we arrived in Manhattan, where we docked in a flurry of excitement and bustling activity. I fear that we gawked like poor country mice, amazed by the sights and smells of the trade goods and the tradesmen on the wharf, until Leah managed to acquire a hansom cab and wrestle our trunks aboard.

I admit to being seriously spoiled by life in the great city. Our visitors brought gifts, ranging from ribbons and lace to tickets for musical revues and boxes of sweet confections. Leah banned the chocolates in a fit of temper when it became difficult to tighten her corsets. Still, we smuggled in our treats, and once Kate and I made off with an entire bottle of champagne, which we drank after Leah had retired to bed.

During our weeks in New York, we met with newspapermen flushed with pomposity, church leaders endeavoring to reconcile their beliefs, and an array of artists, writers, and performers, all curious and itching to participate in the most fashionable activity in town. There was no end of gentlemen jostling one another to spend an hour or two with Leah, who was described in the newspapers as "a vivacious woman of more than average attractiveness." Kate and I were not ignored either. Several young men inquired of my older sister whether "pretty Maggie" would soon be of an age to accept the attention of beaux.

In the fall, Mr. Horace Greeley gently reminded us of our promise to send Kate back to school. The Greeley farmhouse was a short day's travel from Manhattan, just on the outskirts of the city, and Mr. Greeley extended an invitation to house all three of us while Kate settled in. We certainly would have accepted, if we had not at that time received a telegram from Rochester.

In it, Amy Post asked us to return to Rochester without delay. Calvin had taken a turn for the worse.

Our mother was already established in the Rochester house, having come from Hydesville at Amy's request some days before. "Oh, thank the Lord you have come at last!" Mother cried, opening the door to us. "He's been asking for you and will not be comforted!"

Leah swept up the stairs, with me following closely. We passed Amy in the bedroom doorway, and I barely had time to register her grim, drawn features before I hurried in behind my sister and beheld my foster brother.

Sweat glistened on his pale and clammy skin. Except for a red flush in his cheeks, he was colorless, with gray hollows around his eyes. Hearing us burst into the room, he floundered weakly on the bed, trying to raise his head to see us. "Leah…" His voice was unrecognizable, strained for lack of breath, and he managed no more than a word before a hacking cough shook his entire body. Amy rushed forward with a rag, which he pressed to his lips, and I watched in horror as the cloth grew dark, and then bright red in his hands. The smell of blood rose in the close, stifling air of the room.

I fled, pushing past Mother, and burst into the smaller, second bedroom. Reaching with floundering hands under the bed that I had shared with Kate, I barely managed to grasp the chamber pot before I vomited.

After a time, Amy came in and sat upon the bed, placing her hand upon my hair and smoothing it back away from my face. I was still kneeling on the floor, holding the pot in my lap.

"It is consumption," she said.

I nodded. I knew it, from description, although I had never before seen anyone bring up blood in that manner.

"He is in a great deal of discomfort," Amy went on, "although the doctors have tried to ease his pain. He wanted very badly to see you and Leah, and he has stubbornly held on until your arrival." When I raised tear-filled eyes to her face, she nodded solemnly.

She allowed me the dignity of solitude, so that I could gather control of my emotions and my fear. As soon as I was capable, I wiped my tears and composed my face and returned to the sickroom.

Calvin was agitated by our presence, for he desperately wanted to speak to us but could not control his coughing spasms. Leah, still in her traveling clothes, took his hand and sat down beside him and begged him to save his breath. "We are here, and we are not leaving you," she assured him. "There will be time to say what you will when you have calmed down and the coughing has stopped."

Gripping her fingers tightly, Calvin stared plaintively at Leah's face. "There is not time," he whispered, unable to put any voice behind his breathy words. "I have waited days to speak to you…I didn't want to…leave…you until I had asked you…"

Mother and Amy exchanged significant glances over my head. "Perhaps we should give you a few minutes of privacy," Mother ventured.

"No." Calvin put out a pale, shaky hand to stop her. "I want you all to be here...for this." His frame shook lightly as he fought down a cough with his lips tightly pressed together, but his eyes had not left Leah's face. "Ann Leah," he said shakily, sounding suddenly very formal for a man so ill. Obviously, he had rehearsed these words. "You and I have known each other for many years, and in that time you have given me a home and your friendship. There is no way I could ever have repaid your kindness...or hoped that you would feel the way I have felt...but now that I am dying..."

"Surely not," whispered Leah.

"Now that I am dying," Calvin repeated, "there is something I can give to you, to repay in part all that you have done for me, and that is...my name. It is not a grand one...but I can do better than that wretched Bowman Fish, who gave you nothing but grief. If you marry me now, I can leave you the undisputed title of widow...not a divorced woman anymore but a widow. You'll have the respect you deserve...with no more slander of your character..."

Mother was crying quietly, and I kept trying to brush away the tears that spilled over my cheeks. Leah held Calvin's hands tightly, her lips trembling. Amy put out her arms and herded Mother and me from the room, murmuring, "Let us give them some time to talk alone."

The next day, a Methodist minister came to the house and, presiding over the deathbed, joined Leah and Calvin in marriage.

Upon the conclusion of the vows, Leah sat promptly down again in her seat by his bed, to nurse him through as many hours as he could last.

Two days later, Calvin rallied.

In a week's time, the doctors proclaimed him likely to recover, and the household rejoiced. Calvin, thin and shaken but less pale, wore a foolish grin, and Mrs. Ann Leah Fox Fish Brown looked as surprised and befuddled as I had ever seen her. Every time someone spoke to Mrs. Brown, Leah turned around in puzzlement looking for such a person, and I burst into uncontrollable giggles.

For the first time in more than eighteen years, my sister had a real, live husband on her hands.

Chapter Twenty
Maggie

I wondered at first if Calvin's marriage to Leah would make a significant difference in the running of our household, but it was naïve to think that my sister would give over control of the purse strings simply because she was now legally wed. Leah was far too set in her ways. Even if Calvin had wanted to master his wife and assume his place as provider of the family, he was not capable. In spite of his unexpected return from the brink of the grave, we all knew that it was not so much a reprieve as a postponement. Consumption was a chronic disease, known for its lengthy periods of dormancy followed by sudden crisis. For months after his illness, Calvin was as weak as a kitten.

Thus, our family business of spiritual stewardship remained the only means of income for us. Our circuit across the state had brought in a fair amount of money, but our traveling expenses had not been inconsequential either. Once it was certain that Calvin was not in immediate danger, it became necessary for us to resume the spirit circles that provided the means for our subsistence.

When Kate came home for Christmas, we discovered that she had not been neglecting her talent for mischief while away at school. During the hours in which she no doubt should have been studying, she had invented a new spirit trick, which she called ghost writing. In the midst of a spirit circle, Kate would moan and roll her eyes back convincingly, apparently descending into a trance. Her left hand would begin to move in broad, looping gestures. If given a pen and directed to a sheet of paper, Kate's hand would begin to write, seemingly without her volition, in a wide, scrawling backward script. When reflected in a mirror, the writing revealed some communication intended for a person in the room. No matter what was written, be it *I forgive you* or *Trust that your present occupation will serve you well*, someone in the room would claim the message for their own. Hardly anyone who departed from a spirit circle in which Kate participated doubted the validity of what he or she had seen.

⚜

In January, Leah pressed for Kate to return to the Greeley house and attend the next school term. Not only was it important to retain Mr. Greeley's support, but Kate's image of innocence was enhanced by her scrupulous attention to her studies. Kate did not depart without tears, but as usual, she eventually submitted to Leah's will.

The months flew by. Life in Rochester, while not as quickly paced as that in New York City, offered more than enough amusement to keep me busy. I was enjoying the company of a large and varied group of persons, ranging from abolitionist and feminist reformers to newspapermen and mesmerists. I received letters from people I had never met. No less than four letters offered betrothal, solely on the basis of my description. "Hmmph!" snorted Leah, reading these proposals with amusement. "No doubt these gentlemen, if they even deserve such a term, are more interested in the shape of your purse than your figure!"

In the summer and fall of 1850, two terrible events shook our nation. The first was the unexpected death of President Zachary Taylor from a sudden attack of cholera, and the second was the passing of the Fugitive Slave Act by Congress. This great blow to the antislavery movement made it a federal crime to harbor fugitive slaves. The new president, Millard Fillmore, signed the bill, officially turning the Posts into criminals. Our spirit table shook with anger, and Kate, finally returned from her lengthy term at school, transcribed pages of spiritual invective in her eerie, backward script. On one occasion, the spirits wrote, through Kate's hand: *Poor President Taylor—he has left his country with a man who will lead the nation into war.*

Our spirit circle was taken aback by that message, and Leah chastised Kate privately for it. "There is no need to be so grim! Our clients don't like it!"

Kate made no excuses but gazed at Leah with that fathomless expression she used when trying to convey that her spirit messages were real. Leah only snorted in disdain and waved her away impatiently. There was no more talk of war after that, but the shade of the idea had already been raised and could not be banished.

In the late fall, I received a letter from a family we had met in Troy the previous year, inviting me to come and reside for a time in their home and hold spirit circles for the believers who lived in that town. I remembered the Boutons fondly, especially Mr. Bouton's sister Annabel, who was my age. This girl had struck up an acquaintance with me at the time of our visit, and we had continued to exchange letters over the months. Leah was inclined to allow me to go, now that she had Kate back, but my younger sister surprised me with her jealousy and anger.

"I've only just returned!" she cried. "Is my companionship so unsatisfactory that you have to leave Rochester for better company?"

I was shocked and hurt by her words. "Kate! You have been away for months making friends at school, but I have been working all that time, holding the spirit circles and doing Leah's bidding! Don't I deserve an opportunity to travel and meet new people as you have been doing?"

To my consternation, Kate folded up like a rag doll and collapsed weeping upon our bed. "None of those girls was a sister to me! I could never truly be myself! I counted the days until I could return to Rochester, and now you are going away!"

Slowly, I sat down beside her and put my arms around her. I knew my sister well, and while she spoke the truth, she was also trying to bend me to her will. I was approaching seventeen years of age, on the verge of womanhood, and Kate was still a child. Although she was my beloved sister, I was stubbornly determined to seek out a measure of independence.

I had not told Kate, nor did I plan to tell Leah, but Annabel Bouton had written to me that she had an "understanding" with a young banker named John. Her brother would not consider allowing a formal betrothal at her age, but all tacitly agreed that Annabel and John could be engaged when she reached eighteen and married shortly thereafter.

"I would love for you to come and stay with us for a few weeks," Annabel wrote. "I am so happy and I want to share my newfound elation. John has a brother who saw you at a spiritual lecture last summer, and he would dearly like to make your acquaintance. If you were to come to Troy, Maggie, it would be my greatest delight to make the introduction!"

Perhaps it was foolish, but I felt great satisfaction at keeping Annabel's secret engagement from Leah, and the idea that I could meet an admirer during my visit had tantalized me with daydreams of romance. I regretted Kate's unhappiness, but it was not going to prevent me from having my little rebellion.

"Three weeks," I said into Kate's hair, hugging her closely. "I'll be back in Rochester in less than a month." In my heart, though, I knew that once I was out of Leah's clutches, I would stay in Troy as long as I pleased.

"I just wish you wouldn't go at all," Kate whispered. "I can't explain it. I just don't want you to go."

Chapter Twenty-One
Maggie

The autumn foliage was brilliant and vibrant, and the air was crisp. I bade farewell to the elderly couple who had shared my train compartment during the trip, people known to my mother from church who had agreed to chaperone me. They continued to their destination farther along the rail line, and I disembarked at the Troy station, where I was met enthusiastically by all three of my hosts.

The Boutons were a childless couple, cheery and sociable. Mr. Bouton's sister Annabel was a sweet-tempered beauty with a heart-shaped face and masses of chestnut curls. They enfolded me at once into their family, and despite the grime and weariness from the trip, I was excited to be traveling like a young woman with friends of her own rather than as a child carried along as extra baggage.

My first days in Troy were pleasantly busy, and I found my spirit circles quite easy to manage. It was amazing how expansively people could talk about themselves and still be surprised to find that you knew so much about them. Leah said it was because they never expected you to be listening, and perhaps this was true. Most people only politely waited their turn to change the subject to themselves, and if you kept silent during a lengthy conversation, you would learn many things about your companions.

My fourth day in Troy was marred by something that seemed minor at the time but from which we should have taken warning. A letter arrived by post addressed to me in care of the Boutons. I did not recognize the handwriting, and acting as a responsible guardian of a girl in her care, Mrs. Bouton opened it for me and read it herself. I watched her face drain of color, and unable to contain myself, I darted forward and snatched it from her hand before she could protest. "Is it about Calvin?" I cried.

But it was no letter at all, merely one line scratched out upon the page in scarcely legible, ill-formed letters: *Thou shalt not suffer a witch to live.*

At first the meaning did not register, and I turned to the back of the page, then the front again, trying to figure out what I held in my hand. It was only when Mrs. Bouton gently removed it and crumpled it into a ball that I realized I was looking at a threat.

And I was the witch.

"People are ignorant and sometimes spiteful," Mrs. Bouton said in the face of my shock. "Cowards who are too craven to express their beliefs openly resort to nasty letters. Do not let it disturb you, Maggie. Whoever wrote this is sitting at home hoping it has upset you, and the best satisfaction you can have is pretending you never saw it."

She was wrong, as it turns out, but I followed her advice at the time.

The next evening, the Boutons and I took a carriage into the city to attend a performance of sonnets from Shakespeare. I vaguely remember it as an entertaining evening, although it was much overshadowed by the events that came after, and I could never recall it later without breaking out into shivers.

Annabel and I were chattering gaily on the ride home, with Mrs. Bouton smiling fondly at our girlish vivacity, when we noticed that the carriage had been at a standstill for several minutes. We felt the slight give of the carriage as Mr. Bouton evidently jumped down from his seat at the reins. With a frown, Mrs. Bouton opened the door and leaned out. "Is there a problem, dear?" she called.

Past Mrs. Bouton's shoulder, I could see her husband engaged in conversation with someone. Beyond them, the waters of the Hudson River sparkled in the moonlight. After a moment, Mr. Bouton turned and walked back to the carriage. It was difficult to make out his features precisely, but I thought at the time that he looked rather perplexed.

"The ferry is not here," he told his wife. "And I don't see any sign of it on the river at all, which is strange. This fellow—" he looked back over his shoulder with that same puzzled expression "—suggests we take the East Street Bridge."

"Then I guess we had better do that," replied Mrs. Bouton. "The hour is late already, and it would be very vexing to wait here and find that the ferry isn't going to return."

Mr. Bouton nodded, but his expression did not seem to indicate agreement. For one moment, he looked past his wife and directly at me. Then he closed the carriage door. We felt his weight climbing up onto the driver's seat, and in a moment we were under way again.

We continued for a time, jostled slightly by the roughness of the road. Annabel resumed her chatter, but I felt a little apprehensive. Having learned to read emotions in my role as spirit medium, I had heard the fear in her brother's voice when he spoke to us.

After a time, the long East Street Bridge came into view outside the carriage window, but our vehicle showed no signs of slowing down or turning onto its shadowy length. Mrs. Bouton's smooth brow furrowed when she realized we were passing it by, and standing up, she leaned out the window and called to her husband. We heard him reply, but I could not make out his words. Mrs. Bouton heard him, however, and we saw her start and suddenly turn her head to look behind the carriage. Chatty Annabel was only beginning to notice the strangeness of the situation, and her conversation died out as her sister-in-law drew her head back into the carriage and regained her seat, looking as worried and tense as her husband.

"He is taking the long way around to the other bridge," she said. "East Street isn't safe."

"We rode the carriage across that bridge just last week," protested Annabel. Mrs. Bouton did not reply but pursed her lips together and twisted her hands nervously.

The ride back to the Bouton house was considerably longer than the one that had taken us into the city earlier. By now I knew that something very wrong had detained the ferry and deterred Mr. Bouton from using the bridge that would have taken us directly home. Eventually we crossed the Hudson on another bridge, and I was not comforted at seeing Mrs. Bouton close her eyes and move her lips in what seemed to be prayer as we clattered across the structure at an alarmingly high rate of speed. It was almost midnight when we finally turned into the lane that led to the Boutons' house. The carriage rolled to a stop, and we again felt Mr. Bouton's weight leave his seat as he jumped down at once.

"Hurry! Hurry!" he called urgently, throwing open the door.

Mrs. Bouton grasped me by the arm and thrust me out the door toward her husband, who unceremoniously took me about the waist and swung me to the ground. "Run for the house!" he urged, turning back to deliver his young sister in the same manner.

I did as I was told. Flinging open the door, I stumbled inside and retreated into the dark safety of their front room. Annabel and Mrs. Bouton followed swiftly upon my heels, and Mr. Bouton came after, leaving his horse hitched to the carriage and bolting the door behind him.

"Are they there?" gasped Mrs. Bouton.

"They were behind us the entire way, until the very end," he said. "I don't see them now."

"Perhaps they're gone."

Mr. Bouton looked doubtful, and he turned to the window, approaching cautiously and peering around the curtain without pushing it aside in a normal manner.

"Who?" demanded Annabel. "Who was behind us? What is happening?"

"The men at the river, the ones who said the ferry was gone," her brother replied. "They were up to no good, I fear, and they followed us in their own wagon when we left. Girls," he said, turning from the window to face us, "I want you to go to your room and stay there. Do not leave for any reason. I'm sure we'll be safe enough inside."

"Are they out there? What do they want?" Annabel cried.

Mr. Bouton tried to control his features, but his eyes went to me almost against his will. I felt suddenly cold in my hands and my feet, as if the blood had left my extremities. "I don't see them," he said. "Perhaps they have gone."

"Are they robbers?" my friend persisted. "Do they want money?"

"We don't know, Annabel," Mrs. Bouton said in her low, reassuring voice. "Please go to your room and try not to be afraid. Robert has everything well in hand."

It was useless to tell us not to be afraid after they had shown themselves to be so frightened. But we went to our room like obedient girls and lit the lamp and sat upon the bed together, holding hands. We could hear the indistinct voices of Annabel's brother and his wife, although we could not make out their words.

"I wish John were here," Annabel sighed after a time. I nodded my understanding, but I rather wished myself wherever John was now, instead of him here with us in this house. My heart was beating so hard it felt as if my whole body were shaking. Suddenly this place seemed intolerably strange to me, and I wanted desperately to be back in Rochester with my family. What had possessed Leah to send me here, where strange men waylaid us in the street and followed us home with unknown intent?

An unexpected thump outside the walls of the house made us flinch. "What was that?" gasped Annabel. She stood and took up the lamp, moving over to the window.

"No, Annabel!" I cried with sudden premonition, reaching out a hand to her.

The window exploded with a horrific blast, showering us with flying glass. Our screams were lost in the roar of shotgun fire. I flung myself to the floor on the far side of the bed, covered my ears with my hands, and pressed my face to the floor. The gas lamp fell to the floor and rolled, and it was a wonder that it did not break open or catch the bedclothes on fire. A series of loud crashes followed the gunfire, as rocks and bricks hurtled through the broken window to smash the objects on Annabel's chiffonier

I don't know how long the barrage lasted. I heard Mr. Bouton shouting, and the door to the room flung open. "Annabel! Maggie!" he cried.

My ears still ringing from the shotgun blast, I crawled out from behind the bed, seeking safety with Mr. Bouton.

My first sight was Annabel, stretched out across the floor, feebly trying to lift her head. Blood was running in long streaks down her face. I screamed and screamed and screamed until Mrs. Bouton came and shook me into silence.

I passed the next three days in blind terror. We were virtually prisoners inside the house. People could come to us, like the doctor who stitched up Annabel's head and the chief of police, but any time members of the Bouton family stepped outside they were met with flying rocks and pieces of brick. I was locked into a small storage area for my own safety, because it was the only room with no windows. Annabel stayed with me as much as possible, but the resemblance to a prison cell was unmistakable.

The chief of police, a sly-looking individual with a perpetual sneer, was outwardly sympathetic but useless. He claimed to have thoroughly searched the neighboring lumberyard and the surrounding area for the men who were stalking and spying upon us but to have found no one. He was unmoved by Mr. Bouton's insistence that we were under siege, because he himself was unable to find any perpetrators. The best he could do, he offered with his slick smirk, was to place some of his men in the Bouton house to provide us a live-in guard.

The Boutons refused immediately, and once the policeman was gone, Mr. Bouton took action to procure his own source of protection. Soon the house was guarded night and day by a group of men who were friends and associates of the Boutons. Annabel's young man was among them, but I never saw him.

I did not leave my room. I shivered, wrapped in blankets that could not warm me; I wept until I vomited; and I slept when exhaustion overwhelmed me.

"Why?" I cried to Annabel. "Why would anyone want to kill me?"

"I don't know." Poor, devoted Annabel tried to soothe me, although she was the one who had been scarred by the incident.

"Why can't the police find them?" It astounded me that such madmen could act freely in a modern city such as Troy. "Who are they, even?" I wailed. "I do not know my enemies! How many are out there?"

She tried to answer honestly. She never insulted my intelligence by trying to deceive me. "Robert says there were two men who followed our carriage in a wagon. And he saw two more upon the East Street Bridge, which is why he chose not to cross there. So that makes four, Maggie, that we know of."

"How could I have made four mortal enemies?" I sobbed. "I am just a girl. Don't they know I am only a girl?"

Annabel put her arms about me, and we held each other close in fear and dread. "We invited you into danger," she whispered, "but I swear we knew it not. We did not foresee that anyone could find such offense with spiritualism—when there are so many graver sins in our nation."

On the third day, the door to my little prison opened and Leah swept in, looking as fierce as a mother bear. Breaking into fresh sobs, I hurled myself to my feet and into her arms.

Leah turned on Mr. Bouton, her voice tight with outrage. "Why is she shut up in this room?"

"It is the only room without a window," he replied wearily. "We didn't want any more shots taken at her."

Perhaps Leah took note of his worried face, or perhaps she saw for the first time how Annabel's lovely features were red and swollen around the stitches in her forehead. For whatever reason, she modified her tone when she said, "I am grateful to you for keeping her safe."

"We need to get both of you out of town as soon as possible," Mr. Bouton said. "No one accosted you coming in, because they don't know who you are, but if we try to take Maggie out, shots will be fired."

"Men with arms escorted me here from the train station," Leah said.

"Those are associates of mine, but they cannot guarantee protection from sharpshooters. Even the rocks can do substantial damage," he added ruefully, rubbing his head where he had apparently been struck.

"The police?" ventured Leah.

"Are no help," Mr. Bouton finished. "The less contact we have with them, the better. We shall have to smuggle you out."

"The wagon," whispered Mrs. Bouton. At this, there was a long moment of silence while Mr. Bouton and his wife regarded each other. Then they looked at Mr. Bouton's young sister.

"You can trust them," Annabel said simply. "They are supporters of our cause. Amy Post recommends them."

Leah narrowed her eyes and looked questioningly at Mr. Bouton.

"We have a wagon," he explained, "with a false bottom."

And with those words he revealed himself to be a conductor on the Underground Railroad, one of those men who personally transported fugitives from slavery to the border of Canada. This was the reason he had been able to call upon an organized group of men to guard his home. This is why he had not wanted police in the house, and why the police wanted nothing to do with him. Under the Fugitive Slave Act, he was a criminal.

My chatty friend Annabel, who had filled her letters with pages and pages of information about her life in Troy, had never hinted or given me any reason to suspect what they really did here. I did not even know that she knew Amy Post, let alone that I had been recommended to her as a sympathetic friend. I looked around at the tiny, airless room in which I had been kept and realized that I was not the first occupant to seek safety here.

"If you can tolerate the wagon," Mr. Bouton went on, "my associate can conduct you as far as Albany."

"You have done right by my sister so far," Leah acceded. "We will place ourselves in your hands for deliverance."

Chapter Twenty-Two
Maggie

A diversion was needed to get us out of the house. Annabel assured us with confidence that her brother was a master of misdirection. She little suspected that she was addressing two women quite accustomed to deception, and I marveled at the number of secrets that seemingly open people kept from one another.

Robert Bouton planned and executed a double diversion that began with a round of fireworks going off near the lumberyard that served as cover for our tormentors. While they were erupting with a frightening show of light and color, Mr. Bouton drove his carriage practically onto the front porch, and a short-statured person concealed in a hooded cloak dashed from the house into the carriage, which promptly took off in a cloud of dust.

It was supposed to look like me, trying to escape by carriage under the cover of the firecrackers. In fact, it was Annabel's young man, John, nearly bent double to conceal his height, and the carriage was filled with ammunitions. Anyone thinking to waylay a helpless girl would receive an unpleasant surprise. This was the real distraction, and it served us well, for we saw two men take off on foot to pursue the carriage, and shortly thereafter a wagon with two more men appeared on the road careening in the same direction.

Leah and I took this occasion to clamber through a window at the back of the house and into an open wagon waiting nearby. One of Mr. Bouton's friends bade us lie down on our backs in the bottom of the wagon, and then he lay the false floor on top of us.

It was as though the lid of a coffin had been closed upon us.

I panicked immediately as the light and air vanished and thrust my hands out to scrabble at the wooden planks, drawing in breath to scream. Leah threw her arms around me, as best she could in the confined space, and held me down. The wagon lurched forward, and we slid unpleasantly backward in the first moment and then hurtled feet first at an alarming speed, helpless and blind in the darkness.

If I had been in my right mind, I might have felt pity for the others who had traveled in this wagon, fleeing enemies just as single-minded and relentless. Elderly men, women with infants, the injured and the sick had lain here, pressed together, unable to move and much less capable of withstanding this ordeal than a healthy young girl. Instead, I indulged in a shameless terror. Frightened and disoriented, I was immediately beset by a terrible nausea, but I knew that to vomit would only make our situation worse. And so I clamped my lips together and fought the heaving of my stomach.

Shortly, a greater agony overshadowed my need to retch. We lay upon rough planks located directly over the axle of the wagon, and every bump or rut in the road was translated through the wood and into our bones. The pain quickly grew overwhelming as we felt our backbones jarred until it seemed they would break into pieces.

All the while, Leah was speaking quietly into my ear. I do not remember everything she said. I believe at one point she spoke, incongruously, about her butcher in Rochester, whom she believed was shorting her on the weight of the meat he sold. Her voice served as a distraction, an anchor to sanity, as it was meant to do. I might have replied that I did not think we would live long enough for the butcher to cheat her again, but I did not.

How long would we be trapped in this makeshift coffin? Mr. Bouton said it was only until we were out of sight, but surely we should have already reached that point? Did that mean we were still in view of our enemies? Had we been followed? I was tormented with visions of our driver forced off his seat at gunpoint, the wagon driven to the edge of a ravine and pushed over.

Suddenly we came to a halt. Overwhelmed by fear that the worst had happened, I began to scream. Nothing Leah did could quiet me. And then the false bottom was wrenched up and the face of Mr. Bouton's friend appeared in the bright light of day. "Hush, Miss Fox!" he chastened me with a smile. "You're safe now. We're five miles out from Troy, and you can come sit in the wagon like civilized folk for the rest of the trip."

Five miles? It had seemed like a hundred.

It was more than a week before we made it back to Rochester. Leah rented a room in an Albany hotel for a few days to give me an opportunity to recover from my fright. I took to the bed and cowered under the covers, trembling at footsteps in the corridor and gasping in fright at the sound of loud voices on the street. Leah was sympathetic for a time, but her impatience won out in the end and I was roused from bed by a firm grip on my ear and forced to dress myself. We traveled home by train. I was silent and unresponsive throughout the trip, refusing to speak to our fellow travelers, who must have thought I was Leah's idiot daughter.

Something had broken inside me. I did not feel safe at home, and nothing that Kate or Mother could do would repair the damage. I lay upon my bed for days, staring up at the ceiling, wondering whether my enemies would come to Rochester. I imagined that the people in the street were watching the house and sent Calvin, time and again, to hasten away any strangers who seemed to be loitering. This did not please Leah, for the fact was that many people did come to look at the house of the Rochester "rappers," and most of them were merely curious or seeking an appointment with us.

I turned seventeen in December. The family made a great fuss over me, with new dresses and books and hair ribbons, but I remained spiritless.

Mother tried to give me Kate's tonic. Calvin tried to interest me in the phosphorescent "hands" he was making as a new spirit trick. Amy Post came and read me letters about the National Women's Rights Convention.

The only person who brought me any real comfort was Kate, who simply lay down at my side and held my hand.

The winter passed, and I haunted the house like a mournful specter from one of the novels I loved so much. When I caught glimpses of my own reflection in the looking glass, I saw a thin and pale young woman with large brown eyes and a sad, downcast mouth. Sometimes I sat with Kate in the spirit circles, but I no longer felt the stirring of humor when the table danced upon its legs or when my sisters used a collapsible pole to brush the clothes of the sitters in the dark. My sense of mischief had been snuffed like one of the trick candles we employed.

It was Leah, of course, who finally decided to break me of my melancholy.

"I'm sending you to Philadelphia, Maggie," she announced one morning in early June. I looked up from my breakfast dish in some alarm. She wasn't even looking at me but was pouring molasses on her oats as if there was nothing unusual about her words. "There is a community of spiritualists there, and in particular, one Mr. Simmons, who has offered to sponsor your visit to meet with them."

"I won't go!" I gasped.

"I have told him you won't stay at his home." She laid down the molasses and raised her eyes to mine. "I explained *some* of the particulars of the incident at Troy, and he agreed that your comfort and safety would be foremost on his mind."

I shook my head at her, but she simply continued as if I had already agreed. "Mother will go as your chaperone, and Mr. Simmons has reserved the bridal suite at Webb's Union Hotel for the two of you."

"The bridal suite?" I asked in spite of myself.

"It is apparently their finest room," she replied. "Mr. Simmons will personally interview your visitors, and the hotel staff will be instructed to allow no one to your parlor without his prior approval. Truly, Maggie, it should be a restful and pleasant trip. I know how you enjoy a city, and Philadelphia is second only to New York. You will do good for us in the name of spiritualism, and it will do you good to go."

"Can Kate come?" I reached across the table and took my younger sister's hand.

Leah's eyes showed a twinkle of satisfaction as she recognized that I would bow to her will. "You know I cannot have you both gone at the same time. We have a business to run, and every one of us must do her part."

Thus, I agreed to the trip, although not without reservation. I confided the depths of my fears to Kate. "You did not want me to go to Troy," I recalled. "I thought at the time that you were jealous because I wanted to visit Annabel Bouton, but perhaps…" I couldn't believe I was admitting that Kate might have some second sight, but here I was, just like one of our sitters, clinging to the hope that she could offer me some comfort. "How do you feel about my traveling to Philadelphia?" I asked.

"I have no bad feelings about it," Kate replied. "I only have the sense that the trip will do you good, and I scarcely need the sight to know that!"

I sighed. "I wish we could go together."

"Someone must stay and obey Leah's every command," Kate said wryly. "Otherwise she will have no one to bully save poor Calvin, and his fate would be upon our heads!"

It was a restful trip, and we were lucky to enjoy a stretch of warm, early summer weather. Philadelphia, while quite a large city, seemed more personable and warm than New York, and our hotel suite was better than promised, with a sunny sitting room and a spectacular view. We were hosted by Mr. Simmons and a number of spiritualists from his Quaker meeting. They were polite and gentle folk, quite typical of Quakers, and the demand for spirit circles was far less than I had expected. They seemed content to have me there, to meet me, and to talk about spiritualism.

In the afternoons we held public circles at our hotel in a parlor given over to our use. Any of the known Quaker and spiritualist associates could attend for a dollar's fee and converse with the spirits on matters of religion and philosophy. For a slightly larger fee, we also held private meetings with people wanting a more intimate conversation. Mr. Simmons met with prospective clients ahead of time, and it turned out to be quite easy wheedling information from him before meeting the sitters. Leah would have been proud. Mother was a great help, as she was a natural gossip, and her forthright, friendly manner not only put our guests at ease but also encouraged them to talk freely about themselves.

Occasionally, someone of high stature in the city would approach Mr. Simmons, and he would send this person directly up to our parlor without prior warning, never realizing he was lessening my chances for a successful sitting. Such was the case one afternoon in our second week there, when a diffident knock came upon the door and Mother opened it to a stranger.

I was seated in the window seat of the parlor at the time, enjoying the sunny warmth and reading a book. I scarcely looked up when I heard a mild voice say, "I beg your pardon. I have made some mistake. Can you direct me to the room where the spiritual rappers can be found?"

I smiled and turned back to my book while Mother assured the gentleman that he had found the correct room. She invited him in and ascertained that Mr. Simmons had met him downstairs and directed him up, a sure sign that he was an important person. Under those circumstances, it was probably inexcusable that I continued to direct my attention to my book, but I was keenly aware that the visitor kept glancing in my direction as if unable to help himself. It was my first deliberate flirtation since I was in Troy, and after a moment's enjoyment of the old thrill, I put down my book with a sigh and approached the sitting table with a mind toward getting down to business.

He was a man of slight stature, scarcely taller than I was, well dressed, with dark hair. As I seated myself across from him, I noticed that he had remarkable eyes, very wide and warm brown in color. They were kindly eyes, and I smiled naturally at him and watched those eyes widen in reaction. It was easier to manage these unannounced sittings if the client's attention was drawn to a pretty girl instead of being on the alert for manipulation.

"You have come to us today because someone dear to you has died," I said, by way of introduction.

"Yes, my youngest brother, Willie," he helpfully replied.

I nodded sympathetically. I looked at his careworn face, showing the ravages of recent grief and sadness. "You feel some guilt," I went on, "because your younger brother is gone but you have survived him." This was not a difficult guess, but I appeared to strike some deep feeling in the man. He started in his seat and looked nearly overcome with emotion.

"I have never been a completely well man," he admitted. "My health has been delicate for years—although I have never let that prevent me from living my life," he quickly amended, as if I might think less of him for being sickly. "But I always assumed that if any one of us might die young, it would be me. Not Willie."

I had gathered enough information at that point to commence the sitting. Mother drew the curtains, bringing the room to semi-darkness, and we called upon the spirits to join us.

It was not a remarkable sitting. Young Willie appeared and rapped out a message for his brother, encouraging him to continue living as he usually did and to enjoy every day that came to him. There was no need for guilt, and the spirit of Willie expressed surprise that his beloved brother would succumb to such a fruitless emotion.

Feeling that I had the upper hand, I invited the gentleman to ask a question that would prove the identity of his brother's spirit and gave him a pen and a paper on which he could write four answers. Our visitor accepted these items with a strangely anguished look at me, and then bent to his task, quickly penning the words "medicine" and "engineering." He paused a moment, lifting the pen from the paper, and then wrote "languages" and, after another pause, "law." Then he lay down the pen and looked across the table at me with some apprehension.

I smiled, trying to put him at his ease. "You may ask your question," I prompted.

"When I first went away to university, what did I study there?" he asked. I directed him to point at each of his answers in turn and when he reached "engineering," I caused there to be a sharp rap. He stared at me in puzzlement and amazement, and I gazed innocently back at him. My mother and I rose, to signal him that the sitting was over.

It had been a session of rapping like a hundred others that I had done. I was accomplished at my task and used to disconcerting men of intelligence who did not believe I could outwit them. There would have been no reason to remember this man above any other, if he had not turned to me while Mother was bustling toward the door, taken my hand, and looked me directly in the eye.

"This is no life for a young lady," he said, and I recognized in his frank gaze that he had clearly seen through my deception.

"Good afternoon to you, Dr. Kane," Mother chirped merrily from the door, having heard nothing of what he said to me. "And may God grant you respite from your sorrow."

"Good day to you, Mrs. Fox," the gentleman replied, tipping his hat to her as he departed.

I was startled and a little disappointed that I had been unable to fool him. However, I had no idea on that afternoon that I had met a man who would change my life forever.

PART THREE:
THE AFFAIR AND THE
ADVENTURER

Chapter Twenty-Three
Maggie

When we received Dr. Elisha Kent Kane's note on the afternoon following his first visit, my mother was delighted and flattered. Mr. Simmons was quick to advise us on how honored we should be to receive his invitation to a carriage ride in the city. For my part, I had no wish to spend the afternoon with a man who had mocked my efforts the previous day. But Mother insisted that we accept the gracious invitation of the very important Dr. Kane.

I stumped my way down to the entranceway of the hotel with some ill grace, sulking and petulant, but nonetheless dressed in my finest frock. I recalled the good doctor as slight figured, rather sickly, with a too-high forehead. This description did fit him superficially, and yet did not in any way account for the manner in which his personality illuminated him from within. He met us at the door of the hotel with a smile that sprang naturally to his face and bowed us out onto the street toward his waiting carriage.

I was startled at the sight of him, while recognizing him at once as the same man who had come to us the previous day. But he looked different to me somehow. Yes, he had a high forehead but also rich, waving dark hair. His eyes were fiery and intense. He was a man whose attraction came from his personality, and in the absence of his presence, you could forget how remarkable he really was. When he boosted me into the carriage with a hand upon my arm, I could feel the strength of him, and the sudden flush of warmth to my cheeks startled me.

He was not the sort of man who interested me. Any flirtation on the previous day had been solely for the sake of the spirit sitting, to unbalance him and acquire information. So why, then, did my heart beat so rapidly?

A second man was seated inside the carriage, and for a moment I was frightened. Before the incidents at Troy, I would never have so easily taken affright, but my constitution had been sorely tested, and I recoiled in shock at the sight of him. But then he smiled affably, and Dr. Kane stuck his head into the carriage to introduce the gentleman as his cousin, Mr. Patterson.

"I humbly beg your forgiveness," this new person said as the four of us settled into our places, "for my intrusion on your excursion. Heaven knows that I have no need to visit the sights of the Quaker City, but I am in Philadelphia only for a day and have not laid eyes on my cousin in nearly five years. Fearing he might hare off on another excursion to the Arctic before my next visit to the old hometown, I foisted myself upon him for the day, and, as it turns out, upon you."

"I keep telling my cousin that he is no burden," Dr. Kane murmured with a slight smile, "unless he continues to apologize so loquaciously, in which case we might very well expel him from our tour."

"Land sakes, Dr. Kane," my mother simpered, her plump cheeks flushed with the exertion of climbing into the carriage, "we certainly do not mind Mr. Patterson. We are just so grateful and honored that you have extended your hospitality…"

"Are you intending to visit the Arctic?" I inquired, firmly interrupting Mother's rambling discourse before she could embarrass us. I did not want these gentlemen to think we were languishing in our hotel for lack of company!

"Just returned, in fact," replied Dr. Kane with another soft smile, accompanied by a flash of his remarkable brown eyes.

"From the Arctic?" I repeated. "How curious! Whatever were you doing in the Arctic? It is not a typical destination for travelers."

"No, it is not," he admitted, "although it is beautiful nonetheless, and if not so deadly, it would be a worthy addition to any serious wayfarer's itinerary. I was lucky enough to be a member of the Grinnell Rescue Expedition in search of Sir John Franklin's ships and crew."

I blinked at him thoughtfully for a moment and then asked, "Do you mean the English explorer who vanished some years ago?"

It was his turn to gaze at me in momentary discomfort, and he said, "Exactly so," as if he was surprised to find that I knew this.

"It seems unrealistic to launch a rescue at this late date," I remarked with unwitting coldness. "What has it been, five or six years? Surely Sir Franklin and his crew are dead."

"Now, Maggie," muttered Mother.

"Do you know of this through your spirits?" inquired the cousin, Mr. Patterson, brightly.

"Merely common sense," I demurred. "I have no direct knowledge through the spirit world, but if they lived, they would have returned to civilization by now."

"Not necessarily, Miss Margaretta," Dr. Kane replied, and I felt a startling thrill as he spoke my name. My eyes were drawn helplessly back to his own, as though magnetized. "Ships can be lost and, if warranted, abandoned. But there is game to be found, and a living to be made in those lands, if you are determined. Perhaps you have heard of the Eskimo?"

"Of course," I said. I would not stand for being thought ignorant. "I know that Indians live in the Arctic lands. However, if this Englishman and his crew survived, whether by living like savages or not, wouldn't someone have encountered them by now? Did you find any signs of him on your voyage?"

"Sadly, no." The doctor's eyes remained strangely alight. His mouth was curved upward while delivering his unfortunate statement, as though he was greatly amused by the conversation, if not by the subject. "Our ships became trapped near Baffin Island, and we were unable to continue our search."

"Trapped?" chirped Mother. "How does a ship become trapped? Do you mean run aground?"

"No," he said, breaking our gaze and turning to Mother. "The sea around the ship froze into solid ice, preventing us from moving forward or backward and trapping us in our place."

"How horrifying!" she gasped. "You must have been terrified!"

Dr. Kane broke out an unexpected grin. "Surprisingly, Mrs. Fox, the opposite is true. It was the tedium that horrified, for we were perfectly safe, but fixed fast and unable to escape for months. Terror would imply immediate danger, and our circumstance was more on the order of slow, torturous boredom!"

"Only my cousin Elisha," interjected Mr. Patterson, "would complain that being icebound in the Arctic for months was a trial of boredom! Mind you, I imagine that after you've explored a volcano, all else pales by comparison!"

"Has he explored a volcano?" I asked innocently, darting my eyes first at Mr. Patterson and then back to his cousin in an invitation to tell more.

"He has," asserted Mr. Patterson proudly, while Dr. Kane continued to grin sheepishly, murmuring, "It is a foolish story."

It was a matter of moments to convince him to tell us the tale. He made a weak effort to resist, directing our attention out the carriage window to the graceful arch of the Schuylkill Bridge. But we persisted, and with a sigh and a modest shake of the head, he acquiesced, saying mournfully, "The tale does not paint me in a very flattering light."

"All the more reason for us to enjoy it!" quipped his cousin.

"I was in the Philippines," Dr. Kane began. Mother interrupted to ask where that was, and I darted her a look of consternation that she would so cheerfully display her lack of education. But the doctor patiently explained that the Philippines were islands south of China, in the South China Sea. "I was a member of a diplomatic mission to China," he continued, as mildly as if remarking that he had made a journey to the state capital. "From there, I was dispatched as part of an auxiliary expedition to Manila—which is a city in the Philippines," he added for my mother's benefit, "to inspect a cache of military supplies. While in Manila, I met a young German peer of the realm, the Baron Loë, who was an adventurer and traveler—a rather brash fellow known for taking appalling risks with his life."

"Nothing like you, then, cousin," interjected Mr. Patterson, winning a sidelong glance and a devilish grin from Dr. Kane.

"When I met the baron," he went on, "he had arranged an expedition to the volcano at Taal Lake, bribing some native guides with a ghastly amount of local currency. The natives viewed it as a sacred place, you see, the home of angry gods. Before I knew it, I found myself embarking on a thirty-mile hike into the jungles of Luzon with a crazy German peer and a handful of cowering, untrustworthy natives apt to run off with the money and abandon us.

"The jungle was a miserable place, abominably hot, with insects as large as my hand. Taal Lake, however, was magnificent, awe inspiring, with jewel-blue waters and a fog-wrapped shroud over the volcano that rises from its center. The natives paddled us across the lake in the dugout canoe that we had carried—with some difficulty—upon our heads on our jaunt through the jungle. Then we ascended a thousand feet up the side of the volcano itself, onto the rim of the crater, a vast ring two miles in circumference. Looking down from the height of the rim, we could see the most amazing sight of all, a second lake within the crater, surrounded by a beach of volcanic ash and steaming as if the whole thing were part of a tremendous witch's cauldron."

The carriage continued to rattle along on its prearranged tour of Philadelphia, but the sights passed unremarked as we sat mesmerized by Dr. Kane's every word.

"Loë and I speculated on the chemical composition of the lake inside the volcano, and I became convinced that it must be sulfuric acid. Loë disagreed, however, and suddenly I announced that I would descend to the basin of the crater and acquire a sample of it to prove my theory. Even the baron was shocked by such a foolish suggestion, and I am afraid that I became all the more resolved to my course in the hopes that I would impress this seasoned adventurer. Of course," he said, turning to us and smiling ruefully, "it was a dreadfully stupid thing to do. It was, in fact, almost the death of me.

"Loë quickly rose to the spirit of the thing and helped me create a makeshift rope out of bamboo fibers. I directed the natives to brace themselves to support my weight as I climbed down. Thus, I soon found myself descending into the crater, a rigorous venture that I came to regret.

"The basin was a desolate place, humid and ill smelling, and the lake itself was foul. I wandered about for a moment, awestruck by the otherworldliness of the place, when sudden shouts attracted my attention. Loë had attempted to follow me down, but the fellow was fully six feet tall and half as wide across the chest. The fiber rope could not support his weight and had begun to unravel, nearly dumping him into the crater before he managed to grasp an outcropping and clamber back up. At this point, the natives experienced a sudden reprise of their superstitions and, deciding that the volcano god was angered by the invasion, abandoned their positions and scrambled down the side of the volcano, leaving me stranded inside and Loë unable to haul me out by himself!

"Oh, look!" Dr. Kane interrupted himself, suddenly pointing out the window of the carriage. "There is Congress Hall. Surely, ladies, you would like to alight here and see this prestigious building."

Mother and I shook our heads, hardly noticing the bustle of the city square outside. "An historic building or two can hold no appeal over a volcano in the middle of a lake on an island in the South China Sea," I breathed. "Please, Dr. Kane, do not leave us thus, or we shall conclude that you perished there, and that the man before us is only a phantom!"

Mr. Patterson gave a rich laugh, and Dr. Kane's eyes twinkled with amusement as he gazed upon me. "I would be lucky to have such a lovely medium conjure me if I were a spirit, but as you may have surmised, I survived. The baron, thinking quickly, tore through my travel pack until he located my service pistol and fired a shot into the air, halting the natives in midflight.

"In the meantime, I was pacing the length of that beach of ash, trying to find a good line of sight to make out what was happening above. To my great surprise, I found myself growing dizzy, and after a moment of disorientation, I was even more astonished to find myself upon my knees and hands. You see, there were noxious fumes rising from the lake, and because of the bowl-like structure of the crater, these gases were trapped inside, as was I. Awakening to this danger, I struggled to my feet, resolving to climb up the side of the crater by hand, if need be, in an effort to rise above the gases.

Alas, this effort was fruitless. I did not even reach the wall of the crater before I found myself facedown in the warm ash, unable to rise at all.

"The baron at once saw my predicament and, with brute force of will, coerced one of the native guides at gunpoint into descending to retrieve me. This fellow tied the bamboo rope around me, and then hung on behind as Loë and the remaining guides hauled us up with as much speed as the frayed rope could bear. The fibers were snapping and curling away as we ascended, and it was a lucky thing that the native and I together didn't weigh as much as Loë did, or we would never have made it to the top."

"Oh, Dr. Kane!" Mother cried. "I would never have imagined you to be such a daring and fearless soul!"

I arched an eyebrow at the doctor, asking, "And was the lake composed of sulfuric acid as you thought?"

Our host colored with embarrassment, and his cousin guffawed out loud, exclaiming, "This is a young lady who expects results, Elisha!"

"Alas," Dr. Kane told me meekly, "I failed to obtain my sample. And now, ladies, I must insist that you pay some attention to this beautiful city and this fine day, and leave off teasing a poor man about his foolish days of reckless youth!"

The rest of our excursion was spent admiring the sights and enjoying the humorous banter of the two gentlemen. I found myself fascinated with the doctor, who by his slight appearance seemed unequal to the feats of daring he had recounted to us, and yet I did not doubt a word of it. The fire in his eyes when he spoke compelled me to see the strength of his spirit. It was a thoroughly enjoyable afternoon, and I felt sincere regret when the carriage returned us to Webb's Union Hotel.

"I am honored to have made your acquaintance today," Mr. Patterson said as we alighted. "I thank you for allowing me to intrude upon your afternoon, and I will be proud to be able to claim the acquaintance of the celebrated Fox ladies."

Mother assured him that his presence had been no intrusion, but I was watching the two gentlemen closely and clearly saw the glance that was exchanged between them. In that moment, with a flash of inspiration, I knew without a doubt that Mr. Patterson's company had been arranged in advance and was no last-minute surprise. Dr. Kane had invited him deliberately so that his cousin could prompt the telling of stories that would entertain us.

I curtsied my farewell with a scarcely hidden, smug smile, pleased that I had inspired the good doctor to such a transparent ruse in order to impress me.

The amazing thing was that he had succeeded.

Chapter Twenty-Four
Maggie

Dealing with skeptics was something to which I had grown accustomed, and although it was never comfortable, it was best to let them express their opinions and go their way. Likewise, with flirtatious gentlemen, it was advisable to remain aloof and cool, allow them to press their case, as it were, and then withdraw into a retreat of maidenly virtue.

Dr. Kane was a new sort of experience, a skeptic who was also persistently attentive. I was surprised when he turned up at our public sitting the day after our jaunt in the city but not terribly so. Somehow, when he appeared in the doorway of the parlor, hat in hand and looking unsure of himself, it seemed inevitable for him to be present. Even then, I must have sensed that our futures were destined to travel a common path.

I might have been nervous in his presence, but perversely, I was not. If he had come to scoff, I planned on being very angry. And if he had come to catch me in deception, then he would be sorely disappointed. I reminded myself firmly that dashing as he might be, Dr. Kane was merely a paying client, unconvinced as of yet but not beyond hope. Perhaps he wished to engage in flirtations, or thought he did, but more likely his grief for his young brother was driving him to pursue the only relief he knew.

My performance was flawless. Strong raps announced the arrival of the spirits. Candles extinguished themselves without a human hand to aid them. I made use of a handful of small tricks, all so simple and yet unsuspected. Lead balls in my petticoats produced a scraping sound when rubbed together.

Dr. Kane was quiet and unassuming. He spoke politely if addressed, but otherwise kept his silence. It was Mother who insisted on asking about Sir John Franklin, and the spirits replied: *His resting place remains hidden for the present.* In the darkness it was hard to read the doctor's face, but I believe he nodded a grudging respect at the spirits' deflection of the question.

Upon the conclusion of the sitting, the clients conversed amiably among themselves and with Mother and me. The good doctor, however, withdrew to a corner alone and spent some minutes writing intently in a small journal. I tried to ignore him but felt his presence distinctly. Even in reserve, the man possessed a luminous character, and I, poor moth, was irresistibly drawn to him.

At last he stood and with that energetic stride crossed the room to me. "Miss Fox," he said, bowing over my hand, "It has been a revelation to see you at work again."

"I am honored," I replied with demurely cast-down eyes, feeling all the while the folded paper he had pressed into my hand. I turned back toward my other guests, but remained aware of his passage toward the door, his polite farewell to Mother, his leave-taking.

For an hour or more I held off the pleasure of reading his note. But when the other sitters had departed and Mother had retired to her room for a rest, I seated myself in the chair he had occupied and carefully unfolded the paper. I was ashamed to see that my hands were trembling.

A poem for Miss Fox.

Now thy long day's work is o'er,
Fold thine arms across thy breast;
Weary! weary is the life
By cold deceit oppressed.

You have many traits that lift you above your calling, Miss Fox. If you would allow me the honor of nurturing your keen intelligence, I would be exceedingly pleased to have you attend my lecture at the Academy of Natural Sciences tomorrow evening. I will send a carriage for you and Mrs. Fox, with tickets, at seven of the clock.

E. K. Kane

A flush of irritation and pleasure sent the blood to my cheeks, as I did not know whether to be offended by his poem or impressed at his impertinent confidence in slipping it to me. One thing, however, was clear: perhaps I was the illumination and he the moth.

He was not what I had expected for my very first suitor. To begin with, he was from a social class distinctly beyond my own. He was a skeptic who had called me oppressed and deceitful in a poem written for me in his own hand. Did he think I would take that as flattery?

But of course, I did. He had written me a poem, passed it to me secretly, and informed me that he was aware of my trickery. I felt a perverse satisfaction in finally being acknowledged for my cleverness, and because he had not denounced me publicly, he had tacitly colluded with me. Although I had assumed that my first suitors would be young men I met through the spiritual circles, I suddenly realized how difficult it would be to feel affection for a man whom I had deceived.

I pretended to myself for a time that I was considering declining his offer. But there was never really any doubt that I would go.

Mother was delighted at the invitation. She and Mr. Simmons discussed it at length, with Mr. Simmons trying to take credit for introducing us in the first place. "His father is a celebrated judge here in Philadelphia and has served as attorney general of Pennsylvania," Mr. Simmons informed us. "His mother is the daughter of a Revolutionary War hero who was a personal friend of Thomas Jefferson. Truly, Mrs. Fox, your daughter could not find a suitor from a better family in all of Pennsylvania!"

The carriage arrived at seven, and the driver presented an admittance ticket for two to the Academy of Natural Sciences. Scrawled across the back in handwriting I was now bound to recognize were these words: "Please seat with preference—E. K. K." Upon our arrival at the academy, we handed over the noted ticket and were ushered to seats at the front of the lecture hall, sweeping past gentlemen and ladies far more elegantly dressed than my poor mother and I.

I spotted Dr. Kane as I was taking my seat, speaking with a gentleman off to the side of the raised platform. I dropped my eyes immediately upon locating him but did not overlook that he immediately turned in my direction, as though he had sensed my gaze.

When the time came for the lecture to begin, a representative of the academy introduced Dr. Kane in the most glowing of terms, beginning with his illustrious family connections and ending with a summary of his career with the navy.

Indeed, the doctor was attired in full navy regalia for his lecture this evening. He looked exceedingly smart, buttons polished, a high collar over which his thick, curled hair tumbled in a boyish manner at odds with his studied dignity. He approached the lectern with a gracious bow to the academy professor and then a second, deeper bow to the audience.

"Twenty months ago," he began, "I had the honor of receiving special orders to participate in an expedition to the Arctic Sea in search of Sir John Franklin, whose 1845 mission vanished six years ago. As hope begins to wane, many rational persons have begun to assume the worst—that Sir Franklin and his crew have joined the lengthy list of casualties inflicted by the Arctic on courageous explorers since the time of Henry Hudson himself."

Dr. Kane, who had been speaking over my head to the general audience until this point, dropped his gaze suddenly and met my eyes with a startling and personal intensity. "I am here this evening to explain to you why your fatalistic assumptions may be erroneous."

Over the next hour, Dr. Kane laid out his logical groundwork for the existence of an Arctic land in the unexplored regions at the top of the world that was fully capable of sustaining life. He described for us the otherworldly beauty of the Arctic, not excluding the months when the sun disappeared beneath the horizon for the midnight of the year: "Noonday and midnight are alike, and except for a vague glimmer on the sky, there is nothing to tell you that the Arctic world even has a sun. The northern heavens resemble a dome of granite, almost forcing the beholder to imagine himself within a cavern of the earth."

I already knew that Dr. Kane told a great tale of adventure, and I was not disappointed to learn that the frozen wastes of the North were no less exciting than sultry volcanic paradises. "We had more than fifty dogs aboard our vessels," he said, "the majority of which might be characterized as ravening wolves. They were a mixed blessing, desperately needed for overland travel and yet providing their own inconveniences. No specimen could leave our hands without their making a rush at it and swallowing it at a gulp. I even saw them attempt a whole feather bed!

"To feed our canine companions it was necessary to lay in a supply of walrus and seal. One of these little excursions nearly came at the cost of my life!

"I was traveling upon a plain limitless to the eye and smooth as a billiard table when the dogs began to bark at the sight of seal ahead. I had hardly welcomed this spectacle of easy prey when I saw that we had passed from the firm ice of the plain onto a new belt of ice that was obviously unsafe. The nearest solid floe was a mere lump, standing out like an island a mile ahead. To turn was impossible; the dogs had to keep up their gait lest our weight cause the ice to break beneath us. I urged them on with whip and voice, the ice rolling like leather beneath the sled runners.

"The suspense was intolerable. There was no remedy but to reach the floe, and everything depended upon my dogs. A moment's hesitation would plunge us into the rapid tideway.

"This desperate race against fate could not last. The rolling of the water beneath us terrified the dogs, and fifty paces from the floe, they faltered. The left-hand runner went through. The leader dog followed, and in one second the entire left side of the sledge was submerged. My first thought was to liberate the dogs. I leaned forward to cut the poor leader's traces, and the next minute I was swimming in a little circle of pasty ice and water beside him!

"I cut the lead dog's lines and let him scramble onto the ice, for the poor fellow was drowning me in his panic. I made for the sledge, but found that it would not support me, and I had no resource but to try the circumference of the hole. Around this I paddled faithfully, the miserable ice always yielding beneath my weight. During this process I enlarged my circle of operations to a very uncomfortable diameter!" Some nervous laughter acknowledged his little joke, but most members of the audience leaned forward anxiously in their seats.

"My strength was failing quickly. In the end, I owed my extraction to the rest of the dog team, who in struggling against their traces, managed to wedge the sled runners into the circumference of the ice hole. Only then did it bear my weight long enough for me to inch my way out onto the ice. Thus, the dogs saved my life and would have received my duly deserved gratitude, if it had not been understood that only the driving force of their voracious hunger had sent me out upon that hunt in the first place!"

The audience applauded heartily with laughter and relief, as if they had been living the ordeal along with Dr. Kane. After a smooth bow to acknowledge the accolade, the doctor retreated to a corner of the platform, where he retrieved an awkwardly long object wrapped in cloth. "I would like to present the Academy of Natural Sciences," he said as he began to laboriously unwind the cloth, "with a relic of one of those hunts." After a final effort, the cloth fell away, revealing to an audience that gasped in awe a winding, shimmering, spiral horn, fully one foot taller than Dr. Kane. "The tusk, or 'horn,' of the narwhal, a welcome supplement to our diet and the legendary source of the unicorn myth."

The representative of the academy joined the doctor on stage to accept the gift as the audience thundered their approval. Together, the academy man and Dr. Kane lifted the narwhal's horn over their heads and stepped to the edge of the platform to give everyone the most advantageous view. When the applause finally died away, Dr. Kane presented his plea for money.

It seemed that the Grinnell Expedition had not managed to find any signs or clues of the ill-fated Franklin Expedition. And thus, another expedition was planned.

"The search cannot, *will not*, be abandoned," Dr. Kane boldly promised. "That great philanthropist Henry Grinnell has self-lessly offered to provide the vessel, and I will have the honor of commanding it…" The doctor had to pause here to receive and acknowledge the applause of an audience totally under the power of his personality. "It is my hope that the academy will pledge its support to this cause. Our country has stained the plains of Mexico with blood to obtain more perishable honors, and men die daily upon the banks of the Sacramento River in pursuit of gold. But good deeds yield brighter laurels than war, and humanity's triumphs are more valued than gold."

Mother pressed her handkerchief to her eyes to blot her tears, and I could see that she was not the only person in the room to be affected by this patriotic call to nobility. I had no doubt that Dr. Kane would acquire the funds he desired from the members of the academy.

As I joined in the applause and lifted my eyes with a proprietary kinship with the doctor, I understood that he and I were, beyond all expectation, engaged in very similar professions.

Chapter Twenty-Five
Kate

A baby robin, when first emerging from the egg, is wet, bedraggled, and little resembles that which it will become. Its first flights are fluttering, hesitant, and full of risk. Likewise, my emergence as a medium, when little more than a child in Hydesville, was fluttering, hesitant, and full of risk. Begun in childish games, my gift nevertheless made me open to contact with that poor soul buried beneath the Hydesville house. Although I fumbled greatly when trying to rap out his message—and indeed made up many of the details as I went along—it was truly my escape from the shell of the mundane world.

In the following years, my progression toward womanhood, my enforced separation from my sister Maggie, and my isolation at school had all served to temper my gift, much as glass is strengthened through heat. At fourteen, I believed that I had realized my potential as a medium to an extent that I could never have imagined back in Hydesville.

My ghost writing was popular among the clients, and although it was always necessary to manifest some rapping noises, the written word was the best channel for my messages. I can describe the process as a form of mesmerism: a fierce concentration on my task leading to a state of open awareness, in which the messages appeared in my head. The backward writing was a trick I had studied and practiced, but the words themselves came from somewhere beyond my conscious mind.

The spirits, for their part, were very social, although a bit uncertain on details, as if death had severed some of their memories. However, on occasion, I would be seized with an idea so strong and undeniable that I took risks that unsettled Leah. There was a woman who came to us once with her husband, and she had a pinched-up face and a turned-down mouth and she bickered with Leah over the fee for the sitting. My sister set her jaw in a forced bland smile and agreed to the woman's demands, for it was her studied practice to please the clients above all else. The husband of the pair was the true believer, wishing to contact his dead aunt, and the wife was clearly uncomfortable with the whole undertaking.

I knew nothing of these people, save their name and the name of the deceased aunt. They were strangers, people who had read about us in the newspaper and sent their calling card with a request for a private sitting. Yet I looked across the table at the woman, and even in the darkness, her avaricious little face showed such greed and spitefulness that my hand began to write of its own accord: *It is not yours. You are not entitled to it. It is not yours.* The woman recoiled as if some snake had appeared upon the table. The husband snatched up the parchment and rounded on his wife with the outcry, "I told you not to take that pearl ring! She left it in her will to LouAnna!"

His wife, white faced and thin lipped, retorted, "She didn't deserve it! Who nursed the old hag through her final illness? Not your sister!"

"You'll have to give it back!" the husband exclaimed, waving the paper with the spirit writing in the air.

"We told LouAnna it was lost! How are we supposed to give it back now?" shrieked the woman, clasping one hand firmly over the other, shielding her prize.

Needless to say, the two of them left our residence quickly. Leah looked at me in a pained way and explained that this was the sort of situation where she would very much like to slap me but found herself just too weary to manage it.

While we continued to comfort the bereft—and sometimes confound the unbelieving—letters from Philadelphia demonstrated that Maggie was finally recovering from the shock of her experience in Troy. Mother wrote that our morose sister had blossomed under the gentle welcome of the Philadelphia Quakers, who had conspired to keep her well amused, admired, and occupied. There was even, she confided, a suitor for Maggie's affections.

I was taken aback by this disclosure. She was seventeen and clearly the age for it, but somehow it was still a shock. My constant companion for so many years and dearest friend was now eligible for marriage. It was true that one beau did not a marriage make, and a single courtship did not guarantee the end of Maggie's youth. It was the beginning of great changes in our lives, however, and there was no way to deny it.

Leah was also concerned, particularly that all proprieties were maintained and that nothing occurred that might mar Maggie's reputation. Calvin tried to reassure her, pointing out that Mother was there to chaperone any beaux who called upon Maggie. Leah's response was a low, agonized groan. "Mother chaperoned Bowman Fish when he called upon me!" she stated, with no further explanation. However, Calvin and I both knew that Leah had ended up marrying Mr. Fish when she was only fourteen years old.

The letters from Philadelphia were not the only ones we received that spring. Mr. Greeley invited us back to Manhattan. His letter was followed by a dozen more, all from people we had met in New York City the previous summer: the author Mr. James Fenimore Cooper, for instance, and the beautiful singer Jenny Lind. Leah began to make travel plans and discuss with Calvin the possibility of renting a house in the city for a semipermanent residence. "The people of Rochester who would come out of curiosity have already done so," she said. "We are left with only our regular clients and those persons willing to travel to Rochester to see us. It might be an excellent idea to relocate to a city with a fresh new population of sitters."

It did not matter to me. I had my clients in Rochester, and I had my clients in New York City. There were spirits clamoring to speak wherever I resided. Calvin began to dismantle the contrivances he had built in the Rochester house, understanding it would be unwise to leave them where others could discover them, and we prepared for an extended journey across the state.

Our travel was pleasant and lively. We were met along the way by banners proclaiming "Welcome to the Fox Sisters" and treated by the residents of each small town with respect and reverence.

There was no sign of the hostility that had afflicted Maggie the past fall, although I admit we took care to avoid Troy, and we arrived in Manhattan without mishap. With Leah as the gracious hostess, Calvin as our silent watchdog, and myself as the main attraction, we embarked on a successful second season in the busiest city in the United States. Spiritualism was the newest enthusiasm of intellectual people. The requests for sittings were so numerous that Leah immediately began to search for a house that we could rent and so extend our stay in New York indefinitely.

In the midst of this turmoil and confusion, more letters arrived from Philadelphia. Maggie was circumspect and uncharacteristically discreet, but Mother was more than anxious to give us the details regarding the eager new suitor.

When Leah realized who was courting Maggie, she became very worried indeed.

Chapter Twenty-Six
Maggie

Not a day passed without some word from Elisha Kane—a note, a visit, an invitation, or some token sent to our hotel. He observed proprieties meticulously, addressing his flowers and gifts to my mother. A book of verse, for example, arrived with a card for my mother that read, "I could not resist this little trifle for Miss Margaretta. Permit me to place it in your hands for your perusal first." Mother, of course, passed the book along to me without hesitation, and between its pages there was a carefully folded note for my eyes alone:

> Once in the mornings of old, I read in a newspaper that for one dollar the inmates of another world would rap to me the secrets of this one; all things spiritlike and incomprehensible would be resolved into hard knocks, and all for one dollar! With that, I wended my way to a hotel, and after the necessary forms of doorkeepers and fees—by Jove, I saw the spirit!
>
> Bright Spirit, read these verses in the window of the hotel parlor with the light in your hair, as on that memorable day.

The doctor was as eloquent with the pen as he was in speech. His evenings were usually spent behind a lectern and his afternoons engaged in penning letters, all in the pursuit of money for his expedition. I was flattered that he deviated from his single-minded vocation to occasionally inscribe these whimsical little sentiments for me.

I imagine that he and I were the two most celebrated persons in the city of Philadelphia that summer. I collected the grief stricken, the philosophical, and the curious, while Elisha drew in the scholarly, the philanthropic, and the secretly adventurous. On occasion, the two groups intersected.

One evening, Elisha appeared at our hotel just as we were ending a private sitting. The doctor had written me earlier wishing to treat me to a carriage ride through the park. Regretfully, I had been forced to decline, having already committed to clients. As was often the case when I refused his invitation in order to complete my spiritual obligations, Dr. Kane was drawn to the hotel as if unable to resist investigating what occupied me.

In this particular instance, he met our sitters as they were exiting from our parlor, and the gentleman of the couple turned instantly toward him, calling him by name. Elisha immediately transformed from an anxiously waiting suitor into the dashing world explorer and came forward to shake the man's hand. "Colonel Childs! I almost didn't know you, sir, and I am surprised that you would recognize me after all this time."

"I don't often forget my officers," the man replied gruffly. "And I especially remember you, Kane. Not many of my men are decorated with honors from both sides of a war, nor do I have very many officers known for running the enemy through with a sword and then stopping to stitch them back together again. It seems the navy has sent you far afield since the last time I saw you."

Dr. Kane nodded. "I imagine they have loaned me out for exploration in the Arctic so that I cannot cause any more trouble for them."

"They did not value you nearly enough," grumbled the colonel. "Good luck to you, then, in the Arctic. You were a good officer, and Franklin's wife is lucky to have you in charge of the rescue operation." The colonel smiled and turned to include his wife, a petite and daintily featured lady with a dimpled smile, who hung patiently on his arm. "I hope you gain as much from your spirit sitting as we did. It is a modern miracle, is it not?"

"Oh, indeed," Elisha replied with an enigmatic smile and a quick glance at me. "Miracles have definitely taken place here; I cannot deny it."

Colonel and Mrs. Childs departed then, comforted and gratified to have contacted the spirit of their dead son, and Elisha the impertinent unbeliever joined us in our parlor, pleased to have stolen a bit of my time after all. He seated himself across the spirit table from me, leaning against it casually. Mother retreated with a knowing smile to the farthest corner of the room and busied herself with her needlework, a corporeal but not very observant chaperone.

"It sounds like another hair-raising story," I said, nodding my head toward the departed guests.

"Another story that makes a fool of me," he replied with mock curtness. "You seem overfond of that type of tale, Miss Margaretta."

"I have a weakness for adventures," I admitted. "Are you going to tell me the story or not, Elisha? I warn you, if you refuse, I will be left to draw my own conclusions."

"Then I hardly have a choice, do I, Maggie?" The doctor reached absently across the table and laid his fingers lightly across my own. I trembled at the touch and shifted my position so that Mother could not see the impropriety. "It was during the Mexican War," he continued, as I met his steady brown gaze. "I was traveling on horseback with a party of officers led by a Mexican rebel named Domínguez, who was, frankly, little more than a bandit. To my considerable distaste, Domínguez and his pack of thieves were considered allies because they were willing to act as guides for the Americans. When we encountered Mexican forces and engaged in combat, I lost my horse underneath me but nevertheless accounted well for myself, taking down several men, including a young major.

"When the skirmish was over and the Mexican nationals were defeated, Domínguez began to slaughter the prisoners! We were appalled by such a dastardly act—to kill men who had surrendered! We shouted for him to stop, and finally I took up my saber and defended the enemy commander, an old Mexican general, who was trying to shield the major I had wounded. In the end, I had to draw my gun and fire at Domínguez, who cursed me vilely and swore that he would have me court-martialed.

"Thus, I saved the life of the enemy commander, General Gaona, and when it turned out that the young major was the general's son, there was nothing else for it but to get out my kit and perform surgery on the field. I saved the general *and* the major, but I had humiliated our Mexican ally, who caused a great deal of trouble for me when we returned to our command post. The incident was an embarrassment to my commanders, doubly so after General Gaona gifted me with a horse from his own stables to replace the one I had lost. No officer ever made a good military career by endearing himself to the enemy, you realize!"

"But you only did what was right!" I exclaimed. "You did the noble thing, the civilized thing!"

"There is very little place in war for the noble and the civilized," Elisha said. "Privately my commanders approved of my actions, but there was no denying that I had fired a gun at a superior officer. They were greatly relieved when I contracted a tropical fever shortly after the incident and quickly declared me unfit for service and shipped me home. I was unhappy to depart under a cloud of disapproval, and I even had to leave my Mexican horse behind."

"I do declare, Dr. Kane! You lead the lives of ten men! Mr. James Fenimore Cooper should wish his heroes showed half your boldness! Think of the scores of pages that pass by before they have an opportunity to display their courage, while you can scarcely walk down the street without finding yourself in mortal straits!"

His face lit with laughter. "If my ears do not deceive me, Miss Margaretta, you just implied that I am haplessly prone to falling into embarrassing and exaggerated circumstances! I fear you view my life as a Shakespearean comedy!"

"Not at all," I assured him, for in all honesty, I was in awe of his courage and flair. "I imagine you are just living in the harness."

Here I was referring to another story he had told me, just a couple days earlier. Again I was astounded by the simple luminosity of his spirit as he talked about the rheumatic fever that had nearly taken his life a decade earlier and left him with a chronic heart disease. His physician had prognosticated that the remainder of his life would be brief and lived in bed as an invalid. However, his father, the commanding Judge John Kane, had rejected the diagnosis and ordered his eldest son to rise and go about his life. "If you must die, Elisha, die in the harness!" And Elisha had chosen the path his father had recommended, leading to medical university, the life of a navy officer, and ultimately to the Arctic.

"It is the harness in which *you* are living that concerns me," he told me now. "It is a melancholy life, collecting fees from the bereft and desperate. Half the world thinks you are a fraud."

I withdrew my fingers from his touch and pitched my voice low, beneath my mother's range of hearing: "If Mother knew that you occupied that half of public opinion, our acquaintance would be brief, I assure you, Dr. Kane."

"Then I will not address the issue now," he demurred, "except to state that I would rather see you devoting yourself to an education that would prepare you for a higher position in society."

I felt my breath entirely taken away as I imagined what high position he might have in mind for me. My hands trembled as I pressed them together and carefully folded them into my lap. What was I to think?

I was trying to be cautious, like any proper young woman in my position. A girl who gave her heart too willingly to an ardent suitor

might find herself without a husband and without the unblem-
ished reputation she needed to acquire one. Yet what an intoxi-
cating thought, to be the wife of this magnificent man!

Folded in the interior pocket of my skirt, beneath my hands,
was a small measure of sanity. Only that morning, I had received a
letter from Leah. It was typical of my sister to reach out across the
distance in an attempt to keep her thumb firmly upon my neck. I
was well accustomed to her manipulation, but she still knew the
words to write that would give me pause even in the middle of a
flirtation with Elisha. As he rose to take his parting that evening, as
I offered my hand in farewell and raised my eyes to his warm and
passionate gaze, Leah's letter haunted me, rapping its own message
into my skull:

> I understand that you are currently receiving the attentions of your
> first true suitor, an honor that has caused many a young girl to
> lose her sense unless guided by the feminine wisdom of her kin. As
> Mother is not always the best judge of these matters, I thought you
> might appreciate a few frank words from one who wants only the
> happiest future for you.
>
> First, be prudent and modest. Do not confide your heart or
> any other private matters to this man. I mean him no disrespect
> but ask you to recall that young men can be fickle. You need not
> look too far backward in our own family history to see this truth
> for yourself. A man's love is a transitory thing, often shaped
> by circumstance, and not to be relied upon at the expense of
> good judgment.

Secondly, look to your future. Although there may be excitement in finding yourself the favorite of an illustrious hero, consider that you might better be matched to someone of your own background. Your first suitor will not be your last, and I would rather see you married to a man who comes from our own circle of associates and is devoted to the same ideals of family that we value. Heroics are all well and good between the pages of a book, but I imagine the appeal fails in the face of managing a home and children.

Finally, do not forget that issues of social status are not easily set aside. Forgive my bluntness, dearest Maggie, but you would not be welcomed by this man's family, nor would either of you be happy with such a union.

I hope you do not take these sentiments amiss and appreciate that I only hope to provide you with the sisterly advice I was lacking in my own youth. Enjoy your attention from Dr. Kane, whom I understand is quite a charismatic and entertaining gentleman, but comport yourself with the utmost propriety. Do not lose your head, your heart, or your reputation—nor do anything that would injure our family.

Respectfully and lovingly,

Your sister,

Leah

Knowing my sister as I did, I thought that she was less blunt than she might have been and that there had probably been other versions of this letter that had never made the post. I knew that her most pressing and self-serving concern was that I keep the family secret, and thus far I had done so, never confirming those doubts that Dr. Kane had expressed to me.

I might have been angry about the things Leah wrote in her letter, but perhaps my own habit of deceptiveness had made me a skeptic in all things. In fact, her letter was an anchor to which I clung, lest my heart fly away on wings of infatuation, borne aloft by the currents of dizzying possibility offered by one Elisha Kent Kane.

Chapter Twenty-Seven
Maggie

The fall of 1851 came upon us too quickly. Soon we would be finishing our business in Philadelphia and rejoining the rest of the family, not in Rochester, but in New York City, where Leah had rented a house.

Our popularity in Philadelphia had not diminished during our four-month stay. Spiritualists from all across the state of Pennsylvania had journeyed to the Quaker City for a meeting with one of the Fox sisters. Very few of these visitors had ever experienced any supernatural event before. When they arrived at Webb's Union Hotel, it was with the reverence of attending church for the very first time, having only read about worship but wishing ardently to participate. When rapping in Rochester and New York, I had always presumed myself to be something like a performer. But in Philadelphia I understood for the first time that Kate and I, or perhaps Leah, had created a new religion.

This caused a great deal of guilty reflection on my part, exacerbated by Elisha's insistence on the sinfulness of my actions. "You know I am nervous about the rappings," he told me. "I believe the only thing that gives me fear is this confounded thing being found out! I would not know the truth myself for ten thousand dollars."

And he did not, in fact, know the truth. No admission ever passed my lips. I believe at that time it would have been a physical impossibility, my tongue stiffening in my mouth as if by some poison, were I ever to confess the method by which I manifested the raps. Unlike some other skeptics, Elisha never demeaned himself by trying to guess their source.

Dr. Kane continued to attend our sittings when he was able and especially when he had failed to engage my companionship otherwise. Some of the Philadelphia spiritualists began to believe that he was a devoted believer, much to his consternation! However, astute participants commented, "Dr. Kane is far more intent on the medium of communication than the substance of the message," and they would smile indulgently at the two of us. In any case, his continued presence could be interpreted only as tacit approval for the rappings, whether he realized it or not.

Our time together was dwindling, for not only was my visit to Philadelphia due to end, but Elisha was scheduled to speak in several other cities across the Northwest in his crusade to raise funds. In the meantime, he escorted me to concerts and plays, and on two more occasions I attended his lectures as an honored guest. Mother usually accompanied us as our chaperone, although sometimes Elisha invited the wife of his cousin Robert Patterson as an escort.

On a brisk October afternoon, just four days before Elisha was to leave for New York City, he took me on a carriage ride through the countryside with Mrs. Helen Patterson along in place of my mother. I found Mrs. Patterson to be a pleasant and agreeable companion, very elegant and gracious. She kept up a steady, cheery conversation throughout our journey, for once outpacing Elisha, who seemed more quiet and pensive than usual. I put it down to his imminent departure until the carriage rolled unexpectedly to a halt before one of the stately mansions on the outskirts of the city.

Mrs. Patterson stopped speaking, almost in the midst of a sentence, and Elisha indicated the house outside the carriage window. "This is my family home, Rensselaer," he said, in a voice that was uncharacteristically stiff.

I took a startled breath and forgot to let it out. It was a magnificent estate, one that should have awed me with its elaborate gardens and aristocratic entryway, but I was terrified. Afterward I could not have described any part of the house, for in that moment, I was aware only that he meant me to disembark from the carriage and go inside to meet his parents. My legs felt as though weighted with lead. I smoothed my hands over my skirt, a fine new gown for a carriage ride in the country but unable to hold a candle to the elegant lines of Mrs. Patterson's attire. I raised my eyes to Elisha in pitiful dread, frozen like a little rabbit. I was totally unprepared for this encounter.

His face showed the same uncertainty, and he suddenly turned to look at his cousin's wife for guidance. Mrs. Patterson dropped her gaze with only the briefest shake of her head, and abruptly Elisha rapped on the side of the carriage and signaled the driver to go on. "My parents are not at home this week," he said gruffly, "so I am afraid there is no use stopping."

I murmured my understanding, grateful for the lie, beholden to the sensitivity of Mrs. Patterson, my heart thudding in a belated attack of nerves. I could not meet his parents without prior planning, without the proper clothing, without some guidance. I was so relieved that I felt no slight in recognizing that Elisha, too, knew a meeting at this time was not favorable.

We continued on, our chaperone resuming her lonely discourse and Elisha and I answering belatedly, or not at all, as we recovered from what felt like a narrow escape from calamity. Finally, the carriage turned into a carefully tended garden lane and I realized that we were headed into cemetery grounds. This did not seem a typical stop for a country ride, and I turned to Elisha in some puzzlement, but he appeared to have recovered his poise and was smiling proudly. "Just a brief visit," he assured me. "Would you accompany me on a stroll, Miss Fox?"

He disembarked first. As I was the younger lady aboard the carriage, I paused to allow Mrs. Patterson to go before me, but she shook her head with a secretive smile. "I believe I will rest here for the time being," she said. And when I showed my surprise, she leaned forward and put her hand on my arm. "I see no harm in allowing you a few private moments, especially here. Go with him. I expect he will wish to confess his feelings."

With a burning face, I climbed down from the carriage, placing my hand in Elisha's for assistance. Smiling, he kept it even after I was firmly on the ground and tucked it into his arm. "This is not quite the gardens of Rensselaer," he said, "but still family property for all that. It is perhaps best not to overwhelm you all at once, so a tour of the Kane vault will suffice for us today."

It soon became apparent that his hold on my arm was not entirely sentimental. The level ground of the cemetery dropped off abruptly, and Elisha led me to a stone path set into a steep hill. I twitched my skirts aside with my free hand, carefully placing my feet on the steps, but with Elisha's firm grip I knew that I was safe enough. I could see our destination, a stone mausoleum set into the side of the hill, the family name carved proudly above the lintel in tall letters. Beyond the vault the hillside sloped sharply down to the wooded banks of the Schuylkill River.

"When I was a boy, my brothers and I used to ice skate on the frozen river and then climb up here and build a fire to warm ourselves afterward," Elisha reflected as he guided me down the inclining path. "We would sit right on the doorstep of the vault and pitch rocks down the hill. My grandparents are entombed here, and an infant brother I scarcely remember, and, of course, my dear brother Willie."

Approaching the vault with tenderness, Elisha placed a hand on the wooden door. "He was a bright, good child, full of innocence and a love of learning. It broke my heart when he left us. But you…" He turned to face me, taking my hand between his two and holding it between us. "You have been a godsend, more welcome than the northern sun after months of despairing night."

"Elisha, I know you cannot abide spiritualism," I said, pitying his persistent grief, "but your brother loves you still. One does not have to be a medium to believe in heaven and to know that it is the ultimate destination of us all."

"I am a scientific man of facts and data and hard, worldly evidence. I've been trained to believe in what I can measure and observe and touch with my hands. Existence beyond death defies such quantification."

"But for all your facts and measurements, you believe in an Arctic land at the top of the world that you have never seen," I argued. "Can you not muster a similar faith in a paradise for spirits enjoying their just reward?"

"Let us hope it is a brighter, cheerier reward than this." Elisha waved his hand at the family vault. "How much better to look toward the promise of heaven than to reflect upon this stone pallet, destined to be my final resting place, and that of a future Mrs. Kane as well."

"I am sure that the future Mrs. Kane would be deeply honored to lie in a crypt with you," I said carefully, "especially one with such a picturesque view...not that she'd be in any position to enjoy it."

"Do not make me laugh when I am trying to be romantic!" he protested.

"Your romance needs work if you ply your charms in a cemetery at the foot of a mausoleum, contemplating your future tomb," I informed him.

"All part of my plan," he assured me. "What will you do when I leave the city, fair Maggie? Find another young man to twine about your finger with your bewitching eyes and clever conversation?"

"Wherever would I find another companion such as yourself?" I retorted. "I could place a classified advertisement, I suppose. Wanted: a philosophical but skeptical scientist and explorer, to swoon in volcanoes, swim with sled dogs, and dangle headfirst off giant Egyptian statues with one foot tangled in his climbing rope."

"Now, Maggie, I told you that tale in confidence!"

"There are no living ears to hear us," I said, "as you have cleverly left Mrs. Patterson in the rear." I waved my hand at the slope above us. Our heads had passed below the level of the main cemetery, and we were now out of sight of the carriage and our esteemed chaperone.

"Just so." He took a step toward me and stopped, close enough that I had to tilt my head back to look him in the eye. "Miss Maggie, I have brought you here to steal a kiss."

Instinct made me continue with my lighthearted banter, although my ears were filled with the sound of my heart pounding in excitation. "It will have to be theft, as no young lady of good standing would give such a thing away willingly."

But Elisha was done teasing. He placed his hands lightly on my shoulders, stepped even closer, and bent his head toward mine. It was my first kiss, stolen in a graveyard by a man with warm lips and a clean, sharp scent. For a long moment, I was speechless, even after he had stepped decorously backward and dropped his hands to his sides. I just gazed at him, stunned and giddy with emotion. His brown eyes sparkled at me fondly. "I wish I could have a lock of your hair," he whispered, "to take with me when I go. But I am not that brazen of a thief. It would have to be a gift."

I nodded timidly. "Call upon me tomorrow," I said, in a voice rather hoarse with feeling, "and I will see if I can manage it."

He took my arm once more and directed me onto the stone steps, so that in a moment we ascended into the view of the carriage, seeming respectable and modest, as long as the observer did not look too closely at our foolish smiles.

"Will you keep it with the others?" I dared to ask, feeling a sudden need to be bold with him.

"What others?"

"Why, the locks of hair you have collected from other girls that you have kissed in front of the family tomb." I glanced sidelong at him, waiting to see if he would be angry or offended, but he just laughed out loud.

"Wherever would I find another such girl? I could advertise, I suppose. Wanted: a young lady of more than average beauty, a strange mixture of child and woman, of simplicity and cunning, of passionate impulse and extreme self-control. But I fear that such a search would be fruitless. There can be only one of you in all the world."

"Ah, you haven't met my sister Kate. Still, I am pleased to know that any token I give you would hold a place of honor."

"Do you doubt me? You must look deeper."

"Oh, but isn't it true that you are an enigma past knowing, Doctor?" I fixed him with a mischievous gaze. "You know I am."

"You are not such a mystery," he assured me. "You are refined and lovable, and with a different education—one absent of secret rappings and troublesome spirits—you would have been innocent and artless. If I had my way with you, I would send you to school and teach you to live your life over again."

He handed me up into the carriage, ending our discourse, as he usually did, with his persistent advice to give up the spirit rapping.

What could I have replied to Dr. Kane? I pondered it often over the days of his absence as Mother and I prepared to depart from

Philadelphia. We would arrive in New York City only to miss Elisha by a day, as he would be journeying on to meet with financial backers in Boston. Perhaps if chance had allowed us another meeting, I could have confessed my thoughts as a sort of fanciful tale, such as he was wont to do in his little notes to me.

I could have said to him: "Once in the mornings of old, two naughty girls played a prank upon a third girl they disliked. So successful were they that they extended the prank to include their parents, and then their neighbors, until deception became their way of life, continued in desperation lest they be unmasked. At that point, an older sister presented them with a choice: to be revealed in their wickedness or celebrated in their goodness. And the girls chose goodness, turning their prank into an act of kindness, an opportunity to meet influential people, and a means of speaking out for abolition and other human rights. Until the day that a shining hero met one of the sisters and promised her…" What?

That was the problem. He had promised me nothing.

Leah did not hesitate to point that out to me, almost the first thing upon our arrival at her new home.

"I hope that you have comported yourself with modesty and propriety," she asserted primly, "as our business depends utterly on our reputation."

"Land sakes, Leah," said Mother. "I was always with her as a chaperone."

"I am well aware of your shortcomings as a chaperone, Mother," retorted Leah. "All the more reason for my concern."

My mother drew herself up with indignation, barely capable of uttering a syllable in her own defense. I moved in swiftly with assurances. "You are concerned over nothing, Leah. Dr. Kane is a gentleman, and I have been nothing less than a lady. Mother was a fine chaperone, and there was also a relative of the doctor. We were never alone," I asserted, my lips nevertheless burning with his remembered kiss.

Leah sniffed doubtfully and settled herself on the settee, her broad, hooped skirts resembling a hot-air balloon in descent. Kate hovered in the background, eyes twinkling with confidences to share in private. "I suppose," ventured Leah, "that the house will be swamped with gentleman callers, now that Maggie has begun to collect beaux."

"I am not at home to gentleman callers, save Dr. Kane," I stated carefully.

She eyed me shrewdly. "Do you have an understanding with him, then?"

"Oh," Mother interjected, "Doctor is absolutely smitten with our Maggie! Anyone can see that!"

Leah grimaced and waved frantically for Mother to be quiet, while I gave my truthful answer. "No, we do not have any formal understanding at this time."

"I thought not," she said. "He didn't give me any indication of an agreement between you."

I gasped. "He was here?"

"Yesterday," she affirmed.

"He was *dashing*," Kate said appreciatively.

"He came to pay his respects," Leah continued, shooting an irritated glance over her shoulder at Kate.

Mother clutched at my arm. "Maggie, he *is* serious about you! Such an honor, for an important man like him to call upon your sisters, just out of courtesy!"

"He did not state his intentions for Maggie," Leah said firmly. "And I would just as soon not see her lose her head over him. Why, I know five respectable young men who would offer for Maggie's hand with no hesitation, including Amy Post's son Donald—don't make that face, Maggie; his complexion has considerably cleared up! You don't have to put all your eggs in one basket. Dr. Kane is not likely to engage himself to a girl of Maggie's station. You have said yourself that he made no such promises, and I strongly doubt he ever will. He is a self-proclaimed explorer from an aristocratic family who is far more engaged in the pursuit of fame than respectable marriage. He could ruin Maggie's reputation with a few careless words and put her entire future at risk!"

"I liked him," said Calvin.

There was a long moment of silence from a tableau of startled women. Then everybody turned to look at the one person who rarely had a word to say and never, ever contradicted Leah. Up to that point, I had not even noticed he was in the room.

"He was pleasant and courteous," my brother-in-law continued. "He has shown courage and fortitude in his world explorations and has earned his fame as a hero. I am sure Maggie is proud of his regard for her." Calvin graced me with his shy, brotherly smile while Leah looked like she was sucking lemons, and the subject was closed for discussion that evening, firmly concluded by the man of the house.

⟡

Quiet days of solemn spiritual discussion with Quakers and other believers in Philadelphia were decidedly over. New York City embraced me with a whirlwind of social engagements and entertainments. Spirit sittings were a lively affair, with Leah and Calvin expertly coordinating the supernatural phenomena. The dying candles awed the guests, and in the darkness Leah plied a collapsible pole to tip over a pewter jug and wave a phosphorescent cloth in the air.

Mother, being singularly unobservant, remained oblivious to our artifice. She was an inconvenient presence nevertheless, often drawing attention where we did not want close inspection. For instance, she had a habit of fumbling with the candles after a sitting, complaining that she could not get them lit again. Calvin would smoothly intervene in his unobtrusive way, slicing the top off the offending instrument with his pocketknife before someone noticed the missing wick. "Candles touched by spirits are often troublesome thereafter," Leah coolly remarked. It was a relief when Mother finally left for an extended visit to Hydesville.

Meanwhile, Leah seemed determined to marry me off, or at least divert my attention from Elisha Kent Kane. The average age of guests dropped twenty years as a series of engaging young bachelors vied for my attention. These included the dreadful Donald Post but also enterprising reporters in the employ of Mr. Greeley, earnest psychology students recommended by Mr. Capron, and social activists of varied professions. Many of them were quite handsome, and some were very charming, but all truly believed that I was a spirit medium, and secretly I thought them all fools.

Kate had a fair share of admirers herself. My little sister had developed into a winsome fifteen-year-old beauty while I was away. Her fair, translucent complexion and delicate features appeared almost luminous against raven hair and wide-set violet eyes. Grown men neglected their proper manners and stared openly at the first sight of her. One frequent visitor confessed to me, "I think this is all a humbug, but it is well worth a dollar just to bask in the light of Miss Kate's eyes!"

We had a lot of fun. Kate and I blended our wits and our talent for mischief together seamlessly, no matter the months we had spent apart. We flew from one event to the next, accepted invitations to plays and musical revues with Leah and Calvin to chaperone, and reveled in the life of New York society.

But with Dr. Kane's first letter, guilt for my deceptions came flooding back.

Leah called me to her parlor on that day, looking like a thundercloud in the summer, and laid before me an envelope, addressed in a familiar hand that made my heart leap. When I picked it up, the envelope gaped open, the seal already broken. I gasped.

"You opened it!"

"Of course I opened it, as would any married sister of a maiden girl. It is my duty to oversee your correspondence, although I see by your reaction that Mother was not as diligent." Leah's scowl was fierce, and she moved toward me like a steamboat propelling its way upstream. "Dr. Kane seems confident that what we do here is a hoax," she growled.

I trembled, holding the open letter in my hands, and I prayed fearfully that Elisha had not mentioned the kiss in the cemetery or the lock of hair I had smuggled to him the next day. "I swear to you, Leah, I have not told him so. I did not confess a thing. But he has his strong opinions."

"So I see. He seems particularly intent on persuading you to renounce spiritualism and give up rapping."

What could I do but nod? She had already read the letter, and I had not. I had no doubt that Elisha had renewed his plea for me to reform my life.

"And yet he makes no claim upon you, professes no interest beyond kindness and affection. If you are expecting more from him, you will be disappointed."

I stood before her, mute in my suffering. His letter in my hand burned with the need to be read, but, then, why bother? Leah already knew the contents. It would be more preaching and nothing else. A kiss, a passionate gaze, personal tokens exchanged—these things had meant far more to me, an inexperienced girl, than to a sophisticated, worldly gentleman like Elisha Kent Kane. His interest was no more than that of an older brother who simply wished a different kind of life for me.

Leah took pity upon me and invited me to sit beside her on the settee. I did so, still clasping the letter pitifully and trying to blink back the tears that threatened, now that my expectations had been so lowered. "How did you meet Dr. Kane?" Leah asked me in a gentler voice.

"In a sitting." I glanced at my sister's face. "He is not a believer in spiritualism, but in a moment of despair, he did reach out to his late brother."

"Very human of him, for such a grand hero," Leah said wryly, unable to resist a dig at his character. "I'm sorry, Maggie, but my point is that you would never have met this man if it were not for the business of rapping. It is all well and good for Dr. Kane to assert so righteously that our business is not respectable, but I allow that our business is all that affords us the respect and social status we currently enjoy! Your reputation protects you, Maggie. In a way, our names are as well known as his. Without this cloak of respectability, he would never have met you, or if he had, he might have persuaded you to give up your virtue and then cast you aside."

I resented this implication. "You do not know him, Leah. And you do not know me very well if you think me so much a fool."

"I have met him," she countered. "And other men like him. I was once a young girl easily led by an attractive man. You may think me too old for romance, Maggie, but I remember what it was like. A person of goodwill might have warned me of my fate. Sadly, there was no one who bothered, no one who cared enough to intervene on my behalf."

We sat for a moment in silence, with Leah reflecting on her poor, neglected younger self. However, the question begged asking: "If there had been such a person, would you have heeded the advice?"

Leah gazed at me solemnly. I could see her consider a lie, but she seemed to understand that I would never believe it. After a moment, she replied, "No. I would have scolded them for jealousy or spite. I would have followed my heart and ended up just where I am right now, even though I had been forewarned."

Then she laid her hand over my own, the one that held Elisha's letter, and said, "That's why I am so worried about you."

Chapter Twenty-Eight
Maggie

Elisha's letter was not as much a disappointment as Leah had suggested, especially after she had lowered my expectations. He mentioned our last carriage ride into the country, the significance of which Leah did not know. Nor could she have understood his reference to patting his right breast pocket for luck before each of his lectures—the promised residing place of my carefully clipped curl. I embraced these small allusions to his affection, cherishing them all the more for having been told they did not exist.

It was true that he devoted the bulk of the letter to his concern over my calling as a spirit medium.

"Oh, how I wish that you would quit this life of dreary sameness and suspected deceit," he wrote. "We live in this world only for the opinions of the good and noble. How crushing it must be to occupy a position of ambiguous respect!"

I expected this was the comment that raised Leah's ire and caused her to assert so firmly that our role as mediums had brought us respect in society. In truth, I skimmed this part of his letter, simply desiring to devour his words and seek out tender phrases.

He confided in me his worries about collecting sufficient funds for the second expedition. Although his lectures in Boston had been well received, private contributions had not met his expectations. The letter continued, "I present my theories to an uninterested audience, and my pleas for support sound desperate even to my own ears."

Over the next three days, I planned and savored and replanned my reply to him. I did not presume upon his affection but matched the tone in which he fondly recalled our days in Philadelphia. I did make bold enough to comment on his desire to reap more revenue from his lectures. Carefully and most logically, I suggested that he rely less on the scientific theory behind the polar sea and the lands above it and more upon his experience during the expedition. His tale of falling through the ice with his sled dog had enthralled listeners in Philadelphia, and if there were any other harrowing adventures he could recount, I felt sure he would see an increased enthusiasm in his audience.

When my letter was completed, after much revision and several copies, I presented it dutifully to Leah for reading. She declined, waving her hand and saying, "I rely on your good sense."

Leah was very busy with spiritualist business at that time. Most recently, Mr. Capron had invited us to Auburn to visit a newly discovered medium, a young girl named Cora Scott. Leah accepted the offer on behalf of the whole family, feeling that we owed Eliab Capron the courtesy of a visit and the medium Miss Scott a gesture of professional support.

The Capron household was crowded but cozy, overflowing with a passel of giggling girls and the warm hospitality of the plump and amiable Mrs. Capron. Kate was welcomed like a long-lost sister, and after only a few minutes of acquaintance, so was I.

I felt some trepidation regarding our meeting with Cora Scott. I knew, of course, that spirit mediums had cropped up all over the country, but I had never met any. It was daunting and troubling to think of these people who imitated the example set by my family. Did we greet them as devoted believers or as artisans exchanging professional secrets?

Miss Cora Scott turned out to be a tiny thing, very pale with wide-set green eyes and hair the color of dark honey. She spoke hardly a dozen words to us, completely dominated by her hatchet-faced father. Her mother, Mrs. Scott, was a ghostly presence, floating along the perimeter of the room and avoiding eye contact with anyone. We, the guests, were directed to seats in a parlor elaborately overdecorated, cluttered with furniture, and heavily muffled with curtains. The room was uncomfortably close, and the smell of perfumed oil rose from the cushions and draperies.

Mr. Scott required us to place our hands on the arms of our chairs "to await the coming of the apparition" and warned us against moving from our assigned places. The spectral Mrs. Scott fluttered forward and presented her daughter with a cup of pungent tea. Miss Cora sipped delicately, then allowed her mother to remove the cup while she slumped in her seat with a soft sigh. Soon the child's eyelids began to twitch and her mouth worked silently, flecks of froth appearing on her pale lips. Her limbs jerked stiffly and her body began to convulse. I assumed the fit was faked but still glanced at Leah for reassurance. And then Mr. Scott put the gaslight out.

For a moment, we sat in total, impenetrable darkness. Then, with a sudden burst of noise, a powerful light exploded into the room, a harsh, unnatural light that caused sharp pain in our dark-adapted eyes. It was nothing like I had ever experienced, magnitudes of brightness beyond any gas flame and accompanied by a harsh crackling sound. In the center of this supernatural illumination a figure appeared, moving toward us.

A vision of a young woman, veiled and robed in diaphanous silks flickered in and out of existence. The apparition approached us in a disjointed and frightening progression, so that I drew back in my seat with horror. She was bleached of all color in the terrible light, inhumanly pale with dark eyes just visible beneath the obscuring veil, drawing inexorably closer with undulating ripples. Then, just when I thought I might scream, she began to retreat, writhing backward like some feminine snake. She descended into the brilliance, which abruptly popped out of existence, leaving us in darkness with bright images still dancing across our eyes and a harsh smell permeating the room.

Shortly thereafter we were escorted from the house by Mr. Scott, leaving his daughter limp on the couch and his wife hovering nearby. There were no questions to the spirit, no messages, no significance to the ghastly phantasm beyond, apparently, scaring the wits out of us.

We spoke among ourselves in the carriage on the ride back to the Capron house. Leah seemed amused. "Impressive," she said, "but rather a one-trick pony for all that. What did you make of it, Calvin?"

"They used an arc lamp," her husband affirmed with confidence. "It's an electric device, probably run from a battery in this case. If you looked directly into the light, you could see it on the floor."

Look directly into that light? I admired Calvin's fortitude of eyesight while Leah asked questions about the device.

"I saw one demonstrated as part of a science lecture in Rochester. It was some years ago," said Calvin, "but the lack of color in the light and that crackling noise make it unmistakable. Clearly, there was a hidden door or cabinet behind one of those curtains. Their accomplice started the battery and threw open the door. All she did was walk across the floor toward us, then backward away from us. She closed the door and dropped the curtain, then extinguished the battery."

"But she kept popping from place to place," Kate observed, with a tinge of jealousy in her voice.

"The light was flickering, too fast for you to realize. Her movement forward was steady, but it appeared fragmented to our eyes." Calvin turned to Leah. "If you want one, I know where to inquire."

My sister laughed. "I think not. Our business is best done in the dark. Besides, all it will take is one visitor to reach out and grab that spirit, and I expect she will squeal like a stuck pig. It is a doomed venture."

"They will be exposed before the year is out," Kate uttered in the flat, throaty intonation she used for her supposedly true predictions. Leah simply snorted her derision and commented that she did not need the second sight to predict that!

After a week's stay in Auburn, we returned by rail to New York City. Awaiting us, I found another letter from Dr. Kane. This time I sat in the room with Leah while she read it, fidgeting anxiously and trying to interpret the expressions on her face, ranging from raised eyebrow to scowl. Finally, she handed over the letter with obvious reluctance.

Dearest Maggie,

Your letter has been a comfort and a stimulus to long sessions of self-reflection. I can hear your voice in every written word, and I discover that I am bereft of a cherished friendship in your absence. How I miss you when listening to the nonsense of my fashionable friends who flatter and fawn and drown a man in empty praise! Only you, Maggie, have the sharp wit and intellect to puncture a man's folly and sense of overworth and still retain your sweet innocence of expression. Your words are honey, laced with a sharp tonic!

It was a blow when you suggested that "harrowing" tales were valued more than science and philosophy. What a comedown to think that I was simply being paid for an evening's worth of vicarious entertainment! I have chastised you, dear darling, for wasting your youth and conscience for a few paltry dollars, but when I think of the crowds who come nightly to hear wild stories of the frozen North, I realize that we are not so far removed after all.

However, I hasten to add that my accomplishments are true, and however entertaining, my stories harbor no exaggeration. If I must face the reality that the public will open its pocketbooks more out of sensation than humanitarianism, then I will be content to know that my intentions are pure. Can you, Maggie, claim a similar virtue in your rapping?

You say that my last letter was full of preaching, and I know that this one may be similarly received. Know only that I have your best interests at heart, and that my persuasions only serve to divert me from writing at length about other matters…how I long to look—only look!—at your dear, deceitful mouth and your hair tumbling over your cheeks. Better that I devote my attention to your character and your soul than other comely aspects of your precious self.

Thus, I must resign myself to being, fondly…

Your Preacher,

E. K. Kane

I could not control the flush that came to my cheeks nor force down the smile that curved my lips when I came to his final paragraph. I glanced guiltily at Leah, who was scrutinizing me with her stern gaze, but she had no comment to make.

In my reply, I addressed his question, defending myself from the criticism that he had so ably wrapped in silky words. "While I cannot pretend to lofty deeds that will expand the sphere of the globe and the knowledge of mankind all at once, I affirm a smaller, more personal goal in my actions. It is the meek and humble who come to me, broken with grief, racked by guilt, unable to escape the icy grip of despair, and it is to these poor souls I address my efforts." Honey laced with tonic, indeed!

Thus our correspondence continued for several months, as we debated our positions on faith and honor while slipping endearments between the barbs. Leah commented dryly that if I was suddenly so taken with letter writing, then I could assist with her duties in correspondence, and I found myself sitting with my sister daily, writing letters under her direction to the Posts, Mr. Capron, and various spiritualist supplicants.

Elisha's touring schedule took him to Columbus and Cincinnati, then back to Philadelphia before he headed south to Washington. At first he wrote that he planned on diverting to New York City for a few days, and my hopes soared wildly, but a following letter served as apology when his plans changed.

As the weeks and months passed, I worked more and more closely with Leah in her web of connections between spiritualists and abolitionists and feminists. During our daily toil, she began to pressure me to demand some sort of answer from Dr. Kane regarding his intentions.

"You have known the man eight months," she said, "although he has spent most of them hundreds of miles away from you. You are eighteen years old, highly marriageable right now, and there would be suitable young men knocking on our door day and night if it were not known that you were holding out for some mystery man who never shows his face here."

"I cannot ask him if he wants to marry me!" I protested. "That is carrying the feminist cause too far!"

"He continually asks you to abandon your family and quit the rapping!" she retorted. "Yet he has not declared any serious intentions for you. And even if he did, is he really what you want? That man will spend all of his life traveling the world, and any wife of his had better get used to a marriage by post."

It was hard to listen to her words, as blunt and sensible as they were. As his prolonged absence continued, Kate and Calvin ceased to defend him on my behalf, and all the tokens I had from Elisha himself were philosophical arguments and travelogues signed "The Preacher." I did not want ministering; I wanted the romance and excitement of our time together in Philadelphia. I needed to see the fire in his eyes, the quickness of his hands, and the energy in his athletic frame. One day Kate solemnly pointed out a newspaper gossip column that listed a sighting of "the eminent explorer Dr. Elisha K. Kane" at an opera in Philadelphia with "a beautiful, unnamed young woman." It was during the very week that he had failed to come to New York to visit. That's when I finally broke down.

With all his previous correspondence stacked neatly on my writing desk, I composed my carefully worded note. It was very brief and, I hoped, dignified:

Dearest Elisha,

You have spent the last few months trying to reform me from my current occupation, but I have to ask you, to what end? You speak of education in broad terms. Do you wish me to train as a schoolteacher? I know not how you wish me to make my way in the world, because currently the only thing that stands between my family and destitution is our renowned role as spiritual guides.

You have been my dear friend, Elisha, but I cannot continue in such an indeterminate state. I know well that I have no claim upon you. However, I have come to a point where I must know your intention, and while I value the friendship that we have, I cannot turn my back on my family and their calling even for the sake of friendship.

Fondly,

Maggie

No sooner was this missive posted than I regretted my rashness. I spent days in agony, imagining his response. He would profess his love to me. He would be angry at my presumption. He would rush to my side. He would crush my hopes with a laughing rejection. All these and more I spilled out in a torrent to Kate.

"It is not unreasonable that you should ask," Kate said, again and again.

"What kind of woman asks a man for a proposal?" I would reply. "He will think me shameless and grasping!"

"If he is your sincere lover, he will understand," she soothed me. "After all these months, is he your suitor or your brother?"

Restless and miserable, I scarcely listened to her. I could take no faith in the reassurances of a fifteen-year-old girl who laughed at potential suitors behind their backs. I realized that I had been goaded into unwise action by Leah, who wanted the affair ended by my doing or his, and I cursed myself for rising to her bait.

The reply to my demand was two interminable weeks in coming, and when it arrived, it appeared on my bed in the middle of the day with no warning. It was already opened. Leah had read it and left it for me. I understood at once that she did not want me to witness her reaction, and I knew instinctively that I would find the contents very good or very bad indeed.

Tears were pricking at my eyes before I even had it unfolded.

Maggie,

I confess that your letter comes as a shock to me, and yet I chastise myself for having been so childishly credulous in all these months of sharing my thoughts and dreams with you. In all your former correspondence, which I have reread at length, you write to me entirely as to a friend—kind, noncommittal letters. All the warmth and affection seem to be on my side. And now I see that you have viewed me all this time as nothing but a gentleman hypocrite, never really sincere and amusing himself with a pretty face. I suppose the sort of company you keep has conditioned you to a low expectation.

I imagine that you care for me but not enough. Perhaps it is not in your nature to feel that deeply. Rather sternly you chastise me for not putting my intentions forward. All the more fool I was, for thinking they were self-evident.

I am a man of facts and purpose. I will leave after me a name and a success. But with all this I am a weak man that I should be caught in the midst of my grave purposes by the gilded dust of a butterfly's wing. My intentions? My intention is to sail to the Arctic and from there proceed to the discovery of Sir Franklin's fate and the polar sea. No true gentleman would promise anything to a lady under those circumstances; no true lady would require it.

Just as you have your wearisome round of daily moneymaking, I have my own sad vanities to pursue. I am as devoted to my calling as you, poor child, are to yours.

Remember, then, as a sort of dream, that Dr. Kane of the Arctic Seas once loved Maggie Fox of the Spirit Rappings.

E. K. K.

Chapter Twenty-Nine
Maggie

As tempting as it was to blame Leah, I knew the fault was my own. No hand had guided mine when I wrote my ill-conceived demands to him. Truthfully, I was the one who most desired evidence of his commitment. I had challenged his devotion and, by doing so, proved that I was simply beneath his station, as my sister had warned me and as his letter confirmed.

"He was a puffed-up, pompous little man," Leah was quick to say. "He blamed you for his own shortcomings. He was nothing but heartache for you, Maggie. You are better off without him."

I did not answer her, believing that in her bitterness she was speaking of her own lost love more than mine. Leah's true love had rejected her twenty years earlier, and she had married a second time only out of friendship and pity. There was no doubt that for Calvin it was a love match, but Leah was already irrevocably damaged by the man who first abandoned her. And it occurred to me that this dubious honor went not to Bowman Fish at all, but to our own father. Therefore, I let her caustic comments fall into a well of silence, where they lay moldering in their own animosity until even Leah felt embarrassment.

Perhaps my family expected me to take to my bed in hysteria, as I had done after my fright in Troy. Instead I continued to uphold my duties in the spirit circles and in the correspondence Leah had entrusted to me. I had written in my letter to Dr. Kane that I would never turn my back on my family, and I was determined that the last sentence I ever wrote to him would at least not be a lie.

It was true also that I wrapped a shroud of tragedy about myself and let it shield me from the view of others. Perhaps I read too many novels and viewed myself as heroine of my own tale, a sad combination of star-crossed lover and jilted bride. Whatever the source, my tragic demeanor kept the young men who still attended our spirit circles from intruding upon my grief. Their plentiful presence remained, each one eager to detect any sign of encouragement, and in the meantime they were happy to ply their charms on Kate, who toyed with them lazily. For my part, I viewed them all with distaste. Not one of them could hold a candle to Dr. Kane. In fact, being among them was rather like the plunge into darkness I experienced when Cora Scott's electric lamp was extinguished, a sense of being blinded by the memory of brilliance, with faint spots of afterglow still dazzling my eyes.

Spring faded away, and in the early part of summer we received a regretful letter from the Caprons regarding the Scotts, who had been unmasked nearly in the manner Leah had foreseen. Their electric device had failed in midhaunting, and during the resulting confusion of darkness, the apparition had stumbled bodily into one of the guests, thus proving her own corporeality. The tremor of this disaster was felt among the growing community of spiritualists, followed by a tighter binding together of the faithful. We erected a wall of common sense against the resulting wave of doubt. One cutpurse did not make a crowd of thieves, we argued; one false-hood did not make all neighbors liars.

Of an even more personal and intimate discomfort to me was the arrival of August, when Dr. Kane's lecture circuit returned him to New York City. Every day proved a torture. I felt his presence in the city, and even though I expected no contact from him, I found myself uncontrollably holding my breath every time we opened our doors for a public sitting. Newspapers in the household myste-riously became scarce, but I had long since memorized his itinerary and knew precisely where he was lecturing and to whom. My fami-ly's sensitivity was well placed, however, for if any gossip sheet had observed "an unnamed beauty" in his company, I would scarcely have survived it.

In the third week of this torment, we admitted to one of our public sittings a man who introduced himself as Cornelius Grinnell. His name was met with a collective silence and subsequent cool-ness from my family members. The man cast an appraising glance in my direction before deferentially retreating to the background of the party. Leah herded him to a seat as far from me as she could manage without actually shooing him out of the room. This man, Cornelius Grinnell, was the son of Henry Grinnell, who had financed Dr. Kane's first Arctic expedition and who had pledged a ship for the second.

I found myself scarcely able to breathe and totally unable to participate in my established roles. Kate took over for me deftly, and Leah laid a protective hand over mine while I kept my eyes modestly down and tried to maintain a dignified composure.

A well-dressed man in his thirties, with a square jaw framed by fashionable muttonchops, Mr. Grinnell made no overtures toward me and, after that first frank perusal, kept his attention strictly on the rappings and the spirit writing performed by Kate. My family knew that he must be an acquaintance of Dr. Kane, but I knew from my conversations with Elisha that this man was in fact a close friend and confidant of the doctor. His purpose in visiting us, I could not fathom.

Had he come to spy upon me and report to Elisha? Or had he come for the sake of his own curiosity? In my torturous musings, I imagined that my former suitor sent him in humorous self-reproach, saying, "By all means go and see her for yourself so that you can judge what a fool I was!" At last the interminable spirit session came to a close, and after a halfhearted attempt to mingle with the other attendees, Mr. Grinnell bowed his head in a somewhat apologetic manner and departed. I promptly fled the room in the other direction, dissolving into tears.

Later, I agonized over his unexplained presence to Kate. "Perhaps his visit is unrelated in any way to Dr. Kane," she soothed, "an unpleasant coincidence."

"Did he seem interested in the spirits to you?" I challenged.

"No," she replied, "he did not seem overly taken with the experience. I doubt we shall see him again."

Here Kate's prophetic powers failed her, for the very next day Mr. Cornelius Grinnell presented himself again at our public sitting. It was less of a shock the second time, but still an aching pain of renewed grief for me. How many days was I to be thus tormented? Mr. Grinnell seemed almost cheerful this time but studiously avoided my eyes and willingly kept himself distant. Leah frowned at him imperiously, and even Mother drew herself up indignantly, as though his presence was an affront to her poor, discarded daughter.

That night, as I prepared for bed, I despaired at the thought of seeing him a third time. I would not attend tomorrow's sitting, I decided, rubbing my brow to relieve the headache brought on by my pent-up tears. Kate approached my bed, throwing out her arms with an exaggerated yawn and casting down onto my blankets a small bundle of paper. I stared uncomprehendingly at the packet, then turned to look at my sister, who grinned mischievously.

"I dared not give them to you earlier," she said, "lest Leah suspect. But Mr. Grinnell passed them to me in the doorway as he came in today. He said he would have delivered them to you yesterday, but Leah kept too sharp an eye on him."

The letters had been tied so tightly, to make a tiny package, that they sprang apart with some force when I cut the string. With trembling hands I unfolded them one by one, tears blinding me at the sight of Elisha's handwriting.

They were apologies. Abject, heartfelt, self-abasing apologies. He begged me to forgive him for the letter that had torn out my heart. He blamed the demands of his work, the pressure of his family, and finally, in an eerie echo of Leah's words, his "inflated sense of self-importance." One letter had been written from a sickbed in a Washington hotel and begged me most piteously to come to his side. This note, like all the others, was unfinished and trailed off in the middle of a rambling sentence. None of the letters had ever been made ready for the post.

What battles of willfulness and pride must have taken place on the field of his heart! And after months of warfare, what measure of humility must have risen victorious in order for him to bundle all these pitiful notes together and surrender them for my appraisal! In that moment, I could not have loved him more.

A final note, dated yesterday morning, read:

> If you can find it in your heart to forgive me, beloved Maggie, please do me the honor of meeting me at the Tea Room of the New York Hotel, Waverly and Broadway, this coming Friday at noon.

"Will you do it?" Kate asked, curled up beside me on the bed. "You should do it! I will make up some excuse for you."

"No," I murmured, realizing in that moment that I could not.

"What? Do you not forgive him?"

"We must begin as we mean to go on," I explained. "I cannot meet him in this manner. If I did, it would be an appalling act of impropriety, and how would it look in his eyes?"

"It was his idea!" She seemed astonished that I did not run out immediately and lay down against the hotel doors to wait for Friday. My impetuous Kate would have done so in an instant.

"If he ever once sees me as less than a lady, then I will never regain that status. No woman of Philadelphia society would accept this invitation." Climbing out of the bed, I searched for paper and a pen among the various items in our shared chiffonier and then scrambled back onto the bed with a book for a writing surface.

My dearest Elisha,

How desperately I long to see you! There is no need to speak of forgiveness between two people who are matched so well in mind and soul. I cannot make an imprudent promise to meet you without the consent or approval of my family, but I humbly and meekly request that you call upon me at my sister's house. I know you will understand how much this means to me.

Lovingly,

Maggie

Kate's violet eyes showed both her admiration and her approval. "I will deliver it to him," she volunteered.

On Friday morning, Kate went out for a walk. As soon as she was out of the sight of the house, she hired a carriage to the New York Hotel, where she handed a doorman my note addressed for Dr. Kane. With the message delivered, I sat down to bite at my fingernails and await his response.

The first indication came when I heard Leah's voice raised in indignation while Mother dithered with her in excited agitation. Quickly, I gathered my skirts and scrambled down the stairs in a most unfeminine manner. Leah rounded on me as I entered the parlor. My prompt arrival without benefit of a summons gave me away. "You knew about this!" she exclaimed.

"You were expecting it! Have you been in secret correspondence with him? It was that Grinnell man, wasn't it? And here I was, feeling sorry for you!"

She was waving the paper in her hand so vigorously that it took me a second to catch it and pull it from her grasp. It was a note from the doctor, expressing his intention to call upon the house that afternoon. I let out my breath with relief and collapsed onto the settee, pressing the paper against my pounding heart.

"I don't want that wretched dandy in my house!" Leah growled.

I looked up at her. "You must receive him for my sake."

"We discussed at length why he is not an appropriate suitor for you!"

"We also discussed," I answered her evenly, "how matters of the heart cannot be resolved with good advice. Please, Leah, I ask this of you. Otherwise, I will write to him and say that Mother and I will meet him somewhere else."

Thus was Leah outmaneuvered, for she was not about to be left uninformed and dependent on our mother for intelligence. The meeting between Elisha and me would be held under her watchful eye.

~~~

No girl ever dressed more carefully. I chose a gown that was neither the most expensive nor the most elaborate in my possession, but the one I deemed most striking in its elegant simplicity. Kate helped me arrange my hair in the newest, most fashionable style of the city, a complicated twist at the back of my neck that needed nearly four hands to assemble.

In the end, however, I might as well have dressed in sackcloth and left my hair in rag curls. Once our eyes met, for the first time in nearly a year, nothing else in the room mattered. It was only later that I registered his shorter hair, no longer curling on his collar, and his smartly cut new suit. At first sight, I was only aware of his eyes, which held mine with a magnetism and intensity that I had almost forgotten, and his smile, which rose spontaneously upon his face as he realized, in the same moment as I, that our attraction remained unbroken.

Mother actually took his arm to prevent him stumbling over a footstool, for he had turned to look at me as soon as he entered the parlor. I remained seated in a corner of the room, blinking back tears and smiling foolishly at him. With a visible start, Elisha recovered his composure and wiped his own grin from his face. He turned to look briefly at Calvin, seated in his favorite chair with a shawl draped over his shoulders even in the heat of August. But after only a glance in his direction, Elisha directed his bow at Leah, evidently knowing full well who was the true head of this household.

"Thank you for receiving me on such short notice, Mrs. Brown," he began. "I know I have been long absent and silent, and I hope that I have not presumed upon our acquaintance too much."

Leah nodded but kept her lips primly sealed, for which I was grateful. Elisha realized that he could not expect any more greeting than that and, clearing his throat, prepared to continue. Belatedly, my mother tried to offer him a seat with her usual ineffectiveness. "No, thank you, Mrs. Fox, I shall stand for the time being. Some months ago, I was asked a question—a very reasonable question—about my intentions for Miss Margaretta, with whom I had been bold enough to forge an acquaintance and with whom I continued to correspond. After a rather lengthy and undue delay, I would like to respond that my desire is—and has been, almost since the day I met her—to make her my wife. However, her tender age and my rather unorthodox career led me to believe that it was best to keep those wishes to myself, and thus allow her the opportunity to find a match more to her benefit, if she was so inclined. In fact, I was prepared to end my friendship with her, in the best interests of all concerned—" my sister began to nod her head vigorously "—but I find myself utterly unable to withdraw my suit without making a plea to her in my favor."

"Are you asking for her hand in marriage now?" inquired Calvin gently. As the gentleman of the house, it was his privilege to ask.

"Two circumstances stand in the way," Elisha said regretfully. "First and foremost, I am already committed to a lengthy and perilous undertaking. An expedition to the Arctic Circle is set to leave in May of next year under my command. I will be gone for a year at least, quite possibly longer."

May of next year? So soon?

Leah opened her mouth finally and prompted Elisha. "And the second circumstance?"

He shuffled his feet and looked briefly at the floor. "This is more embarrassing," he admitted. "Through no action of my own, I find that an arrangement has arisen between my father and a political acquaintance that I will marry the man's daughter." Elisha turned to speak directly to me when he emphasized, "I have not even met the lady in question! I am sure that she will be as relieved as I to have the contract dissolved, but you can see that such a thing requires delicacy. To announce my engagement to another woman would dishonor someone who has never harmed me. I would like to handle it personally and discreetly."

"So what you are saying, Doctor," Leah inserted, "is that you cannot marry our Maggie because you are leaving on a potentially lethal adventure some years in length, and you are engaged to someone else, besides?"

Elisha flashed her the same bare grin he might have used on the Mexican rebel Domínguez right before shooting at him. "You are correct, Mrs. Brown, with your usual frankness. But I have not come empty-handed." Slipping a hand inside the right breast pocket of his coat, he strode decisively across the room toward me. I rose to meet him, feeling Kate's hand on my back encouraging me. He stopped a few scant inches from me, devouring my face with his gaze and holding between his forefinger and thumb a small ring of black enamel, set with a dainty but brilliant diamond. "This is my promise to you," he said softly, "that if you are willing to wait for me, when I return from the Arctic I shall make you my wife."

"I would wait for you until the end of the earth," I whispered.

He took my hand and boldly kissed my fingers before placing the ring upon one. "My promise," he said again and kissed the ring in its place. Without letting go of my hand, he turned back to his host and hostess. "With your permission, I would like to spend an hour or two with Maggie."

Perhaps Leah was grudgingly beginning to accept the inevitable, or maybe she just could not stand to be in the same room with him a moment longer. Whatever her motives, she helped Calvin to his feet and brusquely signaled for Kate to join them, leaving us with only Mother as our chaperone.

Together, we sank down upon the sofa in the corner of the room, while Mother busied herself with her embroidery, humming happily and occasionally wiping tears from her eyes. Elisha had not let go of my hand since he had taken it, and I had not taken my eyes from his face.

"Maggie," he began, "the things I wrote to you…you must believe me—"

"Let us not speak of it," I told him. "I understand it is customary for young couples to have what is called a lovers' quarrel, which is all thunder and lightning but rains little on them and amounts to nothing. We have had ours now, and the weather is set to be fair from this moment on."

"Wisely and ably spoken, my darling," he whispered and, leaning forward, he kissed my forehead with only a token squeak of protest from Mother.

Chapter Thirty
Maggie

We were not precisely engaged but began to behave as if we were. I wore his promissory ring with pride, blushing anew each time I caught sight of it on my finger. As for Elisha, with his typical contradictory nature, he treated me with the tenderness and possessiveness of a future husband, all the while expressing mild vexation that so many people knew or had guessed our relationship.

"I think your sister has been telling people about us," he said to me as we sat in the park with my mother across the walkway on a separate bench.

"I think not," I replied. "Leah is displeased with the arrangement and does not desire it widely known."

That was an understatement. The hostility between Elisha and Leah had been so palpable during their enforced interactions that on his last visit to me they had exchanged fewer than a dozen words. To be sure, I was myself unhappy about some other woman planning to marry my love. Elisha counseled patience. He had been in correspondence with his father and was trying to clear up the misunderstanding. "I am sure my father was counting on some political favor in this alliance and is loath to give it up. He is probably trying to sell off one of my brothers in my place even as we speak!" Elisha joked brightly.

"If people know our intentions, it is because of your own loose tongue, Elisha!" I chided him gently. "Why, just the other day, you introduced me as 'the future Mrs. Kane!'"

"Oh, Dr. Grey is the soul of discretion! He would not give away our secret."

"There were ten other people in the room at the time!" I laughed.

"Were there?" he smiled. "I scarcely noticed. I am so happy, Maggie! Happier than I have been in the longest time! When I ended our correspondence last spring, I had decided to give up romance entirely and devote myself more completely to the serious business of my mission. But I was so miserable, Maggie, so alone even when the room was crowded with tiresome people, that I regretted my decision within days. Only pride prevented me from taking the first train to your side. I don't know if I was selfish then or if I am selfish now, but I am so joyful I hardly care! If it were not for the inconvenience of courting you under the jealous eye of the Tigress, I would be in heaven!"

Whenever possible, Elisha tried to take me from the house to avoid my sister. In New York, there was never a shortage of places to go, events to see, entertainments to sample, but the problem was acquiring a chaperone. Mother accommodated us as she could, but more and more often she was required to supervise Kate in the spirit sessions while Leah was nursing Calvin. All told, it was a difficult time for the family, and Leah had not hesitated to prey upon my guilty feelings for slipping off with Dr. Kane while her husband was slipping away from life.

Adding to the increasing burdens upon my conscience, Elisha did not waste time in asking me to give up the rapping once and for all. "You must not engage yourself to be my wife unless you can give me all your love and your whole heart," he said to me.

"Of course!" I told him. "I will never rap for the spirits again after we have married. I will devote myself to you, your endeavors, your dreams, and your children."

"No, Maggie, you must give up your calling *before* we can be married. I cannot bring you to my family unless you are beyond all criticism and suspicion. I will tell you—my friend Mr. Grinnell was most impressed by you. Everybody who really knows you is, for you are a lady in all but a finishing education, and after you've had a course in music and French and art, no one will know you as the original spirit-rapping phenomenon."

I found this troubling. "Is that what you want, Ly, that no one should know me for who I am?"

"My darling, you will always be yourself, and all who meet you love you. But to be Mrs. Elisha Kane, you must sever your ties with ghosts and knocks and collecting money at the door."

"How will I live? Who will pay for this education?" I protested.

"Surely after all these years of taking fees, your mother has a tidy sum."

"No. Leah has it all."

Elisha raised his eyes to heaven. "Of course she does. Then I shall pay for your schooling."

"Where will I live?" I pressed on. "I will not be your kept woman!"

He was just as shocked as I was by the suggestion. "Never! But you challenge me with difficult questions, my ever-practical Maggie! On these matters I will ponder. The path of rightness will find a way for us."

Relieved that I had managed to forestall an immediate renounce-ment of spiritualism, I dared to say, "This would be a bad time for me to abandon my family. Leah's husband is so ill…"

"Mrs. Brown has lived off your labor for years," Elisha replied with feeling. "I have no doubt she will feel the loss of your income, and that has been the true reason behind her objection all along. For all your intelligence and considering all the years you have advocated the cause of abolition, it is surprising to me that you do not recognize the shackles you wear yourself."

He gave me much to think about. When I returned to Leah's house that day, I met her coming heavily down the front stairs, looking not at all like a tigress or a slave mistress but merely a very weary woman who had finally lost the vestiges of her youth. "Maggie, I will need you to lead the sittings this evening," she said by way of greeting. There were dark circles under her gray eyes.

"Is he worse?" I asked at once.

"No, he is sleeping now. He is…the same." Leah brushed her hair back from her face. "But I am spent. I must take my rest now, in case he needs me in the night. Mind you, keep a rein on Kate, or she is liable to flights of fancy and wild risks."

"You can count on me to handle it," I assured her, glad for once that Dr. Kane had plans elsewhere in the city that night.

"You're a good girl, Maggie," Leah said fondly, turning to make her way back upstairs, where she would sleep in a chair beside her dying husband.

Perhaps Elisha was right and there were shackles upon me, but they were no more than the bindings worn in any family, and I bore the burden willingly.

❧❧

The months of that fall passed quickly. Elisha was in and out of the city, making preparations for his voyage. He had provisions to order, sailors and scientists to procure, and always money to acquire. When he was out of town, he sent letters and gifts. Leah threw up her hands in exasperation at the embroidered handkerchiefs, music, books, and trifles that entered the house. Elisha was not stingy in his attention and did not forget either Mother or Kate in his generosity.

I was often overwhelmed by the extent of his generosity. I thought the ermine collar he sent me was excessive, until he sent me the canary.

"Wonderful," Leah remarked. "Another mouth to feed."

Throughout November and December, whenever he was in New York, Elisha was a constant visitor, often bringing Cornelius Grinnell along to distract and consternate my sister. Leah disapproved of him on principle, because she knew he had smuggled letters to me from Elisha, but Mr. Grinnell was so frank and amiable that he won unwilling smiles even from my dour sister.

While his friend provided a distraction for Leah, Elisha shared the plans for his expedition with me. Often, he brought maps to show me. Seeing the plans on paper and hearing of the extended preparations under way, I could not help but feel a certain panic as I realized the time of his departure was quickly approaching. He would be gone at least a year—a year! Elisha pointed out to me the hazards, almost without care, but I could imagine my own disasters aplenty. Freezing to death was only the mildest of fates, compared to falling into an ice crevasse, suffering a painful demise by scurvy, or simply vanishing forever like Sir Franklin. I was never able to view those maps without the urge to throw myself against Elisha's knees and beg him not to leave. I refrained from such a pitiful display of emotion solely because I understood that if he had not wanted so desperately to undertake this mission, he would not have been the Elisha I loved.

"What will I do without you?" I whispered in anticipation of future despair.

My love looked up at me brightly, his hand resting upon the map of Greenland, where he would last see civilization before heading into the frozen North. "I imagine you will have your nose in a book, as you did when I first met you. You will be busy enough, dearest, with your studies."

"Shhh," I hushed him, not wanting Leah to hear his words. She did not yet know his plan to send me to school, and I wasn't even sure that I had agreed to attend. Elisha assumed that I would, just as soon as he had made the arrangements. I was not certain what course I would take but hoped that when the time came to commit myself, the path would be clear to me.

"As for myself, I plan to take your image with me." Elisha rolled up his maps and tapped them on the table absently. "I have spoken with several artists, and I have decided to commission a portrait that I can have aboard the ship with me."

I gasped, pleased and surprised. "A portrait of me?"

"I could not bear to be without you," he smiled, obviously delighted by my response. "I will let you know where and when you will sit for the painting."

"Oh, but when do you think it will be? I shall be in Washington for part of March."

"Washington?" Elisha looked puzzled. "Why would you be in Washington?"

I realized that he would not like the answer. "Mother and Kate and I will be the guests of General Waddy Thompson." Quickly I explained that the trip had been planned for some weeks and that originally I had not planned to participate. "But Leah cannot leave her husband, so I must take her place."

Elisha was indeed displeased. Despite my efforts to dissuade him, he sought out Leah across the room and expressed his feelings on the matter with some forcefulness. Washington was a disreputable city, he argued, and we ladies would not find ourselves as protected as we had been in the bosom of the gentle Quakers in Philadelphia. He urged her to cancel the trip at once.

Leah dismissed his concerns curtly, irritated by his interference. "Maggie will do her duty. We have a business to conduct, Dr. Kane, and expenses to meet. Surely you can appreciate that."

"I do not approve," Elisha said firmly.

"With all due respect, Doctor," Leah replied, "your position in this family is not one that commands any authority. Were you truly betrothed to my sister, I would recognize your right to object. But as things stand…"

Elisha's eyes burned in anger. He removed from his inside coat pocket the small daybook he carried, consulted its pages briefly, and then snapped it closed. "I find that I can divert some time from my traveling appointments to meet the ladies in Washington during their second week there," he informed her gruffly. "I will make arrangements to check on their well-being."

"As you wish, Doctor," Leah said, "as long as you do not interfere with their obligations."

Elisha cast me a significant look. I merely wrung my hands in distress and dropped my eyes.

Dr. Kane was correct. Washington was a mean city, rough and unfriendly. Of course, the gentleman who had invited us was warm and generous enough. General Thompson and his friend Senator Tallmadge were keenly interested in spiritualism. They made every effort to include us in their social circle, escorting us to parties and plays most evenings.

Unfortunately, the same gentility was not found in all the inhabitants of the capital. Kate, Mother, and I found ourselves treated with disdain by General Thompson's social acquaintances. The people who inquired at our public sittings were raucous and crude, apparently mistaking us for some kind of curious circus exhibit.

There was only one spirit sitting of any significance. It came late in the afternoon on a day we had planned a shopping trip. Kate and I were putting on our gloves and bonnets when Mother rushed into our room, calling us to come down to the parlor. "We have a last-minute private sitting, girls!" she announced breathlessly. "Come quickly!"

Kate let out a breath of exasperated air. "Any time that we get a chance to have some fun…" she complained.

"Mother!" I called from the top of the stairs. "Can't you bid them to come back another time? We were dressed to go out. The carriage is waiting."

My mother turned back and hissed up at me with uncharacteristic forcefulness. "Margaretta, come at once!" And then, as if it would make a difference, she added, "It is Mrs. Pierce!"

I looked back grumpily at Kate. "Do we know a Mrs. Pierce?" She shrugged, and together we descended to the boardinghouse parlor, stubbornly refusing to remove our cloaks and bonnets.

In the parlor, we found a quiet commotion of agitated people, including Mother, Senator Tallmadge, and the owner of the boardinghouse, all gathered around a central tiny figure dressed in the black of deepest mourning. As she turned toward me, I saw an unremarkable lady with dainty, grief-stricken features. There was a certain familiarity to her, which I could not place, until Kate's sudden gasp of understanding prompted my recognition.

Oh, *that* Mrs. Pierce.

I promptly whipped off my hat and cast my cloak aside. "Madam, it is an honor," I said, leading the way to the table. "Please, come and be seated."

Dr. Kane, when I told him, was appalled. "You rapped for Mrs. Franklin Pierce? You deceived the wife of the president of the United States? Maggie, how could you?"

Surprised by his reaction, I defended myself. "Elisha, the poor woman saw her son killed before her very eyes!"

"Yes, I know. The entire nation grieves for her. It was a terrible tragedy. But how can you justify lying to her—her, of all people? Maggie, this life of yours is worse than bad; it is sinful!" Elisha paced the room in his vexation. "Entertaining strangers for a dollar a head is disgraceful enough, but to take advantage of the deeply bereft!"

"What is it that you think I do, Ly?" I demanded. "The lady was nearly prostrate with grief! I gave her what comfort I could."

"What comfort can you provide?" he challenged me in return. "The train derailed. The child is dead. Can you change any of that? Will knocking out some bogus message—*Dear Momma, do not grieve for me*—will that make any difference? She needs to muster her dignity and look toward her husband, not the grave!"

"Our messages are not bogus." Kate spoke quietly from the corner of the room. Mother was fetching tea for the doctor and taking rather a long time of it. It was just as well, because she would have been greatly shocked by his opinion.

Elisha turned with some consternation to my younger sister. "Miss Incomprehensible Kate, you need not protest your innocence to me," he said. "I will not argue with you over the origin of your peculiar knocks. But I wish your sister to understand one thing. She has long insisted that her spirit messages do good in the world." He turned back to me. "I strongly disagree. To wallow in death, and to fixate on the dead, that only leads us away from the world. We waste life, precious moments of it, when we scrabble after something we can no longer have. Maggie, I know that you think you are helping people, but you must see that you are doing more harm than good."

I was stung by his words. Hurt, I moved away from him and sat down, struggling to keep my composure. I had so looked forward to his visit and had told him so proudly of my sitting with Mrs. Pierce. I had not counted on this criticism raining down upon my head.

Elisha checked his timepiece. "I cannot stay more than an hour," he said. "Somehow I managed to commit myself to speaking at a new museum downtown, and I have to leave for Philadelphia by tomorrow noon. But Maggie—"

He got down on one knee beside my chair. I turned my head away, not wishing him to see my tears. "I am going to leave my secretary, Morton, here for the duration of your stay. I have rented a room on the top floor of this house. I do not like the idea of you three alone in this city, and I will rest easier knowing Morton is here. If you need to reach me at any time, he will know how to do so. Maggie, I need you to make a choice soon. If you do not..."

I expected him to say that if I did not choose the path he had selected for me, he would break off our relationship. When he did not say this, and when the silence continued, I finally turned to look at him. He was staring at me in sincere anguish.

"Maggie," he whispered brokenly. "I *need* you to choose…me… over this life."

Chapter Thirty-One
Maggie

Kate was furious with Dr. Kane.

"He is every bit as insufferable as Leah said," she raged. "How dare he moralize on our work? He spends small fortunes in search of new frozen bits of wasteland to name after himself! What good does that do for the world? Has he ever *met* Mrs. Pierce? She *needed* to talk to us!"

The president's wife had spent an hour brokenly recounting to us every abhorrent detail of the train wreck that had taken the life of her son. She had shared every sight and sound until we could almost smell and taste the smoke of the wreckage.

"No one else would listen to her," Kate reminded me urgently. "They told her not to dwell upon it. But she needed so desperately to speak of it, to express her horror and her grief. And yes, she *did* need to hear it wasn't her fault that she couldn't save the boy."

"But was it us who gave her that absolution—or was it her son?" I countered.

"Does it matter?" Kate said.

I used to think not, but Elisha had shaken my faith.

Washington quickly went from bad to worse. We lasted only three days past Elisha's departure, three miserable days culminating in a visit from a party of twelve congressmen who had come with their own "spirits" and were as drunk as they could be. They made mean, low remarks and plied us with the wine they had brought. I only pretended to sip at my glass, imagining what Elisha would say to find Kate and me and dear, silly Mother entertaining a crowd of drunken senators. To my horror, Kate drank right along with them until she was shrieking with laughter at their crude comments and flirting shamelessly. Mother looked on uselessly, distraught by the situation but unwilling to give these so-called guests any offense.

Finally, in desperation I sprang from my chair and fled the room. I lifted my skirts and took the stairs two at a time to the top of the boardinghouse, where I pounded on the bedchamber door of a man I had never met.

William Morton, Elisha's assistant, proved to be a thin, soft-spoken, bespectacled boy scarcely older than myself. My first impression was that he would not be up to the task, but his practical efficiency proved me wrong. Mr. Morton ejected our drunken guests by the simple expediency of sweeping their supply of spirits off our table and depositing them in the street outside. The men themselves followed, grumbling and complaining. Then, recognizing Kate's condition with a single glance, young Morton dispatched himself to the kitchen to prepare a restorative tisane.

I rounded on my mother. "We are finished here, Mother. We shall return to New York by the soonest train we can manage."

"What will Leah say?" my mother worried.

"If Leah had been here, those men would not have dared to insult us. They would have been escorted to the door in the first half hour." I was so angry I paced the room in agitation. Passing by my sister, I plucked the half-full glass from her hand and removed it to the sideboard. "Your behavior was atrocious!" I chastised.

Kate just giggled. "Leah's spirit is speaking through the medium!" she said and put her head upon the table.

When Mr. Morton returned, I informed him of my decision. "We will be leaving for New York tomorrow. Would it be possible for you to telegraph Dr. Kane and let him know our plans? I have a personal message to send him as well."

"Absolutely, Miss Fox," Morton said with a smile. "I'll be happy to make the travel plans for you. It was Dr. Kane's wish that I assist you in whatever needs you might have until you are safely home."

We waited until Morton had left, then Mother and I took Kate by the arms and helped her to bed. Once she was safely tucked between the sheets and already dozing, I turned with a sigh to my mother. "I am finished with this, Mother."

"Yes," she sighed, "we will leave tomorrow."

"No, I mean I am finished with the spirit business. Dr. Kane wishes me to give up rapping and has offered to send me to school for a lady's education. I have decided tonight to accept." Having spoken the words, I suddenly felt the weight of my decision, the release from my burden of deception.

Mother gasped. "Margaretta! What will Leah say? How can you turn your back on the spirits after all they have done for us?"

"I have given my whole life to the spirits for five years. I think I have done my part," I said to her wearily. "And I am tired.

Look at what happened here this evening. Look at Kate. Is this how I should live the rest of my life? Dr. Kane has urged me to engage myself to better things, and if I do so, he will make me his wife."

"You are over the age for schooling, and I should think you've had enough." Mother's lack of education had never concerned her. She truly did not conceive what there was in the world to learn.

"It's a finishing education he wants," I emphasized, "the kind that young ladies of fine families receive. Music and languages and manners, I expect…the sorts of subjects that will make me a fit wife for a doctor and scientist of his standing. You cannot imagine, Mother, that Dr. Kane's family would like to see his wife taking clients into his home for spirit rapping?"

"No, I guess not," she admitted. "They are a different sort of people."

"All I ask of you, Mother, is that you give your blessing to this, no matter what Leah has to say."

"If your mind is made up, Margaretta, then I will support your decision." Mother took a long, apprehensive breath. "No matter what Leah has to say."

⁂

Kate cried when she heard my plans during the train ride home the next day. She was pale and foul tempered, reaping the rewards of her flagrant overindulgence the night before. "He has turned you against us, that wretched man!"

"No, Kate, he hasn't." I tried to reason with her patiently, but I knew there was little use in her current state. "I am a grown woman now, and I have my own life to lead. If I am going to be a wife and a mother, I cannot continue in a calling that consumes my time and my energy. Marriage must be my new calling. When you meet your future husband, you will understand."

"If you were leaving us to get married, I could accept it," Kate said bitterly. "But he is sending you to a debutante's school. He thinks we are beneath him, and he wants it forgotten that you were ever a spirit medium."

Mother clucked her tongue at Kate. "It is only right that a wife should put aside her own interests for those of her husband," said the woman who had left her own spouse to follow her daughters into the spirit-rapping business. "Dr. Kane has no grief with our family. He is a devoted spiritualist himself."

Kate turned and gave me a sullen, knowing look while I frowned a warning at her. If Mother knew what Elisha really thought, I would lose her support.

Finally, Kate lay back upon the compartment bench and covered her eyes and aching head with a cool cloth. "I suppose Maggie will do whatever she wants, just as she always does," she said dismissively.

If that wasn't the pot calling the kettle black, I don't know what was.

*

We had apprised Leah of our early return by telegraph with only the briefest mention of the cause. Upon our arrival at her house, we found her anxious and worried but not angry. She was relieved to discover that we had strengthened our ties to General Thompson and Senator Tallmadge and was thrilled to hear that we had hosted a private sitting for Mrs. Pierce. But, considering the unruly nature of the balance of our visitors, she agreed it would have been unwise for us to remain any longer.

"I blame General Thompson," she said. "He should have screened your callers for you."

Leah's sympathy quickly vanished, however, when Mother abruptly announced the rest of our news. "Margaretta is done with the spirit rapping," she said, avoiding my eyes and speaking quickly, as if the decision was a burden she was eager to hand over. "Dr. Kane wants to send her to a finishing school, and she has agreed." This said, she and Kate promptly vanished, my sister with her migraine and my mother to nurse her.

I had rather hoped for a stronger show of support.

"I've been expecting this," Leah said, her voice calm but her eyes flashing irritation, "ever since that first letter of his. I am surprised and disappointed, however, that you would abandon us now, with Calvin so ill. Surely you can wait a few months."

"Dr. Kane is leaving for the Arctic in a few weeks," I explained. "He needs to make the arrangements before he departs."

"What kind of arrangements?" she asked shrewdly. "Is he setting you up in lodgings? How will he pay for the schooling?"

"He has not worked it out yet," I admitted, "but there will be no hint of impropriety! I have told him that I will not live in a place that he has paid for. I understand perfectly where that would lead, and how it would be perceived by others."

"I hope that you do! I have worried for some time that your unconventional understanding with this man would lead to the ruination of your reputation. His obsession with removing you from your family has worried me greatly."

"He is not *obsessed* with removing me from my family!" I objected. "But he wishes me to lead a life of greater respectability. I know you enjoy the respect that you have as a spirit medium, but as you have told me time and time again, it is not an acceptable occupation for a member of the Kane family."

"Even a hat shop would be an unacceptable occupation for the Kane family," Leah retorted. "They have no appreciation for the underclass, which makes its livelihood with the work of its hands. And if we did run a hat shop, I could replace you with a hired girl. But we cannot do without your rapping, Maggie. Kate is a talented young medium, but you bring a maidenly grace to the enterprise that is unique to yourself. The spirits are only half the attraction. The clients come because of *you*. Look at me, Maggie! Do you think that anyone would pay a dollar to spend an hour with me?"

My sister held out her arms with frank honesty and let me behold her with the cruel appraisal of my youth. The predilection for stoutness that was so apparent in my mother had begun to catch up with her, filling out her once bony figure. Her complexion, previously so rosy, had grown sallow from long, haggard days of nursing her husband, and her eyes were sunken in dark circles. At nearly forty years of age, she was no longer the "vivacious woman" described in the New York papers back in 1849, and I dropped my eyes with some measure of shame at my own analysis.

"Calvin's illness and the consequent interruption of business have placed us in arrears for this quarter's rent," Leah continued.

"Frankly, Maggie, we cannot afford to have you leave us at this time. It would be better for everyone if you waited until he returned from his trip—better for you, as well. You can't leave your family now, when he is about to sail off on this expedition. He could be gone for years." She tried to keep her expression neutral, but I could practically read the secret gleeful thought she was keeping to herself: *Perhaps he will never return.*

Anger flared within me that she could wish Elisha harm. "This is all about the money! You're not concerned for my well-being. You don't want the loss of income!"

"That income pays for the dress you are wearing and the roof over your head!" Leah snapped in ire. "What do you think—I'm using it to buy rings for my fingers and bells for my toes?"

"Well, bells perhaps. And collapsible poles," I returned smartly. "I am old enough to choose my own path. I thought you of all people would understand. By the time you were my age, you had already married and birthed a child."

"I had also been abandoned by my husband and divorced." Leah's voice took on the aggrieved tone she always used when speaking about her life. "By the time I was your age, I was struggling not to starve. You have no idea what true poverty means, Maggie. You grew up with a mother and a father, sufficiently fed, living in relative comfort. I did not."

I held up a hand in aggravation. Weary from the train ride, still dressed in my rumpled traveling clothes, I had no patience for her self-pity. "Please, Leah, spare me the speech about how poor you were. I've heard it all before. I could recite it from memory by the time I was nine years old." It was a mean and spiteful thing to say, mocking her hardship, and I regretted it almost at once.

Leah recoiled as if slapped, her face registering her deep offense. "What a fortunate child you were that it was only a tedious speech to you!" she retorted bitterly. "I, however, had to live it! You and Kate were never hungry. You never had to worry about where you would live or whether you would freeze to death in the winter for lack of heating. You were never spit upon, taken for a beggar's child."

"No, but I was shot at, taken for a witch!" I shouted.

Leah paused for a moment before replying, "I have not forgotten. Do you remember who came and fetched you out of there?"

I was struck silent by that, shame creeping upon my face. The truth was, I *had* forgotten how Leah had come to rescue me from that ordeal. And as much as I had tried to forget that torturous ride in the false-bottomed wagon, I knew my sister's embrace and calm, steady voice had kept me from losing my mind.

Leah pressed her advantage. "You are spoiled, Margaretta! You have no idea what I have done for you! You live now in the finest city in the world, having made a name for yourself that secures your invitation to the society of celebrated writers, singers, and political figures. You met the president's wife! You are fashionably dressed; you want for nothing. With the slightest smile of encouragement, you could have your pick of the eligible bachelors of New York. Who do you think acquired this position for you? Who planned it and worked for it? I could have left you in Hydesville, and where do you think you'd be now if I did? Probably scratching out a living on a dirt farm with an uneducated husband and two or three farm brats clutching at your skirts!"

"Do you want my gratitude or my servitude?" I asked peevishly. "You say you've given all this to me, but what kind of gift is it when I've provided the labor for it all along? Don't tell me it's for my benefit when you won't let me go now that I want to be married!"

"He'll never marry you."

"What?" I gasped, shocked by the statement, resentful of the implication.

Leah stepped toward me and leaned forward to stare me down. "Do you know what he sees in you? You are one of a kind, Maggie. You are not of his class, but you associate with people who are. You are keenly intelligent, witty, lively, attractive—and shrouded with mystery. You have a connection to a world other than our own; you provide answers for people from a place no one thought reachable. You touch lives with your gentleness and your practical sensibility and change them forever. You are as wild and mysterious to him as his precious North Pole."

I opened my mouth, trying to stammer some interruption, but Leah continued, inexorable and unstoppable. "Being a man, he desires to tame you, just as he seeks to chart his Arctic Sea. And if he succeeds in conforming you to the standard of his class, if he sends you to school for music and poise and polite conversation, what will he have?" Leah's eyes burned with antipathy and hatred. "A pale, common counterfeit. A blacksmith's daughter masquerading as a lady. All that makes you unique will be gone, and so will be the compelling attraction."

I had thought that I could hold my own against Leah, but the depth of her viciousness proved too much for me. Gathering my skirt, I darted around her and headed for the parlor door. She had shredded my feelings with the ease of a cat clawing through fine Italian lace, and I wanted nothing more than to beat a hasty retreat.

Just before I slammed the door closed, I heard her shout after me, "Mark my words, Maggie! He will never marry you!"

PART FOUR:
EDUCATION AND EXILE

Chapter Thirty-Two
Maggie

In the telegram I sent to Elisha from Washington, informing him of our return to New York, I had included a brief statement agreeing to his wishes. I soon received a telegram in return, expressing his delight and directing me to await further instructions in a forthcoming letter.

In the meantime, I lived uncomfortably in my sister's house. Relations between us were cool, and Leah did not speak to me any more than was necessary for daily living. I declined to participate in any spirit circles, instead withdrawing to my room or sitting by Calvin's bedside while the clients were in the house. By silent agreement, not one of us mentioned to Calvin the sudden rift between Leah and me. We would not have wanted to burden him with this unpleasantness, and in any case, he was far too absorbed in a struggle for his life to have wondered why I was no longer needed for the spirit sittings. I knew that Elisha was caught up in the frenzy of preparations for his journey, but still I chafed at the delay in his letter. Having made my decision, I was eager to get away from Leah's house. Even Kate had chilled in her demeanor toward me.

When the promised letter finally arrived, I discovered that Elisha understood the need to remove me from Leah's home as soon as possible:

I can imagine the awkwardness you feel, my darling. In order to expedite matters, I have consulted my aunt Eliza Leiper for advice, presenting you as a young woman of slight acquaintance whom I wish to assist in the matter of education. To further this notion, I have created a fund for your schooling and boarding that will be administered by my associate, Mr. Henry Grinnell, as a sponsorship. As far as my aunt is to know, I have only a scholarly interest in you, desiring to help you better your prospects with a fine education. Thus is your virtuous and maidenly character protected!

My aunt has written to inform me that she knows a perfect arrangement, and provisional to meeting you, she will secure this place and act as your advisor. She does insist upon an interview, but I have every confidence that my aunt will find you as irresistible as I do, darling little spirit! In fact, I suspect you will find each other exceedingly compatible company, as Aunt Eliza is known for her strong opinions on women's issues. My father detests her, but she is quite my favorite aunt, and she will undoubtedly find you up to her standards of intelligence and character.

I have employed a woman of respectable family to travel as your companion on the journey. You can expect the details to arrive by telegraph once the train tickets to Philadelphia are purchased. A carriage will meet you and your chaperone at the station to transport you to my aunt's residence. I will meet you there to smooth over introductions and, of course, to reward myself for weeks of intensive labor with the pleasure of your company.

I shared the plans with my mother, and although she seemed confused and bewildered by Elisha's complicated arrangement, she agreed that all proprieties had been met. With Mother's consent, I telegraphed my readiness for travel back to Philadelphia and awaited further instructions. Leah feigned indifference to my plans, and Kate was still offended by my defection, so my departure within two weeks' time seemed like deliverance from a house of unfriendly strangers.

My companion, a distant relation of the Grinnells named Miss Walters, was a dour woman of about thirty years with a lazy eye and a gloomy disposition. She had clearly not been hired for her conversational skills, and so the journey passed in awkward silence. In spite of Elisha's reassurances, I was anxious about meeting his aunt. I did not know what to make of his concurrent statements that we would find each other exceedingly compatible and that his father detested the woman. It did not bode well for the chances of Judge Kane liking me!

The efficient Mr. Morton met our train in Philadelphia and ushered us to the waiting carriage. Another long, dull passage ensued, with neither my chaperone nor Elisha's secretary feeling the need to fill the intervening time with discourse.

The Leiper house proved to be a pleasant country residence on partially wooded property. Its most wonderful and welcoming attribute was the sight of Elisha waiting for us on the veranda, his feet upon the railing while he wrote in his ever-present daybook. As the carriage turned into the grounds, he sprang from his seat and hurried down the front steps to meet us. I had to remind myself sternly not to cast myself from the carriage and into his arms, for here we would be mentor and prodigy, two persons connected only by charitable kindness.

As it was, he handed me down from the carriage with a scarcely concealed impudent grin. "Good day, Miss Fox. I trust your journey was pleasant?"

"More so in the ending than in the living of it, but I am here now and well, thank you, Doctor." I withdrew my hand and walked beside him.

"It is so very good to see you," he went on, and then added in a whisper, "I only wish that there was a crypt on the grounds, so that we might take a tour."

"Hush, you," I murmured back. "I must meet your aunt. Do not distract me!"

"Do you wish to retire to your room, to freshen yourself after your trip?"

"No," I said breathlessly, "I would like to meet her at once. Or… do you think I need to change?" I looked down over my attire, searching for rumples and stains.

"No, no," he assured me. "You are the loveliest thing I have seen in days. She is waiting for you in the upstairs sitting room."

I had formed a definite image of Miss Eliza Leiper in my mind, based on Elisha's description. Thus, I was surprised to find myself introduced to a tiny and delicate lady who scarcely reached my shoulder in height. She was dressed in a modest and subdued gown of dark green, which complemented her hair, still golden although streaked with gray. I searched for a resemblance to Elisha but could not find one, save, perhaps, in the keen intensity of her gaze.

Our conversation progressed haltingly at first. After the usual pleasantries about the weather and my trip, Miss Leiper inquired about my previous education, which was unimpressive and rather embarrassing in its brevity. I did mention that my sister Kate had attended a prestigious school in New York under the sponsorship of Mr. Horace Greeley, which Miss Leiper found interesting.

When this subject had been wrung of all potential substance, I groped for an appropriate topic and finally asked whether Miss Leiper was acquainted with Amy Post. Miss Leiper was surprised to discover my close relationship with Mrs. Post and was equally impressed by my acquaintance with Elizabeth Cady Stanton and Lucretia Mott. Before long, I had turned the interview on its head and was asking Miss Leiper questions about her work in the cause of women's suffrage. Miss Leiper was an outspoken conversationalist, and Elisha beamed to see us getting on so well. He made several attempts to join in the discourse, but he was so misinformed about the movement and its goals that we all three ended up laughing at his woeful ignorance.

A pleasant hour passed in this manner, and I was entirely at my ease when Miss Leiper finally turned to her nephew and said, "Elisha, I am going to ask you to leave us now. I would like a few words with Miss Fox on her own."

"As you wish, Aunt Eliza," he replied, smiling broadly. "I shall go downstairs and bother the cook about tea. I imagine the end result of all this feminist talk will be just this—that the ladies remain to discuss political agendas while the men fetch refreshments!" He rose and favored each of us with a graceful bow, although I got a wink with mine, and he departed, gently closing the door behind him.

I broke off gazing fondly after him and turned back to my hostess, only to find her shrewd gaze fixed upon me.

"Let us dispense with the pretense, shall we?" she said in a pleasant but businesslike tone. "Elisha has never been a skillful liar, not even when he was a child. And besides, I have a letter from my nephew Robert Patterson and his wife informing me of his relationship with you."

I dropped my eyes in surprise but then raised them and faced her steadily. "It was not our purpose to deceive you, Miss Leiper. Dr. Kane only wished to safeguard my reputation. Everything besides the extent of our acquaintance is true. I wish to renounce my ties with spiritualism and acquire an education that will improve my life. Dr. Kane wishes this also."

"What are his intentions for you?" she asked.

"If I give up spirit rapping and dedicate myself to a proper education, he has pledged that on his return from the Arctic he will announce our engagement and we shall be wed."

"And the ring you wear on your hand?" She indicated it with a wave.

"It is his promise to me."

"I am glad to hear it," she said. "I was afraid after reading the Pattersons' letter that I was being asked to condone an unsuitable situation."

I admit that I was hurt, for I had liked the congenial Mr. Patterson and his cultured wife and thought they returned the affection. "They do not approve of me?" I asked dolefully.

"On the contrary, they were charmed by you, surprisingly so. Now that I have met you, I can better understand. You are a remarkably appealing young woman, and I can see why the Pattersons were concerned for your well-being. It was Elisha's actions that worried them, not your suitability. They did not wish to see you injured by his rather overzealous pursuit of you."

"I cannot imagine that Dr. Kane would ever knowingly injure me," I protested.

"Perhaps not," she said. "But I am accustomed to speaking in a direct manner, and I hope that you are a steady enough girl to hear the truth."

I smiled. "I am quite used to frankness, Miss Leiper, and would not have it any other way."

"Then indulge me while I divert momentarily from the topic. My nephew was quite ill as a young man, expected to die even, although he confounded all the experts by surviving. You know this?" I nodded and she went on. "Since that time, he has reached out for everything he wanted in life with both hands and refused to let go. He finished his education, joined the navy, and traveled the world. Over the years, I have seen Elisha driven by ambition, obsessed by his goals, and exultant in his achievements."

Miss Leiper leaned forward in her chair, her hands folded in her lap, and impaled me with her keen gaze. "But I have never seen him as happy as he is today. I have never seen him laugh so readily, especially not at himself. For these things alone I would approve of you, Miss Fox, even if you were a one-legged dipsomaniac with a glass eye! But, in fact, you are lovely and vivacious, intelligent and witty. I cannot think of a single thing to which I would object if I were Elisha's mother. But therein lies the trouble that prompted the Pattersons to write me."

I sighed. "I suppose they believe his parents will not approve of the match."

Miss Leiper shook her head. "You do not understand. Elisha would rather not tell you this, but I believe it would be a cruel disservice to mislead you. He has already asked his parents for permission to introduce you at their home. They refused. In fact, they have forbidden him from bringing you to Rensselaer."

I felt suddenly sick. Trembling a little, I bent my head in shame and distress. My hands were twisting the fabric of my skirt, and I forced myself to release the grip and lay them flat. "I did not know I was so unacceptable," I whispered. "I am sorry."

"There is no need to apologize to me," she said sharply. "It is I who should apologize for my sister, but I take no responsibility for her behavior. And I cannot regret telling you the truth, for it is essential that you know the entire situation before you commit yourself to any action. Elisha has rejected numerous young ladies from fine Philadelphia families who have been thrown at him over the years and has taken up with a spirit rapper. His parents view this behavior as a deliberate slight against them and hope that you are a temporary infatuation that will pass in time. For myself, I withheld judgment, wishing to meet you, see you together, and determine your suitability for my nephew on your own merits."

"And what have you decided?" I asked, blinking back my tears and marveling at how unexpected it was that my sister Leah and Elisha's parents should be so closely aligned in their opinions.

Unexpectedly, Miss Leiper rose from her chair and crossed the room to sit beside me. She took my hand in a gentle manner and patted it kindly. "My dear, you appear to be a wonderful remedy for my nephew's intensity. Perhaps you will do what no one else has managed to do and provide him a reason to cease his endless wanderings. But I wonder, is he good for you? Tell me, Miss Fox, if you knew there was a chance that Judge Kane and his wife would not accept you even after Elisha put you through this schooling, would you still go through with it?"

"That would be deeply distressing," I admitted, "but I have already given my heart to your nephew, and it is far too late to ask for it back. If Dr. Kane is resolved on this course of action, and if he wishes me to attend this school, then I shall do so, whatever the outcome."

She nodded approvingly. "It seems that my talent at judging character is as astute as ever. So, Elisha, you can come in now."

This last was said without the slightest change of tone in her voice. I looked at the closed door and then back at my hostess in uncertainty. "Miss Leiper, he went downstairs," I told her gently.

"Nonsense. He's listening behind the door. Come in now, and bring the tea."

For about three seconds more the door remained resolutely closed. Then, hesitantly, with some embarrassment, it opened and a sheepish Elisha appeared around the edge of it. "Can't you leave a man his dignity, Aunt?" he asked. When he saw me blotting my eyes with my handkerchief, he swiftly crossed the room and plunked the tea tray on a side table. "Aunt Eliza!" he protested.

"Now, Elisha, your young lady is completely unharmed," his aunt assured him. "Pour out the tea for us and we shall discuss her future."

It seemed that Miss Leiper had chosen not a school for me but a private tutor. She was recommending a woman named Susanna Turner. On Miss Leiper's recommendation, Mrs. Turner was willing to take me on as a boarder in her home and provide an education tailored to my needs.

"To discourage gossip," she said, "it would be best to cast Elisha as a disinterested benefactor, but I think that I can improve upon your story. We shall say that Miss Fox was recommended to me by Mrs. Post and that Elisha has helped to set up a fund for her education merely to please me. That should be enough for Mrs. Turner, and if no one sees how you look at each other, it might even be believed."

The next two days passed by blissfully. Except for a brief jaunt taken with Miss Leiper to meet my prospective tutor in the neighboring town of Crooksville, I spent my days with Elisha, enjoying the spell of fine weather on the Leiper estate. It was heavenly to live for a time in the same house as my love, to take meals together and know that he was always somewhere nearby. Accompanied by the lumpish Miss Walters, we enjoyed long walks on the property. Elisha shared his boyhood memories, pointing out his favorite place for fishing and the tree from which his brother had fallen and broken an arm.

For this fleeting interval, the outside world had no hold on us, although I knew that the Arctic expedition lingered in the background, ready to extend its icy grip and drag him back. In the end, however, it was not his life that intruded but my own.

On the third afternoon, I was reading aloud to Miss Leiper with Elisha seated on a footstool by my side, his head resting against my chair, when Morton knocked apologetically upon the door.

"A telegram has arrived for Miss Fox," he said.

Elisha jumped to his feet and accepted the telegram on my behalf as naturally as if he were already my husband. "Thank you, Morton," he said, neatly slitting open the message with his pocketknife.

I lay down Miss Leiper's book expectantly and waited while Elisha looked over the paper. It was not until I saw his shoulders drop and his face lose its cheerful animation that I realized what the message had to be. I knew it before he spoke. "Maggie, your sister's husband…"

I gasped aloud in sudden guilt, realizing that it had been days since I had given him a thought. "Oh, Calvin!" I cried. "Poor Calvin!"

"I am so sorry, my darling," Elisha said, dropping to one knee beside me.

I took the telegram from his hands and read it, tears spilling freely. "Oh, my poor family!" I looked up at Elisha. "They are taking him to Rochester for the services. I shall have to leave at once and join them."

He hesitated, looking stricken. "I hadn't planned on you returning to your family," he said. "I thought you would start with Mrs. Turner as soon as I left here. But I suppose you will have to go. In fact," he took my hand, "I will go with you."

"Oh, Ly, will you?" I cried gratefully.

"Of course," he said. "Some day it will be my family, too."

Chapter Thirty-Three
Kate

On the evening Calvin died, a portent lit the sky in the form of a shooting star. It crossed the black patch of night outside my window, and I sat up in bed at once, knowing what had happened. Hurriedly, I put on my dressing gown and went down one floor to my sister's bedchamber, where I found her trembling and shaken, drained of all color. "He has left us," she whispered to me hoarsely, "just now." Her hand was still upon his brow, which grew cold and still beneath her touch.

His spirit, I knew, was at peace, well content for having lived four years past his projected death—and married to the woman he loved besides. So I wept only for our sadness, that we would no longer have him among us.

Leah decided that Calvin should be laid to rest in his hometown, and the city of Rochester offered a sympathetic welcome home to its beloved mediums. The Posts opened their home to us, and Calvin's casket lay there for two days while all our good friends came to pay their respects.

Maggie arrived shortly after us. We were glad for her presence, but relations between us could best be described as strained. Leah and Maggie had argued bitterly on the day we returned from Washington, and neither one had gotten over it. Maggie confessed to me that she would not soon forgive the things Leah had said, while Leah told me that Maggie had mocked her in a high-handed manner that could have been learned from only one source.

Dr. Kane himself had come with Maggie to Rochester. Leah tolerated his presence for the sake of dignity and respect for the occasion of our gathering. For his part, Dr. Kane was civil and kind to her, in a cool, bloodless way. They spoke to one another as little as possible—and only with the barest truths.

"I was saddened to hear of Mr. Brown's passing," Dr. Kane said to her upon his arrival.

"Mr. Brown would be touched by your sentiment" was Leah's reply.

For all his talk of a secret engagement, the doctor took no pains to hide his feelings. He stood with the family when greeting guests and often placed his hand familiarly on Maggie's shoulder. No one who saw them together could mistake the relationship between them. My sister Maggie was, as always, the light at the center of the room. Even dressed in mourning black, with her usual bell-like voice pitched low, she possessed more life and color than half the people in the room. Men were drawn to her like bees to a bright flower, and women could not feel jealous of her, for she was so earnest and friendly. Falling in love had flushed her with a joy she could not suppress, even on this sad occasion, but I thought that among all of us, Calvin would have been most pleased to see her this way. He had been a secret romantic, our quiet and bashful foster brother.

I only wondered: If Dr. Kane had his way, would the bright light of my sister's spirit be snuffed out? Would her lively mannerisms and wit be squashed beneath a weight of respectability, so that she faded in among the empty women of society, reserved and lifeless? How could he profess to love our Maggie and still wish to change her? Leah had choice words to say on this subject, and I had heard them aplenty. For my part, I had been fond of the doctor until he had called me a fraud, but even now it was hard to hold a grudge. Like Maggie, he possessed an irresistible charm. He would not be a bad brother, I thought, as long as he did not use his flame to put Maggie's out.

He brought me a cup of tea while I stood at the casket. "It is a shame," Dr. Kane said. "He was still a young man."

"He was only thirty-three," I replied. "But, of course, he was deathly ill a few years ago and expected to die then. The doctors said it was a miracle he lived this long."

Dr. Kane started, and suddenly looked more closely at the man in the casket. The teacup in his hand rattled in its saucer, and I reached out to take it, watching him curiously.

"They said the same of me," he murmured, almost too softly to hear. Then, louder, "He never fully regained his health, did he?"

"He had frequent relapses," I confirmed, sipping at the tea and looking back and forth between Calvin's gray, shrunken features and the suddenly pale countenance of Dr. Kane. The chatter of voices in the room behind us seemed to fade away from my hearing. For that moment, we two and the dead man beside us were the only people in the world.

"Are you all right?" I asked, my own voice sounding tinny and small.

"Yes, quite. I'm fine," the doctor said automatically, his eyes fixed with horror on the casket. But he was not fine. He was seeing his own death upon him, and as I watched him shudder at the thought, I saw it, too.

A shadow passed over him, such as might be made by a reflection in a window that obscures the image beyond the glass. I saw him in his casket, his face waxen with death, haggard and ravaged by illness that left him, like Calvin, old before his time. Then the real man turned away from the coffin, his ghostly image dispersing like tendrils of mist, and with a resolute set to his jaw, Dr. Kane crossed boldly to Maggie's side.

Taking her hand, he drew her out into the center of the room. Interrupted in midconversation, Maggie tilted her head in puzzlement, her eyes searching his face with concern. Addressing the room, Dr. Kane abruptly began to speak of the brevity of life and the precious gift of love. He rambled, making little sense and seeming quite addled in his thoughts, although some of the people who guessed where this muddled monologue was leading began to smile among themselves.

Finally, calling upon the gathering of friends and family to witness his word, he pledged his love to Maggie and swore before all present that he would marry her on his return from the Arctic. Maggie beamed with joy, her face flushing prettily, but the doctor seemed nearly broken by emotion. "I will be true to you," he vowed, his voice choked with feeling, "until death."

Well-wishers closed in among them, although Leah did not, clearly outraged to have her widowhood overshadowed by the happy couple. And I hung back near poor Calvin, shaking in dread.

She was my dearest sister, for all that he had taken her away from us. How could I tell her that I had seen a vision of him in his coffin?

So I huddled with a cup of stone-cold tea by the side of my dead brother and shivered miserably all to myself—cursing my gift.

Chapter Thirty-Four
Maggie

After Calvin's funeral and burial in Rochester, Leah announced that she, Mother, and Kate would be continuing on to Hydesville, where they would visit with the family. "Are you coming or not?" she demanded with her usual bluntness.

I wanted to go, of course, but felt obliged to consult Elisha. Unexpectedly, he gave his blessings. "Go, spend time with your family before you move to Mrs. Turner's. I have a dozen things waiting in New York that need my immediate attention. I will see you once more in the city when you return from Hydesville, and it is there we will have our good-byes. I cannot bear to think of them now."

My brave, bold explorer had been highly emotional for days and, in fact, had unexpectedly proposed marriage to me before the entire congregation of family and friends at Amy Post's house. This led me to tease him a bit afterward, remarking that crypts and wakes seemed to bring out his true romantic nature! In truth, however, I realized that he was suffering apprehension about his upcoming voyage, a sentiment I heartily shared. We had spoken at great length about the future we would enjoy after his return, but we had avoided the topic that preyed upon both our minds: the chance that he would not return at all.

I was not the least bit surprised when Elisha insisted that he still wanted to keep our engagement discreet, even though he had announced it publicly at the Posts' house. "I do not think there is anyone left for me to tell," I said wryly. However, I knew that although Elisha spoke his intentions freely among my acquaintances, he was strictly closemouthed to his own family.

⌘

We returned to New York in the early days of May after three weeks in the country only to find that Elisha had suddenly been called to Philadelphia. I had missed him by only a day. A traveling trunk had been delivered to Leah's house at Elisha's behest, and I began to pack my belongings with a heavy heart.

"I guess I'll be taking you with me," I said to Lovey, my little canary bird. His constant twittering was a nuisance, but I would not have wanted Elisha to know that his gift was unappreciated. Mother and Kate had refused to keep him, and Leah said she would pop him into a stew if I left him behind. "I just hope Mrs. Turner doesn't have a cat," I teased him.

There was nothing else for me to do. I would not depart for Crooksville until I had the chance to see Elisha. Leah and Kate recommenced their spirit sittings, from which I excluded myself. I tried to fill my days with letter writing, reading, and social calls. Mostly, however, I brooded over Elisha's impending departure.

The *Advance* would sail from New York Harbor at the end of May, heading to Newfoundland. From there, it would make its way to Greenland and push northward, along the frozen coast of that wasteland. I traced the route with my finger on one of the maps Elisha had left for me, past settlements with strange names like Fiskenes and Upernavik until the map trailed off into speculation, sketched in by Elisha with only his best guesses.

Although he had been planning this trip since before I met him, delays with supplies and disappointments in funding had caused a mad scramble of frantic activity in the final weeks. The expedition needed to be under way in time to take advantage of the short Arctic summer. In addition, news of a competing British expedition had driven Elisha mad with jealous rivalry. In spite of its established goal of finding the missing Franklin mission, it could not be denied that the second Grinnell Expedition was foremost a journey of exploration. The desire for fame consumed him. If he were able to discover the fate of Franklin or prove the existence of an open polar sea with Arctic lands above it, he would be hailed as the most celebrated explorer of our day.

For my part, however, I could not look at the blank stretches of the polar map without a deep, primal fear. Something in that desolate void had swallowed two British ships and all their crew without a trace. My beloved Elisha could vanish just as easily into that unknown.

Scarcely two weeks before his planned departure, my fiancé returned to New York and came to see me. He arrived wearing his navy uniform and carrying two packages under his arm, one small and the other twelve inches square. Immediately I noticed that he moved with a greatly restrained and impatient energy, like an overwound clock mechanism. Still, he greeted me warmly with an embrace and his usual whispered endearments. The smaller package proved to be a gift to me, a book of verse in which Elisha had inscribed little messages and comments. The larger one, as I had guessed, was his present to himself, the portrait of me. I had finished sitting for it the week before my Washington trip, but I had never seen the completed work.

The girl in the painting was a fragile and delicate creature who resembled me in some superficial features and might have been a romanticized ideal of my person. I bit back a comment that my alter-image looked pale and ready to faint, as if her corset had been fastened too tightly, because Elisha had paid for it and he was greatly pleased. "My Darling Little Spirit," he called the portrait fondly. "This will never leave my side until God brings me back to you!" Smiling appreciatively, I only hoped that this shy and swan-necked girl did not so overtake his affection that the rosy-cheeked sturdiness of the original disappointed him upon his return!

We enjoyed a quiet supper. He entertained us with anecdotes of his travels during the past weeks, recounting amusing antics of fellow train passengers and frustrating experiences with railroad timetables. As much as possible, he avoided speaking of the journey yet to come; nevertheless, it overshadowed everything he said. After the meal, Mother shooed us out the door, encouraging us to stroll around the block to the bakery, from where she had asked us to acquire a small cake. Elisha arranged a cloak around my shoulders and folded my arm into his own as we stepped down into the street.

We did not hurry, even though the air was brisk and the light was fading with the onset of evening. "I did not want to make overmuch of our parting," he confessed to me as we walked. "But seeing you tonight, I only know that I am about to leave you, and I realize how very, very much I love you."

"I have been frightened," I admitted. "And I have been despondent. But those are my own failings, for I have never seen you unsuccessful at anything you have desired to achieve. You will undoubtedly find what you seek and return in triumph. I will not mar your departure with tears nor have you remember me for the next year for my red and swollen eyes!"

"A year is a long time," he reflected solemnly. "You won't forget me, will you Maggie? Marry some other young swain who catches your eye while I am gone?"

I smiled up into his face. "You know I could not."

"No," he said complacently. "You hold half of my soul and I hold half of yours. It is only when we are together that each one of us is complete."

We returned to the house with a luscious lemon cake, which Mother served to us in the parlor with coffee. When at last the time came for Elisha to make his departure, Mother rose from her seat and motioned Kate to the door. "It is a little irregular," she said, giving us a knowing smile, "but, then, your circumstance is a bit irregular, what with Dr. Kane's voyage and a lengthy separation to face. After all, you *are* engaged, so I think a few minutes of privacy would not be unreasonable!" She followed my sister to the door and—after cooing back over her shoulder, "Just a few minutes, mind you"—closed it behind her, leaving us entirely alone.

It can be safely said that those few minutes were well spent, although the tears came after all, and my eyes were indeed red and swollen when he left.

⤜⟡⤛

The next morning Mother and I left New York by train. I was listless and useless after a long night of weeping into my pillow. It was for this reason that I was careless with my luggage and did not realize until the train was well under way that I had left the birdcage with my canary sitting on the floor of the terminal. This new loss set about a fresh round of wailing that Mother could not subdue. "It cannot be helped now, Margaretta!" she kept saying, obviously confounded that I should grieve so much for a bird that had annoyed us all. But Lovey had been a gift from Elisha, and to lose him so thoughtlessly seemed a terrible betrayal. Nothing would comfort me, and I immediately began to compose a tear-stained letter to Elisha confessing my sin, which I posted upon our arrival in Philadelphia.

There was little conversation on the trip, due to my moroseness and Mother's waning tolerance for it. She was still dressed in the deepest black, mourning her son-in-law just as if he had been her own flesh and blood. Her reproach could not have been clearer: my loss could not compare with Leah's, and my continued self-pity was unseemly.

Neither of us was cheered by the sight of the picturesque Turner home with its handsome trees and welcoming piazza covered in honeysuckle vine. Despite hearty greetings from Mr. and Mrs. Turner, we expressed our desire to promptly turn in for the night.

I cannot imagine what Mrs. Turner thought of us, but in her kind-heartedness she forgave us any breach of courtesy and ushered us to our beds. The next morning Mother announced her intention to return at once, and Mr. Turner drove her to Philadelphia himself.

My first week at the Turners was a dark and gloomy one. The weather turned gray and wet, trapping us indoors and drowning the cheerful little honeysuckle blossoms on the piazza. I was tearful and distraught, which Mrs. Turner took for homesickness. In actuality, I was numbering each day until Elisha's departure. There had been no letter from him since my arrival, which probably only indicated his intensive involvement in readying his ship but seemed to me an early taste of the silence I could expect when his expedition disappeared into the North.

On the last Saturday in May, only four days before the scheduled departure of the *Advance*, I was listlessly applying myself to scales on Mrs. Turner's piano. Rain streamed down the windows in a torrent, and so it was rather a surprise when my tutor opened the door to the sitting room and called out, "Miss Fox, here's a guest come to visit you!"

I straightened up and turned around, expecting that Miss Leiper may have come to see me settled in with the Turners.

Instead, standing in the doorway, dressed in a dripping uniform with a self-satisfied grin, was Elisha. He had one hand on the door-frame, and in the other he held up a birdcage, slightly battered and worse for wear but still containing that endlessly twittering canary!

"Oh, Lovey!" I cried, at the last moment substituting the bird's name for his own. I overturned the piano stool in my rush to the door, but then, unable to fling myself into his arms, came to a stop just in front of him and covered my face with my hands. Mrs. Turner must have thought me a brainless fool, watching me sob so heartily for a silly bird.

"The little wanderer has returned to the fold!" Elisha announced, unable to squelch his glee at surprising me. "Make it an evidence of my thoughtful attention to your every need, Miss Fox, and an omen of my own eventual homecoming."

Chapter Thirty-Five
Maggie

On Tuesday, the last day in May 1853, Elisha sailed away from New York in command of his first ship, the *Advance*, on a route to Greenland by way of Newfoundland. The newspapers were full of the story, even in Crooksville. Even before he had accomplished anything at all, Elisha Kent Kane was a hero, a dashing adventurer who had already captured the hearts of Americans with his great feats.

For me, he was a hopeless romantic who had given up a night's sleep amid all his important occupations to bring me a lost bird, one that he had located by the simple expedient of advertising a reward. I was simultaneously overjoyed and embarrassed by this diversion of his attention to duty. "I am shamed to have been so careless," I agonized to him. "I have dragged you away from your ship and your preparations! Everyone who needs you aboard the *Advance* must be furious!"

"I account to no one for my whereabouts," Elisha reminded me. "I am the commander. Besides, I was wishing for a handy excuse…I wanted to see you here, to know by my own observation that you were well and happy. Your mother told me that it was a tear-filled journey."

"I was distraught," I admitted. "But the Turners have been nothing but kind. Their home is lovely and welcoming, and I am content to be at my studies." I turned to Mrs. Turner at this point, to acknowledge her presence and my gratitude, and I was startled to find her observing me shrewdly. It had not escaped her notice that the despondent, weepy student in her house was suddenly flushed with color and come alive with animation.

"I am pleased to be able to depart knowing that you are comfortable and contented," Elisha said.

He stayed only long enough for tea, then departed in his hired carriage for Philadelphia to return by train to his point of origin. All those hours of travel for an afternoon's visit! I tried making a lame explanation to Mrs. Turner regarding his kindly patronage and true friendship.

She was having none of it. "I hope you will pardon me if I am being too forward, Miss Fox, but it is plain to anyone with eyes to see that Dr. Kane holds you in tender regard."

I sighed. "People keep telling us that." That was the end of keeping any secret from Mrs. Turner. It was a relief to admit my feelings, and on Saturday, when we knew the *Advance* was under way, I did not have to hide my tears.

"Now, now, Miss Fox," my tutor comforted me, "you just look at that canary and remember what Dr. Kane said."

<hr />

I lived for letters.

It was not to say that the Turner house was unpleasant. Although I was a paying boarder, I had not been brought up to idleness, and so

I helped with the household duties. My studies had been chosen by Elisha with my consultation, and so were precious to me—in theory. However, in practice, it could not be denied that I had never been a diligent student. I loved to read, but only the things that pleased me, and submitting to another's tutelage at my age chafed a bit.

Letters from Kate came regularly, describing her lively activities in New York with spiritualists and artists and intellectuals. There were letters from Mother as well, badly spelled and filled with inane details of the lives of people scarcely known to me. Still, I read them and was glad for the occupation. Leah was silent by post, thus making known her displeasure at my defection.

Most precious of all were the letters from Elisha. They arrived in Crooksville weeks and weeks after they had been written. By the time they reached my hands, Elisha had already passed out of the known, inhabited regions of Greenland and into the frozen silence of the North. Therefore, it was with some faint shivers of dread that I read his hearty descriptions of the Atlantic passage, his crew, and the outposts of southern Greenland, knowing that for him, these events were long past. I only hoped that during the very same moments that I was reading his treasured letters he was safe and well and somehow sensing my love for him.

⤞⤝

The summer of 1853 passed in a kind of torture by pleasantries, scholarship, and a handful of outdated letters, creased and worn by constant rereading. The lovely and rustic Turner house mocked me with its charm, which had concealed at first its devastating isolation from the world I loved.

As for Mrs. Turner, having learned the true purpose for my education, she decided to include extra tutelage in deportment, to teach me to blend in with the society of the Kane family. "No extra charge," she chirped amiably. One of the first things she wished to change was my outspoken belief in such social reforms as abolition and women's suffrage.

"A lady should be well informed and capable of speaking intelligently on politics, religion, and social issues," Mrs. Turner instructed, "but hold no strong opinions of her own."

"But Mrs. Turner," I objected, "I have never noticed Miss Leiper to hold back her own opinions."

Mrs. Turner pursed her lips as she considered the most tactful way to reply. Finally, she said, "Miss Leiper was born into an illustrious and well-respected family. You, Miss Fox, were not. Miss Leiper has no need, or dare I say interest, in winning the acceptance of anyone. You do. And I might mention that for all her breeding and social standing, Miss Leiper never married. Therefore, one might assume that her plainspoken viewpoints may not have been well received even by her own peers."

I rather thought that Miss Leiper's maiden status was by her own choice, but Mrs. Turner had made her point.

Spiritualism, too, came under fire from my tutor, and not for the reasons one might think. "I express no opinion on messages from the spirit world," she told me frankly. "I care not whether they are a miracle or a hoax. But I will tell you that any activity that places men and women together in a darkened room is a shocking breach of propriety and must be avoided at all costs!"

The green vegetation of the Pennsylvanian summer grew brown and dry through August and then flourished briefly again in the chill damp of September. I despised it in all colors, and with the autumn came a hay fever that brought me low with new misery. I am sure the Turners found me terrible company, and I know that my tutor was vexed by the growing number of excuses that kept me from my work. Toothaches and chest ailments provided one delay after another, not to mention pure peevishness. I was not proud of my behavior, but I had no more control of it than I did my own life anymore.

I spent hours locked in my room, reading all my old letters from Elisha and writing new missives of my own, which I burned when finished. Knowing that he would never read my words, I railed at him for imprisoning me here, for selfishly pursuing his own ambition while caging me as securely as the little canary he had given me. On other days, I poured my unending and undying love for him across the page. I was nineteen years old, soon to turn twenty, and I was dying by degrees of loneliness and despair.

Just when things seemed blackest, when I imagined the early winter ices closing in upon Elisha and dooming me to eternal emptiness, Kate, my darling sister and my closest friend, reached out her hand to me in my isolation and beckoned me to her:

> You must come to us in New York. We have the most delicious
> opportunity to demonstrate our spiritual talents! I know that you
> will not take part, but I cannot bear to think of you pining away in

the country alone without your family. You need not rap nor sit in circles with us, but you must come!

The New York Tribune has offered a reward of $500 to any spiritualist who can prove his or her power to communicate with the other world. Leah has decided to accept this challenge. There are other mediums who will gather in New York for this opportunity, including the Davenport brothers. I expect the entertainment of watching the others will be just as satisfying as proving myself.

I know you will say that Dr. Kane would not approve. I know you will say that Mrs. Turner will not release you from your studies and the Grinnells will not permit you to live under Leah's roof. I have taken measures to overcome all these objectors—save, of course, Elisha, who is quite out of my reach. Still, he who loves you would not want to see you so unhappy. He would let you come and visit with your darling sister (me) as long as you promised to avoid the influence of the Tigress (Leah). Have I judged him rightly?

Bear up, dear Maggie, and await rescue. You will know it when it arrives.

With love,

Kate

I did not know what to make of her letter, although the tantalizing thought of spending the rest of the year in the city with Kate and a flurry of social engagements lifted my hopes. I did not see what she could do to influence Mrs. Turner or Henry and Cornelius Grinnell, but if I had learned anything in all the years since 1848, it was to not underestimate my little sister.

The letters, when they arrived, caused Mrs. Turner some distress. "I wish you had told me, Maggie," she said to me with some indignation, "that your mother has been begging you to come to New York. It makes me seem like a tyrant for not allowing you a visit, when in fact you never even asked me!"

"I am sorry, Mrs. Turner," I replied contritely, feeling my way carefully because I was not privy to the contents of the letter in her hand. "I wanted to do better in my studies. I know that my progress has been slow this fall, as I've been ill so often."

"But if your mother has been pining for a visit and her doctor will not allow her to travel…You never told me she suffered from the gout."

"It comes and goes," I said weakly.

"And here is a letter from Mr. Grinnell imploring me to release you for a month's visit. Release you! As if I had you locked up here! Really, Maggie, this is most unfair. If you had told me about your mother's condition, she certainly would have had no reason to write Mr. Grinnell and ask for his permission."

"No, you are right, Mrs. Turner," I agreed. "I never meant to imply that you would not let me go, only that I wished to honor my promises to Dr. Kane."

"Mr. Grinnell has arranged for you to stay with a Mrs. Ellen Walters rather than at your sister's home. He says that her daughter has chaperoned you in the past." She put down the letter in her hand in order to pick up the other one, the one from Mr. Grinnell.

"Oh, yes, she was a lovely and charming young lady," I lied, casually moving over to take a peek at the letter from "my mother." As I had suspected, it was written by Kate.

I looked up at my tutor earnestly. "I will make it up to you, Mrs. Turner. I will be sure to write my thanks to Mr. Grinnell and let him know that the fault for neglecting my mother is entirely mine." I smiled. "And I promise to study ever so hard while I am gone."

⁂

By the middle of October, I found myself back in New York, seated in the stately home of Charles Partridge, a match factory owner and devoted spiritualist, awaiting a demonstration by the Davenport brothers, the newest team of sibling mediums in the state of New York. Mr. Partridge had kindly offered to host this affair for reporters and interested spiritualists on the week before the official tests.

My return to the city had been a genuine surprise to my mother. She, of course, knew nothing of the letters she had supposedly written to arrange my visit but was nonetheless happy to see me. I was indeed expected to stay at the house of Ellen Walters, the mother of the woman who had served as my chaperone in the spring. Leah was insulted by this slight and blamed Elisha for the offense, despite the fact that he was hundreds of miles away and knew nothing about the arrangement. My relation with Leah was more strained than ever, and my presence at Mr. Partridge's gathering was only barely tolerated.

Being there at all was a matter of some ambiguity. I was attending a spiritualist event, although not as a participant. The Grinnells would have been displeased, and Elisha would not have approved, but technically I was breaking no promises. I was so happy to be in society again that I had no intention of missing out on all the fun. Elisha, I decided, could scarcely begrudge me an evening's entertainment.

Since I had returned to New York, I had enjoyed deliveries of flowers and gifts, invitations to plays and musicals, and a constant stream of callers. My boarding lady, Mrs. Walters, was delighted by the sudden popularity of her house. Unexpectedly, she turned out to be an affable but lonely older woman, confined with an unsociable spinster daughter. The younger woman, Miss Clementine Walters, had not changed a bit since our previous encounter; if anything, she had grown dourer in the intervening months. My presence brought a sudden shower of attention that ill suited her nature, and I thought of her, uncharitably I admit, as a sort of sinister spirit lurking in the background of our sunny days. By contrast, Mrs. Walters, giggling giddily in happiness, welcomed my guests and savored the sudden change in her lifestyle almost as much as I did. If it had not been for my fear that she would report back to Mr. Grinnell, I would have brought her with me this evening, as she would surely have been fascinated by the demonstration.

Kate, my clever rescuer, linked arms with me as we prepared to watch the Davenport boys perform their celebrated talents. We were both wearing new gowns, trimmed in the latest fashion, our hair intricately twisted and curled. "They can't be a day over fifteen," she whispered, eyeing up the competition.

"Rather less, I think," I replied.

"They remind me of us," Kate said reflectively, "when we were young and innocent."

"*You* were never innocent," I retorted.

The Davenport brothers were the newest sensation in the profession. Their specialty was levitation and summoning spirits to play musical instruments while they were bound hand and foot. They worked with the aid of a spirit cabinet, in which they were locked while the phenomena took place.

The cabinet was displayed before us this evening in the ballroom of Mr. Partridge's mansion, where nearly four dozen guests had gathered. It was nothing more than a large wooden closet with three doors on hinges. Inside were two benches, at opposite ends, and a number of hooks and pegs from which hung tambourines, trumpets, and cowbells of varying sizes.

Dr. J. B. Ferguson, the Presbyterian minister who sponsored the boys, introduced the demonstration. "What you will see here tonight is no trickery but a true manifestation of beings from another realm," he assured us. "These innocent boys are only the channel through which the spirits touch our world, and to prove to you that there is no collusion here, we shall ask two strangers from the audience to assist us."

Kate released me and leaned forward in her chair, thrusting her hand in the air and waving like an overeager schoolgirl. Dr. Ferguson could not resist her charms and motioned her to come forward, then chose one of the journalists as well. The two Davenport boys seated themselves on the benches in the cabinet while Dr. Ferguson gave Kate and the other gentleman each a rope and pantomimed how they should secure the mediums. While Kate wrapped her rope round and round William Davenport's legs, I searched for some sign of subterfuge, but I could not detect a thing. Impulsively, I leaned across Kate's empty chair and whispered to Leah, "I miss Calvin."

My sister turned her head to regard me impassively, then looked away without comment. After all this time, I still did not know what depth of feeling she'd had for her second husband, or whether she had married him, as she did so many other things, to further her own purposes.

Kate, meanwhile, was laughing, casting flirtatious glances at the audience while twining the long length of rope through the bench and around the arms and torso of the elder brother. The gentleman from the newspaper finished securing Ira Davenport and came to assist her, taking the rope and giving several sharp tugs before tying it off across William's shoulders. If Kate had been a planned distraction, she could not have done a better job. All eyes were upon her, and even William Davenport seemed taken with her, gazing at her foolishly with his mouth agape. Dr. Ferguson took her hand and thanked her, holding onto her fingers just a moment longer than he needed to, and she saucily swept her smile across the audience before returning to her seat beside me.

"Nothing in the boy's hands," she murmured to me, settling back in her chair. "And nothing up his sleeves." I just stared at her, astounded at her boldness and audacity.

Dr. Ferguson, with the assistance of Mr. Partridge, closed the three doors to the cabinet and locked them. He turned down the gaslights in the room to the merest flicker of illumination, scarcely enough to see the person seated beside us. Apparently, the Davenport boys would perform their miracle not only while locked in a cabinet and concealed from our sight but in darkness as well.

For the next quarter of an hour, we were treated to a variety of perplexing phenomena, including the clamor of a badly played trumpet and an off-beat tambourine, a clatter of bells, and luminous hands that appeared from the sides of the cabinet making strange, meaningless gestures at us. After a time, all fell silent, except for the murmurs and whispers of the audience. Dr. Ferguson rose from his seat and gradually turned the lights up to their full strength. Then he made quite a show of unlocking the three cabinet doors, finally throwing them back to reveal William and Ira, still seated on their respective benches, trussed from neck to feet in ropes as before.

The audience broke into applause, which I joined wholeheartedly, while Dr. Ferguson selected two other persons to come and untie the boys. "Please indicate whether you feel they are sufficiently restrained," he asked them, and the two chosen assistants agreed heartily that the boys were still tightly bound. The young man releasing William's feet even complained, "Miss Kate Fox ties a devilish knot!" bringing a surge of laughter from the assembly.

Finally, when the boys were free, Mr. Partridge thanked the assembly for attending the demonstration and smoothly informed the journalists and other sundry guests that the event was over. The mediums who had gathered to participate in next week's examination were all invited to a late evening supper at the Partridge home, but everyone else was subtly encouraged to depart.

The audience broke into applause. The two Davenport boys scuttled over to their father, who ushered them to the side door, where supper would be waiting. As the company began to disperse, some to the street and some to Mr. Partridge's dining room, I asked Kate whether she had figured out how the boys had escaped their bindings and gotten back into them so neatly.

"I do not know," she admitted, "but I am going to do my best to find out!" With that, she sashayed off in pursuit of William Davenport, a predatory gleam lighting her eyes.

I gathered my cloak and picked my way through the scattered chairs. When I reached the point where I would have to choose my path, toward the front door or toward the dining room, I looked up to find Leah observing me curiously. I paused, and she raised one eyebrow significantly, a knowing smile on her lips. There was no doubt she knew exactly how much I would rather attend Mr. Partridge's supper than return alone by taxi carriage to Mrs. Walters's house.

But I had given my word to Elisha that I would not allow my name to be linked with spirit rapping anymore.

And so I turned away from her, walking with dignity toward the street door, grateful only that she could not see my face.

Chapter Thirty-Six
Maggie

I dragged out my stay in New York as long as possible, and in December when I had run out of excuses and reasons for delay, I returned to Crooksville. I shed tears on the journey but resolved to demonstrate an improved temperament upon arrival at the Turner house. Susannah Turner and her husband had been good to me and did not deserve the brunt of my ill temper.

Besides, I told myself, it was only for six months more.

I had latched on to the idea that Elisha's expedition would take exactly a year and had refused to entertain the possibility of it extending any longer. Thus, in May 1854 I sent a package of letters to the Grinnells for Elisha, asking to have them forwarded to his first expected contact. Then I applied myself to my studies virtuously in the expectation that I would hear from Elisha by June and spent many hours imagining how we would celebrate his return.

My patience chafed, however, as the weeks and then the months passed with no sign of Elisha's vessel. I knew very well how short the Arctic summer was and how briefly the ice floes parted to create a passage for ships. The speculation in the newspapers about the extended silence from Elisha's expedition did nothing to alleviate my growing anxieties.

Months slowly passed, and in the early days of September a package arrived at the Turner house. Seeing that the sender was Cornelius Grinnell, I tore into it with soaring hopes—only to have my heart torn out by the contents. The package was filled with my own letters to Elisha. Young Mr. Grinnell had returned them to me with a brief note explaining that no contact had been made with the *Advance*, and none could now be expected until the following spring. "Whaling vessels report that it has been a very bad year for ice," he wrote. "Dr. Kane will have no choice but to wait out a second winter above the Arctic Circle."

At this revelation, I fell into such a state of fevered agitation that the Turners became alarmed. I locked myself into my bedroom with the unread letters; I sobbed until I was sick and refused to eat or drink. I burrowed into my bed and would not come out, weeping for hours without speaking and ignoring Mrs. Turner's anxious attempts to comfort me. After two days, my tutor and her husband threw up their hands in surrender and telegraphed my family in New York, requesting that someone come to fetch me. Mother and Kate arrived as soon as they could, and after failing to cajole me into a functioning state, they decided to take me with them back to the city.

"Only Maggie," remarked Kate, "needs to leave the country for the city to regain her health."

I had come to abhor country living, and only the unwavering belief that Elisha was going to return this summer and find me hard at work at my studies had sustained me. Now that this idyllic vision of our reunion had crumbled, I fell to pieces as well.

"He is dead," I cried piteously on Kate's shoulder during the interminable carriage ride to the Philadelphia train station. "I know he is dead!"

"He is not dead, Maggie!" my sister reprimanded me. "He knew that he might be gone two years. He said so when he talked of provisioning his ship. Did you not *listen* to him?"

"I listened. But I refused to hear anything that did not have him back in my arms in a year." I pressed my sodden handkerchief to my face. "I couldn't bear it, Kate. I can't bear it now! Another year!"

"Does he expect you to stay in Crooksville for another entire year?" demanded Mother. "You would be happier living with us!"

"I can't live with Leah!" I wailed. "He doesn't want me with Leah!"

My mother sighed. "Those two and their silly feud!"

I turned back to Kate and grasped her hands between my own. "He could be dead, Kate!" I insisted, pleading with her. She knew what I was asking her. I could see it in the way her eyes darted from side to side, trying to escape my gaze.

Finally, she sighed and looked at me directly. "He is not dead, Maggie. I am sure of it."

I let out a breath of relief, followed by an intake of shuddering realization. "You know!" I gasped. "You *know!* What have you seen?"

"When did you start believing I have the sight?"

"When did you start hesitating to tell me what you've seen?" I countered.

Kate shook her head at me, looking distressed and wary. "I do not believe Elisha will die in the Arctic. I cannot tell you any more."

"Cannot or will not?" I demanded.

"My vision is unclear," she insisted. "I only feel certain that he will return from this trip. I cannot give you any reason."

She was lying. I knew she was, and I still did not press her. For I was wise enough to know even in my state of hysteria that if she had seen something worse than his dying in the Arctic, I was not strong enough to hear it.

My stay in New York was destined to be brief this time. Mr. Henry Grinnell, the sponsor of Elisha's expedition and guardian of my living allowance, liked me best in the backcountry of Pennsylvania, buried under a mound of schoolbooks. It did not take long for him to discover my presence in the city and ply his influence to reinstate my exile.

As usual, the son Cornelius was delegated to the dirty work, and it was from him that I received the first warning letter. His first sentence caused my heart to rise up in my throat with panic, but upon reading further, I realized that there was no cause for any more alarm than we already endured.

Dear Miss Fox,

I am sorry to be writing you with an unhappy development that may cause you grief, but it is my sad duty to break this news before you read about it in the newspapers. Remains of the Franklin Expedition have been discovered by the Canadian explorer John Rae on the Boothia Peninsula of northern Canada, and it appears that all of the English explorers are dead. I am further distressed to explain to you that this final trace of the ill-fated group is far to the south of the route taken by the *Advance*, and it is now clear that Dr. Kane is searching in the wrong place.

As there will undoubtedly be increased speculation on the condition of Dr. Kane's expedition, I urge you to withdraw to your quiet country retreat, the better to escape the hurtful and ill-informed opinions of the newspapers.

After all, you and I are in accord regarding our belief that Dr. Kane will safely return from his explorations. When this happy event does occur, I would not like him to think that I allowed you to be remiss in your studies during his absence.

Your humble servant,

Cornelius Grinnell

I was not as ignorant as Mr. Cornelius Grinnell assumed. I knew the location of the Boothia Peninsula. The charted regions of the Arctic had long since been burned into my memory. I quite understood, from the moment I read the name Boothia, that Elisha's expedition would find no trace of Franklin in northern Greenland or any island thereabouts.

What I also understood was this: if the discovery had been made a year earlier, in time to inform Elisha before he passed beyond the areas of human habitation, he still would not have turned back. This expedition was never about Franklin, not really, no matter how the men who had planned, financed, and executed it pretended otherwise to themselves and to others. It was about competition and recognition and, as Kate had so nastily put it, about "naming frozen bits of wasteland." And therefore, the fate of the Franklin party upset me less than Cornelius Grinnell thought it might, because I had never expected it to divert Elisha one degree from what he really wanted to do.

In my reply, I thanked Cornelius for his concern and assured him that I fully understood the implications of this discovery, but I also knew that it had no bearing on the state of the second Grinnell Expedition, hundreds of miles to the north. Furthermore, as politely as I could, I reminded him that in fifteen months I had only twice left Crooksville to visit my family. Surely, Elisha would not wish me to neglect my own mother!

A second letter followed fast upon the heels of my reply. Cornelius explained that his father was greatly concerned about the grim reports trickling into the newspapers as more details of Franklin's last days became known. Both father and son wanted me tucked away in Crooksville as soon as I could possibly arrange it, to shield my delicate sensibilities from the sordid truth about those wretched and desperate men.

In fact, I already knew that members of the Franklin crew had resorted to eating the flesh of their own dead in a fruitless attempt to avoid starvation. I had too many friends in the newspaper business to have escaped that unpleasant knowledge. I knew, also, that with Elisha's ship overdue and assumedly trapped in the ice, speculation was rife about whether he and his crew would, this winter, be reduced to the same depravity.

The Grinnells, in their paternal way, wished to shield me from this conjecture. But I was a practical girl and not given to passing judgment on people whose dire circumstances I could scarcely imagine. I am afraid my opinion on the matter was sharply divided, depending on who was doing the eating and who was doing the dying.

However, one fact was inescapable. Mr. Henry Grinnell was, for now, in charge of my living expenses, and if he desired that I return to Crooksville, then it would behoove me to comply.

Still, my willful nature led me to concoct one small rebellion. I wrote to the Grinnells that I would gladly return to Crooksville as requested, *after* I traveled to Rochester for the wedding of a dear family friend.

❧

It was only a slight untruth. Although he and I had spent several years growing up together while I was a boarder in his home, I had never considered Amy Post's son Donald "a dear friend." But I would not submit completely to these men who were trying to confine me in obscurity. Thus, I accompanied Mother and Kate to Rochester, where we watched a quiet and subdued Quaker ceremony, with the emphasis on quiet, and there was nothing that could be described as ceremonial at all.

The couple merely stood before a handful of close friends and kin and, after a suitably long and contemplative silence, expressed aloud their wish to be joined in marriage. There was no minister to sanctify the union, only the good wishes of any person present who wished to speak. This was marriage in the old way, the common-law manner, which Quakers still practiced.

It was a bittersweet event for me. Ill-complexioned Donald Post was married, and not even to a lumpish fright like Miss Clementine

Walters. The sweet-natured Post bride was a lovely auburn-haired beauty, scarcely eighteen years old.

And here I was, just a few months away from my twenty-first birthday, living an enforced exile from my family, with no prospect of marriage unless the cruel Arctic ice spared the lives of its newest batch of victims.

Chapter Thirty-Seven
Maggie

I returned for a third time to Crooksville, despondent, reluctant, and more than a trifle resentful. I spent long hours of the journey contemplating the fate, not of Sir Franklin, but of his widow. In 1845 her husband had left her for the arms of the cruel mistress of the North, the elusive Arctic Passage, and only now, nearly ten years later, did she finally ascertain that which her heart must have known all along. Would nine years find me forgotten in Crooksville, fluent in seven languages and composing my own music for the piano, a used-up and faded old maid still waiting for the return of my love?

As it turned out, that was not going to be a possibility. Waiting for me upon my return to the Turner house was a letter anxiously held in my tutor's hands, her curiosity barely restrained. Clearly, from the markings, it had originated from the Kane household at Rensselaer.

Naïvely, I was excited by this, my first contact with Elisha's family. I opened it with expectations of commiseration in this time of great apprehension. Having been amply warned by Miss Leiper, I should have known better.

Dear Miss Fox,

I am writing to you at the behest of Mr. Henry Grinnell, who manages the funds held in trust for you. The monies placed in Mr. Grinnell's care will soon be exhausted, and as the protracted absence of Dr. Kane has extended the duration of his guardianship, Mr. Grinnell has sought my recommendation on the matter.

After due consideration I have decided that in deference to the affection I feel for my brother, I will donate my own personal funds to the cause that he espoused: the redemption of a young lady by providing her with the means of leading an honest life and resisting the temptations that beset a poor girl with a pretty face and an already disreputable association. I am certain you will find great relief in this safeguard to your comfortable home and education, but now that I am cograntor of your trust, I will remind you that as a dependent of my brother's kind charity your expenses should be subjected to restraint. As you are neither relation nor mistress to Dr. Kane, you of course realize that this generosity must in due time end and apply yourself to that eventuality.

In the meantime, I would like an itemized account of your expenditures since June of 1853, which you can forward to me through your regular correspondence with Mr. Grinnell.

Your servant,

Robert Kane

"Is something amiss?" inquired the shrewd Mrs. Turner, watching my face closely.

I could not have prevented the flush that burned on my cheeks, but I called upon all the control I had learned in many years of deceit to look up from this letter with an expression of serenity. Even in a moment of acute humiliation my instinct for self-preservation led me to understand I could not let Mrs. Turner know her income was in jeopardy. "Not at all," I said lightly. "Just an amiable letter from Dr. Kane's brother, inquiring after my well-being in light of the recent unpleasant developments in the North. He also asks after his aunt. Do you think it would be possible for Mr. Turner to take me in his carriage tomorrow, to call upon Miss Leiper and commend to her Mr. Kane's regard?"

⚬⚬⚬

"What a detestable young man!" exclaimed Miss Leiper.

I looked at her with some surprise, and Miss Leiper smiled, clearly amused at my reaction to her words. "I know, Miss Fox," she said, bending her head with its still-golden hair to the teacup in her veined hands. "I should not have a favorite among my nephews, let alone a *least* favorite! Yet I can safely say that Robert is a man who would try the most patient and virtuous soul. He is a Philadelphia lawyer, through and through."

"Does he not know?" I asked. "Is he unaware of Elisha's regard for me?"

"Oh, he knows, Miss Fox. I assure you, they all do. Have I not told you that Elisha begged their permission to present you at Rensselaer House? But my nephew Robert Kane would not admit such a relationship in a letter that could be read by others. I hate to slander all lawyers. I am sure there are many men in the profession who are warm and generous and kind to children and dogs alike. But Robert was born a lawyer, or born with the personality of one at any rate, and thus chosen for the role in the cradle."

To the extreme irritation of Mrs. Turner, I spent a week with Elisha's aunt. She was transparently glad for the company. I read to her, and she regaled me with stories about Elisha's childhood, her own youth, and her father's exploits in the War for Independence.

We also worked together on my reply to Robert Kane. I thanked him for his intervention in the matter of the dwindling trust fund and assured him that I would inform his brother of the treatment I received at his hands. I also conveyed to him his aunt's regards and passed along her request to be notified if any further funds were needed, as she had promised Elisha she would treat me as her own niece. Furthermore, I suggested he apply to Mr. Henry Grinnell for a list of my expenditures since 1853, for as trustee of the fund, he certainly must have such a record. Finally, I assured him that I was bearing up well under the strain of Elisha's long absence and that despite the speculations of the press I was certain that he would return in the spring. "It will be a joyous reunion for us all," I wrote, "and I greatly look forward to making your acquaintance during the happy celebrations to come."

Thus, I answered the kindly letter he should have written to me rather than the acerbic one he had actually composed. There was not a single word to suggest the injury I had received from his cold note, or any acknowledgement of the low way in which he addressed my character. However, I knew that he would read between the lines to grasp the meaning I wished him to comprehend: Elisha would learn of any insult he gave to me. I lived under the protection of his aunt, Eliza Leiper, who was fully aware of my true relationship with her nephew. And upon the triumphant return of Elisha's expedition, I would meet Robert Kane on equal terms as the wife of his brother.

I received no further correspondence from Mr. Kane, and money for my expenses continued to arrive from the Grinnells with no interruption.

❧

The months crept on. I had lived so long with the Turners that I had become a member of the family. This meant that the gloves came off, in a certain respect, and Mrs. Turner and I clashed as heartily as any mother and daughter. By turns she cajoled and threatened me.

"I trust in kind Providence that Dr. Kane will return in the course of this next year," she enticed me. "He will expect to find a companion whose conversational powers have been cultivated. I know that you will not wish to disappoint him."

On another day, she spoke with more bluntness, using a variation of that time-honored threat of every mother: "You just wait until Dr. Kane gets home and hears about this!"

This is not to say that I did not apply myself to my studies. But under the circumstances, what young lady could continue day after day, week after week, with no occupation save the endless tasks given by a relentless tutor and no social engagements except visits to a kind elderly lady? I was living the prime years of my life in exile, practically confined to a convent like some maiden of medieval days. While my sister Kate attended plays and operas in the city, I stared moodily out through a pane of glass at a bleak, rainy autumn of bedraggled greenery, a pile of books in my lap and nothing to break the monotony except dire imaginings of Elisha's plight.

The cold was not his only enemy. As lethal and malignant as it was, with its constant threat of frostbite and gangrene, there was also the danger of illness, especially scurvy. The bane of explorers since the time of Ferdinand Magellan, this disease had cost more lives than the forces of nature or mishap in expeditions of the North. Without fresh food, its insidious poison would eat away at its victims, weakening their ability to remedy themselves by hunting for the food that could cure them. I *had* listened to Elisha when he spoke of provisioning his ship. And I knew that his stores of fresh foods must surely have been expended by now. He had known from the start that this would be his greatest deficiency and his most dire need.

I began to pester Cornelius Grinnell obsessively with demands for information on a possible rescue mission. He counseled me to practice self-control and not give way to "female jitters." He promised to apprise me of developments as they became known to him and advised that I commit myself to my studies and leave the matters of men to men.

December buried Crooksville under snow deep enough to make the roads impassable by man or beast, and so I passed my birthday, Christmas, and the end of 1854 in even more solitude than usual. It was not until January that the Turners were able to retrieve their accumulated post from Philadelphia. My first bit of news came not from the Grinnells, but in the form of a telegram from Leah, my first communication with her since the *Tribune* spiritual contest of 1853.

Its message was short, simple, and baffling:

Married Daniel Underhill on Christmas Day.

Because I had never heard of Daniel Underhill and the whole thing seemed so unlikely, I was inclined to think the telegraph office had made a mistake and confused her message with that of someone else. But a letter from Kate followed fast upon the heels of the telegram, confirming the truth of the statement.

Daniel Underhill, president of the New York Fire Insurance Company, had been a longtime client of Leah's. His sudden proposal of marriage had been no less surprising than Leah's prompt acceptance. Kate wryly commented that Mr. Underhill's bank account and fine brownstone home on West Thirty-seventh Street may have had some influence on her answer. Mr. Underhill was an attentive and doting soul, who had kindly opened his home to Leah's mother and sister, but Kate reported that she and Mother would soon be seeking their own private lodgings.

Leah, forty-two years old and as broad as a carriage, was now on her third husband.

It was two weeks before I could manage a polite letter of congratulations to my sister.

Throughout the month of January, preparations for a possible rescue expedition continued to stall. Although Mr. Henry Grinnell and Elisha's father had enlisted the support of the secretary of the navy and several prominent scientists, Congress was slow to give its approval or assign any funds for such a mission. I strove to keep my rising panic from leaking into my letters to Cornelius Grinnell. "What can I do to assist?" I wrote with forced calmness.

His answer was typical:

> You can but do what you are best equipped to do. Work hard at your studies, say your prayers, and look to Providence. Take comfort where you can in the association with others like yourself, women who have trusted in their loved ones and stood ever faithful by their side.

Buried in his useless and condescending reply was one small item of advice, albeit unintended. I sat down promptly and wrote a letter, presuming upon an association with another like myself, a woman sorely tried by circumstances beyond her control. To better ensure the successful delivery of my plea, I enclosed the letter inside a second one to a man of my acquaintance, the kindly and well-meaning Senator Tallmadge.

It was a matter of a few weeks before I received any response, but in the final week of January, a letter in a small, nondescript envelope was delivered to the Turner home:

> Dear Miss Fox,
>   My influence in such matters is slight, but I will do what little I can.

337

May God grant you what you seek,

Mrs. Jane Appleton Pierce

On February 3, which was by coincidence Elisha's birthday, President Franklin Pierce signed a resolution for the relief of the second Grinnell Expedition and allocated one hundred and fifty thousand dollars to the rescue effort.

Chapter Thirty-Eight
Maggie

On the thirty-first of May, two years to the day after the departure of Elisha's expedition, a pair of ships, the *Release* and the *Arctic*, sailed from New York on a mission of rescue. Among the crew were several officers who had served with Dr. Kane on the first Grinnell Expedition and who had requested the assignment out of "loyalty to a brother officer and a gallant friend."

The weeks of the summer passed in a heightened state of excitement and anticipation. I may have been the person most intimately concerned with Elisha's well-being, excepting only his family, but the entire nation seemed to rest on pins and needles, anxiously awaiting news of his fate. The sensationally gruesome end of the Franklin mission made for endless speculation among the American public. Even Elisha's romantic life was not safe from the conjectures of the press, as I discovered in a column from the *New York Daily Whig* harvested by Kate: "A gentleman from this city informs us that Dr. Kane, when he returns from his Arctic expedition, will walk down the aisle with Miss Margaretta Fox, the second sister of the 'Fox girls,' at whose residence in Hydesville, Wayne County of this state, the spirit rappings first manifested."

I cannot say that the articles concerned me in any way other than irritation at their nosiness, but they did prompt Cornelius Grinnell to write me a curt letter asking me to restrain "this self-serving ploy for publicity by Mrs. Brown."

I had to reply that Mrs. Underhill (for the Grinnells were one marriage behind in regard to Leah) had no use for such publicity. Kate had written to me that Leah, in her new role as wealthy and pampered wife, had given up public spirit rappings and only performed as a medium now for private sittings with friends. There was no indication that she had any interest at all in whether I did or did not marry Elisha Kent Kane.

Kate and Mother moved out of Daniel Underhill's home and took lodgings in a house just a few blocks away from my friend Mrs. Walters. "It is not that Mr. Underhill is ungenerous," Kate wrote me, "but we feel like interlopers in Leah's happy state of wealth and prosperity. After all she has done for us, I cannot begrudge her the house and all its stuffy contents."

❦

As June and July gave way to the sticky misery of August, my thoughts turned more and more toward the promise of the future. Schoolbooks sat upon my lap, open but disregarded, while I fantasized various scenes of reunion with my love. I worried, too, about meeting his parents. Although I could usually endear myself to anyone if I set my mind to it, Judge and Mrs. Kane loomed large and frightening in my mind. During my visits to Miss Leiper, that dear lady coached me on my manners and behavior with a mind to making my first introduction to Elisha's parents as smooth as possible. She warned me to expect rudeness that would make Robert Kane's letter seem cordial. "His engagement to you will thwart their plans for him," she explained. "It will be as if he tried to marry the upstairs maid."

That information was not particularly helpful. I alternated between the verge of nervous collapse and overwhelming despair as the summer passed with no word from the rescue expedition. I had been warned by the Grinnells that the *Release* and the *Arctic* could not be expected to return until fall, but I was beginning to wonder whether they would simply vanish as well. Perhaps we would have to send another vessel after them, and another after that one, as ship after ship disappeared in the search for the one previous.

It was thoughts like these that occupied my mind in late August during a Pennsylvania heat wave. I had abandoned my studies and fled from the close quarters of the house to the overgrown meadows of the property. The air was heavy and still, and it was in vain that I sought a breeze to cool my fevered brow. Realizing that there was no relief from the heat to be found out of doors, I made my way back to the house. As the piazza came into view between the tall grasses and shrubs, I heard voices raised in emotion. I recognized my own name, shouted over and over, and at the same moment, I saw Mrs. Turner come out the front door, her husband on her heels. Mr. Turner's wagon was at the front door, with the horse still in its traces. He was home unexpectedly early from the mill, and a sense of alarm overcame me.

Despite the heat, I lifted my skirt from the ground and broke into a run, my heart pounding in panic at thoughts of illness, death, or war. But as I approached the house and as the Turners caught sight of me, the occasion for their excitement became clear. It was evident in the way Mr. Turner slung his arm fondly about his wife, grinning broadly. It was evident in the way Mrs. Turner triumphantly waved a newspaper above her head while cupping one hand to direct her shout.

Now her words carried clearly across the front lawn. "They've found him! Maggie, they've found him! Dr. Kane is alive!"

In the end, Elisha had rescued himself.

While the relief ships dispatched at great cost and effort were pushing their way northward through the ice floes of Baffin Bay, Elisha and his men were trudging southward, by sledge and open boat, through treacherous Arctic water and over great fields of ice. They had abandoned their icebound ship in May and traveled over one thousand miles and for eighty days, carrying their sick and injured, finally paddling into the settlement of Upernavik in the first days of August.

He was alive. He was safe. He was a hero.

It is not an exaggeration to say that the entire nation rejoiced. Reporters from all over the country raced by railway and steamer to Newfoundland, where the *Release* was scheduled to make first landfall in North America, each newspaper vying to carry the first accounts of the expedition.

I cannot describe the transports of joy I felt in those first days, knowing that he was alive and on his way home to me. I knew, distantly, that two of his crew had died and several more were gravely ill, but this scarcely concerned me. All reports suggested that the commander himself was in reasonably good health, and that it was only through his levelheaded leadership that their retreat from the ice had been achieved. He had managed to do what Sir John Franklin had not done: bring his men safely home.

The *Release* docked in September, and crowds of newspaper reporters swelled the population of Newfoundland, Canada, desiring to attend the first interviews with the returning heroes.

It was, as I knew it would be, another hair-raising tale. Headlines blazed: "Dr. Kane Is Home Again!" "The *Advance* Left in the Ice," "New Lands Found," "An Open Sea Discovered," "Life in the Frozen Regions," "Dr. Kane's Own Account."

The newspapers told a tale of bravery, suffering, and endless ingenuity. The *Advance* became ice locked in September of 1853, in a small bay off Smith Sound. At first the expedition suffered only the discomforts to be expected when wintering in the Arctic. In the spring, Elisha and his crew pressed forward in their explorations, until an unexpected drop in temperature caused them to succumb to the cold. Two men died, and many other members of the crew were so badly weakened that further exploration was hampered.

That summer, while Elisha tended the injured men in his capacity as commander and doctor, two of his crew achieved the crowning success of the expedition: a trip to the northernmost edge of Greenland, where a great expanse of open water was discovered. The newspapers hailed this as the open polar sea, so long sought after and finally discovered by two of Elisha's men, including that efficient young man William Morton! Through the achievement of these valiant men, Elisha's expedition received recognition as the northernmost exploration to date.

Unfortunately, the condition of the ice did not allow for the escape of the *Advance* in 1854, and so the expedition was forced to settle in for a second winter. It was during those months that they suffered the most, and as I had anticipated, scurvy was their greatest enemy.

By April, plans were under way for their escape, and nearly simultaneously with the efforts in the United States to supply their rescue ships, Elisha and his men were packing their few remaining stores to begin a perilous journey across glaciers and seawater to achieve their own emancipation.

The newspapers made Elisha their darling, praising him for "the Yankee ingenuity and fortitude" that had enabled him to succeed where his British counterparts had failed so tragically. They also admired his frank modesty, stating, "As well as he has earned his laurels, Kane wears them with a meekness that adds redoubled luster to his fame, for in his own heart he says, 'I did no more than my duty.'"

I laughed. My Elisha knew how to handle an audience. In my mind I could just imagine him, with his self-deprecating laugh and his sheepish grin, saying to the wide-eyed reporters, "No, gentlemen, I would not call it bravery to take on a bear armed only with a knife. Rather it was desperation, born of near starvation. And I expect I made a foolish spectacle when I was forced to turn tail and run from his sharp-clawed embrace, for he was just as hungry as I was!" And there would not be a man present who did not admire this humbleness and wish in his own heart that he could be as courageous as Dr. Kane!

To the great distress of Mrs. Turner, I began to pack my belongings and plan my return to New York. My tutor wanted me to remain in her house, virtuously working on my studies until the moment when Dr. Kane arrived. However, there was not enough patience within me to wait in Crooksville. I was determined to meet him in New York, where the *Release* was due to dock in early October.

The unhappiness of Mrs. Turner was offset by the rapture of Mrs. Walters, who realized that her home would be the setting for a reunion of the renowned Dr. Kane and his love. Mother and Kate descended upon me with a flurry of excitement, and Kate weeded through my out-of-fashion gowns, replacing them with new dresses of her own, graciously sacrificed for her soon-to-be-married sister.

On October 11, 1855, the *Release* sailed into American waters with the little *Arctic* steaming behind. The greeting of cannon fire could be heard at Mrs. Walters's house, where Ellen and Mother had forced me to stay. "It would not do for you to stand at the docks like a common girl," Mrs. Walters insisted. "You must do the proper thing and wait for him to call upon you."

Oh, but it was torture, to hear the cannon and know that I could have been there to see him waving at the crowd and accepting their adulation. I imagined him spotting me among the masses and leaving his post, to push his way through the people and take me into his arms…

"We could tie the bedsheets together and skin down them from the upstairs bedroom window," Kate suggested, only half in jest. Perhaps the old Maggie might even have considered it.

Instead, I waited in my proper place until the lateness of the hour assured us all that he would not be coming for me that night.

The next day we discovered that the crew of the lost *Advance* had been taken to a welcoming party at the Astor House, where family, friends, and admirers had gathered to meet them. I was shocked and wounded that the Grinnells had forgotten to invite me, and Mrs. Walters realized it was possible no one knew of my presence in the city. "They think you are still in Crooksville!" Just as quick as she thought of it, she sent off a note to Henry Grinnell, rectifying this little oversight.

Again, we sat down to wait: Ellen, Mother, Kate, and myself.

There were no callers.

As the hours passed, my distress grew palpable. There was a weight in my chest that I thought had left me forever once news of his rescue had come to me. Ellen and Mother offered excuse after excuse: Dr. Kane must be in high demand; he was probably detained in meetings with the navy, reunions with his family, reports to the backers of the second Grinnell Expedition. But Kate and I looked at each other, and we both knew that nothing could stop Elisha from anything he truly wanted to do.

How long would it have taken to send a note, if he could not come in person?

He had once given up an entire day just to bring me a canary.

And now he did not come.

By evening, I was nearly prostrate with despair. I retired to my room and lay down with a damp cloth over my eyes, trying to quell the doubts and fears in my heart. There were countless silly things that might have delayed him, although I could not understand why he did not send a carriage for me, at least. In spite of my distress, I must have dozed for a few minutes, because when I first heard the voices, it was as if in a dream. Then, heart pounding, I suddenly realized that Mrs. Walters was speaking to someone downstairs; a man's voice responded to her. Throwing off the towel, I flew to the door and nearly tripped down the staircase in my haste, all pretense at being a refined lady gone.

Mrs. Walters was alone and just turning from the front door when I appeared. She looked strangely agitated and red-faced. "Oh, Maggie. I'm sorry if that disturbed you," she said. "It was just a gentleman come on business, nothing to do with Dr. Kane at all."

I burst into tears, and Mrs. Walters put her arms around me. "There, there, child. We shall figure all this out in the morning. Put yourself to bed and do not cry any longer."

It was strange that a gentleman should call on business with Mrs. Walters at this time of the night. But I was too self-absorbed to see it then, and I climbed the stairs dejectedly. In the hallway upstairs, I nearly bumped right into Miss Clementine Walters, who was unexpectedly lurking in the darkness outside of my room. As usual, the socially awkward spinster had been hiding upstairs all day, not liking Kate and my mother any more than she liked me.

Now, after speaking hardly a word since my arrival, she approached me as though she were some confidant of mine, saying, "She didn't give him the letters. She lied to him."

"What?" I said, impatiently. I was scarcely in the mood for riddles. "Who are you talking about?"

"Cornelius Grinnell," replied my erstwhile chaperone. "That's who was at the door. He asked my mother to turn over your letters from Dr. Kane. Mother put him off, telling him she did not think you had any with you, although they are right on your bedside table. She lied for you."

And with that, Miss Walters retreated into her own lair, having laid me low with her words just as surely as if she had hit me with a poker iron.

In the darkness of my room, I collapsed to a seat on my bed and stared at the bundle of precious letters on the side table.

Elisha had not come to see me, nor sent me any word.

But Cornelius Grinnell, that dogsbody of all dirty work, had been sent to retrieve his letters. All Elisha's love letters.

I began to tremble violently, as though I had taken a sudden fever. And all that sleepless night, I thought about what tomorrow would bring.

And what I would do.

Chapter Thirty-Nine
Kate

A change had come over my sister.

In the days following Dr. Kane's rescue, Maggie was ecstatic. Her dreams were destined to be fulfilled, or so she thought, and her world revolved around a man she believed would give up his wanderings for her—just as she had given up her life of excitement and purpose for him.

But now, as I faithfully attended her on the third day after his arrival in the city, I knew that she had received some news changing her perception of the situation. She would not tell me what it was, but her ashen appearance spoke of a fretful, sleepless night, and her usually bright eyes were dim with grief.

Rejecting all the bright new gowns I had given her, Maggie selected a dress several years old, one that Dr. Kane had seen many times. Donning this simple frock, she bid me tighten her corset until she could scarcely draw breath to fill her lungs and she looked as if she might faint dead away. Then, because she could no longer raise her arms, she directed me in the dressing of her hair. Halfway through the process, I realized what she was doing, if not why. She was making herself over in the image of that foolish painting Dr. Kane had commissioned. This was the very dress she had worn for those sittings, and in her pale, breathless state, she looked just like the fragile creature on the canvas. When we were done she sank down upon her bed to wait for the arrival of the man who had consumed her thoughts and desires all these long years. Her lips, as bloodless as the rest of her, moved slightly, whispering, "Please, let me endure this with dignity." Whether she spoke to me or herself or to God, I did not know.

There was nothing I could do for her but sit beside her and hold her thin, cold hand.

Hours passed in silence, and then around noon I heard the clamor of horses beneath Maggie's window and a sharp rap on the front door. My sister closed her eyes briefly and swayed. There were footsteps downstairs and men's voices. It was only a matter of minutes before Mrs. Walters came to fetch us, looking flushed and distressed.

By this time, no one believed that the coming reunion would be a joyous one. Maggie turned to me and met my solemn, sympathetic gaze. "Do not let me faint," she whispered, and I nodded, gripping her arm with my nails pressed against her flesh.

Down to the parlor we went, where they were waiting for us, standing opposite the door on the other side of the tea table as if it were some strong barrier instead of a wobbly old piece of furniture. We had seen Dr. Kane in his naval uniform before, but never like this—in full, formal dress regalia with all his honors displayed upon his chest. In spite of the glamour, he looked dreadful. The Arctic had aged him. His face was weathered and haggard, with cheekbones pronounced by months of starvation. His hair had thinned and receded. I barely restrained a gasp, recognizing these features from my vision two years before. Surely, this was the face I had seen in a coffin!

Beside him stood a man who could only have been a brother. The resemblance was unmistakable. Their facial features were nearly the same, save for the younger man's heavily hooded eyes, which were as cold and unfeeling as his brother's were warm and passionate.

It was the brother who did the speaking. He had brought a document for Maggie to sign, a statement that denied any relationship between Dr. Kane and herself besides a fraternal friendship and charitable funds that were to end immediately. In particular, it stated that there was not, nor ever had been, any engagement of marriage between Maggie and Elisha. This man, this Robert Kane, laid the document on the table with the expectation that Maggie would sign it and testify to its truth.

I would have protested, and Mrs. Walters, standing in the doorway, did sputter some well-meant intervention. But it was as if none of us were present. There was no one really in the room except Maggie and Elisha, whose overwhelming distress reduced the rest of us to vague shadows.

Dr. Kane said nothing but stared at her with undisguised longing. He shifted his weight and opened his mouth as though to speak, but his brother gripped his arm and Elisha subsided compliantly. From my own position, where I held my sister and lent her my support, I glared across the table. It was family against family, that much I recognized, and I blasted Elisha with my derision, wordlessly cursing him for his weakness. Polar bears and icy wastelands may have held no fear for him, but clearly there was something in this world that intimidated him.

Maggie kept her eyes modestly cast down. She was the picture of loveliness and innocence, as pure and virtuous as that painting Elisha had so admired. I was never more proud of her than when she stepped forward, took up the pen without a tremor, and signed her name. Then, deliberately, she laid down the writing instrument and removed the diamond and enamel ring from her finger. She lifted her face and met Elisha's gaze for just one second—then carefully placed the ring beside the document of falsehood and turned away.

She did not see Elisha flinch as though she had struck him. She did not see his brother's hand tighten upon his arm to restrain him. As Maggie passed through the doorway, Dr. Kane's gaze flickered briefly to me, as if to seek forgiveness or understanding, but I just shook my head in disgust. He was not the man I thought he was.

At that moment, there was a small commotion in the hallway and an outcry from Mrs. Walters. Half turning, I realized that poor Maggie's knees had buckled under her and that she had nearly crumpled to the floor in a dead faint, saved only by Mrs. Walters's quick response.

This at last broke Elisha's resolve. He threw off his brother's grip and started for the doorway. But I was quicker, sweeping ahead of him and closing the door in his very face, shutting him off from my sister.

Chapter Forty
Maggie

I lay in bed with the curtains drawn all the rest of that terrible day. I cried until I vomited, and when I was too exhausted to sob any longer, I stared at the ceiling and let the tears roll down my cheeks. Kate stayed with me, and Mrs. Walters, too. Mother heard about it soon enough and joined us.

I had kept my dignity until the very last minute; that at least was a comfort. If I had burst into tears or raged at the injustice and cruelty of it, I would have proved myself to be no more than Robert Kane thought, common and vulgar. At least I had handled myself like a lady, at what cost they would never know.

Miss Leiper had warned me. I cannot say that I had not been warned. And she was not the only one, although I could not bear to think just then about the sister who had foreseen this all along.

But the agony of seeing Elisha after all these months, to have him stand there and say not a word—it was like a horrible nightmare from which I could not wake. It was as if he had died after all.

Kate and Mother and Ellen Walters had nothing but hateful things to say about him. Kate threatened to send a note to Mr. Greeley, telling him that the hero whose exploits were splashed across his newspaper had just dishonorably broken an engagement with a woman he had promised to marry. I grabbed her hand at that and made her swear that she would do no such thing. That was the sort of low-class response they would have expected from me. The day ended as it had begun, with me curled in a miserable ball in my bed, tormented and sleepless. Kate climbed in and slept beside me, trying to comfort me with her warmth and love. But it was not her embrace I needed.

The following morning, I was roused from a stupor that could scarcely be called sleep by Mrs. Walters shaking my shoulder. "Maggie, he is back again! Tell me what to do, child! He is in the parlor, and he says he will not leave without seeing you."

"Why am I not surprised?" muttered Kate as we sat up wearily. I rubbed my eyes, which felt dry and gritty with grief and exhaustion. Kate was red cheeked with sleep but ready for a fight. "Shall I go down and give the wretched man an earful?" she offered.

"Dr. Kane says to tell you that he will not go away until you come down," Mrs. Walters fretted. "He looks prepared to lay siege here all day. And he said to give you this." She held out her hand, and I could see that he had given her the vile document from yesterday, torn into small pieces.

"A pretty gesture," Kate said bitterly, "but meaningless after what he put her through."

"I would agree," Ellen Walters concurred.

I held up my hand. "Please, let me decide for myself. Tell him I will come down in an hour, Mrs. Walters. Let him wait, if he will."

⚜

There was no sense of yesterday's heightened drama. I entered the parlor to find him quietly seated in the shabbiest chair, leaning

354

forward and staring at the ground, his elbow resting upon his knee and his forehead held in one hand. He stirred only slightly at my presence, looking up at me with eyes sunken in dark circles. He had not slept either. Today, the naval uniform was not in evidence. He wore only an old suit, two years out of style and rather ill fitting.

I turned to Mrs. Walters and Kate, quietly asking them to leave the room. My sister scowled and Mrs. Walters looked scandalized. I waved the handful of torn papers at them. "We are nothing but fraternal friends," I said with only a hint of sarcasm. "Leave the door open, and I am sure my reputation will not be damaged."

They did not exactly approve, but they withdrew out of respect for my feelings. "I will be just down the hall," Kate said. "Call out if you need me."

Dr. Kane looked at her in exasperation. "I will not harm her, Kate," he said.

"More than you have already done, you mean?" she returned acidly.

"Hush," I whispered. "Go."

When we were alone, I walked across the room until I was standing in front of him, then opened my hand and sprinkled the torn pieces of paper at his feet. He dropped his eyes in shame, and I retreated to the farthest corner of the room, taking a seat and drawing breath to keep my composure.

We sat for a long moment in silence, and in spite of myself I discovered that I was content to have him here, safe and sound, even under these circumstances.

I waited him out, and he spoke first.

"What can I say, Maggie? I have wronged you terribly." He looked at me in misery, still holding his head in his hand as if he was too weary to lift it.

"If you wished to break our engagement, why did you not come to me privately and say so?" I asked him sadly. "I would have freed you from your promise if you had asked me. Why was it necessary to humiliate me? Did you think I would make a scandal of it?"

"There is no excuse for my actions yesterday," Elisha admitted. "But I want you to understand that I was not in New York two hours before my family and I were engaged in a terrible argument—over you. The newspapers have been reporting our engagement, and my father was beside himself. My mother was prostrate with hysteria. My mother, Maggie! Pulling out her hair in handfuls! My brother Robert thought it was best to act quickly and get from you a statement that corroborated the story my family wished to publicize."

I let out my breath in derision. "The detestable Robert. Your aunt called him that, you know."

"My aunt," Elisha laughed bitterly, reaching into the breast pocket of his suit coat. "My aunt. Heaven knows how she found out so quickly. I received this from her last night." He unfolded a piece of paper, easily recognizable as a telegram, and read aloud: "If you have deceived that young girl whom you placed in my charge, you will never be welcome in my home again." He thrust the telegram back into his pocket, shaking his head. "That's my favorite aunt turning against me for your sake. I'll be hearing from the Pattersons next, I expect."

"Ever since you left, there has been gossip about our engagement," I told him. "The Grinnells have always blamed my family for this publicity, but I swear to you, it has never come from us. You proposed to me in front of a room full of people, do you remember? You cannot blame me or my sisters if your family found out before you were ready to tell them. You have greatly misjudged me if you believed I would injure you to further my own aims." I looked away from him in a sudden surge of distress, blinking back tears. "I wonder, did you ever know me at all? When I saw my name linked with yours in the newspaper, I was proud!" Turning back to face him, I met his eyes with dignity. "But you…you were ashamed, weren't you?"

Elisha was shaken. "I am not ashamed of you," he protested weakly, but he was lying, even to himself.

Once again an awkward silence fell upon us as we each sat miserably in our respective corners of the room. He was as unhappy as I was, but it was his own doing. I was faultless here, and we both knew it.

"Where do we go from here?" he asked finally.

I exhaled and shook my head. "We are not anything more than fraternal friends, brother and sister. We signed a statement, have you forgotten?"

He waved his hand at the floor. "I have torn up that document."

"Your brother is a lawyer," I replied. "I signed that paper before witnesses. It is a legal truth now, no matter what you have done with the paper. Even I know that, Ly!"

The use of his old pet name nearly unmanned him. With a choked cry, he rose and crossed the room in two strides, then knelt down before me and took my hands.

"Maggie, I lost my ship; I lost two of my men; I didn't find Franklin—in fact, I was looking in the wrong place. And through all the adversity and hardship, I had to face the daily truth that those men's lives were in my hands. I was their leader; they looked to me to save them. And there were times, Maggie, when I didn't know if I could manage it. We returned alive, yes, and with the appearance of triumph. But there is much you do not know, of savagery and darkness and violence, stories that we will keep to ourselves…stories we would like to forget. I returned empty, worn down, and that made me susceptible, I suppose, to the counsel of my detestable brother and the theatrics of my mother. When I saw you yesterday, looking just the way I had imagined you all these long months, I realized what a terrible deed I had done, to treat the woman I loved so shabbily."

I stood up and pulled away from him. The urge to embrace him, to kiss him, was overwhelming, but I had to remember what he had done to me.

He climbed to his feet and tried to follow me, but I stopped him with an outstretched hand. "While you were gone," I said bitterly, "I had my own trials to bear, not as deadly or dark as yours, but real enough to me. I gave up the spirit rapping for you and exiled myself from my family. My sister Leah no longer speaks to me, although I doubt you will care about that. I devoted myself to the tasks you set for me. I did everything you asked—everything—but still, I was so far beneath you that you could not even treat me as a lady when you came back to break my heart!"

"Maggie, I cannot bear it!" he cried, taking me into his arms in spite of my protest. "You are right. It was cruel, and I treated you just as my family wanted it done, as if you were no person of value. It was a mistake, a bad one, but I want to make it up to you. We cannot be together right now. My family is violently opposed, and I am destitute without their support. My savings are gone, spent on the expedition. I have nothing except what my parents give me. But when I have an independent income that can support us—then we shall be married. I swear it!"

He kissed my head and my brow and my lips, murmuring my name, while I stood shivering in his arms, fighting a battle with myself. In the end, it took all my strength to disengage, to hold him back with one hand and withdraw.

"I am not the girl you left, Elisha," I said with a shaking voice. "And I am not so easily led as I once was. I love you still," I admitted. "I will never love anyone else. But my trust is cracked beyond repair."

"I will mend it, Maggie," he promised, reaching for me again. "Piece by piece, I will put it back together again until we do not even remember how I broke it."

I stepped backward, shaking my head. "That would be a very difficult task, Elisha."

Apparently, his trials in the North had not robbed him of his impertinence, for he actually dared to grin at me. "Surely you realize, Maggie. Very difficult tasks are my specialty."

PART FIVE:
FOLLY AND FATE

Chapter Forty-One
Maggie

In the following months, everyone was angry with me.

My family, understandably enough, was furious that I continued to accept calls from the man who had broken—in fact, *denied*—our engagement.

"Take one of my suitors," Kate begged me. "Land sakes, Maggie, take three and have some to spare! But, please, send Dr. Kane packing and be done with him!"

My mother and Mrs. Walters, who had come to regard herself as a member of the family, were united in their feelings. They firmly insisted that I should decline any visits from the doctor, for the sake of my health and my reputation. "This emotional turmoil has been very distressing for you," said Ellen. "You have faded away before our eyes!" Meanwhile, my mother feared that my name would be blemished if I continued to accept Dr. Kane's attentions under the current cloud of controversy.

Yet to break off our relationship completely was unimaginable. I could no sooner forbid Elisha from calling at the house or writing his eloquent love letters than I could imagine renouncing light and air.

This is not to say that I succumbed entirely to his charms or that I had forgotten how he had spurned me. I sent back his gifts, and after that one breach of propriety on the day he tore up his offensive document, I did not allow him to kiss me or even hold my hand. As a man very used to getting his own way, he found my coolness nearly irresistible. Elisha certainly had a penchant for pursuing what he could not have, as Leah had once warned me.

Of course, Elisha was angry at me also, because I had expressed my intention to recommence spirit rapping. I had no choice that I could see. It was necessary for me to make a living, and I could neither move into Mother's crowded apartment nor stay in Ellen Walters's spacious house without contributing to the household income of either.

I joined Kate at private sittings, and I found that the old habits came back easily. Together, Kate and I produced an eerie array of simple phenomena. Still, we looked at our sad accumulation of cash with some consternation, wondering how Leah had deftly produced so much more.

Finally, as if it were not enough to have angered my family by association with Elisha, and angered Elisha by association with the family business, the Kanes were still infuriated by the insinuations of the press.

Elisha's family had forced the newspaper that had reported our engagement to retract the statement. Unfortunately for everyone concerned, the matter did not rest there. Several papers persisted in reporting an engagement, or a broken engagement. In the end, it nearly became a battle between reporters of rival papers to acquire the truth. Elisha found himself accosted in his daily activities by journalists, and one tenacious young man attached himself to the doctor as he walked down the street toward Mrs. Walters's house one afternoon and could not be shaken. When Elisha realized that the reporter would not be dissuaded from following him, he decided to change his destination rather than lead the reporter to the house where I lived. Unfortunately, Mother and I emerged from the front door just at the moment they were passing, and I was quickly recognized. An unpleasant scene occurred, Mother chastising both the doctor and the reporter while I tried to scurry back into the house.

However, the damage was done. We scarcely had a moment's peace after that, with reporters calling at Mrs. Walters's house and applying for private sittings with the Fox sisters. It was a terrible nuisance, in spite of the extra income and in spite of Mrs. Walters's secret delight in her new role as my doorkeeper and guardian. The reporters only had one question for the spirits anyway, and it concerned my past, present, and future marriage plans.

The problem was that anything to do with Elisha Kent Kane was news. The newspapers wrote about his expedition, about his last remaining sled dog, and even resurrected the stories of his past adventures. The volcano, his exploits in the Mexican War—all were fair game.

Amid all this public adoration, there was one person who remained unmoved in her opinion of Elisha, and that was my mother. Therefore, shortly after signing a prestigious book deal, he tried to explain to her, as best he could, why he had broken our engagement.

She listened patiently. It was doubtful she understood the complexities of his finances, but she was clearly more concerned about

Elisha's family than his bank account. "Regardless of your financial expectations," she said, "I do not understand your continued attentions to my daughter when your family is not willing to receive her as your wife. I fear I should not allow Margaretta to see you at all under these circumstances. You are young, Dr. Kane, and do not fully appreciate the far-reaching consequences of your actions."

Elisha laughed lightly. "I am old enough to know my own mind."

"You did not know your own mind the day you returned to New York," my mother reminded him, causing him to drop his gaze in shame. "I daresay you may have traveled to the North Pole and back," she went on, once again proving her faulty geography, "but I imagine I understand a little more of life than you do. If your family disowns you, it will be a great misery for you, and I am not speaking of money now. For this pain, you will blame my daughter, if not in the first flush of her bridehood, then in the years to come. And you, Margaretta, will you not learn from the mistakes of your mother and your sister Leah? Must you also choose unwisely?"

I spoke as I knew I must, whether it was the truth of my feelings or not. "I would not see him wretched in that way. If his family will not have me as a daughter, then it would be better if we were parted forever."

As I had expected, Elisha did not warm to the words "parted forever." He stirred uneasily in his chair. "It will not come to that," he assured us. "My mother will bend in time. I cannot imagine she would maintain her disapproval once there were children to be considered."

His mother, I had come to realize, was the true author of the wreckage of my engagement. Robert Kane may have engineered the execution of it, but Mrs. Kane had provided the impetus with her histrionics. I thought I understood her well, thanks to my friendship with Eliza Leiper, and I recognized Mrs. Kane as a formidable enemy. But she could snatch herself bald next time, for all I cared. I hoped never to be bested by her again.

After all, I did have a few advantages when it came to vying for her son's affections.

Elisha was extremely jealous and could scarcely stand to admit that the dissolution of our understanding meant that I was open to the courtship of other men. In spite of my mother's objections, he called upon me regularly and was not pleased if he found another gentleman visitor. On one occasion, I opened the door in farewell to a particular young man and found Elisha on the front step, just preparing to knock. My other caller tipped his hat politely in greeting as he passed, only to be disconcerted by Dr. Kane's unfriendly stare.

"Who was he?" Elisha asked coldly as he entered.

"Mr. Carter?" I said blithely. "Just an acquaintance of mine."

Elisha found his own way to the parlor and stuck his head inside, looking around suspiciously. "And where is Mrs. Walters? Or the esteemed Miss Clementine?"

"Upstairs, I imagine," I replied offhandedly, sweeping into the parlor with total disregard for his displeasure. Of course, Mrs. Walters had been in my company for the entirety of Mr. Carter's visit and had retired to her room only a minute ago. But I did not bother to share that with Elisha. I crossed to the tea table and began to clear the dishes. There were three cups, if he cared to notice, but he was too distracted.

"Was he here for a sitting?"

"Hmmm," I murmured noncommittally.

He moved quickly toward me and spoke urgently. "You are tormenting me, Maggie, and I know you do it on purpose. I cannot bear the idea of you sitting in the dark, squeezing other people's hands. I touch no hands but yours, no lips but yours. Can you say as much?" He reached out and took the tea tray from my hands, setting it back down with a decided rattle of china. "Will the spirit answer?" he mocked me.

"Come now, Doctor!" I said brightly. "Are you saying you did not hold the hand of the lovely lady with the fiery red curls you took to the opera on Tuesday last? What a missed opportunity!"

That brought him up short. He stared at me a moment, then said in a milder tone, "Kate saw me?"

I nodded with a curt smile and watched him bare his teeth in a familiar fierce grin. "It was an evening of fine intellectual stimulation," he declared. "That particular young lady thought the Franklin I went to rescue in the Arctic was *Benjamin* Franklin."

I burst out into peals of laughter. I could not help it. Stricken with a most unladylike hilarity, I collapsed weakly on the sofa and wiped tears from my eyes.

Elisha nodded at me wryly. "That's right, Maggie. Laugh. Just imagine me fumbling in vain for conversation in words of one syllable. I asked you to the opera that night, but you would not come. Do you remember?"

"Yes," I gasped. "I remember. I am truly sorry, Ly, that I condemned you to such company."

"Now," he said, towering over me with his arms crossed across his chest, "I know you are just toying with me, but answer me truly. Who is Mr. Carter to you? If you will not tell me, than I will have to go out now and knock him down in the street."

I sobered quickly, sensing that he was only half joking. There was a dangerous edge to him since he had returned from the Arctic, something I should have guessed was always there, considering the stories he told, but that he had never revealed to me before. "Mr. Carter is a cast-off beau of Kate's, and he wished me to intercede with her on his behalf," I explained obediently. "I had to tell him that I have little influence with her."

The lines of tension ran out of him. "Kate," he murmured, shaking his head slightly. "It is a wonder she remembers seeing me at the opera at all. She drinks too much, your sister."

I looked away. There was nothing to be said to that. It was true, but I could only repeat what I had said before. I had little influence over her. Kate was nineteen years old and a woman in her own right.

Elisha sighed and reached out a hand to smooth my hair, the first touch I had allowed him in over a week. "I still want to take you to the opera," he whispered. "What is a Wagner without someone who can appreciate it? Someone as bright as she is beautiful…"

I gave in, of course. I was walking a precariously thin line, and this game could only be played so long without granting a small reward to the opposite player.

Chapter Forty-Two
Maggie

The weeks passed, and, in some respects, it seemed I had come full circle in my life.

Spirit rapping had been the center of my world until Dr. Kane began to court me and persuaded me to give it up for his sake. But two years of private education had failed to make me more acceptable to his family. My engagement was broken, and I returned to rapping. The same man was even courting me again, so I had to ask myself, in five years, had I accomplished anything at all?

Somehow I believed that I had. When Dr. Kane first met me, I lived under the dominion of my sister Leah. And although she was never as terrible as Elisha made her out to be, there was no denying she directed all my affairs—how I behaved, what I believed, who I met—until the time she sent me to Philadelphia for my own health and lost me to someone else. After I met Elisha, he ruled my life. Yes, he battled Leah for the honor, and he won my loyalty and obedience for a time. However, when he broke his promise to me and cast me adrift, he also granted me a boon, the value of which I had not understood until now.

I was independent.

It was an unusual position for a young woman of my age and background. At twenty-two, I should have been living under the authority of a husband, or my parents if I was not yet married. I had not yet passed out of marriageable age and into spinsterhood, although the prospect was not so far off anymore. And yet I was not unhappy.

I continued to live with Ellen Walters, by her choice and by mine. We were close friends, despite the difference in our ages. The Grinnells may have thrown us together thinking only that Mrs. Walters was a trustworthy guardian, but our mutual affection had blossomed into a treasured companionship. I had moved to the third floor of her house and claimed a parlor of my own. The income I received from my labors went into Mrs. Walters's household account.

I had returned to rapping, but on my own terms and for clients I chose myself. I conducted my business in my own style. Leah's moving tables and Kate's glassy-eyed trances were not for me. My strength was a simple practicality and sensibility. I offered comfort, condolence, and sage advice.

"There now, Mr. Smithfield," I said soothingly in a typical sitting, while the client, an overlarge banker, snuffled like a baby and cried huge tears into a walrus mustache. "Do not despair. It is unfortunate that your brother departed this earth before you could make your amends, but take comfort! He has heard your prayers and accepted your heartfelt apologies. Furthermore, he bids you make no more delay, but make haste to heal any other estrangements in your life before fate robs you of the opportunity."

"Yes, Miss Fox," replied Mr. Smithfield, wiping his face with his handkerchief. "I see the wisdom of your words. We must not waste the days given to us."

"Every day is a gift," I agreed. "We may not realize what doors are open to us until they have closed."

⁓⁓

Meanwhile, Dr. Kane was feverishly working on his book, claiming that the proceeds from the sales would give him the financial independence he needed to make me his wife. Repeated entreaties to his parents had accomplished nothing. They refused to receive me at their house and threatened to disown their eldest son if he actually married me.

"If I have my own income," he assured me, "I would not mind so much. And I am convinced it would be a short-lived banishment in any case. My mother has engaged me in a pitched battle of wills, which she believes she can win with dire pronouncements. Once she has lost the war, her surrender will be prompt and dizzying in its sudden reversal of opinion. She will not cut off any heirs she receives from me, no matter how she has taunted me with Robert's infant."

Robert Kane had produced offspring? What a repugnant idea! Still, Kate was quick to point out that Elisha could end the conflict immediately by making good on his original promise to me. "He is weak," she said caustically. "He is not man enough to defy his mother."

She was wrong, though. Elisha was strong-minded, absolutely positive that he would get his own way in the end. I was the weak one, for I could have concluded the affair myself by sending the doctor away as everyone advised me to do, thus ending our awkward romantic entanglement once and for all.

But I could not.

On two separate occasions, I accepted invitations from other gentleman callers and stepped out with them, accompanied by my mother or Mrs. Walters. Each of these excursions ended poorly, my lack of enthusiasm so evident that neither man ever called upon me again. I had once told Dr. Kane that I would wait for him until the end of the earth, and apparently I was inclined to keep my word. It would be him or no man. I would be Mrs. Kane or a spinster for life.

We conducted our visits in my third-floor parlor alone, against all rules of propriety. I imagine that we felt ourselves above such matters, although Mrs. Walters and Mother were not at all pleased and strove to blunder in on us as often as possible. They never found us closer than two separate armchairs, for we were sensible enough not to tempt ourselves. Often, he brought pages from his manuscript for me to read aloud to him. He liked the sound of his words in my voice, he said, and he usually tipped his head back, closed his eyes, and listened with intense concentration. If he did not like what he heard, he would sit up and ask for the manuscript back, making immediate changes.

Thus, I finally learned the story of his time in the Arctic, at least the parts that he was willing to commit to publication. There was as much hardship and danger as I had imagined, and it was almost painful to read of it. A tale of adventure lost its appeal when your beloved was the protagonist. Some details were distasteful, and I rather thought Elisha was testing my devotion by revealing these intimate secrets.

"You ate rats?" I asked in disbelief, breaking off in the middle of my reading.

"Yes," he confirmed, eyeing me speculatively. "In my soup."

I returned his gaze steadily. "How did you season this concoction?"

"With horseradish."

I tipped my head quizzically. "How curious! That would not have been my first choice."

Elisha indulged in a small grin. "Horseradish was the only seasoning we had left by the time we came to eating rats."

"I will make a note of it," I told him. "As your wife, I will want to be able to prepare your favorite meals as you like them."

We often still spoke of marriage casually, as though the whole world were not set against our union and as though Elisha had not already broken our engagement for his own convenience. On this occasion he laughed brightly, saying, "Then I will make an effort to stay out of your ill graces, lest I find to my chagrin that you're not making a jest!"

He lay his head back against the back of the chair and cast his gaze toward the ceiling. "I made mistakes, of course. We would not have been in such desperate straits if we had not stubbornly engaged so much of our energies toward the scientific explorations for which we had come and too little toward the acquisition of food while it was available. If I had applied more man power to better organized hunts in the summer, we could have laid in enough fresh meat to supply all our wants for the dark time of the year. A starving, scurvy-filled explorer is of no use to himself or to the scientific establishments that commissioned him. I will not make that mistake next time."

Next time.

With two words, my secret visions of a quiet physician's practice in Philadelphia or New York crumbled to dust. Elisha had not made his last expedition to that hellish region of darkness and cold. No mission would ever be his last, until the one that defeated him. Life with this man would be nothing but eternal waiting and agonized apprehension, and even with such foreknowledge, I could not turn away from my fate. I suddenly felt a kinship with my mother's sister, the one who supposedly learned in a dream that marrying a particular man would herald her certain death. I had always considered the story a foolish family folktale, but whether or not Aunt Elizabeth had truly been gifted with the sight was beside the point. I now understood her dilemma.

With all my skill at deception, I allowed no sign of distress to pass over my face or enter my voice as I bent my head and continued to read aloud the Arctic adventures of the man who was destined to break my heart—over and over again.

In the spring of 1856, he was quite ill, stricken with an attack of inflammatory rheumatism. I was in Rochester at the time, visiting with Amy Post when I received his letter. His hands were so swollen that he was unable to write, and he had dictated the words to his secretary, Morton. Consequently, he was a little more reserved and formal than he normally was, and I wouldn't have recognized the extent of his illness had Morton not written his own note at the bottom of the letter—a note that I am certain Elisha had not seen: "Miss Fox, I have taken Dr. Kane to the Grinnells' house for care that I am unable to provide alone. Please seek him there at your earliest convenience. W. Morton."

I left Rochester at once, arriving in New York the very next day. I wasted no time stopping at Mrs. Walters's house to change my clothes or deposit my luggage but directed my carriage driver immediately to the Grinnells' residence, an address well known from many letters to my erstwhile guardians but never before visited.

The servant who answered the door was not at all sure what to do with me, an unknown young woman on the doorstep with her luggage, no chaperone, no invitation, but only a persistent demand to be let in. Luckily, William Morton was attracted by the sound of my voice and soon expedited my entry. I followed the secretary into the inner chambers of the house, noting the pronounced limp he suffered, a result of frostbite and infection in the Arctic. I shook my head in aggravation, wondering at how these men had abused their bodies for the love of such a cruel and deadly land.

Morton introduced me to Mrs. Sarah Grinnell and took responsibility for inviting me. "I thought it best to send for Miss Fox," he explained in his mild manner, and there was nothing Mrs. Grinnell could say to argue with that, for Elisha had already spotted me.

"Maggie, is it you?" he called, struggling to rise from a sofa in Mrs. Grinnell's private parlor. He was clothed in an overlarge crimson dressing gown, possibly borrowed from his host, and he had evidently been dozing when I arrived. He raised one hand to rub at his eyes in some confusion, and when I saw the swollen joints of his wrist and knuckles, I rushed around Mrs. Grinnell with a total lack of decorum and flung myself down at his side.

"Oh, Elisha, please don't get up!" I gasped. "Lay back and rest! I wouldn't disturb you for the world!"

There ensued a small struggle, as I tried to shoo Elisha back into a reclining position and he just grinned back at me and insisted on sitting up. "I am not so bad," he said. "I have been far worse. There is no better cure than fresh air and sunlight, and you are both those things to me!"

After this initial scene of comic behavior, we settled down to a more sedate and respectable visit. A servant brought tea, which I poured out for everyone, deftly taking over from Morton, who, in my outspoken opinion, needed to sit down and rest his foot. Mrs. Grinnell recovered from the shock of my unexpected intrusion, slowly warming to my presence, and Elisha was determined to prove that he was not an invalid. However, by the time an hour or two had passed, I could easily observe how the pretense was wearying him. I pled exhaustion in my own right, then, and excused myself with the need to remove my luggage and myself back to Mrs. Walters's house. "If I am welcome," I said, with a careful glance at our hostess, "I will call again tomorrow."

"You are most certainly welcome," Mrs. Grinnell heartily replied. "You are a remarkable tonic for ill health. We ought to bottle you up and apply you at will!"

Mrs. Grinnell rose to accompany me to the door and spoke privately out of the hearing of the men. "I owe you an apology,

Miss Fox," she said with a brisk manner covering some embarrassment. I looked at her with surprise, and she continued. "I am afraid I had made up my mind about you. With no evidence at all, I was convinced I knew what kind of woman you were. In all those months you were in correspondence with my husband and son, all that time when you might have appreciated a woman's comfort, I never wrote you even once, never introduced myself, never expressed a word of counsel or encouragement. I am quite ashamed, now that I have met you. You are not at all what I expected."

"I am honored to make your acquaintance finally," I replied politely. "And I am pleased if I have gained a small measure of your approval."

"Miss Fox, look at him!" Mrs. Grinnell and I turned, gazing back down the hallway at the open parlor door. Elisha was standing in conversation with Morton, leaning heavily upon a cane, unaware of our observation. "He could not stand this morning without assistance," she told me. "Now, one look at you, and he is back on his feet."

I smiled. "I am sure that your kind nursing and generous care have had much to do with his recovery."

"Miss Fox, I do entreat you to call again tomorrow," Mrs. Grinnell said firmly. "And this evening, I intend to write Judge Kane's wife and tell her of my thoughts on this matter."

I nodded my head respectfully at my hostess and made my way toward the front door. I never knew whether Mrs. Grinnell kept her word, but any letter she might have written Elisha's mother never made any difference.

Elisha improved slowly over the course of a few weeks. I called upon him often at the Grinnell house, and when he returned to his own lodgings, I began to visit him there, bringing Kate along as chaperone and once, when desperate, even coercing the reluctant Clementine Walters into accompanying me.

His two-volume narration, *Arctic Explorations*, was only three-quarters done, but Elisha's publishers were already demanding changes. They were not interested in producing a work of scientific data. They wanted something to satisfy the appetite of the American readers for travel and adventure. "I must attempt to be more popular and gaseous," he complained to me. "They want polar bears and hunting seals and descriptions of the Eskimo's savage way of life. And faster, ever faster, they want it!"

He was pushing his recovery, anxious to complete his writing. There were deadlines to meet, he insisted, and cash advances to earn. His family, worried about the reckless way he was driving himself, entreated with him to come home to Philadelphia. He would not—not without me.

Therefore, it was Morton and I who watched over him, making certain that he ate decent meals and slept enough. To the both of us, it seemed like a task of holding back the sea with a broom. The more Elisha poured his soul onto paper, the less of it there was to sustain his physical body.

Chapter Forty-Three
Maggie

Elisha delivered his completed manuscript to its publisher in the early fall of 1856. "This book, poor as it is, has been my coffin," he said gloomily as he packed it into a leather valise.

"Oh, Dr. Kane," protested Mrs. Walters, who had accompanied me on a visit to his lodgings. "You mustn't tempt fate with such utterings!"

He looked up sheepishly, caught my smothered smile. "My apologies, Mrs. Walters," he said. "I have been depressed by illness, and I'm afraid I am poor company. It is hard to believe, but I think I was healthier in the Arctic—if you do not count the scurvy."

"And the frostbite," I added.

"And the chafing and the itching," he continued, winking at me while Mrs. Walters fluttered her handkerchief in front of her face in distaste.

Although it was easy enough to tease poor Ellen Walters, the fact remained that Elisha could not conquer this latest attack of rheumatic fever. Many years after the original infection that had nearly killed him as a youth, this persistent affliction had disabled him once more. Frustrated by his lack of vitality, Elisha had decided to consult his private physician in

Philadelphia and hand-deliver his manuscript to the publishers at the same time.

I was unhappy to see him return to Philadelphia and into the clutches of his mother, but I could not say this, of course. I had to appear cheery and content to send him off to his family and his doctor, and I did hope, of course, that the latter would have some miraculous cure.

On this particular day, the afternoon before his departure, he had a special surprise to cushion the sadness of his leave-taking. I recognized the gleam in his eye when he handed me the velvet-wrapped box, and so I knew that he expected to enjoy my reaction. Even thus warned, I could not control my gasp.

"It is from Tiffany's," he said, lifting the bracelet from its silk-lined bed, the diamonds winking brilliantly. "I ordered it weeks ago, but I was afraid it would not be ready in time."

"Elisha! What have you done? I couldn't possibly accept such a gift!" Nonetheless, my arm rose of its own accord, and he wrapped it around my wrist. "You cannot afford this; I know that, Ly." I tore my eyes away from the dazzling diamonds set in gold and met his affectionate gaze.

"You cannot turn it down, Maggie," he said. "Are you saying you will not marry me?"

"What?" I murmured breathlessly.

"No promissory ring this time," he assured me. "An engagement, truly."

"Another secret one?" I asked, unable to bite it back.

He paused, wincing. "Discreet, at least. Unless you want the newspaper reporters at your house again."

"No, I do not care to relive that nonsense," I said.

"Will you marry me, darling spirit?" he asked again. "I would get down on one knee, but I am afraid I would embarrass myself trying to get up again. Still, if you would prefer it…"

"No, no!" I exclaimed, gripping his arms when he made as if to kneel.

"No, you will not marry me?" But he was grinning, teasing me.

"No! I mean, I will! You know I will!" Somehow I found myself in his arms, and he kissed me possessively, even in front of Mrs. Walters, who, for her part, blushed and cried out, "Oh dear, whatever is your mother going to say, Maggie?"

"My mother," I moaned, pulling my lips back from his. "*Your* mother! You must tell her, Ly. You must tell her during this visit, or I swear I shall break the engagement myself this time!"

"I will tell her," he promised. And he kissed me again.

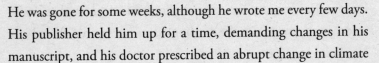

He was gone for some weeks, although he wrote me every few days. His publisher held him up for a time, demanding changes in his manuscript, and his doctor prescribed an abrupt change in climate that necessitated an extended overseas voyage:

> As fond of travel as I am, the idea does not appeal. If I must lie limpidly anywhere, I would rather it be by your side, with your gentle hand upon my fevered brow. However, my physician is sending me to a spa in Switzerland where the high altitude and cold air may alleviate my symptoms. Additionally, my publisher has agreed to foot some of the costs if I will divert

first to England, there to meet with Lady Franklin and the British Admiralty.

They have proposed another mission of exploration and have suggested me as commander, hoping for a collaborative British and American achievement. Do not worry, my darling. I am in no fit condition for such a venture, and besides, I have my obligation to you now, as well. My publisher wishes me to make the trip only to support the great Lady's cause. Thus, a brief stay in England, a recuperative visit to Switzerland, and then home to you, my love. My mother is resigned—or at least I have told her that she must be, by the time I return, for that is when we shall be married.

I admit I despaired to read those words, knowing that I would again have to await his return from a long voyage for the redemption of his promise. To be true, England and Switzerland were not as deadly as the Arctic, but he was not so ill when he left me the last time. It seemed folly to send a man in his condition on such a long trip.

And of course, the last time he left me, I did not know that he would come back and forsake his vow. It seemed a faithless thing to doubt him now. But I did, and it proved impossible for me to hide this from him.

He called upon me as soon as he returned to New York, turning up on Mrs. Walters's doorstep a day before I had expected him. With a cry of joy, I pulled him into the foyer and covered his face with kisses before I had even closed the door. He laughed and caught my hand, turning aside my sleeve. "You are wearing my bracelet," he observed with some satisfaction.

"I never take it off," I told him proudly.

He paused then and looked up at the stairs. We were accustomed to sitting in my private parlor on the third floor during his visits, and the look on his face tore at my heart. I could see that he dreaded the climb.

"We cannot go to that parlor," I said then. "Mrs. Walters has decided to have it painted, and the fumes are unbearable. For my sake, let us sit downstairs."

"Maggie, I always know when you are lying," Elisha said reprovingly. "Even on the day I first met you, I thought to myself, 'This angel, with her luminous eyes and her perfect lips, is deceiving me.' Oh, I was truly consternated that I could not figure out how you were doing it!"

"Then I shall be relentlessly honest with you," I said, standing very close to him. "I do not wish to climb to the third floor, because I want you to save your breath for other things!" I slipped my arms around his neck, pressing my lips against his and thoroughly distracting him from thoughts of staircases and foolish pride, until he came with me to the ground-floor parlor like a docile little lamb, led by the hand.

Elisha spent most of his time with me for the next few days. He brought me several highly personal gifts: a set of handkerchiefs embroidered with his initials—because he had noted how often I misplaced my own—and a locket that had belonged to his grandmother. Because he no longer had the stamina for outings in the park, he spent entire afternoons reclining upon Mrs. Walters's settee while I sat in a chair beside him, reading aloud to him and holding one hand, as requested, upon his brow.

It was—just as he had said—fevered.

And perhaps because of this ominous sign, we both grew more and more depressed by his approaching trip. On the evening before his departure, we were frankly morose. Mother and Kate had come to say farewell to him, and both of them kept trying to meet my eye with eyebrows raised and mouths turned down as if to say, "Whatever is the matter with you two?"

When he finally came to take his leave, I walked with him down the hallway to the front door. My steps came ever slower and smaller until at last I stopped in the middle of the corridor and nearly bent double, suddenly overcome with tears.

"Maggie, dearest, please don't cry!" he exclaimed, turning me toward him.

I turned my tear-stained face up to his. "I am afraid for you to leave me in this condition!"

He took my face between his two hands and stared at me as if trying to memorize my features. "I am such a fool," he said. "I should have married you when I had the chance. How did I ever let my family bend me to their will? I was so sure I could have my cake and eat it, too, that I could make everyone happy and have my own way. Yet here I am, about to leave you again, and I have never redeemed my promise to you!"

I should have reassured him then that I had faith in him, but instead I just continued to cry helplessly, my lips parted but unable to speak. Knowing me as he did, he read the doubt in my eyes, and it wounded him.

"I have left it too late," he said in despair. "Even this week, I could have…and did not. But Maggie, you *are* my wife, my very own wife. No ceremony or magistrate could make you more so than you already are. You *are* my wife, are you not?"

"Yes, I am," I cried. "In my heart, I am!"

"If we pledge ourselves before witnesses, it is as binding as any marriage in a church. It is both legal and sacred as any ceremony before a magistrate." His eyes held my own in thrall. "Would you be willing *now* to enter such a bond?"

I nodded, dumbfounded. He took my hand and strode back down the hallway to the parlor, with a vigor he had not shown in weeks. Mother and Kate were still there, although Mrs. Walters had gone to her room. He should have waited until we could summon her back, but none of us thought of it then.

He expressed his intention to my mother, who was bewildered and confused. "Do you mean…like a Quaker ceremony?" she said.

"Exactly," he affirmed. "It is a time-honored custom in common law." And then he swung me around to face him again, holding my hands between his own. "Maggie—Margaretta Fox—is my wife, and I am her husband. Wherever we are, she is mine, and I am hers. Do you understand and consent to this, Maggie?"

"I do," I whispered. "You are my husband, Elisha Kane, and I am your wife…unto death."

"But I want my daughter married in a church!" Mother wailed, as Elisha kissed me and embraced me.

"She will be," he promised over the top of my head. "We shall do it again properly when I return. You have my word—as your son."

386

I received only four letters from Elisha on his trip. The first came from Liverpool, England, where his ship disembarked:

Dearest Wife,

How truly novel and wonderful to write those words! I shall do it again. Dearest Wife, I have arrived safely and plan a departure to London within the hour. Forgive the brevity of this letter, but Morton is even now arranging our transport. I will write again upon arrival in the great city and apprise you of the address where you may reach me should you need anything.

Your beloved husband,

Ly

The second letter, two weeks later, was of greater length but written in Morton's hand, which immediately revealed how sick Elisha really was. Amusing anecdotes filled the letter, cleverly written with Elisha's recognizable turn of phrase, for all the handwriting was that of another man's. He spoke of his meetings with Lady Franklin, her overwhelming personality and strong convictions: "She would lead the expedition herself, if only the Admiralty would allow it."

He did not speak of his illness, although it was clear that he could not hold his own pen. I sat at home, pacing and worrying and wringing my hands. What good did it do me to be called his wife when I still had no recourse but to wait in the rear for his return?

"I should have gone with him!" I cried to the walls of the house.

The third letter returned to brevity and was once more dictated in his secretary's hand:

My darling Maggie,

I am sent now to Havana—yes, Cuba, rather than Switzerland after all. England was a mistake, for the climate has disagreed with me sharply. All my engagements here are canceled, and I am commanded to seek warmer lands. Cuba is but a week's travel from New York. Will you come if I send for you? Please write me care of American Consul, Havana. Will advise you upon arrival.

Lovingly,

Elisha

By now, I was greatly alarmed. No one could console me. There was no hiding the gravity of his condition. In fact, newsboys shouted it on the streets of New York so that I could not even walk to church or to the park without wanting to cover my ears. "Kane Collapses at London Reception!" they cried. "Arctic Explorer Rushed Aboard Steamer to the Tropics!" What anguish it was, to have my beloved's critical condition bandied about in the press to satisfy the curiosity of the public! Horace Greeley's paper carried a lengthy story regarding Dr. Kane's declining state of health. Even though Mr. Greeley sent me a private note expressing his concern for my state of mind, it evidently did not preclude his making the story a first-page sensation.

I waited impatiently for word to reach me of his arrival in Cuba. My trunk was packed, the same trunk he had purchased for me when I moved to Crooksville. Mother had agreed to accompany me when the time came, although she was reluctant and apprehensive. She had never traveled such a distance and was quite wary of visiting a land where English was a foreign tongue.

When the fourth letter came, it was a shock beyond bearing. It was written in a strange hand, neither Elisha's nor Morton's, with disjointed ill-formed letters and nearly indecipherable spelling. When translated into something approaching sense, the gist was this:

> Why have you not come? I have received no letters from you! I am sick unto death without you—will you not come to me?

I cried out loud upon reading it. He had not received my letters? I had written nearly one a day and sent them to Havana. They should have been waiting for him upon his arrival. I could have been on a steamer already if I had known he was in Cuba. Who was writing his letters, and where was Morton?

For help, I sought the Grinnells. A carriage took me to their home, and a servant placed me in a small parlor to await a member of the family. I would have preferred Mrs. Sarah Grinnell, but was obliged to accept Cornelius, who was located after nearly an hour of impatient waiting.

"My dear Miss Fox," he said breathlessly. "You must accept my apology for your long wait. I know you must be concerned—"

"Concerned?" I broke in sharply. "That does not even scratch the surface, Mr. Grinnell. I have been waiting three weeks for word that Dr. Kane's ship had reached Havana, and now today I receive a letter that suggests he has been there for some time and has received none of the letters that I sent to him. He is very sick…very sick, Mr. Grinnell… and he needs me…" Here I struggled not to break down entirely.

"I don't know what to tell you, Miss Fox," Cornelius stammered. "I know that Dr. Kane arrived in Cuba some days ago. His mother and brother met him there…"

My sharp intake of breath said it all. He broke off at once, and we stared at each other, both knowing why my letters had not reached Elisha and why I had not been notified of his arrival. He was mortified. I was livid. "Please help me," I whispered, my face flushed. "I need to get to Havana as quickly as I can."

"Miss Fox," he replied, in a whisper just as anguished as my own. "You will not be welcomed, I fear."

Wordlessly, I handed him my last letter from Elisha. As he read it, I saw the struggle on his face. He had always followed the dictates of his father, who was in turn strongly influenced by Judge Kane. But here in his hand was a letter from his dear friend, who had not even the strength to write it himself but had made use of some uneducated servant in his desperation to deliver the message. When he looked up, I saw that even Cornelius Grinnell had been moved to tears. "I will buy your passage personally," he said. "I will book you on the soonest ship."

❧

The soonest ship was three weeks away. I nearly died with impatience but had to console myself by telegraphing Havana, care of Mr. William Morton, that I was on my way. I followed this with a letter, vividly proclaiming my love and my urgent concern, again addressing it to Morton in the hopes that it would escape the hands of Mrs. Kane and Robert.

Newspaper accounts continued to be grim, and yet they were so often inaccurate and contradictory. Dr. Kane was still news, and if there was no news to report, the journalists in Havana had little scruples about making it up. I was heartsick and weary of their nonsense. I relied on the good sense of Morton and hoped that I would get a detailed account within days.

My departure for Havana was set for mid-February, just a few days after Elisha's birthday. It would take a week to arrive at best, and I could expect an uncertain reception, but as the date approached, I felt more and more relieved. I would soon be at his side, and once there I could bear anything.

I was seated at breakfast, only two days before my ship was set to leave, when Clementine Walters brought me the newspaper. It was such an unlikely thing for her to do. I should have known better than to take it from her hand with so little thought, hardly looking at her, without recognizing the malice in her little cock-eyed expression.

However, so self-absorbed was I in my misery that I took the offering with scarcely an acknowledgment and unfolded it innocently to the headline page.

The words were nearly one inch high:

KANE DEAD.

NATION MOURNS.

I rose from my chair, gasping for air. The room spun around, swinging upside down. Dimly I heard Mrs. Walters cry out.

The world diminished, blackening around the edges, shrinking, until I could see only those two horrible words—

And then my head struck the floor.

Chapter Forty-Four
Kate

At first we thought Maggie might follow him into the grave. Falling into a collapse far greater than the one she suffered after Troy so many years ago, my sister succumbed to a dangerously high fever. For days she thrashed in her bed, soaked with sweat and rambling incoherently. Our doctor diagnosed it as a brain fever and proscribed laudanum, but this medication sent her into a delirium so deep and disturbing that we soon abandoned it.

Meanwhile, preparations were made to transport Elisha's body from Havana back to Philadelphia. Newspapers reported that a great procession accompanied his casket to the port, where a ship with railings dressed in black cloth was waiting to receive it. All American ships in the port flew their flags at half-mast, and a cannon cavalcade saluted the ship as it departed.

Mother telegraphed the Kane family in Philadelphia, inquiring about Maggie's role in the planned funeral arrangements, but received no reply. By that time, however, we knew that she would not be in any condition to attend, and so we ignored this discourtesy for the time being. While I held my sister's thin hand, she languished in her sickbed, whispering, "Where is he now?" And I would patiently tell her. It was not difficult to keep track.

The steamer landed in New Orleans, and another procession accompanied Elisha's body to the city hall, where it lay in state for several days. From there it was moved to a steamboat on the Mississippi and transported north to the Ohio River. "Strange that even the corpse of the Arctic wanderer is traveling still," reported one newspaper.

When his casket disembarked in Cincinnati, it began an even stranger journey, in which cities across Ohio vied for the honor of hosting the body of Dr. Kane. In each place there was a pause in progress so that his casket could lie in state in the city hall or some other public place. Speeches were made, and thousands of people lined up in the streets to see his casket pass. "Poor Kane was a true martyr to science," spoke the mayor of one city. "There is a genuine sanctity in his coffin, worth the prestige of a thousand conquering heroes."

The wife of Mr. Henry Grinnell called upon us before her departure for Philadelphia, where she planned to attend the funeral ceremonies. She stayed only a few minutes with Maggie, and then left the sickroom quite disturbed by my sister's condition. "The poor child is not in a state to care about this at present," she told my mother, "but I know you are concerned for her future welfare, even if she thinks right now that she has no future. So I want you to understand that Dr. Kane made some disposition for her care before he left for England. On the morning of his departure, I was called to my husband's business chamber to witness a will written by Dr. Kane, in which he left five thousand dollars in the care of his brother, to be delivered to Miss Fox in the event of his death."

"His brother Robert Kane?" I asked, with some concern.

Mrs. Grinnell turned her gaze upon me, and I knew she understood my apprehension, although she was too much a lady to say so. "I understood that Mr. Robert Kane was already the executor of his will, and as this was a last minute change, it was simplest to arrange it thus."

We asked Mrs. Grinnell if Dr. Kane had spoken of the marriage ceremony performed at Mrs. Walters's house the night before he changed his will, and she expressed some surprise and puzzlement. "He never said a thing," she exclaimed. "Why, is that even legal in this day and age?"

That was a question Mother and I asked ourselves daily.

Three weeks after his death, Elisha's body was still in transport on its circuitous route home to Philadelphia. From Ohio the casket had been carried by train to Baltimore, where it lay in state at the Maryland Institute below a banner reading "Science Weeps, Humanity Weeps, the World Weeps." It was early March before the coffin finally boarded a train for Philadelphia, where the grandest and lengthiest services of all were planned. The funeral procession for Elisha Kent Kane, lasting over a month and traversing from Havana to Philadelphia, was the longest and most celebrated in American history. "Not even an American president has received such an honor," proclaimed Mr. Greeley's newspaper, "for no president since Washington has been as universally loved as Dr. Kane, by the North and the South, the East and the West."

When he was finally laid to rest in his family crypt outside Philadelphia, Mother and I, at last, breathed a sigh of relief.

For those of us who knew Elisha, it was astonishing to behold this outpouring of grief from thousands of people who did not know him at all. He was only a man, after all, with virtues and faults like any other person. True, he was bold and daring, generous and charming. He was witty and intellectual in public and also wrote tender poetry in private. But Elisha could also be pompous and sanctimonious, and his ambition was self-consuming. He loved my sister, yes, but not as much as he loved himself.

This is not to say that I didn't grieve for him. I did weep for Elisha, who might have been my brother. I would miss his clever conversation and his irreverent grin. I would miss his sense of humor and fondly recall his talent for mimicry. I would miss the way he used to roll his eyes behind Leah's back, and the kindness with which he addressed Mother, no matter how foolishly she rambled.

However, as I sat by the side of my grief-stricken sister, who lay in her bed as if rehearsing for her own coffin, I could not help but also resent him. "He has taken half my soul with him," she whispered to me, which sounded like some of Elisha's romantic nonsense. Maggie was supposed to be the practical one, but she was wasting away with these morbid, fanciful thoughts. Nothing can take our souls from us, not even death.

He should have married her properly. He should have done it when he returned from the Arctic, over a year ago. The ending would have been the same, for I had known ever since my vision that he would die of sickness at a young age. But at least Maggie could have spent that time as his proper wife, and perhaps there would have been a child to comfort her when he was gone.

My mother blamed Elisha's parents, but I thought he was old enough to make his own decision. Certainly he did not consult his parents in any other aspect of his life. Perhaps they were only an excuse, and the truth was that Elisha feared his reputation as a great man of science would suffer if he took a spirit rapper as his wife.

All the more of a fool was he. What had he accomplished in his lifetime that was truly lasting? All this great display of national mourning, the banners, the flags at half-mast—for what? I could not put my finger on any significant achievement. He made a voyage that failed at its goals and managed to turn it into a heroic endeavor of science and humanitarianism. For all that I had liked the man personally, I could not see anything that justified his treatment as the newest Meriwether Lewis in the history of American exploration.

If one wanted to compare accomplishments, I think Maggie and I had achieved a more lasting success. Hundreds of thousands of people across the world were now exploring communication with the dead, a more worthwhile realm for investigation than the Arctic seas, in my opinion.

I feared that a terrible tragedy loomed on the horizon for our country. The visions came to me more often now, not only in my trances, but troubling my waking moments as well. Repeatedly I dreamed of a conflict so savage and vast that Americans born generations from now would still be feeling its aftereffects. Soon no one would care that Dr. Kane had discovered a patch of water off the coast of Greenland. But thousands and thousands of people would have reason to wish they could speak to their dead.

Poor Elisha. He sacrificed much for his fame, including my sister. But I suspect time will still rob him of that which he held dearer than anything else.

Chapter Forty-Five
Maggie

I should have known it was impossible to keep him. He was like the bright flame of a match, blazing intensely for only a brief time, destined to burn out too soon and scorch the fingers of anyone trying to hold on. If it had not been his valiant heart that felled him, it would have been the Arctic, or some other heroic venture. We were never going to lead a quiet life together, no matter how much we idly dreamed about it. He was not the kind of man to live quietly.

After his death, I was desperately ill. Grief and regret tormented me in turns, piercing my heart. He had died hundreds of miles away, wanting me and thinking that I had forsaken him. Why had I not taken passage to Havana when I first knew he had left England? I could have been waiting for him when he arrived. I could have been with him at the end, held him in my arms, and eased his passing with my tears. There was also the thought, cruelest of all, that my presence might have given him the strength to rally, as Leah had once done for Calvin...

Mother and Kate and Ellen attended me lovingly, all three of them demonstrating patience beyond what I deserved. After all, was my loss greater than that of Mrs. Jane Appleton Pierce, who saw her son crushed to death in a train wreck? Was it greater than Mrs. Granger's, whose daughter was poisoned by her own husband? Was my loss greater than my brother David's, who lost his daughter to a fever in just two days? I had no business thinking that my suffering was more than that of any other human soul in this imperfect world, and yet it was *my* suffering, and as such, unbearable.

Poor Mother tried so hard to comfort me. "Doctor was a devoted spiritualist," she said. "Surely he would send a message to you, if you would just open yourself to receive it." Dear, silly Mother. She had no idea why her words caused me to turn my face to the wall in despair.

Physician, heal thyself. That is the message he would have sent, I think, with that ironic laugh of his. Having spent the last nine years consoling the bereaved with my rapping from the dead, was I able to lighten my own grief?

No. Because I knew I was a fraud.

I had no better understanding than anyone else of whether there truly was a heaven or a fiery perdition either. For all that Kate and I had rapped out messages from a spiritual paradise, blithely promising salvation for all and eternal happiness in another world, I did not know what happened after death. If there was a heaven to be attained, had I earned it by easing the grief of other people, or was I bound for another destination because I accomplished my work through lies?

And what would happen to me, now that the man who had promised to rescue me from this life of deceit had gone to his own reward without me?

My dreams, when I was able to achieve slumber, tormented me with visions of what might have been. In dreams he returned to me, healthy and hale; I could hear his laugh and feel his hands in mine, his lips upon my cheek. But even in the depths of sleep I knew it for a falsehood and whimpered in dread of the morning. The first moments of wakefulness would strike me like a hammer, and I would open my eyes reluctantly on a world where he did not exist.

I did not die of grief. No one ever truly does.

The days spiraled downward, dark and long and empty. Then one day, I found that I could abide my sickbed no longer, and so I moved to a chair and stared blankly out the window. On another day, I could no longer bear to sit idle, and so I picked up a needle and thread. One simple act followed another, until I finally faced myself in the mirror and beheld the hollowed cheeks, sunken eyes, and matted hair of a woman who had wallowed in her misery for nearly eight weeks. That day I said to myself, "The widow of Dr. Kane should not demean his memory with an appearance like this," and I sent Ellen out with an order for two mourning dresses in deep black crinoline.

Everyone was so relieved to see me demonstrate some sign of life that they allowed the dresses to be delivered. Then Kate sat down beside me, gently took my hand, and queried, "How are you going to pay for them, Maggie?"

If I was going to live after all, then it would be necessary to make a living. It seemed a terribly mundane concern, something that should not have mattered in a world where the post would never again bring one of his letters, where I would never again bask in his smile. Yet I was keenly aware that I had lived all these weeks on the charity of my friend Mrs. Walters, and I did not wish to burden her any longer. The time had come, Kate explained, to address the legacy that Elisha had left in his will.

"It is fortunate that you have decided to take an interest," she said, "for I have already written Mr. Kane to inquire about your inheritance." I gave her a look of surprise and suspicion then, which caused her to add defensively, "I did not write in your name, Maggie. I used Mother's name."

"Oh, Kate," I sighed.

"Would you rather I had let Mother write on her own?"

No, of course not. I would not have wanted Robert Kane to sneer at my mother's uneducated scrawl. Kate explained that her initial inquiry had been answered by a curt and disinterested reply. "I can show you the letter," she offered.

"Do not bother," I told her. "I am familiar with his style of communication."

Kate had written him again, persisting in her request for information on the legacy, this time presenting me as Dr. Kane's legal widow. Unsurprisingly, this seemed to catch the lawyer's attention, and he announced an intention to call upon us to discuss the situation.

I did not look forward to it. However, I knew that I could not expect the Kanes to honor my rights as Elisha's widow out of the kindness of their hearts. And so I steeled myself for an unpleasant interview and resolved to behave with the dignity of a lady, however he addressed me as less than one.

I dressed in one of my new mourning gowns for his visit, knowing that the significance of my "widow's weeds" would not escape his shrewd notice. Mrs. Walters and I received him in the parlor alone, as I had decided that the complication of Mother's or Kate's presence was unnecessary. Kate was unhappy to be excluded, but I knew she would not refrain from sharpening her tongue on the man who had treated me so shabbily. And Mother would be bewildered and hurt by the derision of the Kane family representative.

Mr. Kane greeted us perfunctorily and seated himself, crossing his legs with a mannerism that so resembled Elisha it caused a painful stab in my heart. Then he looked up with his cold, hooded eyes and the similarity, thankfully, disappeared. To no one's surprise, he began by announcing he was unable to deliver the money bequeathed to me in Elisha's will.

"My brother did not have five thousand dollars when he passed away," Robert Kane explained. "He was entirely dependent on my father's allowance for his living expenses. I am afraid that the money bestowed upon you in his last-minute codicil does not exist."

"What about his book?" I asked.

"The book has not yet been published. If there were any cash advances, they have all been spent."

"Dr. Kane must have believed the money would come from somewhere," I said reasonably. "He was hardly likely to change his will on the morning of his departure to bequeath a sum of money he did not have."

"Perhaps he did it to satisfy some person's demand," Kane said blandly, "not believing the will would ever be put into effect. I do not think he expected to die on that trip, Miss Fox."

"Your implication is clear, Mr. Kane," Mrs. Walters broke in, "although completely wrong."

For just a moment, Kane looked as surprised as if a mouse in the corner of the room had decided to speak. Mrs. Walters flushed nervously, but pushed up her spectacles and looked at him defiantly. She had resented Mr. Kane ever since he made me sign that document denying my engagement, and she had a few pent-up opinions to express.

"Miss Fox never made any demands on Dr. Kane, although he had raised and dashed her hopes repeatedly. *You* may not have known how sick he was when he left here last October, but I can assure you that *he* did. He was worried and frightened enough to arrange an impromptu marriage on the eve of his departure. He then took the sensible precaution of providing for his new wife in the event that the worst came to pass."

Recovering from his consternation at this unexpected outburst, Kane composed his features into their normal expressionless mask and said, "Ah, yes, this so-called marriage ceremony, done without benefit of magistrate, minister, or document. Did you witness it, Mrs. Walters?" He reached into his coat pocket and removed a small daybook, opening it with a gesture very like his brother. Again I closed my eyes and tried not to dwell upon their close resemblance.

"I am afraid I did not witness it, Mr. Kane," Mrs. Walters confessed. "I had already retired for the evening. But I heard all about it the next morning."

"From my brother?" he asked, making note in his book.

"No, from Miss Fox, and then later from her mother and sister."

"Miss Fox's mother and sister are the only witnesses, then," he confirmed. At Mrs. Walters's affirmation, he turned suddenly to me and asked, "Was the marriage consummated following this ceremony?"

I was shocked into breathlessness by the effrontery of his question and could barely speak to object. "That is certainly not a matter for discussion!"

"No, I am afraid it has a certain legal significance," he persisted. "Did you behave as his wife?"

Flushing with mortification, I cast my eyes down in the semblance of modesty while I frantically considered my answer. To say no might lessen the legality of the marriage, but to say yes would damage my reputation if the marriage was struck down. Appearance was more important than truth here, and only I knew the truth anyway, now that Elisha was gone.

Robert Kane waited patiently for my answer, no doubt enjoying my delicate dilemma. Thankfully, I was saved from a reply by an unlikely source.

"No cohabitation is necessary for the marriage to be legal," Mrs. Walters piped up. Elisha's brother turned his head and stared at her as if the mouse in the room had now climbed up his trouser leg and bitten his finger. My brave little friend was flushed bright pink, her hands twisted together with nervousness, but she cleared her throat and continued. "I inquired last week with a lawyer who attends my church." She glanced at me and drew strength from my grateful smile. "He told me that Dr. Kane knew what he was doing. The common-law ceremony is still recognized in this state, and Miss Fox's mother and sister are perfectly legal witnesses."

"Legal, perhaps," sniffed Mr. Kane, "but not necessarily believable. The problem is credibility. My brother never expressed to his family any intention of marrying Miss Fox, nor gave any indication that he had already done so, and I was with him up until his very death."

It was a hurtful statement, perhaps meant to bait me. I wanted to rail at him and vent my anguish. *I would have been there too, had you not thwarted me at every turn, forbidden our match, and diverted my communication in Havana!* But I knew that it was a useless protest and had steeled myself against it before his arrival. A true lady might be forgiven for losing her temper; a woman who had risen up through the lower classes to present herself as a lady did not have that luxury.

Instead, with great self-control, I replied evenly, "I think you will find he stated his intentions to your aunt, Miss Eliza Leiper. And she is under the distinct impression that he informed his parents as well."

Mr. Kane simply regarded me impassively. "I am very sorry, Miss Fox, but I cannot corroborate that. Perhaps you do not know that my aunt passed away suddenly over a month ago."

That was shocking enough to get a reaction out of me, no matter how I had hardened my heart to this man. I gasped out loud and pressed my fingers to my lips in distress. Miss Leiper, dead? While I lay in my bed and languished in my grief, she had died? For a long moment, I was too distraught to speak. Poor Miss Leiper, that dear lady!

"The Pattersons," I whispered finally, my last hope for a friendly welcome among this cold and forbidding family.

"The Pattersons," he echoed. "The Pattersons never believed my brother would marry you. It seems they knew him a good deal better than you did. I am afraid that Elisha was known in his youth as something of a ladies' man…"

My heart was thudding painfully in my breast, but I carefully modulated my voice to a firm evenness. "You will *not* twist my memory of him, Mr. Kane. I am already familiar with your talent for distorting the truth, and I was also warned by your aunt that you were a 'detestable' man." Here I leaned slightly forward and kept my tone as sweet as honey. "When I repeated that to Elisha, he laughed and agreed."

There may have been a flicker, just a fleeting moment, where his eyes widened in reaction, and I felt rewarded for my small and petty tit for tat. I continued while I felt an advantage. "Besides, Mr. Kane, I have dozens of letters in which your brother discusses our engagement and our intended marriage. There is even one that addresses me as his wife. So do not pretend that you knew his mind better than I did."

We glared at each other in hearty dislike for a second or two, and then Kane cleared his throat and returned to his professional demeanor. "Returning to the matter at hand, I am afraid that you will be disappointed in your expectations, Miss Fox. I am unable to honor my brother's bequest to you, but I can offer you a small settlement from my own funds—five hundred dollars—under the condition that you hand over all of Dr. Kane's correspondence and retract this fanciful tale of a common-law marriage."

I should not have been surprised. He had tried to acquire them once before. Still, I shook my head in disbelief. "You cannot have Elisha's letters. They are all I have left of him."

"Come now, Miss Fox, that is not true. I can see from here that you have a diamond bracelet, purchased at great expense with my father's money, and a locket that once belonged to my grandmother. I am sure you can get a pretty penny for the bracelet, although I would request that you consult me before selling the locket. I would give you more than a pawnshop, seeing as it is a treasured family heirloom."

I placed a hand protectively over the locket, staring at him in wide-eyed shock. "I think it is time you left," I whispered.

He rose but made no move toward the door. Closing his little daybook and slipping it back inside his coat, he said, "You have no hold on our family, Miss Fox. We do not recognize any contract of marriage between you and my late brother. If you take your claims to the courts or to the press, or if you try to make public my brother's letters, we shall take legal action against you."

"Make public the letters…" I repeated incredulously. "Is that what you think of me? Those are personal and deeply private letters, Mr. Kane. I would not sell them to anyone…least of all you. You mistake me for…for someone like yourself, a hard-hearted and vile individual with no human feeling at all!"

I rose from my chair and pierced him with an imperious glare. "You shame yourself, sir, in this callous betrayal of your brother's wishes. I *am* Elisha's wife…in the eyes of God *and* the law. You cannot unmake that sacred bond. Not by wishing it away, and not by intimidation!"

His mouth twisted in an ironic smirk. He turned and bowed politely to Mrs. Walters, who was huffing indignantly at him, then replaced his hat on his head and started for the door. He strode past me as though I were a house servant unworthy of notice, without acknowledgment or farewell.

Mrs. Walters was up and out of her seat in the blink of an eye. "Oh, Maggie," she gasped, taking my two hands in her own, "what a horrid man! I hope I did not speak out of turn…"

"No, Ellen," I assured her, giving her a grateful hug even though I was trembling with belated reaction from head to toe. "You were wonderful!"

"Forgive me, dear," she said, "for I know how much you loved Dr. Kane, but his brother is a nasty piece of work! And from his behavior I would conclude that the rest of his family is not much better!"

"I was warned as much," I murmured, clasping my cold hands to my bosom and gripping Elisha's locket.

Yes, I had been amply warned.

Chapter Forty-Six
Maggie

I did not lack for advice. Everyone had some sort of opinion on what I should do next. It seemed that in the whole of my life, there had always been someone telling me what to do. At last, I had reached the end of my tolerance for it.

Mrs. Walters asked her lawyer acquaintance from church to call upon me and offer his professional counsel. He kindly waived his consulting fee in exchange for a slice of Mrs. Walters's chiffon cake and a cup of tea. I do not know what he thought of his side of the bargain, but for my part, I found his advice singularly unappetizing.

"I think you should take Mr. Kane's offer," he said, with no hesitation or preamble. "Mind you, the Kanes can do better than five hundred dollars. I would not accept less than twenty percent of the original legacy. Nor would I turn the letters over directly to Mr. Kane. Rather, you should place them in trust with a person or bank agreed upon by both parties."

"But you said the marriage contract was legally binding," I objected.

The lawyer raised a finger. "That is true, but you would have to prove it actually occurred. The executor of Dr. Kane's estate is not going to acknowledge the marriage, because you might then claim more than the original five-thousand-dollar legacy. There may be nothing in the estate at present, but when Dr. Kane's book is published, I think you can anticipate that its value will substantially appreciate. I fear that the Kanes would be willing to spend rather more money than you have at your disposal to prevent you from gaining control of that estate."

"Oh, Mr. Blake," exclaimed Mrs. Walters, "that seems so unjust! If she is entitled to more…"

The gentleman shook his head regretfully. "I cannot recommend that a young woman in Miss Fox's circumstances attempt to best a family like the Kanes in court. It would be of no great difficulty for them to drag the case on for years, until Miss Fox's resources are expired. Consider as well that the marriage may be legally binding but not socially acceptable. There are many people who equate the term 'common-law wife' with 'mistress,' if you will excuse my use of that vulgar term. In my opinion, good ladies, it would be in Miss Fox's best interests to strike an agreement with the Kanes over the inheritance and drop the matter of the marriage, lest she damage her future prospects. When given a choice between money and the good opinion of society, a lady must always choose her reputation."

Ah, better poor than dishonored. Not a surprising bit of advice, coming from a man and given to a woman!

Honestly, I did not know what path my life should take. I was cast adrift among equally dismal futures. My father wrote and asked me to return to Hydesville now that my prospects for marriage had been disappointed, no doubt hoping I would spend my spinsterhood keeping house for him. Mother wanted me to forget my "Quaker marriage," as she called it, and find some respectable Methodist husband—although I could not see myself as anyone but Elisha's wife, today, tomorrow, or ever.

One day during this time of uncertainty, I returned from a morning at church, where I failed to find an answer to my troubles, and discovered Mrs. Walters quite worried over a visitor who had come in my absence. I removed my hat and veil with a listless lack of emotion while she dithered incomprehensibly.

"I told him I wasn't sure it was the best thing," she said. "You have been so much calmer, and I would not like to see you upset again! But it's not my place to turn him away. Maybe it will do you some good, but I am quite afraid—"

"Who is it, Ellen?" I asked, hardly caring. I walked around her before she could bring herself to express an answer and entered the parlor. It was William Morton, seated with his hat in his hand and two packages at his feet.

Two opposite emotions gripped me at once. Dread and longing made a painful vise around my poor, afflicted heart. This man had come to tell me Elisha's last story.

He rose politely at my entrance and greeted me simply. "It is good to see you, Mrs. Kane."

I caught my breath, taken by surprise, and my eyes filled unexpectedly with tears. *Mrs. Kane.* He knew, of course. He was the one person Elisha would have trusted with this secret.

Morton was distressed to see me burst into tears. He looked apprehensively at Mrs. Walters, who promptly chastised him. "I told you!"

"No, please!" I said hastily. "I will compose myself. Be seated, Mr. Morton. I...I am glad that you have come."

I sat opposite him, my eye immediately drawn toward the packages. One was a small bundle of letters; the other was twelve inches square and wrapped in an old sheet.

"The last thing I want to do is upset you, Mrs. Kane," the young man said with a wary look at Mrs. Walters, who seated herself discreetly, as always, in the corner. "But I felt it was my duty to come...it is the last duty I can do for him, in fact."

I nodded and blotted at my eyes with a handkerchief. "I cannot promise that there will be no tears, Mr. Morton. But there are some things I must know. I cannot live without knowing them."

"His thoughts were with you to the last, I can assure you."

"Please...he did not think I had abandoned him?" I begged shamelessly. "I had a letter from him...it said he had received no letters and asked why I did not come to him..." I fumbled to retrieve it from my reticule. I had it with me always, unable to leave my guilt behind.

Morton looked puzzled as he accepted the note from my hand, and his brow creased when he saw the coarsely shaped letters and poor spelling. "It must have been a servant at the hotel who wrote this for him," he mused. "I did not know of it, and I was with him nearly always. His mother was also with him most of the time, but he clearly sent this out secretly." Elisha's secretary raised his eyes to me. "I would have spared you the pain of this if I could. Do not think he was accusing you—or that he thought you had not written. We knew your letters had gone missing. I think—the person who wrote this just did not understand what Dr. Kane was trying to say."

"Because he did not speak the language?"

"Because…" the young man sighed and then went on with great reluctance. "Because the doctor suffered a stroke aboard ship en route to Havana. By the time we reached Cuba, he had lost the use of all four limbs and was able to speak only with great difficulty."

I cried then. I could not help it. Ellen quickly moved from her accustomed place in the corner and sat beside me, lending her strength with one arm about my shoulders. But Morton was committed now to telling the tale and struggled onward, as if climbing through drifts in the Arctic. There was little good to it: a rough Atlantic crossing, damp weather and the soot of London, doctors consulting and disagreeing while Elisha became ever weaker. Switzerland was swapped for Cuba, and my husband boarded this second ship on a stretcher, too ill to walk. Still, he directed Morton to write none of this to me, not wishing to worry or alarm me.

"He was convinced even then that he would recover," Morton said. "He planned to send for you in Cuba, hoping that he would have regained some of his strength by the time you arrived. He directed me to find a seaside hotel, but everything changed after his stroke. I ordered a telegram sent to you by way of the American consulate on our arrival. It was lost—or canceled, I suppose. I did not know that you had been left uninformed until you telegraphed me.

"By the time your letter reached us—and it was clever of you to address it to me—Dr. Kane had suffered a second stroke." Here Morton flushed in embarrassment and his gaze wavered, but he went on. "I read your letter to him. The one you enclosed for me to give to him. So, you see, he knew that you had not forsaken him. He knew that you were on your way."

With great self-control, I managed not to wince. It had been a very private letter, meant only for Elisha's eyes. I simply never imagined that he would be unable to read it himself. Still, I lifted my chin and smiled as best I could through my tears. "Thank you, Mr. Morton. There is no other person I would have trusted with it."

"There is something else," the young man said, still uncharacteristically distressed. "I knew by then that your ship was not going to arrive in time, that it wasn't even going to depart from the United States in time. But I lied to him. I told him you were already on your way—that you were only a couple days from Havana. It seemed to bring him some comfort, and I knew that he would not live long enough to learn of the falsehood. Did I do right, Mrs. Kane? It has weighed heavily upon my conscience."

The poor distraught man looked trustingly to me for comfort. Did he know the irony of asking me, of all people, whether it was right to deceive a person in order to ease his pain? "Yes, Mr. Morton," I said to him. "Heaven forgives the falsehoods told in kindness. You were…a good friend to him, William. You have been a good friend to both of us."

"I saved a few items for you," he said then, clearing his throat and making a conscious effort to recover his usual reserved manner. He reached down and picked up the bundle of letters. "These are your letters. They include the last one to Havana as well as those he was carrying on his person at the time of his trip. They are the ones he always carried, the ones he favored. There was a lock of your hair in one of them. I removed it and…" he drew a breath "…it was entombed with him. I saw to it personally."

I accepted the package gratefully, aware of how the tears ran freely down my face. "Thank you," I whispered. Then I nodded at the larger item on the floor. "That cannot possibly be what I think it is."

Morton smiled proudly and for his answer, unwound the sheet to reveal the portrait beneath. It was faded and cracked and worse for wear, but still, it seemed impossible for it to be here at all. I looked up at Elisha's secretary, completely dumbfounded. "I cannot believe it. Surely it was abandoned with the *Advance*?"

He shook his head. "When we prepared to leave the ship and make our final journey southward, Dr. Kane allotted eight pounds of personal items for each man. This portrait used up most of his allowance, but he never considered leaving it behind." Morton's gaze was fixed somewhere over my shoulder and thousands of miles to the north. "You have to understand. Dr. Kane kept his personal life private. He never spoke of you to them—and yet there was not a man among us who didn't know he was carrying that portrait with him. Every time we unloaded and repacked our cargo, we took special care that "The Commander's Little Lady" should come to no harm.

"He took it with him to England," Morton went on, "planning to have it repaired or duplicated. He had the portrait with him in his room at Havana. It was the one thing his mother did not dare take away," Morton's eyes narrowed in remembrance. "After he… was gone…she gave it to me and ordered me to burn it."

Morton met my gaze proudly and lifted his chin. "But she forgot one thing. I didn't work for *her*. I worked for Dr. Kane."

Chapter Forty-Seven
Maggie

Two days after my visit with Mr. Morton, I rose from my bed at dawn and walked out from the house. Five blocks from Mrs. Walters's street there was a cemetery, and at this time of day, I knew that I would be the only living soul on its premises.

The ground was wet with dew, and beads of moisture lingered on cobwebs spun between the headstones. I wandered, directionless, feeling the hem of my dress grow damp as I meandered through the patchy spring grass. I read each name, the dates, the inscriptions, idly noting the stories revealed by the stones. Here lay a husband and wife with one child between them, all deceased within days of each other. An illness, surely, something deadly and contagious. Here lay a man with a wife on either side of him, the first one dead scarcely more than a decade after her successor was born. A second marriage in middle age for this man, with a much younger wife. But he had outlived both of them just the same, surviving twenty years beyond the passing of the second woman.

The graveyard was full of sad stories. Mine was no more tragic than any other. With a sigh, I sat down upon a stone chosen at random, sat and waited patiently. If the ones who slumbered beneath me had any voice to speak, I would listen. I was ready to receive their messages; I prayed for a sign, any sign.

There was nothing, of course. This was not my first pilgrimage and would probably not be my last, but nothing ever came from it, no glimmer of understanding. Even he who was most precious to me could not reach me, and the echoes of his voice in my mind were nothing more than memories.

No, the dead do not return. God has not willed it. I have never done anything but rap out messages from my own willful imagination. I have used my influence to spread my own sentiments and ideals, and however well intended I may have been, I have done nothing but sell lies to the weak, the desperate, and the gullible.

Now Kate…Kate possessed some gift denied to me…or else she was mad. Yes, that traitorous thought had hidden for some time in my mind, fearfully suppressed. She trusted the voices that spoke in her head; she believed the images that flickered across her vision. My dearest sister needed close watching, and I knew it was my duty to be her guardian and confidant, to protect and shield her when this burden threatened to overwhelm her. Kate was my anchor to life. She was perhaps the sole reason I did not flee to Elisha's tomb and pound upon the door, demanding to be let in so that I might lie down beside him…

I lifted my hand, idly wiping a tear with a wrist bare of ornamentation. The diamond bracelet was gone, traded for the money I needed to hire a lawyer. I had literally ground my teeth in frustration as I handed it over at a pawnshop, just as Robert Kane had predicted I would do, and I cursed the man for forcing me to lower myself to his expectation. But my legal suit would be filed at the Philadelphia Orphan's Court within the week, the bracelet sacrificed for the chance to hold my head up as the wife of Dr. Kane.

I had already been told it was a slim chance.

Sunlight crept weakly across the cemetery grounds. Here and there green bundles of pointed leaves thrust upward from the ground where devoted relatives had planted daffodils and tulips beside their loved ones. Life went on. Every inhabitant of these grounds had left someone behind to shoulder grief and struggle on. How many of those little yellow and red flowers were planted here to serve as markers for futures blighted, diverted, and cut short by an untimely death?

He had left me with nothing but a dubious inheritance and an even more dubious marriage. With even the bracelet gone now, I had not the wherewithal to support myself save by that means that he had so despised. It would have broken Elisha's heart to see me back where he first found me, taking money for lying to people in the dark, living a life of sinful deceit and secret shame.

But Elisha had been no saint. Although he had raised money from the public for an adventure grandly titled "the Second Grinnell Rescue Expedition," I knew very well that his eye had been on a more selfish prize—the glory and fame of discovery. Franklin's fate mattered less to him than forging a reputation for himself. He was not as virtuous as I had once naïvely thought, his motives not nearly as pure as he pretended.

We both were frauds. He was a hero in the public eye, and I, a counselor to the bereaved. But in private, Elisha had not enough courage to defy his family, no matter how heartily he persuaded me to desert my own kin. And I was unable to recognize wise counsel when I heard it. I didn't even follow the advice I gave others. We had been a well-matched pair indeed; all our good intentions blended so neatly with our faults that we never anticipated the dead end of the road upon which we walked.

Every decision in our separate lives had led inexorably to this: that he lay on that cold pallet he had so feared, while I remained trapped in a web of falsehood I had woven long ago with an unthinking, high-spirited prank.

If I could have foreseen it, would I have avoided it? At what point would I have paused in midstep and then put my foot down upon some other path?

With a sigh, I rose and brushed idly at my skirts. There was time enough later for pointless speculation and self-recrimination. I had years to reflect on what I had done with my life, and whether there had ever been a moment when I could have diverted from my fate and chosen a happier future. This morning I had an important errand to complete, and my stop in the graveyard had only been to bolster my resolve, to remind me of the consequences of procrastination.

Today I was going to follow a bit of advice that I had given others countless times. I had rapped out this message over and over again to grieving souls, believing it to be sage advice and yet never heeding it myself. For some time, this failure had preyed upon my conscience, and today I intended to unburden myself of at least one regret.

I was going to make my amends to one who had never done me any harm.

❧ ❧

It was a huge brownstone home, larger than I had expected, in a very expensive neighborhood. I faltered for just a moment on the sidewalk outside, then resolutely mounted the front steps, trying to shake out the damp and bedraggled hem of my skirt.

I wondered if I would have to explain myself to some servant and dreaded finding the words to do so, but this much, at least, I was spared. My knock was answered by a tall, portly gentleman with a round face framed by sideburns and kindly eyes. He was trying to button up a waistcoat over his shirt while smiling a puzzled and tentative greeting to his unexpected early morning visitor.

"I'm Maggie," I said simply.

For a long moment he stared at me blankly, and then recognition and astonishment lit his face. He gave up fumbling with his buttons and stammered for an appropriate greeting. "Of course—I should have known you at once," he finally said. "Please, Miss Fox—Maggie—come in."

He ushered me into the house and down a hallway amply adorned with mirrors and sconces and narrow, elegant tables filled with vases of flowers and small china ornaments. These, I supposed, were the trappings of success, but they were not the sort of things that tempted me. I would have traded them all for another day with Elisha.

My host was eyeing me anxiously. "We were just at breakfast," he said.

"I'll be happy to wait in the parlor," I murmured.

"No, no, of course not! I will just set another place—"

I was about to explain that I might not be welcome when we rounded the corner into a large dining room. An oversized table dominated the space, set with candles and tea service and surrounded by nearly a dozen chairs. There was only one person seated there, however.

She looked up quizzically at her husband as he entered, but when I appeared beside him, she laid down her fork hastily and rose to her feet. She was grayer than I remembered and more plump, but her face was unchanged. While I stood there, suddenly struck dumb with too many emotions to explain, her eyes abruptly filled with tears.

"Oh, Maggie!" she cried. "I am sorry! I am so truly sorry!"

And Leah opened her arms wide in welcome.

Afterword

Maggie Fox returned to spirit rapping intermittently after the death of Elisha Kane but was no longer comfortable with or successful at making her living by deceit. Her reconciliation with Leah proved to be tentative and uneasy. The younger woman never again allowed Leah to rule her life, and before long, the two sisters parted ways and thereafter enjoyed no more than a cool cordiality.

Maggie never received any money from Elisha's estate, despite the overwhelming success of his book. Desperate to acquire a means of supporting herself, Maggie eventually did what she swore she would never do and published an account of her romance, complete with Elisha's letters, in a book called *The Love-Life of Doctor Kane*. Unfortunately, Kane's family spent a small fortune to discredit her, and they were so successful that for a long time historians scoffed at the idea of a common-law marriage between Kane and Fox. Modern researchers, however, have found enough evidence in family letters to support her claim.

Kate Fox did marry and had two sons, one of whom was diagnosed in adulthood with epilepsy. After her husband died, she lived a difficult life, battling addictions to morphine and alcohol.

In 1888, Maggie publicly announced that she was a fraud and revealed in front of an audience how she had created the rapping sounds with the joints in her feet and ankles. She apologized to the public at large and disparaged the entire spiritualist movement. A year later, she recanted her confession, claiming that she had made it only for money, which she desperately needed. Belief in spiritualism continued unabated.

Ann Leah Fox Fish Brown Underhill died in 1890, attended by her devoted and wealthy third husband. Kate and Maggie died in 1892 and 1893, respectively, suffering from ill health.

Spiritualism survived well into the twentieth century, when its validity would be hotly debated by such people as Sir Arthur Conan Doyle and Harry Houdini. The Fox sisters are still credited today with the birth and popularity of the movement.

The accomplishments of Dr. Elisha Kent Kane, the most widely celebrated adventurer of his day, were soon overtaken and surpassed. The ice-free water discovered by the men of his expedition was not, in fact, an open polar sea, because no such body of water exists. Eventually the bay in which the doctor's ship had been trapped was renamed Kane Basin. Other than this nominal accolade, his fame soon receded and gave way to obscurity. In the annals of American exploration, he is nearly forgotten.

A Final Word

In the year 1904, beneath the little Hydesville house where the Fox sisters began their career, a crumbling cellar wall finally collapsed, unearthing the hidden tomb of an almost-complete human skeleton.

Want to Read More?

Kane, Elisha Kent. *Arctic Explorations*. Scituate, MA: Digital Scanning Inc., 2008.

Lewis, E. E. *A Report of the Mysterious Noises Heard in the House of Mr. John D. Fox in Hydesville, Arcadia, Wayne County*. Available at http://www.woodlandway.org.

Sawin, Mark Metzler. *Raising Kane: Elisha Kent Kane and the Culture of Fame in Antebellum America*. Philadelphia: American Philosophical Society, 2008.

Stuart, Nancy Rubin. *The Reluctant Spiritualist: The Life of Maggie Fox*. Orlando, FL: Harcourt, 2005.

Weisberg, Barbara. *Talking to the Dead: Kate and Maggie Fox and the Rise of Spiritualism*. San Francisco: HarperCollins, 2004.

Acknowledgments

I'd like to acknowledge all the people who encouraged me to rescue Maggie and Elisha from the shadowy depths of history and bring their unique story back into the limelight. In particular, thanks to...

My husband, my first reader and most ardent admirer, who didn't mind my having a "love affair" with a long-dead explorer and even took me to visit his crypt in Philadelphia.

My parents and my aunt, who became spirited book promoters, and my sister, who emailed me in tears when she read about Maggie's broken engagement. Their enthusiasm provided me with the incentive to keep writing.

All the family, friends, and community members who read this book in one form or another, providing invaluable feedback and encouragement, including the Crists, the O'Donnells, and several book clubs in the Chester County, Pennsylvania area.

My students at Avon Grove Intermediate School, who witnessed the book undergo many revisions and eagerly kept track of the publication process. I need to especially thank Emma, who thought of the title.

And finally, Kelly Barrales-Saylor, who tracked me down because she believed in the story and then guided me through the sometimes painful process of making important choices in the telling of this tale.

About the Author

Dianne K. Salerni is an elementary school teacher, author, and online book reviewer. She has previously published educational materials for teachers, as well as short stories. *We Hear the Dead* is her first full-length novel. With her husband and her two daughters, Salerni lives in Pennsylvania, where she is at work on her second novel.